Advance Praise

"*Immortal Writers* by Jill Bowers is a sensational read. Adventure, creat. and suspense all wrapped into one amazing book. Jill Bowers has the raw power of drawing readers into her plot. I could not stop reading it. The story hooked me from beginning to end. Overall, I highly recommend this brilliant read to all."

- Danielle Urban, *Urban Book Reviews*

"This is an amazing story with even more amazing writing! The way the writers are presented and how they interact with their creations is very well done. The story is unique, different from all the other books I have read. This tale has a very captivating plot; it has action, a lot of suspense, the perfect romance, and dragon slaying shenanigans! Recommend this book to anyone who likes Fantasy/Science Fiction."

- Gabriel Messier, *Reading by the Fireplace* review blog

"Hemingway, Poe, and Tolkien had me laughing out loud! This book was humorous, but not without its serious moments. I would read again and suggest to friends to read."

- Stephanie Jordan, *StephieJoJo Reviews*

"Jill Bowers' *Immortal Writers* is a fascinating adventure into imagination. Dragons, magic, and a thrilling storyline merely scratch the surface of a world where human imagination can cause anything to come to life—for good or for ill. The characters that come into play are thoroughly enjoyable, with both existing authors and characters, as well as a few of the author's own imagination, coming to life and dealing with their foes... All around, *Immortal Writers* is a solid work of art and a worthwhile read. I am excited to see what will come next from Bowers."

- Chad Nielsen, advance reader

"[*Immortal Writers*] is a great mix of reality with fantasy. Who hasn't wondered what it would be like to live in your favourite story? What it would be like to actually meet and interact with these characters? What an interesting and entertaining idea for a book! Great characters, fantastical action, a love story, and a unique plot all make *Immortal Writers* a fun read!"

- Julie Tracy, advance reader

"Interesting start to a new fantasy series about immortal authors whose fairytale characters come to life. I thoroughly enjoyed interacting with some of my favourite authors and innovators in this book. The way Bowers weaved Liz's story and characters around little author cameos was incredible. If you enjoy fantasy and fairy tales, this book should be right up your alley."

- Kelley W, book reviewer

"Absolutely fantastic read. I loved the story and the characters. Would love to see this as a movie; with real dragons."

- Sue Wallace, book reviewer

COPYRIGHT INFORMATION

Immortal Writers

Copyright 2016 by Jill Bowers

ISBN: 978-0-9947321-7-0 All rights reserved

Cover design and graphic: DigiWriting

Editor: Talia Crockett

Published in Canada by Blue Moon Voices, a division of Blue Moon Publishers, located in Toronto, Canada.

The author greatly appreciates you taking the time to read this work. Please consider leaving a review wherever you bought the book, or telling your friends or blog readers about Immortal Writers, to help spread the word. Thank you for your support.

This book is a work of fiction. The characters, incidents, and dialogue are drawn from the author's imagination and are not to be construed as real. Any resemblance to actual events or persons, living or dead, is entirely coincidental.

First Printing November 2016

IMMORTAL WRITERS

By Jill Bowers

To my parents, Leann and Reed, for their support, love, and encouragement.

CONTENTS

ACKNOWLEDGEMENTS

An author never truly works alone… at least, I know I didn't. I have many people to thank for helping me reach this point. Of course, I'd like to thank my family for their endless love and support, and their faith in me and in my writing. To Mom, Dad, Katie, Bill, Emily, and Wendy, thank you for putting up with my wild imagination! To Zoey and Belle, thank you for helping me stretch my mind and my imagination from telling you stories and playing trolls with you. To Max and Clover, thanks for the love and snuggles. And to my dog Jasmine, thanks for loving me unconditionally, even when I can't pay you as much attention as I should because I'm writing.

I'd also like to thank my writing group at work. Ryan, Sharee, and Karina, thank you for taking time out of your week every Wednesday to write with me. I'd especially like to thank Karina for helping me improve my writing so that I could reach this point. You're a wonderful writer and friend, Karina, and I appreciate your support.

I'd also like to thank Chad and Elise for being endlessly enthusiastic about my writing and about me as a person. Thank you, also, to Christie and Liz, after whom I named the protagonist of this book.

I'd like to give a special shout-out to Jennifer. As one of my professors in college and a very, very dear friend, she's always believed in my writing, and never once doubted that I'd make something of it. Thank you for encouraging me to write, even through all of the truly difficult times.

And finally, thank you to the team at Blue Moon Publishers for giving me, and *Immortal Writers*, a chance.

CHAPTER ONE

Liz looked over her shoulder at the cab that had been following her since she'd left the train station. She had seen the man who had been stalking her for the last three months climb inside. The cab hadn't left the rearview mirror since, and Liz could swear that she could feel the man's eyes on her, even though she knew that was impossible given the dark night.

She swallowed against the fear in her throat and sat facing forward. She closed her eyes. What she wouldn't give for some sleep in her own bed, safe and without any worries for the next day's schedule. She had travelled across the country on tour after winning the library-sponsored Best Young Fantasy Author Award, stopping at bookstores and libraries in towns across America. Secretly, she had visited Child Protective Services and donated the majority of the money she'd won upfront from the award. Not even Derek knew how much money she'd really earned, and how much she'd given away. She had kept enough money for several months' rent at her new place, because she needed to escape. She was grateful for the opportunities she had been given, and grateful that she could give back, but if there was anything she knew, it was that opportunity was often exhausting. She'd gotten a lot of attention and a good deal of cash from this award, and she was honoured. Now, however, she just wanted to sleep in her own bed in her new apartment.

Liz's car slowed and stopped at the curb of the restaurant. Liz looked behind her again; the cab that had been following her sped by. She sighed in relief. Maybe she had only imagined that that man had followed her.

Liz tipped the driver and stepped out of the car, her sore feet complaining at the pressure of standing again. Derek had insisted on meeting *tonight*. Not tomorrow, not after she had rested from her tour. Now. When Liz had first met Derek, she had been completely absorbed by him. He was humorous, romantic, honest... everything she thought she wanted... at least for a way out of her destitute life. She loved him, she really did. But he had always been somewhat controlling; he kept track of everything she did, probably afraid that she would slip back into old habits. It was suffocating.

She wasn't sure about Derek, but she couldn't forget the first time they'd met. He had been in the back of a club, reading a book. *Her* book. Eager to show off, she had approached him. He had been clueless as to who she was until their third date. She still smiled at his embarrassment and astonishment. Whenever she questioned their relationship, she went back to that moment, and the fact that she couldn't make it on her own. She needed to be free of her past, and Derek seemed like a good way to do that. It wasn't fair to him, and she knew that, but she did love him. She just wasn't sure if that love was created purely out of convenience, or something more.

Liz shook her head and groaned as she walked toward the restaurant Derek had chosen for tonight. She hadn't bothered to look at the name of the restaurant when he'd texted it to her; she had merely glanced at the address when she read it off to the cabbie. She didn't really care where she was. As long as the service was fast and the food edible, it could be the unhealthiest fast food restaurant in the world for all she cared.

As soon as Liz opened the door and stepped inside the restaurant, she knew tonight would be long and stressful. The building she'd just entered was lavishly decorated in deep red velvets and dark woods. All of the tables in the spacious room were full—Derek must have made a reservation far in advance. It even smelled expensive. Forget the scents of marinated meats and roasted potatoes and aromatic wines... Liz could smell the money in the place—rich woods and leathers and *snobiness*. The service would be good, certainly, but this was not the type of place where dinner could be rushed.

A heavy, balding host in a black tuxedo stepped forward and greeted her. "Do you have a reservation?" he asked, his eyebrows arched at her in confusion.

Liz supposed that the waiter's questioning look was somewhat justified given her appearance. Her dirty-blonde hair was pulled back into a bun and the front frizzed out, making her look like she had just been electrocuted. Her clothes were wrinkled, her makeup was smeared, and she looked like she didn't belong there, which was undeniably true. Liz swallowed against the sudden lump in her throat and forced herself to close her jaw, which had been hanging open at the grandeur of the restaurant.

"Yes," Liz said. "Under Derek Harbor."

The host nodded hesitantly and stepped behind a computer that stood atop a mahogany pedestal.

"Here you are," the waiter said. "The rest of your party has already arrived. If you will follow me."

Liz followed the host past several small tables. No one spoke over a murmur. The lighting, the china, and the overall *richness* of the place forbade loud conversation. Liz cleared her throat nervously. What was she doing here?

Derek stood as Liz and the host approached. The host paused and handed Liz a menu, giving her one last questioning glance, and walked away as Derek and Liz sat at the table, which was next to a large ornate window overlooking the street and, past that, the Hudson River.

"Didn't I tell you we were coming *here*?" Derek asked.

"Yes, I believe you did," Liz said. She glanced at the menu. No prices. Liz hoped she could afford dinner. She had spent all of her money from her books and her award on the centres for children and her new home. Of course, Derek could afford dinner. His father was the executive of a global oil company, and Derek never wanted for cash. Hopefully, he would pay for her.

"Then why are you dressed like that?" Derek hissed.

Liz didn't look up from the menu. "If you wanted me to look better you should have waited to have dinner on a night when I haven't been travelling all day."

"Liz, you look like you're—"

"I don't care what I look like, Derek," Liz interrupted. She paused and took a deep breath. "I'm sorry, I don't mean to be rude. I'm just tired. I do like your suit."

"I bought it for tonight," Derek said. Liz raised an eyebrow and looked up at Derek, finally putting down the leather-bound menu.

"What's so special about tonight?"

Derek's jaw tensed as he hesitated, but after a moment his brown eyes softened. "Nothing. I just wanted to welcome you home."

"A night in would have sufficed."

A young waiter with light brown hair interrupted them. "Can I start you off with a bottle of wine?"

Liz looked at Derek questioningly, and he nodded with a wink. He knew she was too young to drink legally. They must not check IDs here. She hoped he was right.

Liz picked up the wine list that was propped up against the window and tried to read the long names of each expensive wine. She swallowed. Why wasn't there any beer?

"What do you recommend?" Liz asked.

"The Cabernet Sauvignon is excellent," the waiter said.

Liz looked at the list again. *Which* Cabernet Sauvignon?

"That sounds excellent," Liz said. "Whichever one you recommend." She closed the wine list and set it back against the window, staring outside until the waiter left, just in case he decided to look at her too closely and figure out she was too young to drink.

Derek watched the waiter scurry away and frowned. "Are you happy to see me? You seem distracted."

Liz sighed and rubbed her temples, finally turning away from the window. "I am happy to see you, I'm just exhausted from being out of town. I haven't had a full night's sleep for at least a week and my feet are killing me. I don't mean to take it out on you."

"We haven't seen each other face-to-face for a month since you've been so busy doing press for your book. Talking on the phone is great and everything, but with the fires across the States and the storms and me not knowing if you were safe…"

"I know, I know." Liz dropped her hands and held them out to Derek. He took them, still frowning. "I'll try to be happier for you. But please let me get back to my apartment by eleven. I need to sleep."

"Deal."

The waiter returned, clutching a bottle of Cabernet Sauvignon. He uncorked it and placed it on the table, then took out a notepad and poised his pen above the paper.

"What can I serve you this evening?"

Liz looked back at the menu while Derek ordered.

"I'll have the fifteen ounce steak, medium rare," Derek said.

"And for you?"

"She'll have the salmon, blackened," Derek said. Liz gritted her teeth. She did love salmon, but she didn't appreciate Derek ordering for her.

"How was the book tour?" Derek asked. He poured the wine as the waiter took their menus and left. Liz sighed in relief when the waiter didn't ID her.

Liz waited until Derek was finished pouring her wine and then took a sip. The rich, fruity, stinging taste was a welcome one. This wine was surprisingly comforting, although she still would have preferred a cooler.

"Long, but excellent," Liz answered.

"Do you think *Fall of the Dragon Lord* will win you another Best Young Fantasy Author Award?"

Liz set down her glass. "Well, you never know. The critics like the book well enough, but I'm still not very well-known."

"Oh, come on. You're bound to win something. What's her name… your writer friend… Jennifer? She wouldn't have encouraged you to apply for the last award if you didn't deserve it. Maybe this book will even become a bestseller!"

"I'm still shocked I won, and besides, plenty of people don't enjoy fantasy novels."

"Everyone who's read your books has loved them. Speaking of which, what did all of your fans want to know?"

"They mainly asked questions about Curtis."

"Of course," Derek sighed. "Your leading hero. I know you base him off of me."

Liz picked up her wine glass as she struggled not to laugh. Derek was nothing like Curtis Jameson. For one thing, Derek was real. For another, Curtis was brave and heroic, and, well, a good lover, among other things.

Unfortunately, these were not qualities Derek shared.

"I started writing these novels before I even met you."

"But you write Curtis like you're in love with him," Derek protested. "So I assume you've integrated me into his character."

Liz looked out of the window again while she tried to think of something kind to say. A man was standing outside and leaning against a cab, casually looking into the restaurant. Liz couldn't clearly see his face, but she knew who the man was. This was the man who had been stalking her for months. She still didn't know how he'd found her. She'd seen him at every book signing and lecture she had given, and now he was here. Liz swallowed her wine and gritted her teeth. What if he was dangerous? Why was he following her?

"Liz?" Derek prompted.

Liz shook her head and turned her attention back to Derek.

"I try to keep my books and my real life separate," Liz said carefully. "The stories are so real to me. In order to remind myself that they don't belong in this reality, I make sure to distinguish between this life and the one in my books."

"So I'm not Curtis?"

Liz studied Derek. He was tall (which was a plus—Liz was five eleven and was hard pressed to find a man taller than her) and had dark, cropped hair. He had a nice nose and beautiful brown eyes, but he lacked a strong chin. He was in shape, but not extraordinarily well built. He was attractive as far as real men go, but Curtis was perfect.

"No," Liz said. "But that's not a bad thing. I love you. That's what matters."

"Since you love me, are you going to tell me what happens in the last book? How does Curtis beat Kenric?"

Liz glared. "No. Absolutely not."

"Come on. Don't you trust me?"

"I don't trust anyone that much. You'll just have to wait like everyone else."

Liz felt the hair rise on the back of her neck, and she swerved her head to look back out the window. The man was gone. This shouldn't have bothered Liz, but for some reason his absence disturbed her more than his appearance in the window. Where had he gone?

"Here you are," the waiter's light voice said, startling Liz out of her thoughts.

Steaming plates of food were set down in front of them. Liz looked over at Derek's meal. His steak looked divine. Oh well. Her salmon looked good enough. It wouldn't hurt her to try to eat healthier, anyway.

Derek's attention was immediately absorbed by his food. Usually this bothered Liz, but not tonight. If Derek wasn't talking, he would eat faster, and then she could make it home sooner. She wasn't necessarily eager to part from Derek; she just wanted a good night's sleep.

However, she would have appreciated his help, if only for a minute. It was easy enough to tell which glass to drink from; Derek had filled the wine glasses. Liz was confused about the fork situation, however. One was for salad, though they hadn't had any. That left far too many options.

Liz glanced up at Derek and peered closely at his place setting. He had picked up the fork closest to his plate. She picked up her fork, surprised at how heavy it was—was it real silver?—and ate the salmon. She was startled by how hungry she was.

"Ready for dessert?" Derek asked once he had finished.

"I don't want dessert," Liz said as she looked out the window again in search of the man. She feared seeing him there again, but at least then she would know where he was. He couldn't sneak up on her if she could see him. "I want to go home. It's already ten."

"It won't take long. I'll order for you. Here—"

Liz opened her mouth to protest, but Derek had already beckoned the waiter forward.

"Cherries jubilee, please."

The waiter glanced at Liz hesitantly, probably reading her reluctance. She sighed and nodded, and the waiter moved away.

"That wasn't too bad, was it?"

Liz tapped her fingers on the table while she waited for dessert. She wouldn't even look at Derek. Home was calling to her. She was as close as she'd been to it in weeks, but it felt like she would never get there. She would be safe from that strange stalker if she were home. She felt so exposed here in the restaurant by this stupid window.

The flames from the approaching dessert caught her attention, and she barely noticed (or maybe she was blocking out) that Derek was hitting his wine glass with his knife.

The room quieted as the waiter placed the cherries jubilee on the table. Derek stood up.

"Ladies and gentlemen, this is Elizabeth McKinnen."

Everyone stared at them, only one or two impressed by Liz's name. One woman took out her phone and started to play on it, probably embarrassed by whatever was happening. Liz covered her face with her hands, wishing she could escape as well.

"What are you doing?" she hissed at Derek.

Derek cleared his throat and knelt down on one knee.

"Oh, no," Liz mouthed. She felt heat rush to her face.

"Elizabeth Christina McKinnen, will you marry me?"

Everyone cheered, which was lucky, since Liz groaned in horror.

"Derek, I'm only eighteen years old!" Liz whispered.

Derek's smile faltered and he shifted on his knee, proffering the ring. It had a beautifully etched gold band with one large diamond in the centre, surrounded by three smaller stones on either side. She would be proud to wear it, but that would mean she *belonged* to Derek. She didn't want to belong to anyone as long as she lived. Too many people had thought they'd owned her over the course of her life. Of course, if she did accept, no one else could ever hurt her like they had, or think they owned her. Hadn't she been looking for a way out?

She willed herself to say yes, but she couldn't do it. She was too young, and she was too afraid.

"I need to think about it."

Derek cleared his throat and raised the ring higher, as if by making the diamonds sparkle in the false light he could change her answer.

"Come on, Liz," Derek murmured. He shifted his eyes. "Everyone's watching."

"Then you shouldn't have demanded their attention," Liz said breathlessly. She grabbed her bag and stood up. "I'm going *home*, Derek. I'm tired. I… I can't make a decision like this when I'm so exhausted."

"Liz…"

Liz started to walk out, to a chorus of embarrassed murmurs from the restaurant patrons. One group of men laughed to each other and tried very hard not to look at Derek.

Liz had nearly escaped when Derek grabbed her arm.

"Don't leave me like this," Derek said. "I just *proposed* to you."

"I know, Derek, I know, and I'll tell you my answer soon, just please, not tonight. Not tonight."

She twisted out of his grasp and hurried out the door. He didn't follow her. She took a deep breath, taking in the noise of the city and the smell of gasoline and dirty water. She looked around. An empty cab waited at the curb. She didn't even think about the fact that it was the same cab that the stalker had leaned against earlier. Derek's proposal had completely erased him from her mind.

Liz hurried into the cab before Derek could catch her again, and slammed the door shut. The car was surprisingly clean and smelled musky and leathery.

"Where to, Miss McKinnen?" the cabbie asked.

Liz was too distracted to find it odd that the taxi driver knew her name. She gave her address to him and breathed a sigh of relief when he started driving away from the restaurant.

Derek had *proposed.* She hadn't seen it coming. She hadn't known he was so serious about her. He didn't make her feel complete or full. He was just there, a useless appendage instead of an essential organ. She didn't *need* him… except for his money. And there was just too much that she couldn't stand about Derek. But how would she tell him that? She didn't want to hurt him.

Liz looked out of the window and blinked in confusion. The streets were getting less busy as they drove north out of town. Her apartment was to the east. She leaned forward.

"Excuse me," she said, "are we going the right way?"

The cabbie slowed down. Liz leaned back. She assumed that he was about to turn around when the door opposite her opened.

Liz whirled around as a tall, hooded figure slid into the car and shut the door.

"Hey!" she yelled. "You can't get in here. I've already hired the cab."

"It's all right, Liz," said a deep voice. The hooded man took something out of his pocket.

"Who—"

"Sorry," the man shrugged. He pressed a cloth to her mouth with gloved hands. Liz knew she shouldn't inhale, but panic overwhelmed her, and she gulped in a breath of chloroform.

CHAPTER TWO

Liz's eyes snapped open. She sat up and looked around, trying to ignore the way her head spun when she moved. She blinked rapidly, trying desperately to clear her head while she took in her surroundings. She was shocked that she wasn't in a dungeon. Instead, Liz sat on a long black leather couch at the back of a large room that looked like a study overflowing with books. She had never seen so many books packed into one room. She had never seen any room so extravagant in all of her life. The only downside to this room was that it was windowless; that meant there was no chance she could open a window and scream for help.

Liz stood up and ran over to a door, which was easy to spot only because of the lack of books. She twisted the handle. Locked. She backed up and glared at the door. It was a beautiful mahogany door, and was probably worth more than all of the stipends she'd earned from her first book. Maybe she could break it down.

Liz took a deep breath and ran forward, her right side facing the door. She rammed into it and fell to the ground. The door didn't even shudder.

Liz fought off tears and stood, rubbing her shoulder. She gritted her teeth as she stumbled backward, then ran at the door again, this time hitting it with her left side. She cried out in pain at the force of the impact, but managed to stay on her feet. Wiping away tears, Liz kicked desperately at the door. Once, twice, three times, and again and again. She didn't know where she was, but she knew she had to get away.

Gasping, Liz finally collapsed onto the floor in front of the beautiful, unharmed door. It was hopeless. It wasn't going to budge. She was stuck.

She was afraid to think of how long she'd be trapped, but dark thoughts crept into her mind like tentacles ravelling around her consciousness.

Liz closed her eyes and tried to focus on her breathing. It would do no good to panic… at least, not yet. If she could keep her head, maybe she'd be able to talk her way out of here, wherever *here* was.

She sniffed and stood up on sore, wobbly legs. She walked up to a bookshelf across from the door. The books were packed so tightly together that she couldn't pull one out. Maybe there was a trick. Liz fit her fingers around the top of a leather-bound book and pulled, leaning her back away from the wall. The book wouldn't budge. Liz let up, and then tugged again.

Suddenly, the book careened out of the bookcase, followed by half of the shelf. Liz shrieked and ran to the middle of the room, nearly tripping over the ornate rug that took up most of the space.

Liz stifled another cry and collapsed into the middle of the room, curling her hands over her head in a futile attempt to protect her mind from the onslaught of dark thoughts threatening to smother her. She stared at the large symbol in the middle of the rug to try to distract herself from her situation. The symbol consisted of two quills that crossed over each other diagonally inside of a large circle. Liz tried to keep all of her focus on the quills, but as she stared, her mind numbed and she stopped seeing what was in front of her.

She wasn't sure how long she stayed there, staring at the symbol, but still no one came into the study. As much as Liz feared finding out who had kidnapped her and what they wanted, she was tired of waiting. She knew the power of her imagination. She was probably making up scenarios that were worse than reality.

But how could she be sure? She had just been *kidnapped*. They could rape her. They could torture her for years. They could kill her.

Liz shook her head. All of these ideas were unlikely, despite the brutal manner in which they had brought her here. They probably just wanted money. She certainly didn't have enough to offer them, but maybe Derek did. If he would help her after she had spurned his proposal. She blinked back tears, sat up, and glanced around the room again. It didn't look like they really needed money. But maybe this was how they made their living: kidnapping people, blackmailing them, and then robbing them blind.

Liz forced herself to stand and return to the couch where she had slept off the chloroform. She wanted to appear stronger than she felt to her captors—and she couldn't do that crumpled in a ball on the floor. Maybe if she just sat on the couch and tried to look poised, the people who had taken her would think she was stronger than she really was.

She had just sat down when the door squeaked open. Liz sat up straighter and glared at the man entering the room, hoping she could prove that she wouldn't let them get to her.

The man's hair was receding from his forehead, but what was left of it was dark and straight. He had thick eyebrows and a ridiculous-looking mustache. He wore a basic black and white suit with a thin black tie. Liz couldn't place it, but the man looked familiar. Where had she seen him before?

The man sat in the dark red chair behind the desk and smiled at Liz.

"Well, well, well," the man said. "Elizabeth McKinnen. We've been trying to get you here for a while, but you've been away. Your disappearance would have been a little too conspicuous if we'd taken you while you were on your tour."

"What do you want?" Liz demanded, silently thanking God that her voice was only barely shaking. "Money?"

The man laughed. "I have no need for money, Elizabeth."

Liz's heart sank. She had feared as much. She should have known. This room was worth more than her entire apartment. What was this man going to do to her?

"What do you want?" Liz repeated.

"I want you to take care of a problem for me," the man said. He leaned forward and clasped his hands together on the table. Liz waited for him to explain further, but he simply scrutinized her.

Liz stared back resolutely. She had learned long ago that people who wanted to hurt her liked it when she cowered in front of them. She refused to give this man that satisfaction.

"Well?" Liz finally broke the silence. "What is it?"

"I'm not sure you're ready," the man said.

"Believe me, I'm ready," Liz growled. She stood and walked closer to the desk, trying to hide her trembling hands. "You had a taxi waiting for me and then you hired some man to meet up with us to kidnap me. I want to know *why*. I have a book to finish editing and a deadline to meet. Edits have to be in by next month or I lose the contract for the last book. I don't have all day."

"I plan to keep you much longer than a day," the man said.

Liz swallowed against the sick, sticky feeling in her throat. It was bad enough that she was in this predicament, but if she missed that deadline, she'd never be able to keep her new home. She had been so proud of it. "Why? What do you want? Who are you? I'd like to know the name of my kidnapper."

The man leaned back and heaved a sigh.

"You wouldn't believe me if I told you," he said.

Liz put her hands on the desk and leaned forward. "Try me."

"I am the great writer William Shakespeare."

Liz stepped back and gave a short laugh. Admittedly, he looked *exactly* like the pictures she'd seen of the great author. Maybe that's why she had recognized him. But why would anyone go through the trouble of trying to look like William Shakespeare?

"Based on the décor in this office, I'm assuming you have enough money to buy help for that delusion."

"I do have plenty of money." The man spread his arms wide and gestured to the grand room. "But no doctor can help me."

Liz glared. "Who are you *really*?"

"William Shakespeare."

"You expect me to believe that you're the greatest writer to ever live? That you did not, in fact, die in the seventeenth century? If you're William Shakespeare, why aren't you speaking in poetic verse? You should come up with more believable lies."

"I *am* William Shakespeare. I was forced to fake my death in the year 1616 for… practical reasons. It was time for me to disappear. And then I created this place."

"A camp for hostages?"

"A Castle for the Immortals," Shakespeare said.

Liz gritted her teeth and pinched the bridge of her nose. Why wasn't this man just being honest with her? Was he trying to toy with her? Make her uneasy? It was certainly working. She felt her stomach twist with dread. How crazy was this man? Did he actually believe what he was saying? What did that mean for her if he did?

"You're insane."

"No," Shakespeare sighed, "I think you'll find I'm not."

"You think you're the greatest writer who ever lived."

"I'm afraid centuries of being called that has made me believe it somewhat. I am not nearly as humble as I used to be."

"If you were really William Shakespeare you wouldn't be speaking to me like this. You'd be talking in metre. Or at least Old English."

"I've been alive a long time, Elizabeth," Shakespeare said. "I've adapted to the times. I prefer Old English—the sophistication, the nuances—but any writer knows that he has to write to his audience at least a little. I've changed my language to match the new age. Believe me, I'm not the man you've read about in your history books."

Liz crossed her arms over her chest and shook her head, biting her lip. "Tell me what you want. Tell me what I have to do to get out of here."

Shakespeare stood up. Liz backed away slightly. Maybe she had pushed him too far. He was clearly unstable.

Shakespeare walked to the door and opened it. A tall man, probably about six-foot-three, stepped over the threshold. Shakespeare shut the door after the stranger had entered, while Liz stared at the newcomer. His face was hidden in a black hood, but she still knew it was the man who had kidnapped her. The build and hood were the same.

"You can show her your face," Shakespeare said. "She insists on knowing."

The man threw back his hood.

Liz stared at him. He had sparkling blue eyes and thick, curly blond hair. He had a strong chin, a straight nose, and a long scar on his right cheek that only added to his rugged attractiveness. He was well built and his muscular body, which was accentuated by his leather clothes, looked photoshopped and unfairly perfect. He was without a doubt the handsomest man she'd ever seen. Liz had just spent the previous evening comparing his loving skills with those of her boyfriend. She idly wondered if her speculations were correct, probably letting her mind wander a little too far, then mentally smacked herself for getting distracted.

Liz laughed.

"You found the perfect man for the job," she said. Her voice sounded strained. "If I ever option my books to Hollywood, you'll be the ideal actor for the part. I mean... I'll just tell them my kidnapper can play Curtis. What's *your* name? Ernest Hemingway?"

The man smiled. "Ernest Hemingway is elsewhere in the Writers' Castle."

Liz stopped laughing.

"My name is Curtis Jameson."

"Your *real* name."

"That's the name you gave me. That is what I am called."

Liz ran her hands down her face in frustration. "I'm surrounded by crazy people. You're all nuts."

Shakespeare sat down at his desk again. "His name *is* Curtis Jameson. He is the character from your books."

"He just looks like the hero from my books."

"No," Shakespeare said, "he is your character come to life."

Liz gestured to the man who claimed to be Curtis. "Curtis isn't real. I made him up. He's in my head. This man just looks like him."

"Exactly like him," Shakespeare said. "Exactly the way you pictured him, don't you think? Down to the cleft chin and the shade of blue in his eyes. His height, his build, even the battle scars you gave him."

The man rolled up his right sleeve. Part of the skin on his arm was red and rough with rugged scar tissue. A burn mark from a dragon.

Not from a dragon. Of course not. This wasn't real. This man was just the craziest fan she'd ever met—he'd even burned himself extensively to achieve the perfect Curtis façade. She hadn't known people would do something like this just because they liked her novels. If these people were willing to go this far, perhaps it was best and safest for her to give in.

"You clearly want me to play along," Liz said. "So explain this to me. How did my character go from being an idea in my head to living in the real world?"

"It wasn't just your idea that created me. It was the way you phrased everything. Your *words*," Curtis explained.

"You know, of course, that words are the most powerful form of magic?" Shakespeare asked. "You've heard that words are immortal?"

"Of course," Liz said. "It's part of what drew me to writing."

"Well, it's true to an extent most people don't understand," Shakespeare said. "All words are immortal. Some writers have such a gift that they also become immortal."

"That's how he's still alive," Curtis interjected, nodding at Shakespeare.

"No one's immortal," Liz said.

"Not many," Shakespeare corrected, "but there are some. The most gifted writers use words so expertly that the words become part of them. They transform them into something more than what they were. This group of talented authors is known as the Immortal Writers. You're young, Elizabeth, which is unusual, but you show great potential as one of us."

"Okay," Liz said, ignoring the comment on her youth. Everyone always said she was too young, and she wasn't sure what that had to do with this man claiming he was William Shakespeare. "Let's just assume I believe all of that. That explains *you*, Shakespeare, but not Curtis."

"The writers and their characters are connected. We know when a writer becomes immortal because their characters come to life when their words cross a certain line."

"A line?"

"Between fantasy and reality," Shakespeare explained. "Some writers' words are so powerful that they become real. The writer becomes not only a creator of words, but also a creator of creatures and people and histories.

They come from what we call the Imagination Field and cross into the Reality Field."

Liz stared at the man who called himself William Shakespeare. He was crazy. He had to be. None of this could be real. Still, she liked the idea. She was a fantasy novelist, after all. It would be wonderful if something like this *could* exist. Maybe she would write a book about it after she got out of this mess. Assuming she *ever* got out of this mess.

"So you, William Shakespeare, are an Immortal Writer. Does that mean Hamlet's roaming around somewhere, speaking only in iambic pentameter?"

"Unfortunately, yes," Shakespeare sighed. "I've regretted writing so many plays in iambic pentameter. I can't get my characters to speak normally. You have no idea how annoying it is."

Liz gaped. "Seriously? Hamlet's somewhere around here?"

"Along with Puck, Macbeth, King Richard, and others."

"King Richard? But he wasn't someone you... I mean, the *real* Shakespeare... made up. He was a real king."

"In a manner of speaking, you are correct," Shakespeare replied. "But you're a little out of order. I wrote the plays first, before they happened in real life. History makes up for our characters' appearances. In some cases, it moves time around so that things make better sense. Those plays, *Richard III, Henry V,* et cetera, were all written *first,* and when they came to life, history rearranged itself to fit the stories inside of it. The only real History I wrote was *Julius Caesar,* but individuals who have actually lived on this earth cannot come back to life through words, thank God. Can you imagine the confusion? The political and religious upheaval?"

Liz took a deep breath and looked around the room. This was intriguing, but she was growing tired of it. She had to get to the bottom of what he wanted from her.

"Okay," Liz said, "let's say I believe all of this. Why kidnap me? Why not just let me find out for myself that I'm immortal? Why do you need me?"

"I'm not the only character that's come to life," Curtis said. He took a step forward and looked Liz in the eyes. "Healer and Rob are here, too. But your main problem is Kenric."

"Kenric?"

"Yes," Curtis said. "The dragon lord you made my arch nemesis."

"I know who he is," Liz snapped, "but who cares if he's come to life?"

"As you know, he has a fierce temperament and a greedy eye," Curtis said. "He wants dominion over the world."

"Over Shethara, yes," Liz said.

"Shethara is the nation you created for him to overthrow before he tried for world domination," Curtis said, "but he's not in Shethara. Shethara didn't come over into this world. The only world Kenric has access to now is Earth. And he wants it."

"So you think Kenric will take over the world with his dragon horde?"

"We know he's planning it," Shakespeare said. "His activities have grown conspicuous enough that we had to bring you in. We had no other choice."

"What activities? I haven't noticed anything."

"Haven't you? How about the sudden fires, just blocks from where you were on your tour? The uncanny lightning storms when there were no clouds, where the lightning struck down buildings with unnatural precision?"

"You're saying those weren't natural phenomena, but dragons?"

"Yes. That's why it was crucial we brought you in as soon as possible."

"And what's so special about me that I can defeat him, assuming he's real?"

"You're the writer," Shakespeare said.

"So?" Liz replied. "Curtis is the hero. He takes care of Kenric just fine in the books."

"It's different in real life," Shakespeare said. "The hero isn't enough. The writer has to step into his or her own story and become a hero as well. You created Kenric, so you have to finish him. It has to be you."

Liz stared at the two men. They seemed to absolutely believe what they were saying. She folded her arms against her chest and looked at the ground.

So. Two rich, crazy men had captured her. It sounded like they wanted her to kill someone for them, someone they had convinced themselves was Kenric.

"I won't kill anyone," she said to the floor.

"That's because you don't believe us yet," Shakespeare said, "but you will. We will prove it to you tomorrow."

"Tomorrow?"

"Yes," Shakespeare said as he half-heartedly tried to straighten a stack of papers on his desk. "It is late. You slept long and hard upon your arrival, but I suspect you're still tired. Curtis will show you to your room."

"How long do you plan to keep me here?" Liz asked as Curtis put a gloved hand over her wrist. Liz tried to wrench herself from his grip, but he twisted her arm behind her back and wrapped one hand around her waist.

"That's up to you," Curtis growled.

He dragged her away.

CHAPTER THREE

Liz looked at the clothes laid out for her in absolute horror. Leather? Wasn't it bad enough that these nut jobs had kidnapped her and that they wanted her to kill someone? Now they wanted her to wear skin-tight *leather*?

She turned away in disgust and caught sight of herself in the mirror. She looked awful. Her own clothing was wrinkled from travel, kidnapping, and sleep. And it didn't exactly smell good. She needed to get out of it.

Liz studied her room in an attempt to ignore the fact that what she was putting on was far outside of her comfort zone. She had been surprised when Curtis had brought her here, and even more so that he hadn't blindfolded her. She had been expecting a cell, but instead she found a nice queen-sized bed with an elaborate headboard, a nightstand with a bamboo plant decorating its surface, scarlet-coloured walls, a rustic fireplace, a sturdy wooden desk, and a comfortable recliner. A large, extravagant mirror decorated the right wall, and a bathroom was just off of the room to the left. Everything looked expensive and well taken care of. She had to use a great deal of effort to control her facial expressions in reaction to how lavish everything was. She had never seen anything so *rich* in all of her life. If she hadn't been scared out of her mind, she might have been enjoying herself.

She had just finished putting on a pair of absurd leather boots when a knock came at her door. Liz jumped but managed not to cry out. She hadn't expected to be left alone forever, but it was frightening to think about facing her captors again. Who knew what they had in store for her?

Liz steeled her shoulders and cleared her throat. *Please don't let my voice shake.* "Come in." *Damn it.*

The door opened slowly. Curtis peeked his head in. He offered her a crooked smile that nearly made her heart stop. He looked exactly like she had always pictured her character. Why? How was that fair? He was too attractive to be maniacal.

"Good morning, Liz," Curtis said in his deep voice. "I brought you breakfast."

He stepped all the way into the room, balancing a tray laden with fruit and pancakes. He kicked the door shut and crossed over to the desk, laying the tray down.

"Those clothes suit you," Curtis said, eyeing her. "Do you like them?"

"No," Liz said.

"Do you like them on me?"

Liz gawked while Curtis flexed. His clothes were similar to hers. All leather. But she definitely didn't mind the leather on him. She was glad it was skintight.

He's crazy, she reminded herself. *He kidnapped me.*

That doesn't mean you can't enjoy a little eye candy, she snapped back at herself.

"It's still leather," Liz grumbled.

Curtis grinned at her and gestured to the food. "Go ahead and eat. I want to show you something."

Liz glared at him and then glanced at the food. She was awfully hungry, but despite Curtis's good looks, she didn't trust him.

"I'm not hungry."

Curtis raised an eyebrow. "Sure you are. You just think it's poisoned."

Liz swallowed. "I'm not hungry," she repeated firmly.

"Suit yourself," Curtis said. He grabbed the tray and sat down in the recliner. "I'm happy to eat a second breakfast."

Liz watched with squinted eyes as he cut off a piece of pancake and stuffed it in his mouth.

"Nice and fluffy," he said around a mouthful. "Shame on you for not having pancakes be a food in Shethara. I didn't know what I was missing."

He had barely swallowed when he shoved a strawberry into his mouth. "Mmmm, juicy." He licked his fingers. "At least we had good fruit at home."

Liz glared. Clearly it wasn't poisoned. She was so hungry, but she didn't want to give this man the satisfaction of giving in.

"Wow, these blackberries!" Curtis said. He popped three into his mouth. "I am so glad you didn't want this, Liz. I mean, I didn't need more food but it never hurts to—"

"Fine!" Liz snapped. "Give me breakfast!"

Curtis smiled and swallowed. "As you wish." He hopped out of the chair and walked over to her. "Enjoy."

Liz took the tray and sat down on her bed, careful not to look at Curtis's grinning face. She could tell he was having the time of his life annoying the hell out of her.

He stuck his gloved hands in his pockets (How? How did his hands fit inside pockets? Those pants were *tight*.) and meandered back over to the chair, whistling. Liz rolled her eyes as she ate. He was exactly like her character. He must have studied well.

Which made him all the more attractive.

And crazy.

"What are you showing me today?" Liz asked between bites.

Curtis stopped whistling. "More proof."

"Proof of what?"

"That everything Shakespeare and I told you last night is true," Curtis explained. "I know it's hard to believe right now. But you'll see. We wouldn't lie to you."

"But you'll kidnap me and ask me to kill someone?"

"It's for your own good," Curtis shrugged.

Liz held her tongue and continued eating. Curtis resumed whistling. She didn't recognize the tune, but it was quite pretty. She probably would have liked it if Curtis hadn't been annoying her.

She managed not to snap at him the rest of the time she ate. It was hard with him whistling and drumming out a beat on the arms of the chair, but she did it.

"Ready to go?" Curtis asked. He stood up and stretched. He looked good when he stretched.

"Where are we going?" Liz asked hesitantly. Who knew what "proof" meant? Was it some kind of brainwashing? Would it be painful?

"To the courtyard," Curtis said. He strutted forward. Liz followed. At least he hadn't said anything about a dungeon or a torture chamber. What could be that bad out in a courtyard?

They walked in silence through long, twisting corridors and enormous, richly decorated rooms, including the largest library she had ever seen. Everything was so extravagant and glamorous. What would it be like to have money like this? Money to spend on decorations and art and woodcarvings? And the books... all of the wonderful, wonderful books.

It was a full minute before Liz realized her mouth was hanging open in awe after seeing the library. Everything was beautiful. She was impressed even though the beauty terrified her. Obviously these people were running some sort of lucrative operation, an operation of which they wanted her to be a part. Couldn't someone with their own castle just hire a hit man to kill the person they were calling Kenric? Why did they need her to do it? She had made many mistakes in her life, but she'd never hurt anyone else. She didn't want to hurt anyone else. No matter what they said, she wasn't going to do their dirty work.

"Ready?" Curtis asked, stopping at a rustic-looking white door.

"No."

"Oh, sure you are," Curtis said as he opened the door.

Liz shielded her eyes as sunlight flooded into them. She blinked rapidly as she adjusted to the light. Liz had to admit that the courtyard was beautiful. Roses, lilies, and wisteria covered the edges of the expansive courtyard. Honeysuckle and lilac bushes bordered a large circular stone path that surrounded the outside of the square. Just past the stone circle, fruit trees stood guard to what looked like the entrance to a labyrinth.

Curtis and Liz walked to the centre of the large stone space, which was about fifty feet wide in any direction. Liz looked up at Curtis and squinted in the sunlight.

"You brought me here to show me flowers?"

"Nope," Curtis said. "It's much better than that. Watch."

He looked up to the sky and whistled long and loud, then looked back at her and winked. "You'll love this."

Liz followed his gaze up into the sky. Love what? She couldn't see anything.

But then she saw a little speck of silver in the sky. It came steadily closer, and soon Liz could make out wings. She could tell that whatever was coming toward them was not a bird. It was much, much too large.

"What is it?" Liz asked, glancing over at Curtis.

"You'll see," Curtis said. "And you'll love her. Just make sure you don't touch her."

"Her?"

She looked back up at the sky, and then took a couple of steps back in surprise. It had come a lot closer in just a few seconds, and it definitely wasn't a bird.

An enormous pegasus landed in front of them. Curtis grinned and walked up to it, hand outstretched in greeting. Liz stood frozen where she was, her mouth gaping open in shock. How? A pegasus couldn't be standing in the middle of a courtyard on *Earth*. It had to be some sort of trick.

But it was a very convincing trick. Liz took a hesitant step forward.

"Come look," Curtis said. "Just don't touch her."

Liz hardly heard him. She circled the pegasus carefully. It looked real. She could see its sides moving in and out with its breaths. Its wings fluttered out and shook, shimmering silver in the sunlight, then neatly folded back into its sides. Its tail flicked and its head nodded as Curtis petted the pegasus on the neck.

Liz continued to circle the magnificent creature. Everything about it was exactly the way she had imagined. There was one patch of black hair on its left flank in the shape of a crescent moon.

"Penelope?" Liz said, astonished.

The pegasus looked over at her, her sapphire eyes full of intelligence and recognition.

Without thinking, Liz reached out her hand and felt Penelope's side. She was real. She could feel the body heat, the sweat, the breathing.

"Liz, no!" Curtis shouted. He lurched forward and then stopped, a violent shiver passing through him.

Liz jerked her hand away. "What's wrong?"

Curtis rubbed the back of his neck and groaned. "No. No, no, no!"

"What?"

"I told you not to touch her!" Curtis yelled.

"I wasn't listening!" Liz yelled back.

Curtis rolled his eyes.

"Get on Penelope. Now."

"What, I can't touch her but I'm supposed to ride her?"

"You've already touched her. You might as well." He sounded angry.

"What's the big deal?"

"You weren't supposed to touch any of your creations, not until you were ready."

"But you touched me when you kidnapped me," Liz retorted.

"I was wearing gloves! I knew I couldn't let my skin touch yours!"

"Why?" Liz demanded.

"Because—"

A horrifying cry rent through the air, cutting off Curtis's reply. The scream didn't sound human.

Curtis froze and looked up at the sky.

"What is it? What was that?" Liz asked, following his gaze into the clouds. A small, dark dot swooped toward them. It didn't look malignant now, but Liz could tell from its screaming that it wasn't anything friendly. Curtis seemed panicked by its approach.

"Get on. Get on now."

"Explain what's happening!"

"I will, just get on Penelope!"

Liz walked to Penelope's side, but before she could even try to figure out how to mount her, Curtis picked Liz up and swung her onto the pegasus. He climbed up easily in front of her.

"Hold on to me," he said.

Liz threw her arms around Curtis's waist and stifled a cry as the pegasus took off into the sky. Penelope's wings pushed powerfully against the air, and Liz was overcome by the wind in her hair and a sense of freedom. Even with the fear she felt in her gut she found joy in flying.

She heard that horrible cry again. It sounded like a thousand nails scraping against old glass.

"What is it?" she called to Curtis.

"You weren't supposed to touch any of us," Curtis began to explain. "If you touched any of your creations, we'd all feel it. We'd all know you were here. We're all connected because we're a part of you."

"That's why your body shook when I touched Penelope?"

"Yes. I was reacting to the physical knowledge that you're with us."

"Why does that matter?"

"Because now Kenric knows you're here."

"And that's bad?" Liz asked.

"Oh yes," Curtis said. "That's bad."

The cry came again, and this time it was closer. Liz wanted to turn around but couldn't force herself to do it.

"What's making that noise?"

"One of Kenric's dragons," Curtis said. "He's been patrolling around here for a while. He knew we'd bring you in. And now that he knows you're here…"

The roar was so loud that Liz couldn't hear what Curtis said next. The scream unfroze Liz and she turned around despite the fear in her gut telling her not to. She opened her mouth in terror. A dragon. A real, flying, fire-breathing dragon. Right. There.

"Curtis!" Liz shrieked. "Why did you bring me up into the air when there was a dragon? Are you insane?"

"I have to get you to the north side of the castle. There's a place there with a special shield that can protect you."

"That's crazy!"

"Crazier than a dragon chasing you?"

The dragon opened its jaw and shot fire forward. Its flame was narrow, and would have hit Liz squarely on the back if Curtis hadn't swerved Penelope out of the way. The dragon had remarkably good aim. Just as she had written it.

"Curtis, it's real!"

"I know!" He kicked Penelope's sides. "Come on, girl. I need you to fly! We have to get Liz to the shield!"

Penelope beat her powerful wings. Liz knew she was fast. Supposedly nothing could keep up with her, but seeing the dragon that close made Liz doubt the pegasus's speed.

The dragon was long, brown, and sleek, with strong leathery wings that had sharp pincers at the ends. It was one of the smaller species, called a Raknar. There was no way that any amount of money had created a flying, breathing pegasus and a terrifying dragon. Could it be real?

All remaining doubt fled from her mind when the fire hit her back. Liz screamed as her body tensed up and she tightened her grip on Curtis. The burning spread.

"Liz?" Curtis called. "What's wrong?"

"The dragon," Liz panted, "it got my back."

Curtis muttered a curse and spurred Penelope onward.

Tears streamed down Liz's face. She tried not to think about the pain. The leather of her shirt was melted, seared onto her back. She felt herself sway from lightheadedness as the pain and fear intensified.

"Hold on!" Curtis yelled. "We're almost there!"

But as Penelope dove, Liz felt herself lose her balance.

She started to fall.

"Curtis!"

Curtis twisted around, and as he saw her falling, his face contorted into a mask of terror.

Liz's back screamed in protest as the dragon's claws cut into her, grabbing her from the air. Liz just had time to see Curtis and Penelope turn toward her before everything went black.

CHAPTER FOUR

"We're lucky the damage wasn't worse," a rough voice said.

"It would have been better if there had been no damage."

"Agreed. But Healer has already taken care of the worst of it. She should be waking up soon."

Liz's eyes fluttered open. She stared up at the ceiling of a large, orange and pink silk tent. Soft sunlight streamed in through the fabric above her.

"It's about time," a deep male voice said. "I was starting to wonder if she'd ever wake up."

A woman chuckled. "I hope you have more faith in me than that."

"You're right," the man said. Liz recognized his voice now: Curtis. "I forgot you were all-powerful."

Liz opened her mouth to speak but was instantly inhibited by the sick, sticky feeling in her mouth.

"Thirsty?" the woman's voice asked.

Liz nodded. She heard footsteps and hesitantly sat up, making sure she moved her burned back as little as possible.

Someone offered her a drink. Liz looked up and was about to thank the person, but words escaped her as she looked into a kind face she knew well.

The woman had light brown hair, tinted with little bits of grey. Her bright hazel eyes were kind and had wrinkles around the edges, proof of years of laughter and good humour. Her face was round and the woman herself was plump. She was short, but carried herself with a sense of purpose and power that made her seem taller than she really was.

"Healer?" Liz asked. Her voice croaked a little more than she would have liked.

"Hello, Creator," Healer grinned.

Liz took the drink of water from her and sipped it, amazed at seeing one of her characters come to life. Of course, she had already met Curtis, but at the time she hadn't believed the story that he and Shakespeare had told her.

But she believed now.

She might have passed Penelope off as impressive animatronics or some other science she knew nothing about. She could've believed Curtis's looks were due to a lot of tanning and plastic surgery. But after actually riding on the pegasus and being burned and taken by a dragon, she couldn't help but believe what Curtis and Shakespeare had been telling her. It was all too real. The pain in her back was definite proof of that.

"It's true, isn't it?" Liz whispered.

She caught Curtis rolling his eyes, but Healer was the one who answered.

"Yes, dear," she said. "I know it's a lot to take in, but it's all true. We're really here."

Liz looked around the room: Curtis, Healer, William Shakespeare, and...

"Rob?" Liz said in surprise. "Hey, you're the one who was following me on my book tour!"

Curtis's best friend, an old chariot driver who always took Curtis on discreet missions, smiled from a chair and waved.

"It was my job to keep an eye on you," Rob said. His voice was deep and rough. It had been permanently damaged by acid on one of his missions with Curtis. Rob grinned at Liz and ran a hand through his hair, which used to be black but was now mostly grey. "I'm sorry if I scared you."

Liz turned her astonished gaze to Shakespeare, who stood in the corner of the room, a grim smile on his face. "And you... you're really the great William Shakespeare?"

"Yes," Shakespeare said. "Although 'great' might be a bit of an overstatement."

"Don't pretend to be modest now," Curtis said as he stood up from the chair he had been lounging in. "We all know you think highly of yourself."

"When everyone considers you the greatest writer of all time, it does tend to go to your head," Shakespeare admitted.

"Curtis, how did you get me away from the dragon?" Liz asked.

"It wasn't hard," Curtis said nonchalantly. "I was close enough to my sword that I was able to call it with my mind—you know, because my sword and I were connected back when—"

"I know," Liz interrupted. "I wrote it, remember?"

"Oh yeah," Curtis said. "Well, my sword came to me and I went after the dragon. He was no match for Penelope's speed, so we caught up to him fairly quickly. I went for his wings from behind and put a few holes in them. He swung around to fight me, which was exactly what I wanted." Curtis mimed the fight as he spoke, swinging an invisible sword in the air. "I dodged his fire and then dove under him, right behind the fist where he held you. After I tore through him with my sword, he couldn't help but let you go."

Liz smiled. "I'm very impressed, Curtis."

"You should be." Curtis lifted his chin proudly.

"Don't feed his ego," Rob said. "He doesn't need it."

"How are you feeling?" Healer asked.

Liz grimaced. She had been trying not to think of her singed flesh.

"The pain… isn't as bad as it was before I passed out. But it's still there."

"But is it bearable?"

"I suppose," Liz said, "but I'd prefer no pain at all."

"Of course you would," Healer said, "but you know my magic can only do so much. It only helps your own body's magic."

"I have magic?"

"Everyone does to some extent," Healer said. "Anyone who can heal from any sort of wound has magic running through them—the magic of life. But you have even more magic than the average human. I've sensed it in you."

Liz knew some of the rules to magic, seeing as she had written those rules herself, but she hadn't expected to possess any.

"But I'm... human," Liz said hesitantly. "A regular mortal. Not a sorcerer."

"Human, yes," Shakespeare said. "But not mortal. Not anymore."

"The other night... you said I was one of the Immortal Writers. What does that mean, exactly? That I'll never age? That I can't die? Surely I can be killed by something. I thought for sure that dragon could do me in."

Shakespeare hesitated. "You will never age, Elizabeth... but given the right circumstances, yes, you can die."

"Are my characters immortal, too?"

"Yes," Shakespeare said. "They don't age, but they are capable of being killed."

"Don't worry about it, Creator," Healer said gently. Liz looked over at her. Liz had written her as a mother character, someone she ardently wished her own mother had been like. "We'll deal with death when the time comes, if it ever does. For now, you need to focus on healing the rest of your body."

"But you said I have magic," Liz said. "I want to know what kind of magic I have. Is it strong? When can I start learning how to use it?"

"You do have magic," Healer affirmed. "It's strong. I haven't felt an aptitude as strong as yours since... well, since *I* was tested at the Academy and received the highest marks in a century."

Liz knew how high that was. It was next to impossible. "Really?"

"Really."

"How do I use it?" Liz demanded.

"Both Curtis and Healer will be training you," Shakespeare said.

"Curtis? But Curtis isn't the best magician..."

"No, Healer will be teaching you magic," Shakespeare said, "but Curtis will be teaching you how to fight."

Liz swerved to look at Curtis, a scared expression on her face.

"Don't worry," Curtis said with a cocky grin. He leaned back on his heels and folded his muscular arms. "I'll go easy on you."

"No you won't," Liz said. "I know how you train people."

"It's your own fault for writing me that way, then."

Liz stared desperately at Shakespeare. "Do I *have* to train with Curtis?"

"If you want to stand a chance against Kenric, you have to train with both Healer *and* Curtis."

"What is Rob going to do?" Liz asked.

"I'm going to provide extra protection for you," Rob said, "but all of your lessons will come from Healer and Curtis. I have nothing to teach you that will help you defeat Kenric."

Liz looked down at her hands. "I really do have to fight Kenric, don't I?"

There was a brief moment of silence.

"You know him better than any of us," Curtis finally said. "What do you think?"

Liz looked down and picked at the blue blanket that covered her. She didn't know what to say. Obviously he would have to be defeated, but could she really *kill* him?

Shakespeare spared her from answering. "We can discuss this later. For now, you need to get ready."

Liz gave Shakespeare a quizzical look. "For what?"

"Now that you believe, you have to be initiated."

"Initiated?"

"Into the Immortal Writers."

"What is this, a sorority?" Liz scoffed.

Shakespeare frowned. "Think of it as an opportunity to meet other authors, people you've studied and looked up to your whole life."

Liz's tone turned excited. "Who's going to be there?"

"Go see for yourself," Shakespeare said. "But just to warn you, some of them are quite… strange."

"Strange how?"

"You'll see," Shakespeare said. "Now, go clean up. Curtis will show you the way to the initiation."

Shakespeare swept out of the tent. Only when he had left did Liz realize that she should probably be afraid to meet all of the writers. Who was she compared to the greatest authors in the world? She was so young, just a kid… that's what all of her critics said. How could she associate with people like Shakespeare?

"Are you ready?" Curtis asked. He stood next to her bed, hand extended.

Liz took his hand and, grimacing, gingerly stepped out of the bed. Liz swallowed against the pain. She would have to learn to deal with it.

This was only the beginning.

CHAPTER FIVE

"What do you mean you're not coming in with me?" Liz demanded.

"This is exclusive to writers," Curtis responded, an enormous grin across his face. "No characters allowed."

Liz shook her head frantically. "But I won't know anyone in there!"

Curtis shrugged. "I guess you should have studied harder in school."

Liz glared at him. "Studying someone and knowing someone are not the same things."

Curtis raised an eyebrow. "What did you do during your English lessons?"

Liz sighed in exasperation. "You know what? I'm *glad* you're not coming." She turned away from him and stomped toward the golden, ornate double doors that led into the ballroom.

"That's the spirit, Liz!" Curtis called after her. Liz ignored him and pushed through the double doors, muttering under her breath as she went.

She stopped short at the sight in front of her. A group of at least one hundred people mingled before her. A string quartet played music in the background. Some of the writers in front of her danced, some ate while they spoke with each other, and some stood off by themselves. Edgar Allan Poe was especially easy to spot. His black hair was parted on the right, his mustache fully covered his upper lip, and he wore a black suit with a white cravat tucked underneath the jacket. He wandered around, muttering under his breath. No one stood next to him.

Women were dressed in various outfits, from t-shirts and jeans to simple skirts to extravagant gowns, probably based on what was popular in the time they were brought into the Immortal Writers group, Liz figured.

She looked down at her fighting leather with a frown. Couldn't Shakespeare have provided her with something better to wear? Based on the look of the Castle and especially this ballroom, with its Grecian pillars, crystal chandeliers, and stained glass windows, he certainly could have afforded it. At least she had a new, undamaged shirt.

"Miss McKinnen, it's a pleasure to meet you." Liz looked up from her leather to the man speaking to her. Her jaw dropped.

An older gentleman with white hair and a short white beard stood before her, his hand extended and a smile on his face.

"Ernest Hemingway?" Liz gaped.

His smile broadened. "The one and only."

"It's an honour to meet you."

"Likewise, Miss McKinnen," Hemingway said. He leaned closer to her as he released her hand. "You can close your mouth now."

Liz pursed her lips and lowered her head in embarrassment. Hemingway patted her shoulder and motioned toward a long table in the centre of the room. "Help yourself to some chocolate."

"Chocolate?" Liz repeated. "Not exactly the hors d'oeuvres I was expecting for a fancy party like this."

"It's not just any chocolate," Hemingway said. "Roald Dahl's Willy Wonka made it."

"Well, that changes everything," Liz laughed.

"It really is quite good," Hemingway said. He smiled at her and walked forward, took a piece of chocolate, and sauntered away, swaying slightly to the music.

Liz started through the throng of people and approached the table. It was loaded with various types of chocolate: brownies, cakes, truffles, chocolate-covered fruits, and other candies that Liz was keen on investigating. She was about to take a scrumptious-looking chunk of chocolate when a woman with black hair piled on top of her head in an elaborate bun took her by the right elbow and started leading her away. Liz shot a longing look toward the chocolate before she realized who the woman in the extravagant blue gown was.

"Jane Austen, dear, lovely to meet you," the woman said as she smiled.

Liz resisted the temptation to drop her jaw again.

"Elizabeth McKinnen," Liz introduced herself.

"I've enjoyed reading your novels, dear," Austen said. She paused and stuck her empty champagne glass under one of the streams of chocolate at the fountain. Liz tried to take this opportunity to snag a brownie, but was pulled away right as her fingertips reached a buttered edge. "But couldn't you make your stories a tad more... romantic?"

Liz blinked in surprise. This wasn't what she had expected from Austen. Wasn't the heart of her work making fun of romance? "Well..."

"Now, now, Austen, don't bother her," a deep voice said to Liz's left. She turned to a somewhat short man with black hair and a thin black mustache. He extended his dark hand toward her.

"Langston Hughes," the man said. "Welcome to the Immortal Writers."

"You're the father of jazz poetry," Liz said as she shook his hand. "I studied you in school."

"I'm so sorry," Hughes laughed. Liz grinned.

"Pardon me," Austen cut in, "but I was speaking with Miss McKinnen."

"Sorry, Jane."

"As I was saying, you really should make your novels more romantic."

"I'll keep that in mind," Liz said politely. Maybe meeting all of her leading men had made Austen more into the romantic she had mocked in her classic works.

"Your main character—Curtis, isn't it?—is quite charming," Austen said. She took a sip of chocolate. "He has a certain roughness about him that most women find attractive these days. But he goes gallivanting about and never sticks to one woman. Why is that?"

Liz opened her mouth to answer, paused, and tightened her lips together. She frowned. "I'm not sure," Liz said. "He just... never seemed to find the right one."

Austen cocked her head and narrowed her eyes slightly, clearly disappointed with Liz's answer. "You may want to look into that, dear."

Liz nodded and smiled tightly. "I'll be sure to do that."

"All right, you've pestered her enough," Hughes interrupted. "If you'll come with me." He steered Liz away from Austen, for which Liz found herself grateful. She didn't want her books gushy and romantic. It wasn't her style.

"*Now* you can try some chocolate," Hughes said once they had reached the table. He handed her a chunk of white and dark chocolate. Liz accepted it gratefully and took a bite. It was the richest, smoothest chocolate she had ever tasted, and the blueberry pieces added just the right amount of tartness to the treat.

"Since you're a fantasy writer, I'm surprised you're interested in folks like me," Hughes said conversationally.

"Are you kidding?" Liz said after she swallowed. "You're one of the greatest poets to ever live."

Hughes smiled modestly. "The Harlem Renaissance was an important time in our country. I was glad to be a part of it."

Liz bit off another chunk of chocolate as she looked around the room. "I don't recognize everyone here," she admitted. "I guess I'm not as educated as I thought."

"I hardly knew anyone when I first arrived," Hughes said, waving his hand dismissively. "Everyone feels a little lost when they first join us."

Liz gestured to the crowd mingling around her. "Is this everyone? Are these all of the Immortal Writers?"

"Not even close," Hughes said. "These are just most of the writers who are currently residing in the Castle. There are thousands more across the world. Many choose not to join with us. Writers can be an antisocial bunch sometimes. As it is, I only come to visit every so often. I prefer to be alone."

Liz looked around the room, trying to see if there was anyone she recognized. She finally noticed a man with thick brown hair and brown eyes standing a little ways away.

"Is that—?"

"Douglas Adams," Hughes nodded. "One of our more recent additions, relatively speaking. And don't ask me why, but he always has that ridiculous towel with him."

Liz looked closer at Adams and noticed that he had a yellow towel draped over his pale yellow shirt. Liz grinned.

"And over there is John Tolkien." Hughes pointed, and Liz followed his gaze to see an older man with white hair and bushy eyebrows standing in a corner smoking a pipe. Strange shapes emerged in the smoke in front of him.

"I wouldn't recommend talking to him unless you know Elvish," Hughes said, shaking his head. "He slips in and out of it all the time."

Liz made a mental note to talk to Tolkien later and have the best conversation of her life.

"Over there you'll see—oh, no," Hughes mumbled.

"What?" Liz asked, turning to face him.

"I'm sorry," Hughes said. "But he tries his best, he really does."

"Who?"

"I am Edgar Allan Poe," a low, morose voice said from behind Liz. Liz turned around and smiled.

"I know who you are," Liz said. "I love your horror stories—"

A shriek interrupted her. Liz looked up, startled, as a large black bird landed on Poe's shoulder.

"Is that... the Raven?"

"Ah, yes," Poe nodded. "I know characters aren't allowed into initiation but I simply couldn't leave him behind."

"Nevermore," the Raven croaked.

Liz swallowed.

"I wondered, Miss McKinnen, if you might desire to accompany me on my yearly sojourn?"

"Your what?"

"My annual journey to my grave, of course."

Liz stared.

Poe gave a dramatic sigh and explained. "They've been talking about it ever since I 'died.' A masked man goes to Westminster Hall in Baltimore and leaves a bottle of Cognac and a rose on my grave on the anniversary of my death."

"And you want to go watch?"

Poe glared. "I am the masked man, of course."

"Oh."

"Would you be so kind as to accompany me? Perhaps it will give you inspiration on what you would like to do when it's time to stage your own death."

"Um…"

"I'm sure she'd love to go, Edgar," Hughes intervened, "but William is keeping her here until she's trained up a bit. There are dragons out looking for her. She can't leave."

"That's right," Liz said, shooting Hughes a grateful glance. "I'm afraid I'll have to miss it this year."

Poe nodded and took Liz's hand in his. "Until we meet again, Miss McKinnen." He gave her hand a papery kiss and walked away.

"Nevermore," the Raven called in farewell. Liz shivered.

"Thank you," Liz whispered to Hughes.

He winked. "You're welcome."

More authors came by and greeted Liz. Most seemed to have read her books, and at least some of them had enjoyed them. The majority did not offer suggestions for revisions, but a few did. Douglas Adams wanted more satire; Jack London wanted to know why there were absolutely no wolves in her novels; Theodor Geisel thought they should be more child-appropriate but still found the novels enjoyable; some women wanted more sex and other women found the idea of the sex that was already in her novels appalling. Most of the writers, however, simply wanted her out of the way, but she could not justify leaving the chocolate table.

After several hours of mingling and even a couple dances, a tinkling sound came from the centre of the room, and all of the noise diminished. Liz turned toward the light sound of glass and saw Shakespeare standing there in his traditional gilded suit and ruffle. She had to admit she liked him better in his modern-day attire.

"Welcome, fellow writers," Shakespeare said, raising a glass of champagne. "Thank you for joining me this evening in welcoming our newest author into our midst: Elizabeth Christina McKinnen."

The room erupted into applause. Shakespeare beckoned Liz forward, and she uneasily made her way up to him. Shakespeare raised a hand and the room quieted. He smiled and lowered his hand to Liz's shoulder.

"Elizabeth is here because, like all of us, her words have stretched beyond the page, beyond story, beyond metre, beyond language itself. Her words have been etched into the very fabric of reality, changing it to make room for her stories and her characters. Her words have made her immortal. She is one of us!"

The crowd of writers applauded again. Liz ignored the urge to run away or look down at her feet, and forced herself to gaze out into the room of brilliant wordsmiths. *She* was one of *them*?

"Who will join with me in welcoming Elizabeth into our ranks? Make yourselves known."

A pregnant silence followed Shakespeare's words until footsteps to Liz's left caught her attention. She turned. Hughes walked toward her with a smile on his face.

"I welcome you," Hughes said as he put his hand on top of Liz's shoulder.

"I welcome you," Poe said, seemingly coming out of nowhere.

"Nevermore," the Raven squawked.

"I welcome you," Hemingway said, placing his hand atop Hughes's.

"*Amin creoso lle*," Tolkien said as Liz tried not to hyperventilate.

Several more authors came up and placed their hands on her shoulders. Soon there were so many writers surrounding her that Liz could barely breathe.

"Do the rest of you welcome her as your friend and equal?" Shakespeare proclaimed.

"We welcome her," a chorus of voices chimed together.

Liz smiled at the sound, but her stomach twisted. She couldn't be one of them, not really. She was so inexperienced, and so young… but what worried her the most was that her past wasn't as clean as she wanted it to be. She certainly wasn't heroic.

But she could never let them know.

CHAPTER SIX

t felt like Liz had only just fallen asleep when the banging on her door woke her up again.

Bang. Bang. Bang.

"Liz!" someone shouted. "Get up! There's so much to show you and so little time!"

Liz propped herself up on her elbow and glared at the door. She didn't care who was waking her up. She was going to kill them.

"Liz!"

She grunted and swung her legs out of bed, ignoring the pain in her back from the burns and the pain in her stomach from too much chocolate, stomped toward the door, and threw it open.

"*What?!*"

"Put your hand down, you look ridiculous," Shakespeare said. "You wouldn't really punch a famous old bard in the face, would you?"

"I might," Liz said as she lowered her fist. "What do you want? I swear I just laid down."

"You've had about two hours of sleep, I believe." Shakespeare sighed happily. "That was a splendid party, don't you think?"

"A party that ended *at two in the morning,*" Liz countered, though she had certainly enjoyed herself at the initiation. "There had better be a good reason you're getting me out of bed right now, Shakespeare."

"Consider it part of your initiation," Shakespeare said. He stepped to the side of the doorway and beckoned for Liz to join him. "I want to show you around the Castle."

Liz slumped back against the open door. "A tour? Now? Can't it at least wait until dawn?"

"Most of the writers are asleep right now," Shakespeare said, "and that will make this easier. Besides, you might even enjoy this. You never know."

Liz sighed. "Fine. Let me get dressed."

Shakespeare frowned and narrowed his eyes. "If you go back to sleep I will wake you up at four in the morning every day this week," he warned.

"You're a horrible person." Liz shut the door in Shakespeare's face and changed into her leather gear. She wanted to get this over with as quickly as possible so she could come back to bed.

She splashed cold water on her face and stared into the mirror for a moment. She was about to go on a castle tour with William Shakespeare, and all she wanted to do was sleep. Anyone else would forfeit sleep for a year for this opportunity. It was amazing how kidnapping, dragon burns, and Willy Wonka chocolate could change your priorities.

Liz opened the door and stepped out into the hallway with Shakespeare. He smiled at her.

"Ready to go?"

"Lead the way, bard," Liz said.

Shakespeare started down the long, dim hallway. Moonlight streamed in through the tall windows, making everything look ethereal.

"Is all of the Castle decorated like this?" Liz asked as she wove her long hair into a braid. "All of the colours in this hallway are so… rich. Emerald, sapphire, ruby…"

"No, it's just this way in the Fantasy Wing," Shakespeare said.

"Fantasy Wing?"

Shakespeare nodded. "We try to keep you all organized and try to play to your interests. You are a fantasy author so we keep you in the Fantasy Wing of the Castle. Everything here is rich and colourful. The art is played to your tastes: dragons, wizards, treasure, magic. Tolkien is down this hall, along with Lewis Carroll, Roald Dahl, C.S. Lewis… hundreds of writers have passed through these halls. Not all of them stay. Most authors use the Castle as a retreat."

"You mean you didn't kidnap them and force them to stay?"

"Oh, I did at first," Shakespeare reassured her. "But once the villains are defeated, and once the author's safety is ensured, they are free to do as they please."

"So what other wings—"

Shakespeare grabbed Liz's arm and yanked her to the left.

"What is wrong with you?" Liz shouted.

"Be quiet, it's four o'clock in the morning," Shakespeare reprimanded.

"*What is wrong with you?*" Liz hissed in hushed, dangerous tones.

Shakespeare pointed to the floor. "You almost went down the rabbit hole."

Liz looked down. A person-sized dirt hole disrupted the floor, and it looked like it went down a long way. Liz couldn't see the end of it. She could have easily fallen in.

"I know you have the money to fix that," Liz said.

"It's not a matter of fixing anything," Shakespeare said. "That's *the* rabbit hole. When Wonderland came through to our reality, we had an awful time trying to control everything. It was a nightmare keeping the general populace from noticing what was going on. Eventually, after an enormous amount of hard work and growing and shrinking and white rabbits, we managed to contain Wonderland to the basement of the Castle. Unfortunately, the rabbit hole likes to roam around the Fantasy Wing."

"Roam around?"

Shakespeare nodded to the ground and Liz looked down again. The hole was gone.

"Where did it go?"

"It's off to ensnare some other author," Shakespeare sighed. "And while I'm sure you'd love a trip to Wonderland, please put it off. You don't have time to fight a Jabberwock. You need to learn how to fight dragons."

Shakespeare and Liz continued down the hall. Liz paid special attention to the artwork now that Shakespeare had pointed it out. She was surprised that she'd previously missed the common fantasy theme in all of the art. She supposed she had been too traumatized by her kidnapping and dragon burns, and too impressed by the grandeur of everything else, to have noticed before.

"Does the murder mystery wing have pictures of dead people?" Liz asked.

Shakespeare laughed. "Our Thriller Wing is certainly unique... but I think you'll find that the authors behind the murder mysteries aren't so much attracted to the macabre as they are attracted to the psychological functions behind such heinous deeds. We have abstract art in that wing. It fascinates the writers. I think Edgar Allan Poe is the only author there who owns portraits of death."

Liz and Shakespeare reached the end of the hallway and came into an enormous room that rivalled the size of the ballroom where the initiation party had been held. Mahogany bookshelves lined the walls, which shot up at least four stories.

"This is the library," Shakespeare said. "We have millions of books, and if you can't find the one you want you just have to enter it into the computer over there," Shakespeare pointed, "and it will print a brand new edition for you. The computer even comes up with new artwork for each print. The science fiction authors created that feature."

"I thought your office had a ton of books, but this is ridiculous," Liz said. "Has anyone actually read all of these?"

"You'd be amazed what you can accomplish when you can live forever and you're not overly fond of sleep," Shakespeare said. "I have read every book in this library."

Liz gaped at the vast amount of knowledge all around her. How did Shakespeare keep all of that information in his head?

"The library is the central point of the Castle," Shakespeare said. "You can reach any part of the Castle from here."

Liz frowned and looked around. "But there are only two hallways: the one across the room and the one we came from."

"We just came from the Fantasy Wing, didn't we?" Shakespeare grinned. "Look down the hallway again. Think about the art in the Thriller Wing."

Liz poked her head in the hallway and gasped. This wasn't where they had come from at all. Instead, the colours on the walls were muted neutrals and the art was abstract. She didn't understand any of it, but she recognized a Jackson Pollock piece farther down the hall.

She retreated into the library.

"How did that happen?" Liz asked. "That was the Fantasy Wing a minute ago."

"The Castle is highly improbable," Shakespeare said. "So improbable that it borders on impossible. We have an entire world in our basement and we can house up to a million writers at a time. Dragons and pegasi and phoenixes live here, we house spaceships and jets, and we even have our own prison for criminals when we catch them and don't kill them."

"The Castle is that big?" Liz asked.

"Only some of the time," Shakespeare replied. "It always exists, but its existence is scattered so that everything can fit. The library keeps everything together in a large directory. As long as you can find your way to the library, you can reach any part of the Castle you need."

"How did you make that work?"

"I didn't," Shakespeare said. "The science fiction authors did."

"I bet the Sci-Fi Wing is impressive," Liz mused.

"It's a little overbearing if you ask me," Shakespeare said, "but the authors themselves definitely have their uses."

"So this hallway changes to wherever you need to be?" Liz verified.

"As long as it is within the Castle, yes," Shakespeare said. "Except for Wonderland in the basement. The science fiction authors couldn't really wrap their heads around that place."

"What else is in the basement?"

"The prison," Shakespeare said. "You'll probably have to kill Kenric; there will most likely be no other alternative. But for many of the thriller authors, killing their villains is unnecessary. Still, we can't have them wandering around massacring the people of Earth. So, we keep them here."

"What is the prison like?"

"Each cell and each punishment is left up to the author of the antagonist," Shakespeare said. "But I often wonder if we should just kill the villains instead of incarcerating them. They are stuck there forever. They never die, unless they commit suicide. Are we leaving them to a worse fate by locking them away, with no chance of escape, even by death, and no progression? Would it be kinder to end it for them? I wonder."

Shakespeare fell silent as he pondered. Liz shifted uncomfortably, wondering about the possibilities of the dungeon beneath her feet. Who could be down there? What would it be like to be stuck in one place for all eternity, trapped and unable to move forward with an endless life?

After a moment or two, Shakespeare looked up and smiled. "My apologies. Shall we continue?"

He stepped away from the ever-changing hallway and they crossed the spacious, polished wood floor of the library, their footsteps echoing lightly off of the walls.

"The central part of the Castle, made up of the library, the writing rooms, the Imagination Room, the cafeteria, and various recreation rooms, always stays in the same place, so you don't necessarily have to use the library to reach the different areas here. We have three different writing rooms: one room with computers, one with typewriters, and one with paper and pens and quills. You can be surrounded by whatever writing element comes most naturally to you.

"This is the dining room," Shakespeare said as they exited the library. The dining room looked less like a high school cafeteria than Liz had expected. There was nowhere to prepare or serve food. Instead, the extravagant dining hall was full of elegant tables and impressive art.

"Where do you cook?" Liz asked.

"You don't," Shakespeare said. "It's a perk of magic and science fiction mixed together. Food just appears. Are you hungry? I could demonstrate."

Liz cradled her stomach. It still ached from the embarrassing amount of chocolate she had consumed at the party.

"It's a little early for food, thank you," Liz said.

"Suit yourself," Shakespeare said. "In any case, all you have to do is sit down and a menu and keyboard pop up in front of you. It's interactive. Just select what you'd like and it will appear on your plate."

"No wonder writers like to come stay here," Liz said. "Why does anyone leave?"

"Writers can be an odd group." Shakespeare shrugged. "Sometimes authors just want to be around normal people for a change."

"But what about their characters?" Liz asked. "Are they not normal enough for the writers?"

"In essence, they are just a figment of their imaginations," Shakespeare said. "Many authors get along with their characters; many do not. Some people find that they do not like their minds as much as they thought they did."

Liz wondered if she would get along with her characters. She hadn't interacted with them much, at least not yet... but Curtis did get on her nerves. At least he was nice to look at.

"The most impressive thing I want to show you is the Imagination Room," Shakespeare said, leading Liz toward the exit door on their right.

"The Imagination Room?"

"It is probably the most useful thing the science fiction authors have come up with, at least in terms of helping the writers with their creativity," Shakespeare said, pointing to some high-tech silver doors in front of them. "I'm not very adept at your modern technology, but let me see if I can remember this properly... the Imagination Room reads your mind, mostly by monitoring your brainwaves and scanning the pathways in your brain, and presents a three-dimensional interactive interface in which you can create anything. The interface will respond to your actions and change the scenario based on the laws written in your head."

"The laws in my head?"

"For you, those laws would be the laws of magic, the laws of how certain dragons are killed. The program in the Imagination Room would pick up on these laws and react accordingly. You can have mock dragon battles in this room. The software will read your magical and physical limits and test those against the dragons'. The laws you've set up in your books will not be broken. All of the rules apply as they would in real life. The laws are known. For example, if you're not magically strong enough, no amount of imagination on your part will make you defeat Kenric."

"That's comforting."

"It just shows you why training is so important. Speaking of which, you have training with Healer in three hours."

"I only get three more hours of sleep?" Liz complained.

"You mean you don't want to try out the Imagination Room?" Shakespeare asked. Liz looked from the silver doors to Shakespeare and bit her lip.

"I love sleep," Liz whimpered.

"Learn to love magic and swordplay," Shakespeare said. "Maybe learn to love the Castle. It's not too bad."

"It is pretty impressive," Liz admitted. "And I promise to try the Imagination Room soon. I just don't think anything would pop up if I were to go in there now. I am brain dead."

Shakespeare rolled his eyes, but he followed along when Liz took a hesitant step toward the library.

"Am I confined to the Fantasy Wing, or can I investigate the other wings from time to time?"

"You're not confined anywhere," Shakespeare said. "You are not a prisoner, but I think you'll find yourself most comfortable in the Fantasy Wing. Stay put for now. Focus your energies on learning from Healer and Curtis. You have to be ready to fight Kenric."

"How long do I have to prepare?" Liz asked as she and Shakespeare entered the library.

"I don't know," Shakespeare said. "Hopefully you will have adequate time to prepare yourself and feel confident and comfortable, but that will ultimately depend on Kenric."

"What do you mean?"

"He may need to be stopped before you feel ready," Shakespeare said. "I have faith that you can prepare yourself in time, but I prefer that you have faith in yourself before you go off slaying dragons and sorcerers."

"And you think he'll act quickly?"

Shakespeare frowned. "You would know best, Elizabeth. But from what I've read, I would guess that giving you a fair chance isn't in Kenric's best interest. He's mostly a selfish person. And he's not exactly patient, is he?"

Liz swallowed.

"No," she said. "No, he isn't."

CHAPTER SEVEN

Liz cleared her throat. "Healer?"

Healer looked up from some papers she was writing on and smiled at Liz. She set down her pen and pushed away from the desk that sat at the back of her elaborate pink and orange silk tent.

"Hello, Creator."

Liz grimaced. She felt like the term "creator" was far too important to be used on her. She didn't want to make Healer feel bad, though, so she rocked back and forth on her heels uneasily.

"So... how do we start?"

"I was going to ask you the same question." Healer smiled. "The way I would normally teach magic would be to start with the laws that define it. But you already know all of those laws. Would you like me to skip over them?"

"Could you remind me of the magical laws?" Liz asked. "I do know them, but I'd appreciate the refresher. It's possible that I've forgotten something important."

"Yes, that's perfect," Healer said. She pointed to a plush, light-brown chair close to where Liz stood. "Please, have a seat."

Liz sat while Healer spoke. "I think you're right: a refresher can't hurt. It's important to fully grasp the laws of magic before you try to practise it. There are three different types of magic. The most common is Elemental. Individuals with this type of power can draw from the elements and use them to their advantage. Fire, water, air, and earth will readily respond to these magic users and do their bidding, but, as with all magic, this comes with a price. The elements are all around us. It's easy to draw from them and use their strength, but an Elemental user has to give the elements power to do their will. There are a lot of Elementalists who have wasted away because they don't bother to maintain their body like they do their mind. That's why most institutes of magic spend time strengthening the body as well as the mind and soul."

Healer raised her arms and started drawing in the air with her hands. As she did, sparkling lines appeared in front of her. An image of fire shimmered in the air, along with an outline of a human body.

"Fire is the element that takes the most from a sorcerer. It sucks away heat and air so that it can survive." Liz felt blasts of heat and a sudden breeze as she watched bright red lines pass between the silhouetted magician and the flames in the air. "This can damage the lungs and it lowers the effectiveness of the immune system. While fire does the Elementalist's bidding, it leaves the physical body of the Elementalist vulnerable. Many Elementalists pass out from the fee fire exacts. If the sorcerer were in a battle where they had to participate in hand-to-hand combat along with magic, they would not survive. Most Elementalists don't think it's worth the risk."

With a wave of Healer's hands, the fire outline faded from the air and was replaced by the silhouette of a large tree.

"Earth requires some of the Elementalist's physical strength to give it motion. The amount of strength varies from task to task." Green lines passed between the body and the tree. The tree branches swung violently, like swords lunging for prey. "Unlike fire, earth never takes more than it needs. Its effects are rarely painful for the magician as long as the sorcerer has kept his or her body in peak condition. Most Elementalists use earth more than any other element."

The tree faded and was replaced by waves that continuously crashed against an invisible shore. "An Elementalist has to be careful of how much water they use. Water can become suffocating if used in excess. It takes liquid from the Elementalist. It will suck water out of the person, leaving the magician dehydrated if they're lucky and shrivelled and bleeding if they're not careful. If they don't have enough water in their system for water's purpose, then blood will be sacrificed in its stead." Blue lines passed between the body in the air and the waves. The waves grew more powerful and violent as the magician's sweat and blood passed into them. "Many Elementalists will gladly pay this price because water is easily controlled and contained. It is a very powerful element; not as volatile as fire, yet not as gentle as earth."

The waves in the air were replaced by what looked like a tornado. "Air is the hardest of the elements to control. It takes an enormous amount of willpower to keep it on task. Should you fail in your attempts to control air, it will take a terrible price from you. After it does your bidding, it will surround you and take strength, oxygen, and just the slightest bit of sanity."

The tornado moved over to the body and surrounded it. Grey lines spiked out from the body and surged into the tornado.

Healer waved her hands and the images in front of her disappeared.

"Elemental Magic is the most common type of magic, but it is also the most savage. It is mainly used for battle.

"The next type of magic is Body Magic. This is what I specialize in. Body Magic is mostly defensive. With it, a magician can create shields around themselves and others; they can read the magic in their opponents and therefore predict an attack; and they can heal others' injuries and wounds. Body users have to sacrifice their own physical strength and often their wellbeing so that they can give that strength to others. Like Spirit users, we can also illustrate our thoughts in the air, as you just saw.

"The last type of magic is Spirit Magic. It is a mix of defensive and offensive power. Some think it is the most useful type of magic, but it is exceptionally rare. Spirit magicians can read others' thoughts, move things with their minds, and even plant ideas in other people's heads.

"Spirit Magic demands a price that is often paid by whomever the magic is being used on or against. It saps away physical and mental strength for every minute that the magic is used. While some Spirit users detest hurting others with magic, there are many Spirit users like Kenric who revel in abusing their power to bring others pain. For example, Kenric has manipulated dragons to follow him by using Spirit Magic. Their strength and willpower have become so miniscule that they wouldn't know how to live if he set them free. It takes an immeasurable amount of time for magic to wear someone down that much, but he has consorted with these creatures for so long and been so cruel that he's made it possible."

Healer gave a delicate shudder and fell silent, no doubt reminiscing over Kenric's power. Liz had written him to be the most powerful Spirit user alive. Healer knew how powerful he was; with her Body Magic being able to read another person's abilities, she had been able to ascertain his magic levels when he was under her tutelage at the Academy. Liz questioned why she had allowed herself to give him so much power.

"So," Liz said after a moment of silence, "what kind of magic do I have?"

"I'm not sure yet," Healer said. "I can feel that you have magic, but I can't read your abilities fully until you prepare to attack."

"Attack?" Liz repeated. "But I don't know how to attack anyone."

"I know," Healer said. "That's why I'm here. I can't give you very specific instructions until I know what kind of magic you possess, but I can give you basic guidelines so that you can access your magic. I understand how scary this can be. When I discovered *I* had magic… well, you already know."

"Tell me again. Please."

"When I found out I had magic, I was scared of myself. I didn't know if the magic would change me. Would it make me become a bad person? Someone who enjoyed hurting other people? Could I use magic for good? How could I find out if I had any real talent with magic? Father didn't have the money to send me to the Academy."

"But he managed," Liz said.

"Yes." Healer smiled. "He figured it out. He took care of me. Once I was at the Academy I discovered that the magic wouldn't change me; it was already a part of who I was. Now I know that it's a little different for you; you didn't even know that magic was possible before a couple of days ago. But it's always been a part of you."

"No it hasn't," Liz disagreed. "Not until I became immortal."

"No, your magic began long before that," Healer said. "It was just a different type of magic."

"I can't have always had magic; my books didn't come to life until recently."

"You've always created with words, haven't you?"

"Yes, I suppose so," Liz said. "But they're not magic."

"Aren't they? Words are the most powerful and basic form of magic. The words you've strung together have impacted and changed lives, and they even brought us to life and made you immortal. You, as a writer, know the power of words and stories. How can you say they're not magic?"

"I guess I've just never thought about them that way before."

"You've always had magic. You just have a little more now." Healer stepped around the desk and motioned for Liz to stand. She did, taking a deep breath. She was nervous to touch her magic, but she was excited, too. She hoped she wouldn't fail. The way she had set up magic in her books did not guarantee her success. Many aspiring magicians failed.

"I want you to close your eyes," Healer said. "Now, take several deep breaths. Focus on how the air feels as it goes in and out of your lungs. Notice how it cools your throat and passes through your nose. Pay attention to the way your heart is beating, how it pumps blood through your body. You can feel your pulse in your fingertips and your neck. Focus on that sensation." Healer paused, giving Liz time to focus on her breathing and her heartbeat. "Good. Now as you feel your heartbeat, look deeper. There's something directly behind your heart. Focus on that space."

Liz tried. She knew that this was where magic resided: close to the magician's life source. Magic and life were intertwined. But could she find anything there? That was the important question.

She tried not to think and focused instead on feeling.

It took several minutes of searching, but finally Liz felt a tug in her chest right behind her heart. Some sort of expanse was there, calling to her. Liz gasped. Her magic was real, and it was alive.

"Excellent," Healer said, her voice still soothing. "Now try to take ahold of it and prepare to attack me."

Liz's eyes shot open. "Attack you? I'm not going to attack you."

Healer smiled. "I can defend myself. Besides, you won't be able to attack me yet. You aren't experienced enough. You just need to *try* to attack me so that I can get a read on what type of magic you possess."

"But—"

"I'll be fine, Liz," Healer said. "Now close your eyes and find your magic again, just like I taught you."

Liz took a deep breath, shut her eyes, and focused on her magic again. It took a moment before she found it.

"Imagine yourself reaching out and grabbing it. See if you can hold on to it."

She tried, but it was slippery. Liz's magic wasn't used to being noticed. It didn't know how to respond to her touch.

Come on, Liz thought. *Come to me. Trust me. You're part of me.*

Her magic resisted, but slowly, bit by bit, it came. She could feel a small piece of magic ravel around what felt like a spiritual fist, ready to be flung in any direction.

"Now throw it at me."

Liz steeled herself and hurled the magic at Healer. She heard a crackling sound and opened her eyes. Healer had her hands up in front of her, surprise on her face.

"What happened?" Liz demanded. "Did I hurt you?"

Healer lowered her hands. "No, of course you didn't. But you actually did manage to throw magic at me. I could have been damaged if I wasn't a Body magician. Luckily, I was able to put up a shield."

"I'm sorry, Healer, I didn't mean to—"

Healer held up a hand to silence her. "It's all right, I'm fine. I just didn't expect it to work. You inflicted no damage, so please do not worry."

Liz swayed as a rush of dizziness took over her.

"What's going on?" Liz asked as her head pounded and she crashed into the brown chair.

"Effects of your magic," Healer explained. "You have to pay a price."

Liz nodded. "What type of magic do I have?"

"You're a Spirit user," Healer said. Liz was surprised. There were usually only ten or so in a generation. They were a dying breed. "And you're at least as powerful as Kenric."

Liz's jaw dropped. "But that's not possible. *No one* is as powerful as Kenric. I made him superior to everyone else."

"But you didn't put yourself into the equation. Trust me. You might be even more powerful than Kenric."

"Really?" Liz rubbed her temples and stood back up.

"Really," Healer said. "But don't think that he'll be defenseless against you. I'll train you as best I can, but Kenric will always be far more experienced than you."

"Let's start training, then," Liz said. "What do I need to do?"

"Right now? Nothing," Healer said. "But I'm assigning you homework. I want you to practise accessing your magic. Work on it until you can reach it with a single thought instead of taking several minutes to get to it. The fact that you were already able to throw magic at me means that you're unusually proficient, so it probably won't take you very long to master this. I'll meet with you again in two days."

"So all I'm doing tomorrow is trying to get ahold of my magic?" Liz checked.

"Oh no," Healer said, shaking her head. "For most of tomorrow, you'll be training with Curtis."

Liz grimaced. Curtis might be attractive, but she knew he was a hard instructor.

Healer laughed. "Yes," she said, "I'd look scared too if I had to fight him all day."

Liz smiled and shook her head. "Thank you, Healer."

Healer had stopped laughing, and stared off into a void above Liz's head.

"Healer?"

No response. Liz walked toward Healer slowly, a frown on her face. Healer didn't even blink.

Liz grasped Healer's shoulders. Still, Healer stared ahead.

"Healer!" Liz shouted. She shook Healer slightly, and then noticed her eyes.

Something was off about them. Weren't they hazel? Now they were dark, almost black.

Liz shook Healer again, and Healer collapsed in her arms. Liz half carried, half dragged her over to a chair and propped her up.

"Healer?" Liz said softly.

Healer opened her eyes and smiled like nothing had happened.

"What am I doing over here?" Healer asked.

Liz frowned. "You... went blank. Into a trance or something. Then you collapsed. What happened, Healer?"

Healer sat up. "This has happened once or twice, but never in front of anyone else." She seemed almost embarrassed.

"Have you told anyone?" Liz asked.

"No, no," Healer said. "There's no need to worry anyone else."

"But Healer—" Liz began.

"I'm fine," Healer said. She stood up on sturdy legs to prove it. "I've just been tired. Now, go practise your magic."

Liz hesitated, unsure what to do. She'd never written anything about Healer collapsing. Whatever was going on, it was new.

"Go on," Healer said kindly. She put a hand on Liz's shoulder. "I'm a Body magician, remember? I would know if something was wrong with me. Now go."

Liz bit her lip, but nodded and headed toward the flap of the tent. She shot a look back at Healer, who had her back to her.

Those hadn't been Healer's eyes she'd seen a few minutes ago. They had been Stan's.

But Stan was locked up. Put away for over four years. He couldn't be any part of Healer. Could he?

Liz left the tent. No, it couldn't have been Stan.

Still, something was terribly wrong.

CHAPTER EIGHT

"What do you want to bet he has her bleeding in the first five minutes?" Fyodor Dostoyevsky called. The bearded man stood atop a wooden bench in the courtyard surrounded by six other authors. Langston Hughes leaned against a statue, hands in his pockets, and winked at Liz. Liz gave a tentative smile back and shot a worried glance up at Dostoyevsky.

"Come on," Dostoyevsky said to the small crowd. "A new author against her protagonist! What do you say? The losers have to go with Poe to his grave this year."

The crowd groaned.

"I'll take that bet," Hughes said. "He'll have her bleeding, I'm sure, but not in the first five minutes."

Liz frowned.

"No way," Anne McCaffrey said. She leaned around John Tolkien and shrugged at Liz, who was hiding in the doorway that led out to the courtyard. "Sorry, McKinnen, but you have no experience in swordplay and Curtis is a champion. It's nothing personal."

Liz's frown deepened, but she could hardly argue with the first woman to ever win a Hugo Award.

Tolkien laughed. "I'm going against Hughes on this one, as well. Curtis is going to slice you to bits."

"I'm usually quite pessimistic, but I'll bet he's easier on her, at least for the first five minutes," Sylvia Plath said. "I'll take your bet, Dostoyevsky."

"Anyone else?" Dostoyevsky asked. "Hemingway? Twain?"

"I'm content to watch," Hemingway said. "I'm not willing to risk going with Poe to his grave this year. I'm depressed enough without going there, thank you."

"I had to go three years ago, and it was atrocious," Twain said. "I'm not taking the chance."

"Come on, Twain!" Dostoyevsky complained. "I'll buy you a riverboat."

"I can buy one myself," Twain said. "You should think of something more clever."

"*I* should think of something more clever?" the Russian laughed. "Your penname is slang for twelve feet of water. *You* should be more creative."

"I'm not gambling with you again, Dostoyevsky," Twain said firmly.

"So be it," Dostoyevsky sighed.

"Come on, Liz," Curtis called from the courtyard. Liz thought his smirk couldn't look any more smug.

"Yes, please do go on," Dostoyevsky said. "I'm anxious to win."

Liz bit her lip.

"Liz, let's go!" Curtis waved her forward. Liz slowly stepped out onto the courtyard. Hughes nodded to her encouragingly while Dostoyevsky stepped down from the bench. He took out a pocket watch and the other authors turned to observe Liz's approach.

"Are you ready?" Curtis asked when she reached the courtyard. Liz tore her eyes away from the group of gambling authors and focused on Curtis.

"We're not using real swords today, are we?" Liz asked.

"We sure are." Curtis smiled. He picked two swords up from the ground and tossed one to her. Liz backed away before the sword reached her and it clattered to the cobblestones. Dostoyevsky laughed.

"Lesson one: don't be afraid of the sword," Curtis said with a frown. "Go on, pick it up."

Liz stared at him. "But I don't know how to use this thing. You'll kill me with the sword you're holding."

"I am awfully talented," Curtis admitted, "but I'll try not to hurt you too much."

"I'd rather you didn't hurt me, period."

"Then you'd better pick up your sword and defend yourself." He lifted his sword and took a step forward.

Liz stepped back. "You could kill me with that thing! Can't we start with sticks or some—ow!"

Curtis had lunged forward and smacked her side with the flat of his blade.

"I told you, it's only a matter of time," Tolkien said.

"She's not bleeding yet," Plath replied.

"Forget the swords," Hemingway called. "Punch him in the face, McKinnen!"

"Her villain is going to have a sword, Hemingway." Twain rolled his eyes.

"I could still give her a few boxing tips," Hemingway countered. "They could come in handy."

"What was that for?" Liz yelled at Curtis. "That'll bruise!"

"That was for stalling," Curtis said. "You know that I don't go easy on my pupils. They end up learning quickly for that exact reason. Now pick up your sword."

Liz squatted down and picked up her weapon, her eyes on Curtis just in case he tried to attack her again. He didn't. She stood back up, sword in hand. It was heavier than she'd expected.

"All right," Curtis said. "Now raise your sword and try to block me."

"Wait—"

But Curtis had already begun. She managed to deflect his first two hits before he nicked her cheek. Hughes and Plath sighed. Plath sounded particularly depressed.

"Dammit," she muttered.

"It was inevitable," McCaffrey said.

"Ouch!" Liz cried. "You cut me!"

Curtis nodded. "You're very observant."

"*Why* did you cut me?"

"To make you want to avoid being cut again," Curtis said.

"I'm pretty sure I tried to avoid that."

"But now you're going to do a better job defending yourself," Curtis said. "Now you know that I'll actually hurt you. Not seriously, of course, but I'm not above little scratches here and there."

Liz raised her hand to her face and wiped away some blood. She shoved her bloodied hand toward Curtis, careful not to look at it.

"You call *this* a little scratch? I'm bleeding all over the place!"

"It's not that bad," Tolkien called out.

"I seem to recall several people saying that to you when you had trench fever," Twain mumbled to Tolkien. Tolkien glared at him.

"You can do it, Liz!" Hughes said, ignoring the authors. "It'll stop in a minute. Don't worry about it and get ready to go again."

Liz frowned and shot an annoyed glance at Tolkien but raised her sword.

"Before I attack, let me correct you on a few things," Curtis said. He walked over to her. "No, don't put your sword down. Stay there and let me show you how you should be handling yourself." Liz stayed still as Curtis approached her side and put his hands around her waist. He twisted her around until she faced him. He pointed her sword arm out and then turned her head in the direction the sword was pointing. "When you face an opponent, you want to show as little of your body as possible. You don't want to give your enemy a large target. That's why you should stand to the side like this. Your body is better protected this way. Since you're right handed, your heart is out of the way as well." Curtis walked away from her and hefted his sword. "Ready?"

"No."

Curtis smiled and lunged toward her. She managed to block about five jabs before he cut through the leather on the side of her ribcage and scratched her.

"Twice in less than five minutes," Dostoyevsky noted with a satisfied smirk. Liz gritted her teeth, but directed her frustration at Curtis.

"Do you *really* have to do that?"

"Yes," Curtis said soberly. "I am sorry for your pain."

Liz snorted. "You are not."

"I am a little."

Liz rolled her eyes. "So you've told me how to stand with a sword. Can't you show me how to block you? I can only do so much through sheer willpower."

"You can do a lot with willpower and desperation, but you're right— you could use a few pointers."

Curtis walked to Liz's side and lifted his sword. "First of all, hold your sword closer to the guard on the hilt. The higher you hold it, the more flexibility you'll have. You'll maintain a good grip as long as the majority of your hold is through your thumb and index finger. Keep the rest of your hand light against the sword. That'll give you stability while still allowing you to move your weapon."

Liz adjusted her grip according to Curtis's instructions. She tried moving the sword around and was surprised to find that Curtis was right about its mobility. Still, it was heavier than she would have liked. She wasn't built for this.

"Good," Curtis said, nodding. "Now try a basic cut. It's just a chopping motion, like this." Curtis paused and demonstrated. She frowned and brought her sword down. "Close. Watch again. You want to be sure to land on the edge."

"Landing on the edge would help," Tolkien snickered.

"Give her a chance," Hemingway reprimanded. "You weren't that great when you started either, John."

Liz tried some cuts with Curtis until he deemed her ready to move on. "Good enough. Now, I want you to try to disengage. Basically, you move your blade in a circle, like this. It's a good defensive move. Try it."

Curtis watched her disengage and gave her several pointers before he decided she was ready for more.

"Good. Now try an envelopment. It's similar to a disengage, but instead of avoiding the parry, you're taking your opponent's sword in a circle."

Liz tried it until she had mastered it well enough for Curtis to move on to other techniques like an interception, a mal-parry, and a riposte. Eventually Liz's arm felt like it would never work again.

"Stop," Liz panted. "I'm too tired. My arm is exhausted."

"It's just a sabre," Curtis said. "It's not *that* heavy."

"I'm not used to this like you are," Liz complained. "Give me a break. I've learned a lot today and gotten several bruises and cuts thanks to you."

"I know you're tired, but we're not done yet."

"Keep entertaining us, McKinnen!" Dostoyevsky shouted.

"Come *on*," Liz muttered to Curtis, trying her best to ignore the Russian author. "Just give me a minute to rest."

"Do you think your enemy would ever give you a break?" Curtis countered. "Do you think you can just complain that your arm is tired and Kenric will let you go? No! So get your sword up. I've shown you enough moves for today; now you need to put them into practice before you forget them."

"Curtis…"

"Come on! Get your sword arm up!"

"Oh good, they're going to fight again," Tolkien said. Hughes straightened against the statue in interest.

Liz glared at Curtis but raised her sword. The sabre shook in her grasp. This would definitely result in more bloodshed on her part.

Curtis leapt forward and Liz parried his blow. She enveloped his sword on the next lunge and forced the tip of the sabre away. Curtis stepped back to his En Garde position before lunging forward. Liz crossed back and avoided his blow altogether. Curtis smiled and cut down onto Liz's sword; once, twice, three times. Each blow forced Liz's sword farther and farther down. She couldn't force herself to pick it up to where it had been before. Her arm was too tired.

Liz thought that Curtis was going to cut down again, but just as his sword moved he feinted and went for her face. She couldn't bring her sword up in time and he drew a line of blood from her neck.

Liz dropped her sword, utterly exhausted. She tried her best not to cry.

"That lasted longer." Tolkien nodded in approval. "She's improving quickly."

"Let's go," Hughes said, studying Liz's face. Liz was grateful for his intervention. She couldn't stand to have the authors watch her break down. "I think she's exhausted and done for the day."

"But—" Dostoyevsky began.

"She can't get the sword back up," Plath interrupted. "Let's… leave her be."

The authors slowly trickled away. Hughes gave Liz an encouraging smile before shutting the courtyard door behind him, much to what seemed to be Tolkien's disappointment.

Liz wiped blood off of her neck and collapsed down to the ground, gritting her teeth against the sting in her throat. She tried to push herself up, but noticed the blood on her hand.

Blood in general didn't bother her. She could watch movies with gore, but seeing her own blood hurt her in ways she had never shared with anyone.

Everything went dark.

The courtyard faded away.

Blood, all over the bed.

Sobbing.

Stan above her, buckling his belt together again.

"Keep your mouth shut," Stan says softly. He kisses her head.

Liz screams—

Liz gasped as she found herself back in the courtyard, tears streaming down her face. Curtis removed his hands from her neck.

"How did you get me out?" Liz asked.

"Out of what?" Curtis asked.

"I've never come back so quickly."

Curtis paused. "I healed your neck," he said, "but there was something else in your mind. A darkness, starting to cover it. What was that?"

Liz wiped tears off of her face, careful to use the hand that wasn't covered in blood.

"Liz, what's going on?"

Liz pursed her lips and remained silent.

Curtis took Liz's hand and gingerly helped her sit up.

"Was it the blood?" he asked.

Liz couldn't look at him. She stared at the statue that Hughes had been leaning against a few moments earlier.

Curtis reached under her chin and made her face him. His blue eyes were kind and concerned. She'd never seen anyone look at her like that.

"What's wrong?" Curtis asked again.

Liz hesitated. She couldn't tell him. Not yet. She'd never even told Derek.

"I can't do this anymore," Liz muttered. She'd tell only half of the truth. "I'm tired. This is all a lot to take in—this new life, meeting all of you, finding out you're real, being attacked by a dragon, learning about magic. I can't handle being cut up and bruised by you!"

Curtis moved his hands away from Liz's face and put his muscly arms above his knees. He frowned at the ground, like he was trying to decide how to respond. He knew Liz wasn't telling him everything.

He sighed. "I know, Liz. I know how hard this is for you. But I'm trying to prepare you. I've fought Kenric. I know how talented he is. I can defeat him in the books, but not here. You have to do that in this world, but in your current state you don't stand a chance. You don't have much time before Kenric makes his move. That is why I'm being so hard on you. Kenric won't stop at scratches. He wants to draw as much blood as possible. If he can weaken you like that he'll have more access to your mind, no matter what you've done with Healer to prepare yourself magically. You have to be ready."

Liz wiped away the tears that had escaped her eyes. "I know why you're doing it. But that doesn't mean I can handle it. I'm weaker than you. I'm not strong enough."

"You are strong enough," Curtis said. He smiled at her. "You're picking this up rather quickly, to be honest. Even Tolkien said so. I know it doesn't seem like it, but give yourself a chance, okay? You *can* do this. I have complete faith in you. I'm impressed with how quickly you picked up the techniques I showed you. You just need practice. You also need to get used to holding a sabre. It will take some time, but you can do it."

He scooted closer to her and put his hands on her head. He closed his eyes. His hands seemed to get warmer the longer he held them there. That might have been because he was so close to her and he was so damn attractive. But when he opened his eyes, Liz noticed that her mind was calmer, and the flashback he had saved her from seemed farther away than it had ever been. He had healed part of her mind with Body Magic.

"Thank you," Liz said softly. He didn't know what was wrong, but he had still expended some of his energy on helping her. No one had ever treated her like that.

"You're welcome," Curtis said. His hands stayed on her cheeks as he looked into her eyes.

Just as Liz's heart started to race, Curtis pulled his hands away and stood up.

"Do one hundred pushups every three hours," he said as he walked away. "You need to increase your strength and stamina."

Liz swallowed and shuddered as she looked at the drying blood on her hand. She was grateful for his intervention, but Curtis would never be able to heal her from everything.

CHAPTER NINE

Curtis may have healed her physical wounds, but Liz was still sore. She was bruised, and the pushups Curtis had her doing were agonizing. She had considered herself in shape before, but now she was questioning all of the exercising she had ever done. What good had it all been if she hurt like this?

"Sorry I'm late," Healer said as she swept into the tent where Liz had been waiting. Her brown-grey hair was frazzled and her silk clothes were wrinkled, but she still wore a brilliant smile that lit up her face.

"Is everything okay?" Liz asked. She squinted at Healer's eyes. They were definitely her own.

"Oh yes." Healer waved the thought away. "Nothing to concern yourself with. A character from another set of books was badly injured and Shakespeare called me to deal with it."

"Your magic works on other characters?" Liz was surprised. For some reason she had thought that the magic she had written would only work within the universe of her books. She had never considered that everything from every Immortal Writer's books could exist everywhere at once. It seemed a little overwhelming.

"Yes," Healer said. "Just because not every character can wield the magic you've written does not mean it won't have any effect on them. I'm probably the most proficient medical personnel on the Castle grounds."

"I bet that keeps you busy," Liz noted.

"It can," Healer agreed, "but I enjoy it. I like using my magic, especially to help other people. But I do apologize for being late."

"I don't mind," Liz said. "Who were you helping, anyway?"

Healer sighed. "Edgar Allan Poe has been writing again and I swear his stories get worse and worse. Those poor characters. They can't help being, well, a little insane. They're always getting into trouble."

"Aren't you glad *I* wrote you?" Liz teased.

"I'm very grateful for you." Healer smiled as she undid her soft, worn leather boots. Liz felt a tug of guilt. She would have to change something in that last book before it was published. She hoped she would have time. She made a mental note to talk to Shakespeare about getting in contact with her agent before more time passed. She needed to finish her edits, anyway. She really didn't have much time left.

"All right," Healer sighed after a moment. "I think I'm ready to start our training for the day. The question is, are you?"

"I'm not sure," Liz admitted. "I don't know what to expect. I know you'll be teaching me how to attack with Spirit. What if I hurt you? I don't want to do that."

"You won't be hurting *me*. I enlisted someone to help us today so that I could focus on monitoring and instructing you instead of defending myself from you."

Liz breathed a sigh of relief. "Good. I like you too much to hurt you."

"Thank you, Creator." Healer paused as she stood and stretched. Liz had the impression that she hadn't slept for a while, except for when she passed out. Liz frowned.

"Okay," Healer began, letting her arms fall to her sides. "Have you practised accessing your magic?" Liz nodded. "Good. Let's see how long it takes you to grab hold of it. Go ahead. Try."

Liz closed her eyes. It took her only a second to find her magic, but a few moments more to grab hold of it.

"Open your eyes, but keep a hold on your magic."

Liz did. Her magic wavered, but she managed to hold onto it.

"Now let the magic go."

With a feeling of deep regret, Liz relinquished her hold on the magic.

"You grasped your magic a lot faster than you did last time," Healer said, "but it is still taking too long for a battle. That's probably because your magic doesn't think you're actually going to use it. Today will change that. We will begin with—"

Healer's words were cut off as Curtis strolled into the room.

"Hi there, Healer." Curtis grinned. "Hey, Liz. How's that arm of yours holding up?"

Liz scowled at him. Curtis's smile intensified. "Now, now. Don't give me that. You'll get your payback today. Probably."

It took Liz a minute to catch on to what Curtis was saying.

"I'm going to attack *him*?" Liz exclaimed.

"Don't worry about it," Healer said. "He'll be all right."

"Oh, I'm not worried," Liz snickered. "This'll be fun. He owes me after yesterday."

Curtis shrugged. "I think you're overestimating your abilities. You think you can get through my shield, and I just don't think you're—"

Liz grabbed ahold of her magic and thrust a fistful of it at Curtis. It knocked him back into a bed. He gaped at her for a minute and then laughed.

"Careful there, Liz," Curtis said. "You may have the upper hand in magic, but I'm going to get back at you tomorrow."

"Hold on, hold on." Healer stepped between the two of them, hands extended. "Liz, you can't just attack him like that. You should know better. Don't you feel the effects?"

Liz swayed a little bit and then shook her head. "I forgot..."

"Spirit usually takes its fee from the person the magician is attacking, but if you just throw it around with no real direction or reason then it will take the price from you simply because it doesn't know what it's doing," Healer explained. "You need to focus on *controlling* your magic, not getting even with Curtis."

Liz staggered over to a bed and sat down. "Just give me a minute."

Healer nodded and stepped away. Curtis smiled. "Hey, that was a great attack. I didn't see it coming and it takes a lot to catch me off guard."

Liz smiled. "I know it does. But your arrogance has always been a downfall."

Curtis spread his hands in a shrug. "Hey, I can't be blamed. You wrote me that way."

Liz frowned. "Does that mean you have no agency?"

Curtis laughed. "Even though this won't help my argument... yes, I still have agency. When you were writing my story, didn't it just come to you? How much control did you feel you really had over what happened in your books?"

Liz thought about it for a minute. "Not much, really. The story just... revealed itself to me. I could tweak and enhance things, and of course revision was more than necessary, but I just *knew* how some things had to be and it felt like treason to change them."

"See? When you wrote about me you were writing like you knew what choices I'd make, not like you were making the choices for me. It's the same way with Healer and even Kenric. You didn't take our agency away; I'd say it's more like you gave us access to our choices." Curtis sighed. "So I guess all of my arrogance is on me."

Liz smiled at his admission and then turned her attention over to Healer. "The dizziness has stopped. I think I'm ready to try again."

Healer nodded. "All right. Stand up and grab hold of your magic. This time, don't release it until I say you're ready."

Liz stood and, keeping her eyes open, seized her magic. It came more readily to her this time. Healer must have been right: it was more anxious to cooperate when it knew it would be used.

"Do you have it?" Healer asked. Liz nodded. "Okay. I've explained what Spirit users can do. For this exercise, I want you to try to move something with your mind. When you figure out what you want to move, think of it in terms of a weapon instead of just an object. Your focus needs to be on Curtis more than anything else. That way the Spirit Magic will take its price from Curtis... assuming you can breach his shield."

"What if I can't break it?"

"Then Spirit will just hang in the air until it either succeeds or is called back. It's dangerous to leave Spirit Magic out in the open. If you can't force your object past Curtis's wall, call it back to you. Spirit will take its price from you if that is the case, but it's better than the destruction Spirit Magic will cause if left unattended." Healer nodded at Liz. "Go ahead. Find an object and try to move it toward Curtis."

Liz looked around. There weren't a lot of sharp objects in Healer's tent, but there were plenty of loose, heavy items that could potentially inflict damage. Liz spotted a thick book and released her magic.

The book flew toward Curtis, but just as it was about to reach him, it stopped and shuddered. Liz squinted, trying to exert her will to force the book through Curtis's shield. She could just see the shield's faint shimmering outline in front of him. The book tipped inside of it, trying to find a way through, but it just seemed to bend the shield rather than break it.

Liz noticed that the shield only covered Curtis's front, leaving the rest of him vulnerable. She let the book drop and immediately sent a small lamp from a corner behind Curtis hurtling toward him. Curtis extended a hand and a shield shot out behind him, barely stopping the lamp in time. Liz frowned. Curtis was too quick for her. Maybe she should try something smaller and harder to see.

She started to look away from Curtis to find something else to throw at him when she noticed a knife hilt sticking out from the top of his leather boot. If Curtis was focused on the lamp behind him and didn't notice what she was doing, would he be able to stop the knife from getting him?

There was only one way to find out.

Liz dropped the lamp, and just as Curtis looked around for the next blunt object, she forced her magic to the knife in his boot. Curtis squinted, probably using his Body Magic to figure out her attack. His eyes widened momentarily. Liz was already past any shield he could erect. The knife swooped up and twisted a long gash on his leg. Curtis swore and Liz let her magic go.

Curtis shook his head back and forth. "Ugh. Spirit effects. They're never pleasant."

Liz frowned. "Why aren't you almost passing out like I was? That was a lot of Spirit Magic."

Curtis shrugged as he sat down on a bed to inspect his leg. "I'm stronger than you and I'm used to the effects of magic. You'll get used to it in time, but for now it makes sense that I'm more resilient."

Liz focused on the blood that oozed down his leg. "Sorry about that. That looks worse than I meant for it to be."

Healer stepped forward and inspected it. "It's pretty deep. But I can heal it."

She put her hands on his leg with a look of determination on her face. Liz wondered if she had the strength to heal Curtis, having just healed at least one of Edgar Allan Poe's characters only an hour or so before. But Healer removed her hands, and all that was left on Curtis's leg was a scar and dried blood. Healer looked tired but strong. Liz had made her very powerful.

"There you go." Healer smiled.

Curtis kicked his leg out. "Good as new," he beamed, "with an awesome battle scar!"

Liz rolled her eyes.

"Are you ready to go again?" Healer asked her. Liz nodded.

She practised planting thoughts in Curtis's mind and moving objects for an attack. They practised for a good five hours. By the end, all three of them were exhausted. Curtis had been injured time and time again (though he never complained), Liz had had to take in a lot of magic at Healer's command so that she could get used to its effects, and Healer was drooping from having to repeatedly heal Curtis. He had insisted that Healer didn't have to help him, but it wasn't in Healer's nature *not* to help.

One thing Curtis would not let Liz do was try to read his mind. Liz had started to ask him why, but then thought better of it. She wouldn't want anyone invading her mind, either. She liked her thoughts private. But was there anything Curtis could really hide from her? She knew everything about him, but apparently it didn't matter. His thoughts were his own. Healer even seemed surprised by his defiance, but she didn't push it.

"I think that's enough for now," Healer finally said. "Liz, even though you won't be attacking anyone I want you to practise moving things with your mind. You'll have to take Spirit's effects since no one else will be around to take them, but that should strengthen you in the long run."

Liz nodded, panting from exertion and exhaustion.

Healer gave a small smile, clearly ready to rest. "Then go," Healer said. "I'll see you again in two days."

"Two days?"

"You're mine again tomorrow," Curtis smirked. "Prepare yourself. You have a lot to answer for."

Curtis turned to go, but Healer stopped him. "Your back is all scratched up," she said. "Let me help."

"It really isn't necessary," Curtis said. Healer just smiled and placed her hands on his back.

And then she flew backwards as her control over her magic exploded.

CHAPTER TEN

Liz cried out as she skidded across the floor on her raw back. She gritted her teeth and struggled to sit up.

Curtis was already running toward Healer where she lay on the ground, her eyes wide. She was seizing.

Liz struggled up and hurried to where Curtis knelt next to Healer.

"What happened?" Liz demanded.

"I don't know," Curtis said. "Nothing like this has ever happened before. I don't know what's wrong."

Liz grabbed Healer's wrists and forced them down. It was difficult to keep them in place; Healer was stronger than she looked.

"Hurry, Curtis," Liz said. "Heal her."

Curtis put his hands on either side of Healer's face, his middle fingers brushing the temples of her head, and closed his eyes. Liz looked from Curtis to Healer and hissed through her teeth. Healer's eyes were gone again; Stan stared back at her.

Liz startled back, letting go of Healer's wrists. Her arms flung up and hit Curtis. His eyes opened and he stumbled back.

"Why did you let her go?" Curtis demanded.

Liz forced herself to calm her breathing and looked away from Healer's—Stan's—eyes. "Something's wrong," she said.

"You think?" Curtis demanded.

"No, Curtis," Liz said. She pointed to Healer's face. "Those aren't her eyes."

Curtis looked back to Healer's face, but she had stopped seizing and her eyes were closed. He scooted toward her and pried open one of her eyelids. A glazed-over hazel eye stared back at him.

He let her eye shut again. "Looks like Healer to me," he said.

Liz frowned. "But they weren't her eyes, they were—" Liz stopped herself. No. She wasn't going to tell anyone that story.

Curtis frowned and placed his hands on either side of Healer's face again. Liz sat in silence as his eyes closed and he focused on healing her.

After a few minutes, Curtis's eyes opened. He scowled as he removed his hands.

"What's wrong with her?" Liz asked.

"I can't sense anything," Curtis said. "There's nothing wrong."

"She just had a *seizure*," Liz pointed out.

"I know. But I can't find the problem. I don't know what caused it."

"Then what do we do?"

Curtis stood up, then squatted and picked up Healer. He carried her to a bed and covered her with a blanket. "I guess we take care of her the normal way."

Liz stood awkwardly to the side as Curtis sat next to Healer. She didn't know what to do.

"What did you see in her eyes?" Curtis asked.

Liz hesitated. "It must have just been my imagination."

Curtis turned to her and frowned. "Whatever you saw might be useful. You want to help Healer, don't you?"

That was a classic argument. Tell to help someone else. But it never helped Liz.

"It's nothing," Liz said. She walked toward the flap of the tent.

"I don't know what's going on, Liz," Curtis said. Liz paused. "But maybe I could help. I can tell something's going on in your head."

Liz gritted her teeth. "You won't let me in your head," she said. "I'm not letting you in mine."

"Liz—"

Liz stomped out of the tent, her eyes closed against a surge of memories she didn't want to face.

So she didn't notice the dragon until it wrapped its claws around her waist.

CHAPTER ELEVEN

"Curtis!" Liz screeched at the same time the dragon did. It was another small Raknar. Liz idly wondered why Kenric didn't send something bigger to collect her.

The Raknar snapped its jaws at Liz, and she decided that was a stupid thing to wish for.

She kicked her legs and struggled backwards against the Raknar's strong pull. Ignoring her protests, it drew her in closer and snapped its jaws at her again.

Curtis ran out of the tent and stopped short at the sight of Liz struggling in the Raknar's grasp.

"Hello," Curtis said. "Kenric sent another one of you, did he? You didn't get enough last time?"

The Raknar growled and turned its face toward Curtis.

"Yeah, I'm the one who killed your brother," Curtis said. "I guess Kenric doesn't care about you, because he sent you to be my next dinner. I do so enjoy dragon meat."

The Raknar shrieked and dove for Curtis, its teeth grazing Curtis's shoulder. He didn't even flinch, just raised his arm as his sword flew into his grasp.

He swung forward and sliced off the arm that held Liz. She fell to the ground, trying to pry the claw open so that she could get away from the blood gushing from the limb.

The Raknar stomped on Liz just as she escaped the claw, and Liz struggled to breathe under the dragon's weight.

"I wouldn't hurt her if I were you," Curtis said. He pointed to his bloody sword. "This sword is thirsty. I have no problem giving her more dragon blood."

The dragon flapped its wings and flew toward Curtis. Curtis ducked and rolled under the dragon's belly, stabbed upward, and then scrambled out from under the beast before it collapsed to the ground.

Curtis ran to Liz and picked her up. "Are you okay?"

Liz stared at him. She wasn't used to people saving her, and Curtis had done it twice now.

"Liz?"

"Do you…" Liz could barely think. What was happening? "Do you really eat dragon meat?"

Curtis laughed. "I think you're in shock. Come on—"

A shriek erupted from the sky, interrupting Curtis. He looked up and swore.

Two dragons torpedoed down on them, spiralling in their descent toward their target: Liz and her protector, the one who had killed the dragons' sister.

"Sorry, Liz," Curtis said. He took her hand and ran toward the castle.

"Aren't you going to fight them?" Liz asked.

"Of course I am," Curtis said. "But not while you're in danger."

"You can protect me," Liz said.

Curtis's eyes softened as he glanced at her. "I'll always protect you," he said, "but I think the Castle can protect you better than I can right now."

They reached the door to the courtyard. Curtis flung it open and all but threw Liz inside.

"Find Shakespeare," Curtis commanded. He turned back toward the courtyard.

"Curtis, you can't fight them yourself!" Liz hated how panicked she sounded. She sounded so weak. She was completely useless.

"I've got her, Curtis," Shakespeare said. Liz spun around.

"Where did you come from?" Liz asked.

"This will make you a little sick," Shakespeare said. He pressed a round piece of metal with a black button into her hand.

"But Curtis—"

"Now!" Curtis shouted.

Shakespeare pushed the button, and Liz felt herself disintegrate.

Every piece of herself dissolved away, like her entire body had gone to sleep at once and then separated into tiny fragments. She might have felt sick if she had had any idea where her stomach was, but instead all she felt was tingling. She was surrounded by too much air. Her body was too exposed. Where was her body? Did she have one?

Then she materialized into another courtyard on the opposite side of the Writers' Castle, Shakespeare beside her.

She suddenly wished she still couldn't feel her stomach.

She bent over and heaved, highly aware that Shakespeare was watching her.

"Sorry about that," Shakespeare said. "I know it's not very pleasant. Even I'm not completely used to it."

Liz straightened up and wiped her mouth. "What just happened?"

"We teleported."

"We—what?"

"Teleported."

"Is that possible?"

"Yes," Shakespeare said. "The science fiction authors are highly useful."

"Where's Curtis?"

"He's still in the east courtyard, where we left him," Shakespeare said.

"Fighting the dragons? Alone?"

"He can take care of himself," Shakespeare said.

A loud screeching reverberated across the courtyard. It wasn't human.

"Are you sure?" Liz said after a moment of silence.

"What help would you have been?" Shakespeare asked. "You just started training."

Liz blinked. "I... I could have done *something*," she protested.

"You were their target. Kenric sent them for you. We needed to get you somewhere safe."

"And this courtyard is safe?"

Shakespeare bent down and picked up a small pebble. He winked at Liz, and then threw the rock. He had a surprisingly good arm for such an old man. It flew ten feet before it disintegrated into bits.

"What just happened?"

"This courtyard is surrounded by a shield," Shakespeare said. "You're safe here because nothing can get in without being disintegrated."

"We got in," Liz pointed out.

"Yes," Shakespeare said. "But we were already disintegrated, weren't we?"

Liz opened her mouth, then closed it and frowned.

A horrible shriek sounded from the other end of the castle.

Liz's stomach twisted. She shouldn't have called out for Curtis. What if he got hurt? Healer couldn't help him. And what about Healer? She was alone in the tent, completely unprotected.

Shakespeare put a hand on her shoulder.

"They'll be all right," he said.

Liz shrugged away from him, trying to believe his words as horrible cries rebounded across the mountains from the other end of the castle.

CHAPTER TWELVE

L iz looked up from her omelet and sighed as Curtis slid into the seat across from her in the dining hall, clanging his and Liz's swords onto the table. Hemingway and Willa Cather, who were across the room, looked up from their breakfasts, startled, but Curtis ignored them.

"Can't I at least eat before we start training?" Liz complained. She was still mad at him for sending her away a week ago when those dragons had come to take her. She knew it had been to protect her, but she had felt so useless, and he had taken his sweet time before letting her know he had survived the battle and was all right, and that Healer hadn't been harmed while she'd lain helpless in her tent. "Breakfast is the most important meal of the day, and I really should have my strength up."

"You can eat," Curtis said. He gestured to her omelet and mimed her eating. "I'm not stopping you."

Liz took a bite of omelet and a swig of coffee. "What are you doing here with swords?"

"I thought we'd try something a little different for training today... once you're finished, of course."

"Something different?"

"You've been here two weeks and you haven't even looked inside of the Imagination Room," Curtis said. "Shakespeare is complaining about it. He's really quite proud of that room, you know."

Liz swallowed some more coffee. "I had somehow forgotten about the Imagination Room. I was so intrigued by magic and sword fighting that I didn't even think about it."

"Well, I've been dying to try it out," Curtis said. "So I'm excited to go in there with you."

"With me?"

"I'll still be training you," Curtis said. "Things will just seem a little more... real."

Liz silently prayed that she wouldn't think of anything embarrassing in the Imagination Room, like imagining Curtis naked or something. What kind of thoughts did the room pick up?

"So... what? We'll just have a sword fight in a place of my choosing?" Liz asked. "Or will Kenric be there?"

"I don't think we're ready to face Kenric just yet," Curtis said. "I was actually going to teach you how to fight each breed of dragon. I want you to be prepared the next time dragons come for you—and they will come. I know you're mad at me for sending you away. I wouldn't have if you could have protected yourself. So I'm going to teach you how to kill the dragons. I know you wrote about them and you're sort of the one who taught me how to fight the dragons... but you've never actually faced one in real life, except for the time you were burned so badly you passed out and the time I sent you away. I think a little review would be helpful, don't you?"

"How realistic is this Imagination Room?" Liz asked. "Am I going to get burned again?"

"Shakespeare said it doesn't actually inflict injury, though it makes you think you're injured at the time so that it's as life-like as possible," Curtis said.

"Great," Liz muttered. "I don't want my back baked again."

"I plan to show you fighting techniques on the dragons slowly. That way you'll be a little better prepared when you attack them."

Liz pushed her plate away. "Just thinking about my back burning up again, real or not, has made me lose my appetite."

"Ready to go, then?" Curtis asked, standing up and grabbing the swords.

"I guess," Liz mumbled. She stood and followed him out of the dining hall and into the room with the high-tech silver doors. Curtis stopped just short of the doors as an older gentleman with dark grey hair stepped up to them.

"Elizabeth McKinnen," he said in a pleasant tenor. "Shakespeare told me you'd be coming here today. I'm surprised it's taken you so long to visit. Most authors can't wait to try out the Imagination Room."

Liz cleared her throat. She recognized this man. She did. But she couldn't place him. What was his name? What did he write? Probably science fiction, since he was here. Why couldn't she remember?

"I've been distracted..." Liz began.

"With dragons and magic," he laughed. "I think that would distract me, too."

Liz searched for something to say. She knew she should know who this man was, but she couldn't think. "How does this work?"

The man grinned. "You'll need to be the first one to touch the doors, not your strapping young friend here. When you step into the room, and again you'll need to be the first one through, a brain scanner will surround your head and read your signals, then send them out into the room. The walls are designed to reflect your thoughts and brainwaves."

"Will the brain scanner be around my head the whole time?" Liz didn't like that idea. She could be claustrophobic.

"No," the man said. "It will just get a basic reading from you. Then, once it has familiarized itself with your mind, it will be able to monitor your brainwaves from a distance, allowing you to interact with the three-dimensional interface that will present itself in the room."

"I can be in there too, right?" Curtis asked.

"Yes," the man answered. "The brain scanner won't read you, but you will need to touch the door handles after Liz so that the door can read your body. That way the images produced from Liz's head will be able to read your movements and interact with you accordingly."

"Thank you for your help," Liz said. She wished she could remember this man's name.

"No problem," the man said. He started to turn away.

"Liz is terrible with introductions," Curtis said. "I'm new to this world. I'm Curtis Jameson, dragon warrior. Who are you?"

"Gene Roddenberry," the man said. Liz wanted to slap herself. Of course she knew who this man was. "I'm the creator of a popular science fiction television show." He nodded toward the doors. "Go ahead. I'll stay out here for a moment to make sure everything runs smoothly, and then I'll leave you to it."

Liz, still ashamed of herself for not immediately recognizing Roddenberry, stepped up to the doors and placed either hand on the long silver handles. She froze, tense, as an electric shock coursed through her. She let go of the doors and stepped back as they opened.

"What was that?" Liz demanded.

"An electric shock just went through your body, infusing you with microchips that will allow the scanner to read you."

"Thanks for the warning," Liz mumbled.

"I didn't want you to be nervous," Roddenberry said. "Then you'd get sweat all over my doors. But in any case... go on in, and good luck. I overheard your friend—Curtis, correct?—telling you that you'd be facing dragons today. You must have quite the imagination. That's a wonderful strength, but it can be dangerous in there."

He motioned to the Imagination Room. Liz took a deep breath and stepped inside, vaguely aware that Curtis had stepped up behind her and had placed his hands on the door handles.

Two halves of a large metal orb descended around Liz's head, hovered for a moment, and then snapped together. Liz sucked in a breath, suddenly scared. She couldn't see anything. She was completely closed in.

Light blue horizontal lines faded in on the metal orb, moving up and down the smooth silver metal. Liz swallowed as the metal closed in a little tighter around her head. She closed her eyes.

There was a loud cracking noise, and Liz's eyes snapped open. She looked up. The orb had separated itself and zoomed up toward the ceiling of the tall Imagination Room until she could no longer see it.

Curtis stepped up beside her and she looked over at him. "Damn electric shock," he murmured, rubbing his hands together and grimacing. "That orb thing didn't shock you again, did it?"

"No," Liz said. "It just read my brain waves, I guess."

"It appears that everything is in order," Roddenberry called from outside of the room. "Good luck."

The doors swung closed and the room went black.

"Well that was dramatic," Curtis mumbled.

"What happens now?" Liz asked.

"Look over there."

"I can't see where you're pointing, moron."

Liz could practically feel Curtis rolling his eyes. "Look out into the room. There's a light in the centre."

Liz looked. A light was starting to spark in the middle of the room, like a firecracker struggling to go off. It was dull at first, but soon it blazed and filled up the room, which was revealed to be white and empty.

"That was somewhat... anticlimactic," Liz said.

"You're thinking about what you're seeing and the room is reflecting what you're thinking about, so nothing is happening. Use your imagination."

"What should I think about?"

"I don't know. How about a place in Shethara? I wouldn't mind seeing my homeland again. I miss it."

As soon as Curtis said "Shethara," the white walls flashed and spun around them, colours slowly swirling into them, until the room showed a large map of Shethara. Curtis and Liz currently stood on the star where Arryn, Shethara's capital, was located.

Liz saw the word "Arryn" and thought of her favourite place in the capital: a temple to the Shetharan gods. Water ran through the entire temple in rivers and streams that fed trees and bushes. Sunlight flowed through the windows and lit everything with golden hues. Liz loved picturing it, and now she could actually see it in front of her, and hear the water and smell the flora around her.

"The Arryn Temple," Curtis murmured. "This is where I was ordained a dragon warrior."

"Yes," Liz said. "It's one of the best places I created, I think."

"It is beautiful," Curtis agreed. He crouched down and stuck his hands in the water, then lifted them up and drank. "You can even taste the water."

"I've always wanted to taste temple water," Liz said with enthusiasm. "It isn't like normal water; it's infused with spices to please the gods and it's supposed to be—"

"I know, Liz," Curtis laughed. He grabbed her arm and pulled her down next to him. "Take a sip."

Liz made a cup with her hand and dipped it in the cool water, then brought it up to her lips. It was the most refreshing water she had ever tasted, with a hint of rose and mint. It was supposed to rejuvenate the mind and purify the soul. She felt her thoughts focus.

"This is beautiful, Liz," Curtis said, "but it's hardly appropriate for dragon fighting. I would hate to destroy the temple, even if it is just in the Imagination Room and not really in Arryn."

Liz nodded, and the scene swirled around and changed to a meadow surrounded by large oaks and willows. A mountainous castle could be seen in the distance.

"This is where Kenric first turned against me," Curtis said. "An appropriate venue."

"This isn't going to bother you, is it?" Liz asked.

"No," Curtis said, waving his hand in dismissal. "This is fine. As I said... it's appropriate.

"Now, can you pull up images of the seven dragon species? Maybe not images... think of to-scale statues of them. Then we'll bring in the real ones. First I need to show you some basics."

Seven statues appeared before them. Some were about as big as Curtis; others were big enough that they could have easily smashed Liz.

"Good." Curtis nodded and walked over to the second statue in the lineup, which was of medium build and was brown and sleek. "We'll start here, with the Raknar. That's the dragon you met a couple of weeks ago, and again last week."

"I remember," Liz said, wincing at the memory of the pain in her back.

"Tell me what else you remember about the Raknar," Curtis instructed. "Try to recall what you've written."

"The Raknar is a typical fire breather," Liz said. "Its wings are leathery, not scaly like the Rokur's or the Crystime's. Raknars aren't very fast... but they can breathe fire a good distance away."

"You have to watch out for the pincers at the ends of the wings," Curtis added. "They're poisonous. You're basically dead if one of those touches your skin, so don't get too close. That's why, while other dragon warriors will aim for the wings, I usually go for other weak points."

"The belly and the neck," Liz said.

"Correct," Curtis affirmed. "Those are common weak points on most dragons aside from the Rokur, but the Raknar is especially vulnerable in these areas because they aren't scaled—they're just leathery. Instead of worrying about taking flight away from the dragons and avoiding those pincers, I just use their leathery quality as a disadvantage in these two areas."

"I should know this, but... how do you get close enough to either of those areas while avoiding the fire, especially since they breathe such long distances?"

"Raknars have trouble changing direction when they're breathing fire," Curtis said. Liz nodded, remembering. "They can't turn their necks quickly because of the heat. Penelope and I are much quicker. If we can get them to shoot fire at us, I can go in for the kill while they're still aiming for me.

"I'll demonstrate. Make this Raknar come to life. Just the Raknar, though. I don't want to fight seven dragons at once."

The dragon roared as Curtis hefted his sword. It spread its wings and the pincers on the points of its wings pinched together, hungry for Curtis's skin. Curtis positioned himself in the middle of the Raknar's line of sight, within easy range of the beast's fire. The dragon reared back its head and opened its jaws. Fire roiled ahead, and Liz held her breath as Curtis dove out of the way. He tucked himself into a ball and rolled forward, just out of the dragon's reach, and stopped underneath the dragon's neck. He hefted his sword, jumped, and swung his blade in a wide arc, killing the Raknar in one swift stroke.

Liz blinked. "It didn't even have time to realize you were gone," she said in awe. "How did you move that fast?"

"I knew what the Raknar was going to do," Curtis said. "A dragon will almost always go for the kill."

"Almost always?" Liz asked.

"Sometimes Kenric sends the dragons out to fetch something, but not often. It's best to assume that they are going to kill you. The easiest way for the Raknar to do that was to blast me with fire. I offered it an easy target and it took the bait. So, lesson one: expect the dragon to kill you. Lesson two: be smarter than the dragon. And lesson three: be faster than the dragon. Lesson three is probably the most important lesson."

"I've never been very fast," Liz admitted.

"We'll add that to your training," Curtis said. Liz frowned but nodded. "For now, let's move on."

Curtis turned to the first statue, which was of a medium-sized, purple-scaled dragon.

"This is the Crystime," Curtis said. "Tell me what you know about it."

"Its breath weapon is lightning, not fire," Liz said. "It's the most aerodynamic and fastest dragon in all of my books."

"Good," Curtis said. He pointed to the Crystime's throat. "You said its breath weapon is lightning. This has its pros and cons. Fire spreads around more, so it's more likely to hit you than lightning; and luckily the Crystimes aren't terribly accurate when they fire. Still, it all comes down to being faster than lightning."

"That sounds like a cheesy catchphrase," Liz said.

"It is also impossible, unless you talk to certain superheroes around the Castle," Curtis said. "I can't use the same tactics fighting a Crystime as I use with a Raknar. If I did, I'd be dead the moment the Crystime opened its mouth. I'll have to use my considerable wit to defeat this dragon."

"Where do you aim when you're trying to kill Crystimes?"

"Their scales keep them fairly well protected," Curtis explained. "That's part of what makes them so formidable. Unlike the Rokur, though, the Crystime's weak points are known." Curtis pointed to each spot in turn.

"The eyes, the underbelly, the undersides of the wings, and the bottom part of the neck. If you try to decapitate a Crystime from the top of the neck you won't get anywhere; the scales are too strong from that side. But come up from the bottom, and you're set."

"Which of those areas do you usually go after?" Liz asked.

"Whichever one I can reach first," Curtis said. "And I try my best not to fight Crystimes on the ground. I'll have more speed with Penelope under me. Can you imagine that she's in the meadow with us?"

Penelope snorted from behind Liz, and Curtis walked up to his pegasus and scratched her under her neck. "Hey, girl." Penelope whinnied as Curtis swung on top of her. Together, they pranced toward the statue of the Crystime.

"Bring it to life," Curtis called.

Liz hadn't even blinked before the Crystime was in the air. Luckily, Penelope was a match for the dragon. She shot up and swerved, darting every which way in order to avoid the lightning shooting from the Crystime's mouth. With every blast of lightning, a loud crack resonated across the room. Liz cowered with fear as she watched Curtis and Penelope just barely avoid strike after strike.

"Pay attention to the way I'm moving," Curtis yelled down. "What am I doing?"

Liz watched more carefully, more objectively. She noticed that Curtis and Penelope steadily drew closer to the Crystime. It hadn't backed up at all. It was focused on hitting its prey.

Between two lightning strikes, Curtis and Penelope leapt to the Crystime's right. It moved its reptilian head at almost exactly the same time that they surged forward, but Penelope was just a little faster. Curtis dove off of Penelope, but the Crystime was focused on the pegasus since it was the larger prey. Curtis slid his blade through the soft tissue under the dragon's neck. Penelope veered to the left and caught Curtis just before he hit the ground.

"Can you imagine that the carcass and the blood are gone, please?" Curtis said, spitting blood out of his mouth. "I don't like to be covered in this stuff if I can help it."

Liz willed it away, and soon the meadow was calm and clean again.

"How long did it take you to learn to fight like this?" Liz asked.

"You know the answer to that question, Liz," Curtis said. "I started learning when I was five, and I was ordained a dragon warrior when I turned seventeen."

"Then how am I supposed to learn all of this in... however long I have before Kenric attacks?" Liz complained. "There's no way I'm going to be ready in time."

"It will come naturally to you," Curtis said. "You're the one who created all of this. Your mind already knows what to do. Your soul has been creating this world and how you would interact with it for years and years, maybe for your whole existence, whether you knew it or not. You just have to convince your body that your mind knows what it's doing. You can do this." Curtis folded his arms and looked back at the dragons. "Now, pay attention, because pretty soon I'm going to put you up against a couple of these dragons."

Curtis introduced her to the fire-breathing dragons that were left: the Caller and the Rokur. The Caller was the smallest dragon, but it was dangerous because it could get inside of anyone's head by recreating the person's weaknesses with its voice. Liz practised shutting the Caller out, and then Curtis had her fight it. Within seconds she was screaming, and Curtis vanquished the Caller for her.

"Well, you tried," Curtis consoled.

"If this was real I would be dead," Liz panted in pain.

"That's why we're practising," Curtis said. "Here, watch me take on the Grinliss and the Sampar. Then we'll give you a Raknar to fight. They're the easiest to take out."

Liz watched as Curtis expertly avoided the jaws of the Grinliss and stabbed it in the heart. He shielded himself against the Sampar's radiation breathing and quickly and efficiently decapitated it. It was beautiful, watching him kill things. It was like he was dancing. Liz was fairly certain she looked ridiculous when she faced dragons. She would never achieve his grace, she was sure of it.

"The last dragon is the Washer," Curtis said, pointing to the largest statue in the meadow. It was the only dragon without wings, and it coiled around the meadow evilly. "It is the only dragon I have never fought. There was only one in existence back in Shethara, and Kenric had control over it. I don't know if it came over into this world or not, but I'm hoping it didn't. I'm not sure what I would do if I came against it. But in any case… are you ready to try out a Raknar?"

Liz gulped and rubbed her back again. "No."

"Too bad," Curtis said. "Summon one up."

"But—"

"I promise to actually be more helpful this time," Curtis said. "Just listen to what I say and you'll be fine. We'll come to this room, oh, every other training session or so, and we'll practise some more. By the time we go fight Kenric, you'll be more than ready to face the dragons."

Liz nodded and closed her eyes, imagining a living Raknar in the field. She opened her eyes to see it charging toward her.

"Keep your eyes on the dragon!" Curtis reprimanded. "You're over too far to the left, it'll be able to get you with the pincers on its wings. Centre yourself… good."

Liz could feel the sweat beading down her brow as she faced down the Raknar.

"Steady, steady," Curtis said. "You're trying to bait it, to get it to take the easy shot…"

The Raknar reared its head.

"It's going to fire, Liz. Go! Go!"

Liz tried ducking forward like Curtis had, but she wasn't fast enough. Fire singed her hair and licked her back, and she screamed on the ground beneath the Raknar.

"Ignore the pain, Liz!" Curtis called. "Get up! You're being too slow! Get up!"

Liz hefted herself up on one elbow but was knocked to the side by the base of the Raknar's wing. She landed on her back and looked up at the Raknar just as the pincers in its wings came down on her…

But then Curtis was there, cutting the pincers away and killing the beast for her. The Raknar fell to the ground in front of Liz, leaving her gasping and trembling. Thankfully, the pain began to dissipate almost immediately after the Raknar was dead. Liz was grateful that the Imagination Room didn't allow the pain to last like it would have in real life.

"We've got to build your pain tolerance and your speed," Curtis said.

"I'm sorry," Liz defended herself. "I've never fought dragons before."

"I'm not yelling at you," Curtis said, holding up his hands, palms forward, as a peace gesture. "You did well enough for it only being your second try. You would have succeeded if you were just a little faster. Your brain is in the right place; we just have to train your body to respond better."

"How long is that going to take?"

"With me as your teacher and your natural ability?" Curtis cocked his head and thought. "Not long. Mind you, you're not going to like it."

"I didn't think I would," Liz sighed.

"I think you've had enough for one day," Curtis said. Liz could have cried in relief. "Let's go. We'll come back in a couple of days and try again."

They stepped toward the doors of the Imagination Room. As they neared the exit, the lights dimmed and everything faded to black.

"Is your head suddenly empty or is the room shutting down?" Curtis asked.

Liz smacked his arm. "The room's shutting down, smart ass."

Curtis and Liz laughed.

But then the room lit up and white walls surrounded them, a small bed in the corner, and ponies on a dresser against the wall.

Liz froze.

"Where are we?" Curtis asked.

"We have to leave!" Liz whispered. She ran forward, but was surrounded by the white walls of her old bedroom. She ran to the door, but stopped before she opened it.

"Liz, where are we?" Curtis asked again.

Liz backed up.

She knew what was behind that door.

She knew *who* was behind that door.

A knock.

"Liz," Stan whispered.

He opened the door, and Liz's stepfather came inside her room, then closed and locked the door.

"Liz, where are we?" Curtis demanded.

Liz sobbed as Stan approached the bed.

CHAPTER THIRTEEN

Curtis stepped in front of Liz and held his arms out.

"I don't know what's going on," Curtis said. "But I know this man scares you."

Liz grabbed Curtis's arms and pulled him back against the wall with her. She appreciated that he stayed in front of her, guarding her, but it didn't feel like enough.

Stan paid them no attention. He just stalked toward the bed, a hand on his belt.

He knelt by the bed and pulled down the covers.

Liz turned away when she saw a younger version of herself cowering there.

Curtis hissed in a sharp breath. He drew his sword, stomped forward, and impaled Stan.

Stan didn't notice.

Liz whimpered as Curtis tried to pick up the young Liz and move her, but he couldn't touch her.

The real Liz curled up in a corner of her old room, scratching at the sides of her face. Curtis ran back over to her.

"Liz, stop," Curtis whispered urgently. He grabbed her hands and forced her nails away from her face. "*Stop.*"

"I can't watch this, Curtis," Liz said. "I can't see this again."

Curtis repositioned himself so that he blocked Liz's view of what was happening on the other side of her room. Slowly, Liz's gaze focused on him.

"I can't help her," Curtis said.

"What?"

"I can't help your younger self," Curtis said. "Your mind... the Imagination Room seems to have picked up that I wasn't there in the past, so I couldn't save you then. But maybe you can save yourself."

Liz shrank against the wall. "I just want to leave."

"And leave that little girl there?" Curtis asked. "You have a sword. Whoever this guy is, he's no match for you now. Go save yourself."

"I *can't*," Liz cried. "You don't understand. He's too strong."

"He's not really here," Curtis said. "He's just in your head."

"He's *everywhere*," Liz whispered. She closed her eyes.

"Come back," Curtis said. He shook Liz's shoulders. "This room reflects what you see. Maybe you don't attack him with the sword. Maybe you can't do that. But you can change what happens here."

"It already happened."

"Liz." Curtis cleared his throat and looked down. Liz shuddered as her younger self's scream was muffled by a pillow.

"Liz." Liz looked back at Curtis. His eyes were shining with unshed tears. "Have her fight back."

"I'm too weak."

"You were a kid and you couldn't fight back, but *you,* the you that you are *now*, can tell young Liz how to fight back. Come on, Liz."

Liz shook her head and closed her eyes.

Curtis put his arms around Liz. "Come on, Liz," he whispered.

Liz opened her eyes and forced herself to look at what was happening past Curtis's shoulder. She swallowed the bile in her throat, then entered her younger self's subconscious.

Fight back, she said.

What? young Liz asked.

Punch him in the throat, Liz said.

I can't, young Liz said. *He's too strong.*

I'll help you.

Liz surged Spirit Magic into young Liz, and watched as she punched Stan in the throat. He staggered back, tripping over his pants, which were around his ankles.

"You little bitch," Stan growled.

He advanced again.

Liz shrank back.

"Come on, Liz," Curtis said. He stroked her hair.

Stand up, Liz said. She sent more Spirit Magic to young Liz. *Can you feel the power? Use it against him.*

Liz felt young Liz's bewilderment, but she helped her younger self throw Spirit Magic at Stan. He stumbled back.

Again.

He flew against the dresser. The ponies fell over as young Liz bashed Stan's head in again and again.

"Liz, that's enough."

And again.

"Liz."

Again.

"Liz!"

The room went black as the flashback disappeared. Liz gasped in shock. She'd done it. She'd beaten Stan.

Curtis still held her in his arms.

"Shhh," he said. "I've got you, Liz. I've got you."

She didn't realize she was sobbing until he found her face in the darkness and wiped the tears away.

"You're safe," Curtis said. He held her again, and she wept quietly in the darkness. Liz felt a brief moment of peace.

And then she remembered how she kept slamming Stan's head into the corner of the dresser, and how she had enjoyed it.

CHAPTER FOURTEEN

"Come on, Liz," Healer encouraged from the ceiling. Liz had tried to ask her how she was feeling since the seizure and blackout, but Healer continuously refused to admit it ever happened. Surprisingly, she seemed perfectly healthy now. "You have to be able to handle magic's effects in battle or you'll never be able to defeat Kenric."

"I know," Liz said through gritted teeth. "But I can't do anything else this time."

She was already lifting half of the beds, all of the lamps, and Healer into the air. She was taking all of the effects of Spirit and the pain was getting to her. It was too much.

"You *can*," Healer said. "Take a deep breath and lift one more bed into the air. Just one more. Then we'll take a break, I promise."

Liz grunted and wrapped a tendril of Spirit Magic around a bed, hefting it into the air. The pain immediately overwhelmed her and she fell to her knees as her brain threatened to explode.

"Healer…" Liz gasped. "I've got to let it go."

"Exercise just enough control to let us all down slowly and carefully."

Liz wiped sweat off her brow and focused on bringing Healer down from the ceiling. Each time Healer moved an inch downward the pressure in Liz's head increased. By the time Healer reached the floor, Liz couldn't do it anymore.

The beds and lamps clattered to the ground, the lamps spewing across the floor and a few light bulbs breaking.

Liz collapsed to the ground and tried to breathe deeply as the pain in her head began to lessen. "Sorry… about your lamps…" Liz muttered.

Healer came and sat down next to Liz. "It's quite all right, my dear," she said. "How are you feeling?"

Liz groaned.

"If it makes you feel any better, you're lifting twice as much as you were a week ago," Healer pointed out. "It's like you broke some sort of barrier to your magic. Your power is growing stronger every day. We just have to keep working on it."

Liz flipped over and looked up at Healer, ignoring her comment about the barrier. She had never brought up what happened in the Imagination Room, and Curtis, thankfully, had never asked her about it. However, she felt stronger than she ever had, now that she had faced her past and beaten it.

"But not right now, right? You promised me a break."

Healer smiled. "That I did. What would you like to do?"

"Could we take a nap?" Liz suggested.

"It isn't wise to sleep immediately after using so much magic," Healer said. "It's like using your leg muscles after you run… if you run a lengthy race and then don't move your legs for hours, your muscles will cramp. Your brain is the same way. You have to give it time to recover before you completely stop using it."

Liz sighed. "Then as long as it doesn't involve magic, I don't care what we do."

Healer smiled broadly. "I've been dying to play a new game that Shakespeare taught me. It's supposedly quite popular on Earth."

Liz propped herself up on an elbow and slowly sat up as Healer stood and walked to her desk.

"What is it?" Liz asked.

Healer pulled out a fancy game board.

"Chess!"

Liz frowned. She didn't particularly like chess, especially with a migraine in the works. She didn't want to use that much brainpower. Still, she wanted to make Healer happy. Healer was important to her.

"Of course Shakespeare likes chess," Liz sighed. "That seems appropriate, somehow."

"I can't remember how to set it up," Healer said as she laid the board on the table and took out marble chess pieces. "I get the knights and the bishops confused."

Liz slowly rose from the floor and walked over to Healer's desk, gently massaging her head.

"I'll help you," Liz said. She set up the black pieces while Healer mimicked her motions with the white set.

"White goes first," Liz said as she sat across from Healer.

Healer moved a pawn two spaces forward. "I love learning new games," she said enthusiastically.

Liz smiled and promptly checked her king in six moves.

Healer frowned. "Well that wasn't very nice."

"Sorry, Healer," Liz laughed. "Want to try again?"

They set up the board.

"Do you miss Shethara?" Liz asked as she moved a pawn forward.

"Of course I do," Healer said as she stared at the chessboard. "It's my homeland, and I miss its beauty. I miss the Shetharan temples. The Shetharan gods don't exist here, and I've always been a true believer. I don't know what to do without my faith." She shrugged and moved a pawn forward one space.

"I'm sorry you're not in your homeland anymore," Liz said as she took Healer's pawn. "And yet... I'm really glad you're here."

"And I'm glad to meet you," Healer said. She frowned at her lost pawn. "Even if you do know more about chess than I do."

"I've lived on Earth my whole life," Liz said. "I'm more familiar with this game than you are. With time, I'm sure you'll learn to beat me at chess. I'm not actually that talented." She took another pawn.

Healer sighed. "I wish more of Shethara had come over to Earth with us. I don't understand why only Curtis, Rob, Kenric, and I made it here. There are more creatures here from Shethara than people. It's lonely. We have such a small group of people with whom we can discuss our home."

"I don't know how it all works," Liz said. "From what I understand, though, you four are the characters I developed the best, and only the best come through."

"The others weren't underdeveloped to me," Healer said. "I miss them."

Liz moved her bishop closer to Healer's king. "I understand. Maybe I can try to write them a better backstory, and perhaps they'll cross over to our world."

"That would be wonderful, dear," Healer said as she took Liz's bishop. Liz blinked in surprise. "But I understand if you can't make it work, and I don't mean to complain. I am happy to be here, to have met you, and to be teaching you magic. You are worth leaving Shethara."

Liz moved her knight. "Thank you, Healer. You know, I based you off of my mother."

"Really?" Healer asked, interested.

"Well… not my mother, exactly," Liz clarified, "but the way I wish my mother had been. She never played games with me."

"I can see why," Healer said as she knocked her king over in defeat. "You aren't letting me win."

Liz laughed. "Now that you're here, I don't know what I'd do without you. You being here is like having a second chance at being part of a normal family."

Healer reached over and patted Liz's hand. "Then I am of course honoured and happy to be here."

Liz smiled and opened her mouth to speak, but was interrupted by a voice at the tent door.

"Sorry to interrupt," Rob's gruff voice said, "but I was wondering if I could steal Healer away from you, Creator."

Healer tried to hide her smile, but Liz caught her face light up when she saw Rob. Looking between the two of them, Liz decided she had better step out.

"We're done training, aren't we?" Liz asked Healer.

"Yes," Healer said. "I think we've tortured you enough for today."

Liz stood and walked toward the tent door, passing Rob on the way. "Can I go to sleep now?" Liz asked over her shoulder.

"Yes," Healer said, standing to greet Rob with a hug. "I think you'll be fine if you do."

Liz left Healer's tent, ignoring the inquisitive feeling in her gut about Rob and Healer and focusing instead on how comfortable her bed would be.

"But, Liz?" Healer called from inside the tent. Liz poked her head back in. "Don't sleep too long. You need to practise your magic five times a day."

Liz nodded and sighed.

It would never end.

CHAPTER FIFTEEN

Two months had passed and Liz had barely noticed the time go by. She had been able to kill the dragons in the Imagination Room, and felt far stronger than she had ever felt before in her life. Her flashbacks happened less and less, and when they did come, she was able to help her younger self defeat Stan just as she had in the Imagination Room.

Her days were taken up by magic and combat training, and she had gotten to know several of the other writers at the Castle. She tried to avoid Poe. He made her feel uncomfortable with his dark stare and questionable sanity. She also tried to avoid Jane Austen. She was too attached to romantic ideas to have time for reality, and Liz didn't have the patience for it. Plus, she didn't like the way she looked at Curtis, though why that should matter to Liz, she didn't know. Liz got along fairly well with Langston Hughes, John Tolkien, and several of the other authors. Remarkably, they had all enjoyed her novels and couldn't wait for the next installment.

Liz had managed to get her edits in to her publishers in time, thanks to Shakespeare allowing her access to the Writing Room computers (Liz had been surprised that the Castle had internet), but had all but forgotten about getting in touch with them since she had submitted the revisions. She idly wondered what had happened with them. They were probably trying desperately to get in contact with her. The publication date was only another month away and there was still so much to do.

But now was not the time to worry about her publishers. She had just reached the courtyard and Curtis was waiting for her. The group of authors that had attended her training sessions at the beginning of her time at the Castle no longer bothered to show up. It wasn't entertaining to them anymore. Liz had improved in her combat skills. She and Curtis practised often. He had even taught her how to fight in the air mounted on a pegasus. Liz's steed was named Sinsus, and was the pegasus that was Penelope's mate. Liz was delighted every time she rode him, and it was clear that Sinsus loved her. Liz had killed off Sinsus's previous owner in her second book, and the pegasus had been lonely ever since, but now Liz and Sinsus were an epic duo. Even Curtis was impressed with them. While he still won most of the battles in the air, she managed to defeat him a few times, and that was a few times more often than most people. Curtis was a master swordsman and had been studying ever since he was a little boy. Liz had only been working for two months and was almost caught up with him. She couldn't help but feel a little smug.

"It's about time, Liz," Curtis called. He hefted her sabre and tossed it into the air. She caught it easily. It no longer felt heavy in her grasp. She was much stronger now. Shakespeare had explained that being immortal had enhanced her ability to progress and improve, and Liz couldn't argue with that. She was amazed at how far she had come in so short a time.

Liz didn't wait for Curtis to attack. She jumped forward and lunged. He countered her attack easily and they continued to go back and forth between offensive and defensive positions, constantly looking for the upper hand.

This particular battle lasted at least twenty minutes. Liz *barely* lost. She had taken half a second too long to parry a blow and it had cost her an unfortunate stab to the side. Curtis had given up on scratches a while ago; he insisted that she was too advanced for simple pain like that. He was right: the fear of pain helped her to improve quickly. Still, she never liked it when he actually stabbed her.

"Damn it, Curtis," Liz mumbled. She let her sword fall and clutched her side. "I think that's the deepest you've ever gone."

"It's not *that* bad," Curtis said. "I promise. I wouldn't do any serious damage. Besides, I can heal it quickly."

He sauntered over to her and gently moved her hands away from her wound. He placed his hands over her side and Liz immediately felt warmth trickle through her. She wasn't entirely convinced it was just due to his healing powers. Liz had found herself growing increasingly attracted to him. Of course, she had *always* been attracted to him, but being around him almost constantly, learning from him, and watching him had changed something for her. It had finally hit her that this perfect man, the man whom she had created for herself (and not just for the blogging fan girls who followed her), was real. Yes, he was arrogant. He could be harsh and he liked to push people to their limits. He was sarcastic and at times could be extremely annoying. And yet, all of these things were just more endearing to her.

"You're staring at me," Curtis noted.

Liz blinked. "I'm just dazed, that's all. You *stabbed* me."

"Yes, but it's all better now."

Liz looked down. He wasn't touching her anymore, and aside from the hole in her leather and a dark red scar, her skin looked completely normal.

"I'm not sure if I should thank you or not," Liz said. "I mean, I'm grateful you healed me and everything, but since you're the one who stabbed me in the first place…"

Curtis laughed. "I'm always game for a little appreciation."

"Well then, thank you."

"You're welcome."

Curtis was unusually close to her. Liz wondered if she had ever written about him having issues with people's personal space, but then realized that she didn't necessarily mind that he was so near.

Then he took a step back, and Liz tried not to sigh in disappointment as a grin lit up his face.

"I have to admit, you're doing exceptionally well," Curtis said. "We had a long bout. Most one-on-one battles won't last nearly so long. You're doing a great job at keeping your strength up. Your endurance has certainly increased, as has your talent for swordplay. So I want to try something a little different, just as a test."

He started to unlace his leather jerkin.

"What are you doing?" Liz asked as she stood up. "Please tell me we're not fighting naked."

"Not a bad idea," Curtis said. He finished unlacing his shirt and then took it off. "But we'll have to save that for another time, I'm afraid. Today, I just want to distract you." He threw his shirt to the ground.

Liz was certainly distracted. Men just weren't made this way in the real world. Liz tried desperately not to ogle him but it proved difficult. He looked so sexy it was hard to focus on anything else.

Until he whacked her on the head with the flat of his blade.

"Ow!" Liz complained. She gingerly touched her head. That would swell up. She was sure of it.

"Focus, Liz," Curtis reprimanded.

Liz bent down and picked up her sword. How was she supposed to focus when he looked like *that*? It was like he had set her up for failure.

Curtis swept forward and attacked. Liz just barely had time to push his blow away. She had been so distracted by the way his muscles moved when he lunged that she had almost forgotten how to—

"Ouch! Damn it, Curtis!"

Curtis had lightly stabbed her leg. She hopped on the other one, frustrated.

"Don't let my sexy exterior distract you," Curtis said. "I'm lethal." He paused and considered her. "You're completely overpowered by my looks, aren't you?"

"Well, I… no…"

Curtis stepped forward and leaned in to her. His gaze was intense and he was so close they were touching. She could taste his breath.

"Come on," he said in a husky voice. "I know you're attracted to me."

Liz swallowed, trying very hard to look only at his eyes instead of… well, everything else.

Just as she was about to make some very sappy and probably embarrassing remark, Curtis whacked the back of her head with his sword again.

Liz fell forward, stumbling into him. His chest and arms were sweaty. She didn't get to hold on to him for long. He gently laid her down against the cobblestones. They felt especially cool to her flushing, overheated body.

Curtis started to heal her, which, she had to admit, was probably a good thing since she was so dizzy.

Soon the pain went away and she was able to sit up again.

"You need to work on your focus," Curtis noted. He stood up and winked at her. "I'm happy to take my shirt off anytime to help you with that."

"In my defense, I bet you wouldn't do so well either if *my* shirt was off."

Curtis looked her up and down and then met her gaze with a smile. "You know, I bet you're right. But since we both know you're not that brave, I think I'm pretty safe."

Liz glared. "I'll distract you somehow."

Curtis pivoted and walked away.

"Good luck with that," he laughed.

"TODAY WE'RE going to practise mind reading," Healer said.

"But Curtis doesn't let me access his mind."

"Curtis won't be joining us today," Healer explained. "Instead, you'll be practising with me."

Liz had to admit that she was grateful for this. She wasn't sure she could face Curtis again today. That last training session had been brutal. It was so *obvious* that she was attracted to him, and it didn't seem fair that he humiliated her with that weakness. Worse, she couldn't tell if he was attracted to her. Sometimes she thought he might be, but Curtis was such a flirt that she couldn't be sure what his real feelings were. Liz secretly wondered if Curtis thought of her as a mother. She had created him, after all. The idea of him seeing her that way made her shudder.

"Are you ready?" Healer asked. She was leaning against her desk, studying Liz. "You seem... distracted."

"No, I'm fine," Liz said. She shoved her thoughts to the side and drew on her magic.

"This will be similar to what you've done with planting thoughts in Curtis's mind," Healer said, "but instead of exerting your will, just allow the Spirit Magic to explore my consciousness. Don't try to be invasive in any way. If you are, it'll be easier for me to detect your magical thought strands, erect defenses, and push you away. Minds don't like to be invaded. Stay curious, but not controlling. Ready?"

"Ready," Liz said. Healer nodded at her and Liz saw the faint glimmer surround her that indicated a shield. Liz had become proficient at breaking past Curtis's shields, but Healer was stronger than Curtis was, and Liz wasn't sure she could get past her magic. Still, she knew she had to try.

Liz's Spirit Magic curled around the edges of Healer's shield, trying to find a weak point, but it was flawless. Liz frowned. Apparently this would be a battle of will.

Her magic pushed against the shield. For a while Liz felt like she was trying to push a car uphill. The shield didn't want to break or even move. It started to bend inward but didn't show any sign of letting her through. Liz pushed harder. Healer was strong, but Spirit Magic tended to be stronger than Body Magic. Still, she wasn't sure *she* was strong enough.

It was a stalemate for a while. Liz was getting frustrated, but then she noticed that Healer was starting to sweat. Apparently Liz was making more headway than she thought. She just needed an extra push.

Liz felt for the magical cavity in her chest. It felt so empty, but she kept searching. Surely there was more magic. Even if it was only a little bit... there. A small strand of magic was still hiding inside of Liz. She scraped it up. If Healer was having trouble keeping the current magic at bay, she probably wouldn't be able to hold back a higher concentration of it.

Liz flung the extra magic at Healer and her shield broke. Healer gasped and slumped against the desk. Liz paused, studying Healer for a moment. She didn't seem to be in danger of collapsing or seizing again.

Liz moved her magic closer to Healer's head, but hesitated before entering her mind. If she put all of that magic into Healer's mind, she would be sure to feel it. Liz took back some of her magic and felt the depleted cavity in her chest fill up again. She gritted her teeth against a wave of dizziness and focused again on the task at hand.

Healer was clearly tired from their magic battle. Liz let Healer breathe and start to relax before she slipped her magic into Healer's mind. She tried to be gentle and she told her magic to be curious and not controlling, just as Healer had recommended.

Healer's mind was calm and seemed quite organized. It had a homey feel to it, like sunshine and fresh-baked bread. It was comfortable to be in Healer's head. Liz reached farther into Healer's mind, gently exploring, but not prodding.

There was something in the back corner that caught her attention. It felt like a shadow and it didn't seem like it quite belonged. It felt different to Liz; it didn't have the same tenor as the rest of Healer's mind. Liz sent tendrils of magic out to investigate. It was familiar, somehow, but it definitely wasn't Healer.

Liz was about to push her magic farther into the shadows to investigate when Healer's thoughts distracted her.

She's strong, Healer's voice whispered in Liz's head, and Liz jumped a little at the suddenness of it. *Stronger than I expected. I'm worried about that power. This is the kind of power that corrupts. What will we do if she becomes like Kenric? But no, she won't turn into him. She's good. I've seen her goodness. She would never hurt me, or Curtis, or any of us. She has to be on our side.*

Liz swallowed. She wouldn't join Kenric, but apparently Healer was concerned. Why? Just because her power was so similar to Kenric's?

It *was* similar. Liz had noticed it herself. But what her characters didn't know—*couldn't* know—was that there was a very real explanation for the connection. She worried that Healer had picked up on some resemblances that Liz had tried to hide. What had she seen?

Healer's eyes shot open. Liz frowned and checked her magic. While she had been worrying, her magic had become a little more invasive than she had wanted. She tried to control it again, but her magic was already trying to delve deeper into Healer's psyche, and Healer had noticed.

She felt Healer push back, and Liz started to panic.

It was the panic that did it.

She felt the magic surge into her, urged on by Healer's mind. It was a risk with this type of magic—since she had placed it in Healer's mind, Healer could temporarily control it. It didn't help that Healer was far more skilled in magic than Liz was.

Liz felt Healer start to read her mind. She tried to push down thoughts about her similarities to Kenric, but by the troubled look on Healer's face, she knew she hadn't been quick enough.

Healer let the magic go and both she and Liz collapsed onto chairs to rest, Liz still reeling over that last image: her and young Liz smashing Stan's brains into the corner of the dresser.

Liz avoided Healer's gaze, choosing instead to stare at the green upholstery on the arm of the chair where she had collapsed. What would Healer say? Would she understand?

"Liz…" Healer began.

But whatever she had been about to say was cut off by a horrible screech outside.

"What was that?" Liz asked as she stood up

Whatever it was screeched again. Healer's brow furrowed and she stood as well.

"It sounds like Kenric has sent more dragons," Healer said. She ran toward the tent door, Liz on her heels.

"I thought we had defenses set up? I thought Shakespeare expanded the shield."

"He must have gotten past them somehow," Healer said. She opened the flap and stopped, her mouth open.

Liz looked past her.

The courtyard was bursting in flames and the sky was clouded with a swarm of ferocious dragons.

CHAPTER SIXTEEN

"Don't just stand there, Liz!" a voice shouted from the air. Liz looked up. Curtis was astride Penelope, a trembling magical shield surrounding him and a bloodied sword in his right hand. His eyes were wide, his curly blond hair was dirty and dishevelled, and he was breathing hard with excitement and adrenaline.

"What do you want me to do? Hide?" Liz asked in disbelief.

Even from where she stood, Liz could have sworn that he rolled his eyes. "Obviously not," Curtis shouted. "I want you to—"

A horrible shriek distorted the rest of his words.

"What?" Liz called.

"Go get a sword and fight!" Curtis shouted. "We need you!"

He took off. Penelope's wings were beautiful against the sea of black above her, like moonlight reflecting off of water. Liz tried to watch where the pair went, but they were soon swallowed up in the dragon swarm.

"You don't have to go if you don't feel ready," Healer said beside her. "Remember, you are the one they want."

Liz thought back to the last dragon attack, when she had been forced to run and hide, and the one before that, which had left her back so badly burned. She still had a large scar despite Healer's care. The thought of facing another *real* dragon scared her, but not as much as she thought it would have. She felt better prepared and she didn't want the Castle—which already felt like a kind of home—to be destroyed. She also didn't want Healer or Curtis or even Edgar Allan Poe to be hurt.

"No," Liz said, "I need to go. I can help."

Healer nodded. She looked resigned but proud at the same time.

"What are you going to do?" Liz asked her.

"People are going to be hurt. I'm going to help. Now go. You're right; they need you."

Liz didn't need any more prompting. She took off, looking up at the sky as she ran. Other characters fought amidst the swarm of dragons. There were characters on broomsticks with wands, a few iconic superheroes, and authors in the sky, battling for their lives. Liz recognized Tolkien on the back of a large eagle, screaming in Elvish and waving a long sword in the air.

Movement proved to be difficult. Debris trashed the courtyard and ash clouded the air. Even though it was only dusk, the sky looked almost black with smoke and dragon wings. Liz would have found it hard to see if not for the immense fires that devoured the beautiful courtyard. She had to find a new path to the labyrinth behind the stone clearing where she and Curtis fought, but she made it. She entered the labyrinth at a run, choking on smoke. Liz knew the way to the stables but found her usual route blocked by flames. Blazing branches fell into her path. The flames reached high into the air, forcing Liz to backtrack and find a different route through the labyrinth to the stables.

She made a right hand turn and ran forward, praying she was going the right way. She had almost made it out of the labyrinth when someone screamed behind her. She hesitated. She really didn't have time to go back and help whoever it was. Healer would find them, she was sure of it. She *had* to get to Sinsus. She needed to get up in the air and fight.

The scream rose again, urgent and agonized. It sounded like Langston Hughes. He had been so kind to her. Liz gritted her teeth and turned back.

"Where are you?" she yelled.

Another scream answered her. No words. Just pain. It sounded like it was coming from her left. Liz started to run. Hughes was in trouble. She had to help if she could.

"Tell me where you are!" Liz yelled. "I can help you!"

Another scream, this time over to the right. Liz rounded a tall hedge, narrowly avoiding a falling, flaming branch. She jumped back, coughing into her arm as smoke smothered her lungs.

Hughes screamed again. He was close. Liz closed her watering eyes and jumped over the branch, her leather boots singeing slightly as she leapt over the flames.

Liz rounded another corner. She couldn't see clearly. Her eyes were tearing up from the smoke.

She heard another scream. Liz stopped, blinking rapidly to try and clear her eyes. She could only just see a dark outline in front of her.

"Are you all right?" Liz choked out. "Where are you hurt?"

There was no answer. Fearing she might be too late, Liz wiped her hand against her eyes and closed them for a moment, trying to clear them of the excess moisture that had clouded them.

She opened her eyes.

And promptly stepped back.

"Shit," Liz moaned.

She should have expected this. She should have known. How had she forgotten?

Langston Hughes hadn't been screaming at all. It was a Caller. It was crouching down in front of her, staring at her malevolently. The smallest of the dragons she had created, it was spiky, sleek, and a very dark red. It had its name for a good reason. It knew how to call its enemies. It could make any sound as long as that sound would coerce its foes to come to die.

The dragon lifted its front legs and beat its wings powerfully. She stumbled back from the wind from the wings.

I have no way to defend myself, Liz thought desperately. *This is it. I'm going to die.*

Then Liz realized that Kenric's objective probably wasn't to kill her, but to capture her.

Liz knew that she could not let that happen.

She seized her magic and called her sword. Liz felt a rush of dizziness as her magic took its toll.

A sword wouldn't be enough. She needed her pegasus. She gathered more magic and sent a thought to Sinsus, who was still in the stables. She prayed that the pegasus would come.

The Caller growled and leapt forward. Liz narrowly avoided its claws as she backed into a large bush that, luckily, had not yet been burnt to a crisp.

The dragon inhaled and shot out a burst of blue flame on Liz's left. The bush behind her lit up and the fire spread quickly to where Liz stood. She jumped away from the crackling foliage, but not before her left sleeve caught on fire.

Liz screamed and beat out the flame with her hand, singeing it. She wasn't hurt too badly, but of course that had not been the Caller's plan. It had wanted to distract her.

The Caller flew forward and tackled Liz with its front legs. Its claws raked down her left side as Liz struggled to get up. She couldn't let the Caller take her. She couldn't go to Kenric.

Something clattered to the ground on Liz's right. Liz looked over, her teeth gritted against the pain the Caller was inflicting. Despite the agony, Liz's face lit up. Her sword was *right there*. She just had to reach it.

The Caller didn't seem to have seen the weapon. It was completely focused on getting Liz in its clutches so that it could take her and go. Liz lifted her knee and met the dragon's belly. The Caller loosened its grip for a moment, but not enough for her to wriggle free.

Liz squirmed as much as she could. She managed to get her left arm free and rolled over to reach her sword, but the dragon's leg snapped down onto Liz's back and pinned her onto her stomach. Its foot kicked into her back again, knocking the breath out of her. Liz tried to army-crawl out from under the dragon, but the Caller extended its claws and pierced her back, confining her to the ground.

Liz's screams blocked out the sounds of wings above her. Sinsus careened into the Caller, yanking the claws out of Liz's back and forcing the dragon off of her. The Caller shrieked and tried to blast the pegasus with fire, but Sinsus was too quick and managed to dodge the flames. As the Caller took another breath, Sinsus swept forward and hit the dragon in the snout with a hoof. The dragon tumbled backward, its feet and tail thrashing as it tried to flip itself right side up again.

Sinsus flew over to Liz and urgently nudged her with his nose. Liz groaned, but managed to grab her sword with her right hand. She put a shaking hand on Sinsus's side and slowly stood up, gasping in pain. Five claw-wounds were enough to make anyone weak. Even Curtis would be struggling right now. But Curtis had taught her some resilience to pain. It was part of his training.

Liz forced herself to tighten her grip on her sabre. She patted Sinsus, and the pegasus bent down so that Liz could more easily mount him. Liz gritted her teeth and swung on, grasping Sinsus's brilliant golden mane to steady herself.

An angry snort emanated from the dragon and Liz looked up. The Caller was back on its feet. Its nostrils flared and smoke curled away from its snout in long waves. It blew out a jet of fire and Sinsus took off into the air. The dragon quickly followed suit.

Sinsus stayed low, close to the ground. He didn't seem to want to get too close to the dragons above them before they had dealt with the Caller. Liz looked behind her. The dragon was a good distance behind them now, but it wasn't giving up. Liz knew she had to kill the dragon so that she could help take care of the others. She couldn't leave the Caller unattended or it would trap her while she tried to dispatch another foe.

Liz grabbed Sinsus's mane and turned him around, urging him toward the Caller. The dragon snarled and blasted out a burst of flame. Liz waited until the fire had almost reached her and then grabbed her magic. She took control of the fire, twisting it and throwing it back toward the dragon. The Caller was fire-resistant, but the flames still served as a surprise and a distraction, obscuring the dragon's vision.

As the flames blinded the Caller, Liz urged Sinsus forward. They passed the flames and shot past the dragon, then turned around behind it.

The dragon absorbed the heat into its body, completely unharmed. It snorted and looked around, clearly confused about where Liz had gone. It breathed out heavily, wings flapping slowly in the air. It looked to the left and right but saw nothing.

Liz led Sinsus to the dragon's underbelly, the only place it wasn't armoured. The Caller twisted, trying to get a good view of them, but it was too late. Liz thrust her sword up into the dragon's belly, groaning in pain due to the wounds in her back and side.

The Caller shrieked. It no longer sounded human. It sounded bestial and wild.

Liz wrenched out her sabre and stabbed the dragon again. The Caller cried and Liz pulled out her sword. She brought Sinsus out from underneath the beast just in time. The Caller started to lose altitude. It struggled to stay in the air, wings flapping frantically, head whipping around in panic, but it was mortally wounded. Liz had aimed for the heart. It wouldn't last more than a few minutes.

The dragon finally fell, its screams growing fainter as it died.

A hole opened up in the ground as the Caller reached the labyrinth floor. From the hole came a monstrous, reptilian head. It opened its jaws and, with a snicker-snack, it grabbed the Caller in its maw. It seemed to grin at Liz from below and then sank back into the pit. The rabbit hole disappeared.

"You ready to take on some more?" Liz asked Sinsus in amazement.

Sinsus snorted and surged into the sky toward the remaining dragons. Several dragons had already fallen, but there were eight more wreaking havoc on their opponents. Liz looked around. Three people on broomsticks surrounded a large green dragon. Tolkien and McCaffrey were each taking on their own dragons, McCaffrey on the back of a dragon herself. Two flying superheroes were massacring the dragons they fought. Liz smiled at their enthusiasm.

Curtis was off to the right, battling a purple, snaky monster. That left two dragons, and each was destroying the Writers' Castle and grounds. All of the landscaping surrounding the Castle was aflame. The grove of trees to the west was clouded with smoke and the flower garden to the north was being used as kindling for the enormous fires. Castle turrets had been torn to the ground, and the lake just south of the Castle looked like it was boiling due to the enormous dragon that blew fire into it. That would probably kill the mermaids, naiads, and even some of the sea monsters living there.

Liz was furious. Even if they defeated these dragons before they managed to do any more damage, would anyone be able to repair all of this destruction? Liz was grateful that magic actually existed. With any luck, that would make the cleanup from this disaster easier. Still, they wouldn't be able to replace the lives lost today, and it was all her fault.

Liz directed Sinsus toward the dragon above the lake. She wanted to save all of the creatures in the water that she could, though she knew it might be too late. Liz knew she had to distract the monster quickly before it killed anything else. She gathered her magic and flung a thought toward the dragon, trying to get its attention.

Hey! she mentally shouted. *Aren't you supposed to be capturing me, not torturing innocent water sprites?*

Liz shrank back as the dragon swerved toward her. She felt a sickness in its mind. Kenric's magic had infected it. The dragon didn't belong to itself anymore. Kenric had poisoned it until it no longer had a will of its own.

Liz had no time to pity the poor creature. The dragon seemed to have realized that the Caller had failed in compromising her, and now it was desperate to capture her itself and earn Kenric's favour. It didn't take long for Sinsus and the dragon to meet in the air. Liz tried to direct Sinsus to bait the dragon, but not get too close. She was dealing with a Rokur. They were desirable battle-dragons because they were impossibly hard to hurt and kill. Their sapphire coating protected them from magic, so Liz would find her power next to useless. Her main weapon would be her sword, if she could just find where to use it. Rokurs only had one weak spot. The heart was completely covered, as were the neck and head. Its main weakness was somewhere on its back—just one small, tiny nick where rock didn't protect the creature. It was different on each Rokur, but if Liz could find it, it would prove fatal to the dragon. It was an Achilles Heel to the monster. One solid strike and its life force would be gone.

Liz just had to find it.

Sinsus swerved away from a claw and climbed up toward the dragon's back. The dragon flipped around and met Sinsus head-on. It seemed to know what Liz was trying to do and was eager to protect itself from an attack.

Again and again Liz tried to lead Sinsus away from danger and toward the Rokur's back, but the dragon was too smart and too swift. She tried tricking the dragon by feinting one way and going the other, but it wouldn't work. Sinsus tried to fly under the dragon, but the Rokur wouldn't give them any headway. Why had she made this thing so impossible to kill? What had she been thinking when she made that up?

They were at it for a while, swiping and dodging and feinting. Dimly, Liz noticed that Curtis had dispatched his dragon and was going after the last one. The characters on broomsticks had nearly subdued their dragon, and the characters on their friendly dragons were faring well. The superheroes were done with their foes and were now helping the victims on the ground. Liz was the only one who was struggling. She was the only one who was failing.

Sinsus was tiring. He was a strong pegasus, but Liz could tell that his muscles were cramping. His wing beats were getting slower and slower. Liz couldn't keep doing this to him, but she hadn't come close to finding that one vulnerable spot on the Rokur.

Finally, Sinsus just wasn't quick enough. A claw caught him and he plummeted. The Rokur would get them if Liz didn't act quickly. She tried desperately to see some sign, *any* sign, of weakness on the dragon's back, but it was too dark for Liz to find anything.

Sinsus crashed to the ground and Liz was thrown aside. She grunted in pain as her back hit the dirt beneath her, but she didn't have time to focus on her wounds. The Rokur had followed them down and now hovered above Liz. She reached out for her sword, fingers blindly searching the ground, but she couldn't find it. She looked away from the dragon and over to her right, searching desperately for her weapon.

The dragon took its opportunity and plunged down onto Liz, pinning her with its claws. Liz's eyes snapped back up to the dragon as its talons encircled her.

Within seconds she was air born. She screamed, but no one could hear her over the sounds of battle. She was weaponless and utterly helpless in the dragon's grasp. What could she do? She didn't even have a sword.

Liz huffed out a breath in annoyance at her stupidity. She could use magic to call her sword. It might not do her much good against the dragon but at least she wouldn't go to Kenric empty-handed.

She called her sword with her Spirit Magic and felt a slight wave of dizziness as her wishes were carried out. Within seconds her sword slapped into her grasp, stinging her hand from the force of impact.

The Rokur looked down at her, its eyes malicious and victorious. It had served its master well and would be rewarded.

She looked into the dragon's eyes, her own gaze wide and afraid.

But then she realized: its eyes.

Liz hefted her sword and threw it with all of her might. The dragon flinched back, surprised and annoyed, but not very concerned. What could a sword do against its armour?

Liz thrust her magic around the sword and guided it to the dragon's right eye. It slid in without much resistance. Liz forced the sword farther in, deeper and deeper until it had lodged itself securely into the Rokur's brain.

Liz saw the life leave the dragon's eyes as it started to fall. Its claw loosened and Liz found herself freefalling toward the lake as the dragon flailed in the air, desperate to live. She tried to call Sinsus to her with her mind, but she could feel that Sinsus was too weak to even register her summons.

Liz crashed into the lake and water enveloped her. She tried to scream; the water was still boiling. The pain was unbearable, unmatched even by the dragon burn that had injured her in her first dragon encounter.

Liz clutched at her magic and surrounded herself in Spirit. She shot herself into the air, gasping at the cold air on her burning skin.

Liz crashed to the ground next to Sinsus, still screaming. She couldn't hear anything. She could barely see. She had lost so much blood, and third-degree burns covered her body.

Something grabbed her shoulder. Liz screamed louder. She couldn't bear to have anything touching her skin.

"Liz!" Curtis yelled. His voice sounded distant. "Liz!"

Curtis knelt in front of her and placed his hands on her back. Liz writhed at the contact but the pain dissipated as Curtis's magic rushed through her. When she could breathe without feeling like her body was going to explode, she shrugged away from Curtis's hands and gestured to her pegasus.

"Help Sinsus," Liz moaned.

"But Liz, you aren't—"

"Please. Help Sinsus."

Curtis turned to Sinsus, his hands outstretched. The steed's right wing was bloody. The situation didn't look promising. Curtis's magic wasn't as strong as Healer's, but Liz prayed it would be enough.

Curtis healed Sinsus and shakily took his hands away. Liz could tell that the pegasus was exhausted, but he seemed better than before. Still, Liz didn't dare ride him again. Not yet. She wanted to be sure that he was fully recovered before she put him into action again.

Liz was about to thank Curtis for healing him when she noticed Shakespeare running up to them.

"Thank God," Shakespeare panted once he reached them. "I thought they might have taken you. As it is, you look awful. You shouldn't have fought them. You should've hidden and let us protect you."

"She's the hero of her own story," Curtis said. "And she did brilliantly. She took on a Rokur all by herself."

"Was anyone hurt?" Liz asked, panicked.

"I don't know yet," Shakespeare said. He didn't sound very optimistic. He nodded at Liz's healing wounds on her back and side. "Did the Rokur do all of that to you?"

"The Caller inflicted the wounds," Liz said, "but the Rokur made them worse, and then I was burned in the lake."

"You killed two dragons?" Shakespeare asked.

"Not bad for my first real battle, right?"

Shakespeare frowned. "No, not bad. But I still would have preferred that you had exercised caution. I know you've drastically improved, but maybe you weren't ready."

"I think the dragon carcasses beg to differ," Curtis protested. "We needed her up there tonight. She could take on Kenric now if she wanted to…" Curtis turned to look at her and then frowned. "Well. Maybe after she lets Healer or me take care of her."

"No," Liz said. "You've done enough. The burns are gone, at least. Better to let you and Healer take care of whomever else is injured."

Curtis shot Shakespeare a desperate look, but the old author shook his head.

"No, Liz is right," Shakespeare said. "I'm not happy that she's hurt, but she can take it for now. There may be some other people in more serious condition."

"And the creatures in the lake," Liz said, pointing behind her. "I think they're hurt, too. The Rokur was boiling the water. I don't know if anything survived."

Shakespeare nodded. "Curtis, you're a good swimmer. Put a shield around yourself to protect you from the heat. I want you to go into the water and help as many creatures and characters as you can. I'll have Healer take care of things on land."

Curtis nodded and ran into the lake. Liz wished he would've taken his shirt off on his way into the water, but alas.

"What about me?" Liz asked. "Can I do anything?"

Shakespeare shook his head. "You have to have your wounds bandaged. I'll take care of that while Curtis and Healer care for the others. Then I will oversee the raising of more defenses and you will go rest."

"But maybe I could—"

"No," Shakespeare said. "You have to get your strength up. I agree that others take priority over you right now as far as magical healing goes, but you need to take care of yourself tonight. You have a lot of work to do."

"Like what?"

"We have to go on the offensive. Tomorrow I want you and Curtis to go to your apartment and gather all of your notes about Kenric."

"Why? I know everything there is to know."

"You might not," Shakespeare said. "Whatever you decided to put in the books is definitely real, but anything, *anything* you wrote down in your notes might also have come true. You might have forgotten one miniscule detail that could change everything about Kenric. He could have a power you have forgotten about or a weakness we could use to our advantage. We need everything you have."

Liz nodded, suddenly nervous. She knew some of what her notes mentioned about Kenric and she wasn't sure she wanted Shakespeare, or especially Curtis, to know the horrible truth.

CHAPTER SEVENTEEN

Liz stared at her red and blue plaid shirt, dreading putting it on. Despite her qualms at the beginning, she had grown to like her leather fighting gear, but she knew that if she and Curtis were seen walking around the normal world dressed like dragon warriors they'd attract a lot of unwanted attention.

Liz grimaced. Her back was raw and the bandages felt like they were barely keeping her skin together. She didn't want to stretch her arms up or put anything over her back. Everything was tender and sore.

So she was standing there in nothing but her bra (which was also uncomfortable) and some jeans when Curtis walked in. He wore a green polo shirt and jeans. He didn't look bad, but Liz preferred him in leather. He stopped and stared at her appreciatively for a moment before he realized Liz was blushing.

"Oh... sorry," he murmured as he turned away.

"It's fine. I'm just... I'm scared."

"Of a shirt?"

"No," Liz snickered. "I'm scared of hurting my back. It's killing me and I'm worried that putting my shirt on will aggravate it."

"You could let me heal you better now," Curtis suggested. "Everyone else has been taken care of and I'm recovered enough to help you."

"Are you sure?" Liz asked. "I don't want to drain you."

"It's fine," Curtis said. He turned and walked over to her. Liz blushed again under his gaze and turned away so that her back faced him. "Besides, it'll keep your shirt off longer."

Curtis put his hands on her back and Liz flinched. Even that slight pressure hurt.

"Sorry," Curtis murmured. Liz felt heat surge through her body. It was painful at first but soon turned soothing. She felt her back and side relax and she breathed a sigh of relief as her skin knit together.

"There," Curtis said as he took his hands away. "You'll have some serious scars, but you'll be fine. You can take your bandages off."

"Not while you're looking at me," Liz said.

"Fine, fine," Curtis laughed. It sounded like he turned around, but Liz wasn't sure. It would be just like him to sneak a peek. She kept her back to him just in case, unwrapped her bandages, and quickly slipped her shirt on.

"Okay," Liz sighed. "I'm ready."

She turned around. Curtis really was turned away from her, but of course he was facing the mirror in her room, which gave him a great view. Liz glared at him and Curtis gave her a brilliant smile in return.

Curtis kept that ridiculously handsome grin on his face. "Are you ready to go?"

Liz nodded. "I think it'll be strange to go back to my apartment after all of this."

"Why?" Curtis asked as they walked.

"It will be the same, of course," Liz said, "but everything in my world has changed. You're real. Healer's real. Dragons attacked us last night. I have magic. If I didn't know better I'd say I was crazy. Other people would think I was."

"It's probably best to keep this to yourself," Curtis agreed. "Other people would think you were losing it. But I doubt you'll see anyone today."

"You're right," Liz said. "No one knows where I've been. They don't know we're going to my apartment."

"Exactly," Curtis said. "Just focus on the task at hand and pray that we don't have to fight any more dragons today."

"Amen to that," Liz murmured.

They walked past the expansive, charred front lawn and toward the long, winding driveway that led away from the Castle.

"How are we getting to my place?" Liz asked. "I'm assuming Penelope and Sinsus aren't meeting us in the driveway. We're not teleporting, are we? That was awful last time."

"Shakespeare thought you'd say that," Curtis said. "Remember that taxi I kidnapped you in?"

"How could I forget?"

"We're taking that."

"Perfect," Liz said. "I've missed it."

"It's the same driver and everything."

"Who *is* the driver?"

"You didn't notice last time?" Curtis asked, eyes sparkling.

"Clearly not."

"I guess you weren't expecting to see him. It's Rob."

Liz laughed. "Of course. He would get a kick out of a chariot that moves by itself."

"His driving skills and his combat skills make him an excellent companion for this trip."

"Does he have a sword hidden in the glove compartment or something?" Liz asked.

"No," Curtis scoffed. "His sword, along with mine and a replacement for yours, are all in the trunk."

"I hope we don't get pulled over."

"We won't."

Curtis opened the door for her and Liz slid into the back of the cab. Someone else sat there. H.G. Wells waved at her.

"Don't mind me," Wells said. "I'm only here in case of emergencies."

"Emergencies?"

"As one of the science fiction authors, he knows how to work the teleporter they developed," Rob explained from the driver's seat. "If we're attacked, Wells can automatically bring us back to the castle."

"I do not want to use the teleporter," Liz said.

"You're a fantasy author," Wells replied. "You're not tough enough to handle this technology."

Liz frowned and turned toward Rob, keen on ignoring Wells.

"Hi, Rob," Liz said.

"Hello, Creator," Rob said as he turned around to face her. His smile touched his dark eyes, which crinkled at the corners. "Sorry about what happened the last time you were in here."

"I've forgiven you," Liz said. "But how did you learn to drive? There aren't cars in my books."

Wells scoffed at the lack of technology.

"I learned pretty quickly." Rob shrugged. Curtis opened the passenger door and slid into the seat. "It wasn't hard. Driving chariots is more difficult. At least with cars you're not trying to control something living and breathing."

"You know where to go," Curtis said. Rob nodded and pulled out of the twisting driveway.

It took a while to get to the dirt road that would lead them down the mountain. It didn't look like it had been used very often. Liz figured that Shakespeare probably tried to keep things as secret as possible. If people found out about this place... Liz could only imagine what would happen. Fandoms everywhere would explode.

They wound down the mountain, passing beautiful red spruces, yellow birches, eastern hemlocks, and other trees Liz couldn't remember the names of. Liz tried to focus on the sunlight streaming through the trees and the beauty surrounding her rather than the twists and turns that seemed to bring them precariously close to steep drop-offs and dangerous-looking ravines. She gripped her seatbelt and tried not to hyperventilate.

Curtis picked up on her anxiety. "You were a lot calmer on the way up here," he teased.

"Maybe you should drug me again," Liz suggested.

Curtis laughed. "Unfortunately, you need to be coherent when we reach your apartment."

"How far away are we, anyway?"

"Pretty close," Curtis said. "It'll only take three hours to get you there."

"Strange," Liz said. "Doesn't it seem odd that the Castle would be so close to where I live?"

"It's not strange," Curtis disagreed. "Many Immortal Writers end up drawn to their characters. It's some sort of subconscious drive that brings them together."

"But not all of the writers at the Castle lived in this area during their normal lives," Liz said.

"You don't think we stay in one spot the whole time, do you?" Wells interjected. "The Writers' Castle moves around. It's easy with all the magic and technology at our disposal. Sometimes we end up on secluded beaches, or in forests, or—most often—in mountains. We were in the Himalayas before we ended up here. We have to keep moving so that no one finds us."

"It's all so incredible," Liz said. Wells didn't answer; he just stared out of his window.

"Especially me, right?" Curtis checked.

"Of course," Liz reassured him.

Curtis chuckled and started talking to Rob. Liz supposed she should have been interested in their conversation—these were her characters in *real life* talking about their adventures, after all, and how often do people get to hear that?—but Liz was still tired from the previous night's battle. Eventually, despite her fear of careening off the mountainside and her annoyance at Wells, she drifted off to sleep.

THE GENTLE hum of the taxi was interrupted by Rob's gruff voice. "What's going on? Can I even get in there?"

"Liz," Curtis urged. "Liz, wake up. We need you to let us in."

"What?"

Liz looked up and started smoothing down her hair. She yawned and straightened her shirt.

"McKinnen, *look*," Wells said impatiently.

She finally started to pay attention to what was going on outside the cab. They were basically at her apartment complex, but the way was blocked off by police tape. Cops roamed around the front of the building's open gate, and several more were on the property.

"What are they doing here?"

"Well, you were kidnapped," Curtis pointed out.

"Yeah, but they don't know that," Rob said.

"I can't tell the police that you kidnapped me," Liz said. She started to panic. "I can't tell them the truth. They'd institutionalize me."

"You're a writer," Wells interrupted. "Make up a cover story."

"But I can't just come up with—"

A police officer knocked on Rob's window. He obligingly rolled it down and smiled at the man.

"Yes, officer?"

"Can't you see the police tape out here?" The cop pointed. "You need to move on."

"My passenger lives in this complex."

The officer looked over to Curtis, but he shook his head and pointed at Liz.

"I don't have time for guessing games," the policeman growled. "You need to get out of here. This is a police investigation."

Liz didn't know how to explain where she'd been, but she knew she had to do something before Rob was arrested. She just hoped that her face and her anger would do the work for her.

She opened the cab door and stepped out.

"Miss, get back in the cab," the officer said without looking at her face.

"What right do you have to tell me to get away from my own residence?"

The cop sighed and turned toward her.

"We're investigating a crime. One of the tenants here has gone missing, and..." He trailed off, finally realizing whom he was addressing.

"What were you saying?"

The policeman gaped, trying to recover from his surprise. "Miss... Miss McKinnen, we thought you were missing."

"Clearly I'm not," Liz snapped. She put a fist on her hip. "What right do you have to force me away from *my own home?*"

"We thought you were in trouble," the policeman tried to explain. "We were investigating..."

"What proof did you have of any of this?"

"Your fiancé said he hadn't heard from you for over two months—"

Liz had almost completely forgotten about Derek. "I don't *have* a fiancé."

"You don't know Derek Harbor?"

"I know him," Liz said, "but he is not my fiancé. It looks like you need to be thoroughly checking your information."

"Your agent and publisher also said they hadn't heard from you." The cop seemed desperate to defend himself. "With your book coming out in so short a time, there seemed to be reasonable cause for us to believe..."

"Clearly you were *wrong,*" Liz said firmly. She sent tendrils of Spirit Magic into the cop's brain, hoping to make him panic so that he would leave. "I'll talk to your supervisor now."

"I am the supervisor."

Liz scrutinized him with clear displeasure, heaving a sigh of disgust. "Fine. I trust this won't happen again?"

"No, miss."

"Good." She dropped her fist from her hip and leaned closer to the cop. "Now get away from my building."

The cop nodded and hurried away, speaking frantically into his radio. Several of the other policemen's heads popped up, looking at Liz in confusion. Liz ignored all of them and slid back into the cab, slamming the door behind her.

"Well done," Rob said. Even Wells looked almost impressed.

"Fiancé?" Curtis asked.

Liz grimaced. "I do *not* have a fiancé."

Curtis frowned but turned back toward the front of the cab. The four of them were silent as the police took down the caution tape and trickled back into their cars. Finally the last of them drove away, several shooting glances at the cab as they left.

"Permission to drive onto your property?" Rob asked.

"Of course," Liz said, surprised. "You know you can go ahead."

"I just thought I'd check," Rob said as he drove forward. "I'd hate to be on the receiving end of your wrath. That poor cop."

"At least she didn't have a sword," Curtis interjected. "She would have cut him to ribbons."

"I wasn't really mad," Liz protested. "I actually appreciate that they were here doing their jobs. What if something bad really had happened to me? I just had to act angry to make them go away."

"Trust me, Rob," Curtis stage-whispered, "you don't want to make her mad. Whatever you do, don't drive on her grass."

"I've never been more careful in my life," Rob vowed.

"Oh, for heaven's sake," Liz mumbled. She settled back into the seat and folded her arms across her chest.

Rob parked the taxi and turned it off. "Here we are," he said. "Liz, would you prefer me to stay here?"

"You can come in," Liz said.

"I'll stay here," Wells said. "Keep watch, that type of thing."

Liz shrugged. She opened the door and stepped out onto the walkway, studying her condo building. She loved the Castle, but she had a special connection to her own home. It was painted blue with black accents, and had large bay windows.

Liz walked up the sidewalk that led to her front door and took her keys from her pocket. She had been relieved to discover that they hadn't been lost during her kidnapping and her stay at the Castle. She wasn't sure how she would have gotten in. Of course, she could have called Derek since he had a key, but she didn't feel like facing him. How would she explain why she had neglected him for so long? How could she justify her disappearance? Did she even still want him in her life?

She swung the door open and stepped inside, followed by Curtis and Rob. Light streamed in through the bay window in the large front room off to the right, lighting up a dusty kitchen.

"Nice space," Rob said as they walked farther into the house.

"I don't know, Liz," Curtis said as he looked around. "You need to dust in here."

"I've been *gone*," Liz reminded him.

"Oh yeah," Curtis muttered.

"So where are your notes?" Rob asked. "I feel too exposed out here. I'd like to get back to the Castle."

"Not that it's safe there any more," Curtis said.

"It's better there than here. We have no way to defend ourselves here."

"Come on," Liz said. "It's upstairs."

Liz, Curtis, and Rob climbed the stairs to the second floor. A large red beanbag, which was Liz's favourite, was off to the side of a beige couch that sat in front of a television. They turned left and walked down the hall to Liz's office, which was a fairly small room covered with messy white boards. A desk sat against the south wall and was covered with papers. Two large black filing cabinets were in the left corner.

"So this is your secret lair," Curtis said, clearly unimpressed.

"I'm not made of money," Liz defended herself. "I just barely got this place. I paid three months in advance with my award money, which is the only way I've been able to keep it while I've been with you. If I had it my way, I'd have a secret office hidden behind a huge library. Maybe one day."

"It's just not as spectacular as I expected it to be," Curtis said as he strolled inside.

Liz glared. "It's not supposed to be extravagant. No one really sees it except for me."

"Well, I think it's great," Rob said. "What do you need us to do?"

"Everything for your series should be in the filing cabinet on the right," Liz said. "Look for Kenric's character profile in there. I'll sort through things on my desk."

They set to work, reading through papers quietly. They had been working in silence for about an hour when Curtis suddenly spoke up.

"Ooooh, there's my character profile."

Liz froze in the middle of shuffling through some papers. "Why would you need to read that? Put it away and focus."

"I've got time," Curtis said. Liz turned around to see him pulling out a thick stack of papers.

"Let's see... backstory... I know all that... relationship with father... definitely know that... oh yes, character description." He cleared his throat. "'Curtis is tall, about six-foot-three. He has thick, curly blond hair and astonishing blue eyes.' Oh, *astonishing*. Thank you."

"Put those back," Liz growled. She walked over to him and reached for the papers but he moved them up and out of the way.

"I'm having too much fun," Curtis said, turning his attention back to the papers. "'Curtis is perfectly muscular—' So you think my muscles are perfect, do you?"

"Curtis—"

"'And if he were alive, he'd probably be the most attractive man on the planet,'" Curtis read.

"Does it really say that?" Rob interrupted.

Liz's face was red. "No, of course not."

"Sure does," Curtis said, pointing to the papers. "And thank you, Liz. I appreciate your admiration."

"I was just—"

"Oh, and look at this," Curtis continued. "'If he were alive, I'd probably be in love with him.'"

Curtis put the papers down and peered at her. "So. I'm alive. What do you think?" He flexed.

Liz rolled her eyes at him. "Just so you know, I—"

"Shhh," Rob said. "Did you hear something?"

"Not now, Rob," Curtis said. "She was about to say she loves me."

"I most certainly was not," Liz sputtered.

"Quiet!" Rob said harshly. "I'm serious. Listen."

Curtis paused and then frowned. Liz tried to listen, but her heart was pounding too hard from embarrassment for her to be able to hear anything.

"You're right," Curtis said. "Someone's in the apartment."

Liz quickly forgot her shame. "Could it be Kenric?" she whispered.

Curtis shook his head. "No. I doubt it, anyway. I guess you know him better than I do, but he wouldn't just come in here and take care of you quietly. He likes to make a scene."

"Liz!" a voice called from the living room down the hall.

"Oh no," Liz whimpered.

"Who is it?" Curtis asked. "What's wrong?"

"Liz!" the voice called again. It sounded angry.

"It's Derek," Liz said.

"Your fiancé?" Curtis asked.

"He is *not* my fiancé!" Liz hissed.

"I'll take care of him," Curtis said. He took a step forward.

"No." Liz stopped him. "I should probably talk to him."

"But—"

"I think she'd better take care of this," Rob said. "Just let her go."

"What if it's a Caller?"

"In the middle of town?" Rob sounded skeptical.

"It's Derek," Liz said. "I'll get rid of him. You guys keep looking for notes on Kenric."

Curtis didn't look happy, but he nodded. "Fine," he said. "But we're right here if you need us."

Liz walked out of her office and down the hall, coming face to face with Derek, and Wells trailing him.

"What do you want me to do, McKinnen?" Wells asked.

"It's okay, Wells," Liz said. "I just need to talk to him."

Wells leaned against a wall and folded his arms.

"Where the hell have you been?" Derek snarled. "Who is this guy? Did you hire him to fend me off? I've been worried sick, but the cops say you were just... what, on vacation? Avoiding me?"

"Things have been complicated, Derek, and I—"

"You could have at least said no to my face!" Derek spat. "You didn't have to run away! I thought something had happened to you! How could you do this to me?"

Liz felt her anger bubble to the surface. Derek had always only cared about himself. He wasn't even making sure she was really safe, and that nothing had happened to her. He just wanted to make her pay for rejecting him.

"Do this to *you*?" Liz snapped. "You have no idea where I've been or what I've been through or why I left. You may be a lot of things, Derek, but you are not so powerful that you could make me run away."

"Don't make yourself out to be a victim," Derek said. "For all I know you've been seeing someone on the side the whole time, and you ran away to be with him."

"What?" Liz yelled. "I have *never* cheated on you. And how dare you accuse me of that when I found you with Julia—"

"Don't start throwing things in my face—" Derek yelled back.

"You're not even giving me a chance to tell you what really—"

Curtis cleared his throat from behind Liz. "Is there a problem here?" he asked.

Derek gaped at him, mouth open and eyes wide in astonishment.

"He's just helping me with something," Liz said quickly. She licked her lips. This couldn't look good. "And Curtis, everything's fine, we just—"

"I bet he's helping you with something," Derek snickered. "I guess I was right, wasn't I? You have been cheating on me. You're with this guy."

"That's right," Curtis said, striding forward and putting his arm around Liz. She stared at him. "We've been together for a while now. She was just professing her undying love to me when you so rudely interrupted."

Wells arched an eyebrow in interest. Liz ignored him.

Derek gritted his teeth together, eyes slit and fists clenched. His breathing was heavy, and he looked like he wanted to strangle Curtis.

"I was *not*," Liz said, throwing Curtis's arm off of her. She stepped away from him and glared. "Stop making things worse than they already are."

"Oh, I'm sorry," Curtis said, his smile disappearing. "I was just trying to clear up any confusion."

"There's nothing to clear up," Liz said. "You were helping me find something in my office. End of story. I need to finish things with Derek. Alone."

"No you don't," Derek snarled. "I think we're already finished."

"Yes," Curtis stated. "You are."

"Get back in the office and *find the paperwork*," Liz hissed.

"Rob's got it already," Curtis said. "We're ready to go."

"So you're not even staying?" Derek said. "You're just going back with him? With him and your security guard *and* some other guy? I didn't think you were that kind of girl anymore, Liz."

Liz's lips pursed together. How *dare* he bring that up.

"They are both helping me. There is nothing going on between any of us."

Curtis lifted his chin and folded his arms against his chest, taking a step back.

"Save the lies, Liz," Derek said as he stepped closer to her. "It won't save us."

Liz leaned toward him, her arms folded tightly against her chest. "I'm not lying," she said, her voice low, "but you're right; nothing will save us. If you knew me at all you'd know that I'm telling the truth. But all you've ever cared about is yourself. You said I couldn't say no to your face? Listen carefully. No. *Hell* no. You don't just get to burst into my place and yell at me for something I didn't do. So give me back my keys and get out of my home and out of my life. We are done."

She held out her hand, waiting for her key. Derek stood there, his mouth set in a firm line. They stared at each other for a full minute before Derek uncurled a fist and took the key out of his pocket. He walked up to her and dropped the key into her hand.

"And to think I thought you were the one for me," Derek said. "Thank God I was wrong."

He turned his back and walked away. Liz had never been so glad to see someone walk down the stairs before.

Wells stepped away from the wall. "I'll go back to the cab," he said quietly. He left Liz alone with Curtis.

Liz didn't realize there were tears streaming down her cheeks until Curtis spoke up a moment later.

"I don't see any reason to cry about it." His voice was cold. "You didn't love him anyway."

"I loved him once," she whispered. She wiped her tears away and turned to glare at Curtis. "And you. What was that all about? You made that a thousand times worse!"

Curtis shrugged. "Sorry." He turned and poked his head down the hall. "Let's go, Rob."

Liz glared at Curtis as he walked ahead of her down the stairs. Rob walked beside Liz in silence, watching Curtis's retreating figure with old, wise eyes.

"What's going on?" Rob whispered as they walked together down the stairs and out of the building. He carried a large stack of papers in his hands.

"I don't know," Liz grumbled. "Men suck."

"Well that's not fair."

"Not you, Rob," Liz amended. "I've always liked you."

"That's comforting," he said. "But what happened?"

Liz shook her head. "I don't even know. Derek was upset, but then Curtis just... he was so *stupid*. He made things worse."

"I heard some of it," Rob admitted. "I wasn't trying to eavesdrop, but it was hard not to hear what happened."

"I wouldn't be surprised if the cops came back," Liz joked.

Rob smiled. He paused outside of the cab. "So you really don't know why he's upset?" He gestured to Curtis, who was sitting in the front seat of the cab, head back and eyes closed. Wells sat behind him, not saying a word.

Liz shook her head. "I'm the one who should be mad. Not him."

Rob looked down at the ground and shuffled his feet. "No offense or anything, Liz, but I think that for a writer you're remarkably unobservant."

Liz looked up. "What is that supposed to mean?"

Rob kept his gaze on the ground. "It's not my business," he said. "But Curtis is a good man. He's probably going to be the best friend you have in your new life as an Immortal Writer. You might want to make peace with him."

"I will," she said. "But I'm still angry."

Rob finally looked up. "I know," he said, "but be careful. Even a fictional character's heart is capable of breaking."

Liz looked past Rob at Curtis's closed-off face. What did Liz have to do with Curtis's heart?

"I'll apologize," Liz said.

"He should, too," Rob said. "Just be... patient with him. He's not a very humble man."

"I know."

"Are we going or what?" Curtis shouted from the car.

"Or patient," Rob sighed.

Liz shook her head and slid into the cab. Maybe she could talk to Curtis on the way back to the Castle.

But he never acknowledged her, and Liz never spoke up. She didn't know what she'd done or how, but she seemed to have just ruined things with the one good man in her life. It seemed as though the past was always doomed to repeat itself.

CHAPTER EIGHTEEN

Shakespeare, Curtis, Healer, and Liz were all gathered in Shakespeare's office. They hadn't been able to talk Rob into coming. He had always loved action, but he hated planning it.

Healer sat beside Liz on the couch where Liz had slept off the chloroform two months earlier. Curtis sat on the opposite side of the room. Liz had tried to talk to him, but he hadn't paid any attention to her. She had apologized for how harsh she'd been to him when he'd tried to help her, but he'd still said nothing. Healer seemed to have picked up on the fact that something was wrong, but aside from a quizzical look, she hadn't reacted to the tension in the room.

Shakespeare flipped through the notes that Rob, Curtis, and Liz had found about Kenric. After a moment, he squeezed the bridge of his nose and squinted his eyes shut. "To save some time, why don't you start by telling us Kenric's story?"

"But you all know it," Liz countered.

"I've read your books," Shakespeare said as he looked up, "but you didn't include all of Kenric's history in them. Healer and Curtis—especially Curtis—are more familiar with Kenric, but I think we could all use a refresher. We need to know everything about him. The more we know, the better prepared we will be to fight."

"All right," Liz said, "where do you want me to start?"

"Start at the beginning of his life," Shakespeare said. "I want to hear everything."

Liz looked down at the blue and green rug for a moment, focusing on its swirling patterns and the Immortal Writers symbol in its centre while she organized her thoughts.

"Kenric was born in Tantos, a black market city where dragons were bred," Liz began. She raised her hands and painted pictures in the air, similar to the way Healer had taught her about magic. A small village appeared in sparkling blue in front of her. "According to Shetharan law, dragons were not allowed to be bred or housed. They were considered majestic but wild. Most Shetharans respected them too much to even consider buying them from a place like Tantos, but dragon lords were selected based on skill, and some people needed the extra boost to be chosen. Tantos thrived on overzealous social climbers. It was seedy, grimy, and unsafe.

"Kenric's mother ran away from Tantos when Kenric was seven years old." Liz waved her hands, and the scene before her changed. The image of a young woman, still shrouded in sparkling blue from the magic, ran away from a small, run-down home. "He still has some memories of her and he resents them. He hates his mother for leaving him with his father, Henry, who was a cruel man." A young man with dark hair and green eyes stared at them from the magical picture Liz changed to reflect the story.

"Henry had tried to become a dragon lord but had failed. The other dragon lords had recognized his cruelty and they didn't think he was adept enough to become a lord. Henry was determined to make his son a dragon lord in his stead, and so he made Kenric steal a dragon egg." A young version of Kenric, with dark hair like his father and dark eyes, caressed a silver dragon egg as large as the boy's head.

"Little did Kenric know that he had stolen a Sampar, the dragon that breathes out radiation. This type of dragon was hard to breed and so this egg was extremely rare, and worth at least a million gold pieces in the black market. Henry recognized it for what it was and was proud of his son, but Henry's pride only made him crueler. While they waited for the egg to hatch, Henry taught Kenric how to fight, and he never spared his son injury."

The scene before them changed again to Kenric and Henry sparring in an abandoned dirt street at night. Kenric doubled over in pain as Henry jabbed at his belly.

"Curtis hurts his pupils when he teaches them," Shakespeare said. "How were Henry's methods different?"

"Curtis doesn't wound without a reason," Liz said. "He does it to motivate the student and to build up a resilience to pain. Plus, Curtis stops. Henry never did. When his son went down, he kept cutting him and hurting him until Kenric passed out."

Henry walked toward his son, and with the flat of his blade, beat down on Kenric's back. Once, twice, and again until Kenric passed out from the pain and fell face-first into the dirt road.

"He was teaching his son many lessons: fighting and pain endurance, yes, but also that his opponents would be without mercy, that he needed to fight without honour, to not only defeat an enemy but to destroy him, and that the only way to win was to annihilate.

"Kenric hated training with his father, but he did it. He wanted to make Henry proud. He also secretly hoped that if he were good enough, his mother would come back to him and take him away. But of course, she never came back. He didn't see her again until much later, when he was a dragon lord. He killed her then."

Shakespeare, Healer, and Curtis watched in fascination as the egg shattered open and a small white dragon crawled out, coughing and appearing far too innocent for what it would later become.

"Eventually, the dragon egg hatched and a small Sampar was born. Sampars don't begin to breathe out large amounts of radiation until they're a year old. The Sampar granted Kenric immunity to radiation. Only a Sampar can give someone that ability, and they can only do it once in a lifetime. Kenric loved the dragon and named it Paratheon. It was his best friend and most trusted ally. It is the only thing, aside from power, that Kenric has ever truly loved."

The scene changed to an almost-happy one. Kenric rode the Sampar, a small smile on his face, while the dragon ran down the crowded streets of Tantos, snapping its jaws at passersby.

"When the dragon was large enough, Henry taught Kenric how to ride it. Kenric caught on quickly. He was gifted and could communicate easily and clearly with the dragon through his magic. It was by watching his son's relationship with Paratheon that Henry realized his son possessed Spirit Magic. A son with a magical gift, especially a Spirit gift, enthralled him. Kenric's Spirit Magic meant that he would almost certainly become a dragon lord, which would greatly improve Henry's social status.

"Kenric didn't realize it was Spirit Magic he used to send and receive thoughts with Paratheon; he simply thought that he and the dragon had a special bond. Henry never told Kenric that he had magic. Instead, he experimented with his son's power subtly and secretly.

"Henry manipulated Kenric to anger and used his Body Magic to monitor how quickly Kenric subconsciously grasped his magic. Every time he did, Henry used his Body Magic to measure Kenric's gift. Henry's mind reeled over the possibilities of Kenric actually using that much magic consciously."

The scene changed again. Henry disarmed Kenric and turned toward the watching Paratheon. With a smirk on his face, he sliced the beast up the side of its belly.

"During a training session, Henry harmed Paratheon to make Kenric angry. Fearing for his dragon's life, Kenric reached out and slammed magic into his father."

Kenric picked up his sword and, turning, saw the blood pouring from his dragon. Dropping his sword in shock, he ran up to Henry and grabbed him by the collar. Henry plummeted to the ground, his shirt tearing as waves of blue crackled from Kenric's hands into Henry's body.

"This attack nearly killed Henry. He punished Kenric, but the damage had been done. Henry would never be able to use his right arm again, and Kenric was grateful. That was the arm he used to strike him with most often.

"When Kenric harmed his father, he finally realized that he possessed powerful magic, and he understood that his father had been manipulating him and controlling him. Kenric sought out private instruction from an old woman in Tantos named Syrlia." An old woman with deep wrinkles, glittering eyes, and a balding head smiled before them. "Syrlia was kinder than his father, but still manipulative. Kenric recognized that she, too, was trying to use him for her own purposes, hoping to mold him into something she could use, but he was too smart for her. He refused to be controlled. One day, Syrlia pushed him too far. She tried to control him with her own Spirit Magic and Kenric fought back."

The old woman backed up in the scene in front of them, her hands outstretched and her mouth wide, like she was screaming. Kenric bounded in, surrounded her in blue waves of magic, and then Syrlia went limp.

"Without realizing what he was doing, he killed her. He had never killed someone before. It scared him. He felt horribly guilty. He hadn't particularly liked Syrlia, but he had never taken a life before."

The young Kenric looked at his hands and stepped back from the body, blinking tears away from his eyes. He turned and ran.

"Kenric ran home and sought comfort with Paratheon. Normally, a dragon would have been a source of strength, but the Sampar had been affected by Henry's cruelty, and this had changed it. Instead of offering Kenric sound advice and wisdom, the Sampar justified his actions and encouraged him farther down a dark, bloody road. Since Kenric trusted Paratheon, he slowly started to be proud of what he had done. He felt powerful. He felt invincible.

"His father soon found out that he had been seeking instruction from Syrlia. Henry also knew that his son must have been the one to kill her. He tried to punish Kenric for his involvement with Syrlia, but now Kenric knew that he was powerful—powerful enough to kill. So Kenric fought back, and this time, he knew how to defeat his father. He brought Henry to his knees and made his father look up at him as he used his magic to kill him."

Henry looked up from a dirty, bloodstained floor, his hands clasped together and tears streaming down his face as he begged.

"It was not a quick death. Kenric invaded Henry's mind and forced it to shut down all of Henry's organs one by one. It caused Henry extreme pain, but Kenric never flinched from his task. He listened to every agonized scream until his father finally died."

Liz let the scene in front of her fade and lowered her hands as the images went away.

"Kenric put on a good show for everyone in Tantos. He pretended to mourn his father's passing, but in truth he and Paratheon were proud. As soon as his father was put to rest, Kenric and Paratheon set out for the Academy, where Kenric could learn more magic and train to become a dragon lord."

"I met him there," Healer said. "I taught at the Academy."

"Did you know what he was when you met him?" Shakespeare asked.

"No," Healer said. "He was talented at hiding his... darker tendencies. And no one knew that he came from Tantos. We didn't even know where he'd come across Paratheon. We thought they'd met on the road one night while Kenric was travelling to the Academy."

"But his bond was unusual since he wasn't a dragon lord, correct?" Shakespeare checked. "Why did no one suspect anything?"

"You haven't met him," Curtis interjected. "Kenric is a very good liar and has an excellent façade."

"Many of the most evil people put on the best faces," Liz said. Curtis gave her a glance, but quickly looked away when she saw him.

"Go on, Liz," Shakespeare prompted. He sat back in his chair and folded his hands on his lap.

"Paratheon was a colossal influence in Kenric's life," Liz said. "Considering its upbringing, it is unsurprising that it helped corrupt Kenric. But most of what had destroyed Kenric was the way his father had treated him, and the overwhelming need Kenric felt to be stronger than the man who had abused him and controlled him for years.

"Still, Kenric didn't stray from the path his father had set for him. He wanted to be a dragon lord. He might have changed course if not for his connection with Paratheon, but he wanted to be able to stay in touch with his dragon. Without the status of dragon lord, Paratheon would be taken away from him."

"And he was accepted as a dragon lord as soon as he graduated from the Academy," Curtis said. He rubbed his jaw, eyes downcast, as he thought.

"I met him there. I was a dragon warrior, of course, and not a lord; I kept the dragons in line and treated them with fear and respect, while the dragon lords created laws with the dragons to keep the peace. Still, as a dragon warrior, I associated with Kenric. I was the only one who would even go near him."

"I thought he had a good façade?" Shakespeare said.

"He did," Curtis affirmed, "but Paratheon didn't. Everyone tended to stay away from the Sampar—just one attack by that dragon and they'd die a very painful death. The Sampar's radiation works faster than normal radiation. It acts as a poison that spreads through the body and provides exquisite pain until the victim dies. Naturally, everyone was scared of Kenric's dragon, and Kenric didn't ever let Paratheon get far away from him."

"Curtis thought Kenric was fascinating, and he made an effort to get to know both him and Paratheon," Liz said. "Kenric and Curtis quickly became friends. Curtis was aware of Kenric's darker side, though he didn't know the extent of it. He didn't know his friend was a murderer."

"No one knew," Curtis said. "None of us had any idea. He was intimidating, sure, but that was because he was powerful."

"How did you not see it?" Shakespeare asked.

"You always look for the good in your friends," Curtis murmured.

"Curtis and Kenric sparred often," Liz said. "Curtis proved to be the better fighter, but Kenric was formidable with magic. Curtis only managed to protect himself because of his skill with shields. Without them, Curtis would have realized more quickly what kind of man Kenric was, because, like Henry, Kenric didn't like to stop and he never backed down.

"Kenric grew in status with the dragon lords and was respected, though certainly not loved. No one knew that he was sending money to Tantos to buy more dragons. Not even Curtis knew that he was amassing an army."

"I remember the day that he revealed his legion of dragons at the dragon lord council," Curtis said. "I was keeping guard. Kenric called with his mind and they all came flocking into the hall. They wouldn't even all fit. He had complete control over them. I knew then that he was corrupt. I couldn't deny it anymore, even to myself."

"The dragon lords told Kenric to let his dragons loose," Liz said. "Each dragon lord was allowed only one dragon companion. They couldn't allow Kenric to have control over so many beasts. They worried about what Kenric might do with so much power. They foolishly hoped that he was just being over-eager because he was so young.

"Kenric pretended that that was exactly the case. He agreed to dismiss all of his dragons aside from Paratheon and he apologized for his actions."

"But he lied," Curtis growled. "I knew he hadn't banished his dragons, but I still hoped that he might come back and be the friend I always thought he was. I hoped so much that I was blindsided when Kenric attacked the rest of the dragon lords a few months later. He had attacked wisely, when most of the dragon warriors were absent, fighting a battle that he had staged as a distraction. I was still there because I wanted to keep an eye on Kenric. Not that I did much good." Curtis hung his head.

"Less than half of the dragon lords survived, and they, combined with the available dragon warriors, forced Kenric out of the dragon lord castle," Liz continued quietly. "Curtis gave Kenric chase, determined to talk with him. Kenric was furious at Curtis for standing with the dragon lords instead of with him. Curtis tried to tell Kenric that what he was doing was wrong, and he begged Kenric to make amends, and to stop."

"It didn't make a difference," Curtis said. He kept his head turned down and rubbed his scarred arm. "Kenric had become dark, power-hungry, and vindictive. He turned against me and attacked. I fended him off and Kenric left on Paratheon, severely wounded… but Kenric made sure I'd paid for betraying him. Paratheon breathed a powerful dose of radiation on me before I raised a shield. It hit me on this arm and spread through my body. I was dying."

"That's when I met Curtis," Healer interrupted. "I found him lying there and I healed him."

"I still owe you for that." Curtis smiled at Healer.

"Where did Kenric go?" Shakespeare asked.

"He flew to some caves in the East Mountains," Liz said. "Fifteen of his dragon swarm came with him. He laid low for a while, buying more dragons from the black market and building his army. His plans grew more and more ambitious. He waged a war against the Shetharan government and eventually succeeded in overthrowing the dragon lords completely. He enslaved many people and outlawed magic after killing all of the students at the Academy. He wanted to be the only one with power. Curtis started a rebellion and the two have been battling it out for years. You've read the rest in the books."

"From Curtis's point of view," Shakespeare said. "Is there anything you can add from Kenric's perspective?"

Liz shrugged. "I've never written the story from Kenric's point of view, but it's easy for me to tell where his motivations come from and what his reasoning is. Anything that makes him feel vulnerable reminds him of how he felt with his father, and he'll do *anything* to avoid feeling that way. He wants to be all-powerful so that he never has to feel victimized again. He's made all of his choices with a warped sense of self-defense. He wants control and he'll go to any lengths to be sure he has it. He's controlling hundreds of dragons now. The fact that Kenric has so many under his control should scare you. He's powerful."

"But so are you," Healer said. "You have more Spirit Magic than he does."

"But I don't have as much experience with it," Liz said, "and I know when to stop using my magic. There are things I will not do. Kenric has no limits."

"What else can you tell us about Kenric?" Shakespeare asked.

"I think I've told you just about everything," Liz said. "What do you want, exactly? A character profile? He's five-foot-eleven with dark hair, olive skin, and—"

"No," Shakespeare interrupted, "I know what he looks like. But I want to know if you can tell me anything that maybe didn't make it into your final draft of the character. Is there anything else that Kenric might be able to do? Any other advantage he might have?"

Liz thought for a while. "It's all in the notes," she said slowly. "I never threw anything away. But I can tell you that when I started writing him,

I wrote him as an Elementalist instead of a Spirit user. Is it possible that he could have both forms of magic?"

Shakespeare frowned, but it was Healer who answered. "It's highly unlikely. I haven't heard of anyone with two types of magic before. But anything is possible. We should be prepared, just in case he's even more powerful than we first thought."

"Anything else?" Shakespeare prompted. "Was there ever a different backstory for him? Anything that might change the way he makes decisions, or something of that nature?"

Liz hesitated. "There... are some other things about him... but I'm not sure they're important."

"I need to know everything," Shakespeare insisted. "Kenric is too powerful to battle in ignorance."

"I won't be ignorant going against him," Liz said. "I know him too well. Better than any other character."

"Why is that?" Shakespeare asked.

Liz took a deep breath. "Because... I based him off of me."

There was a moment of uncomfortable silence. Healer took Liz's hand and squeezed it. Healer already knew this—she had known it since the day they had practised mind reading in her room.

"But you're not an evil dragon lord," Healer finally said.

"No," Liz agreed, "but our backstories are... similar."

"Explain," Shakespeare said.

"I changed his a bit," Liz said. "They're not *exactly* the same. But I grew up in an abusive home. It wasn't easy. So I can understand Kenric's desperation."

"But a comparable backstory doesn't make you the same," Curtis said. Liz looked at him, surprised he was speaking to her. He wasn't looking directly at her, but she could still read the concern on his face.

"I chose a different path in the end," Liz said, "but I wasn't always a decent person. I'm by no means perfect right now, but I'm better than I was."

"I highly doubt you've ever killed anyone," Curtis said.

"I haven't killed anyone," Liz agreed. "I exaggerated my own struggles and amplified my faults in Kenric. I made him the example of what I could have been. So I know him. I know him intimately. In too many ways, he's like me. In all of the other ways, he's like the man who abused me."

"So that's why you have such a similar magical ability to Kenric," Shakespeare mused. "You would be quite similar to him in power if you're based off the same history."

"Yes," Liz said. "I've noticed the similarities. So has Healer."

"I hate to ask this," Shakespeare said, "but will you be able to do what's necessary when the time comes? If you've based Kenric off of yourself, will you be able to kill him?"

"He's not me, exactly," Liz said. "He's the darkest parts of me. He's what I would have been if I hadn't changed my life. I want to get rid of those reminders."

"I have to know you're up to the task."

Liz bit her lip. Could she kill Kenric? She had never killed someone before. And wouldn't killing him make her even more like him?

But Healer spared her from answering.

"I read her mind during a training session," Healer said. "She has similarities to Kenric, it's true. But we all have our dark sides; we all have our own struggles. I know that Liz can do what she has to do. I have faith in her."

Liz smiled at Healer and then looked at Curtis. He quickly looked away, avoiding her gaze. Apparently he was still angry. Or maybe now he thought she was evil. She wasn't sure she could bear it if he thought that.

"I'm glad to hear it," Shakespeare said, interrupting her thoughts. He looked back down at the notes on his desk. "I think I'm going to spend some time reading through these to see if there's anything else I can glean from them. Can we meet back here tomorrow evening? Once I've read everything, I'd like to make a plan of attack."

"Will we be attacking soon?" Liz asked, afraid.

"I think we have to," Shakespeare said. "Casualties were high from Kenric's last assault, and we can't afford for him to keep coming after us, or rather, after you. We need to be on the offensive *now*. I want to make sure you're prepared. Curtis, Healer, train with her tomorrow before we meet. Test her and see if you think she's ready to fight Kenric. As much as we need to defeat him, we can't just march into battle unprepared. Agreed?"

"Agreed," Healer said. Curtis nodded.

"Then I'll dismiss you for now," Shakespeare said, turning his attention to the papers in front of him. "It looks like this will take me a while."

Curtis stalked out of the room, still rubbing his right arm. Liz swallowed against the bile in her throat.

She didn't need them to test her.

She would never be ready.

CHAPTER NINETEEN

Instead of testing Liz separately, Healer and Curtis decided that they would assess her magic and combat skills at the same time. It was mid-morning. Curtis stood in front of her, holding his sword in his hand. Healer stood to the side, ready to read Liz's magic as she fought. Rob sat on a bench to Healer's left, eating an apple and twirling a sai absent-mindedly in his right hand. Several Immortal Writers surrounded the courtyard, watching in interest. Once again, Dostoyevsky was taking bets on who would win this battle. He had betted against her, but Tolkien and McCaffrey were rooting for her this time. Liz had no idea how the authors had found out that she was being tested today, but she was determined to beat up whomever had told them. She could grudgingly accept that Hughes was there; he had been friendly to her from the moment they'd met. But she still didn't like an audience, and Jane Austen still looked far too interested in Curtis for Liz's liking.

"Curtis has said that you're proficient with the sword," Healer said. "Just add the magical element now. It's important to be able to use magic and swordplay together."

Liz nodded, glancing nervously at Curtis. He was looking at the ground instead of at her. Liz wished she could understand why he was so upset. It wasn't like Curtis to hold a grudge. Liz didn't think she had done anything wrong. He had been the one to cross a line.

She reached out for her magic and found it waiting eagerly, squirming in excitement.

"Are you ready?" Healer asked.

"I'm nervous," Liz admitted.

"Don't expect to be perfect this first time around," Healer said gently. "Magic and swordplay are very different types of combat. You are quite skilled at both of them; you just need to learn to use them together. You can do it, Creator."

Liz offered Healer a small smile in response, then shifted her weight forward and hefted her sword. It had a slightly different balance than the one she used to have. She regretted losing her old sword in the Rokur's brain, but she didn't necessarily mind the new weapon.

"I'm as ready as I'll ever be," she said.

"Good," Healer said. "Remember that Curtis has his shield up. It'll be harder for you to hit him, whereas your body is mostly undefended. Be prepared for that."

Liz nodded.

"When you're ready."

Curtis lunged at Liz. She was taken aback by the suddenness of his attack, but managed to parry the blow just in time. She forced him back, but he didn't stay back long. He leapt forward again and Liz blocked him. Curtis swung to his right, but he had left himself open on the left side and Liz took the bait.

She swung but hit his shield with such force that she stumbled backward a few feet, failing to avoid Curtis's blow to her left shoulder. Liz grunted and gritted her teeth together as the authors groaned for her. Dostoyevsky cheered. Liz shook her head in frustration. She had somehow managed to forget about the shield already.

"Use your magic," Healer called as Curtis and Liz's swords met in the air again. "You need to push past his shield, and you don't have time to do that with a sword."

Liz grabbed ahold of her magic again. It sensed the adrenaline inside of her and pushed itself eagerly against her grasp. It wanted to be used. It wanted to fight.

But holding her magic had distracted her from the sword fight and she earned another nick, this time to her right thigh.

"Concentrate!" Curtis yelled. He flew forward again.

Liz met his sword in the air, barely blocking him as she tried to balance her magic and her sword. Curtis batted her sword away easily and started to come down on her head. Liz swerved to the side, but it wasn't quite far enough. She flung her magic outward, surrounding Curtis's sword. She forced it away until it hit Curtis's shield, sending him flying back.

Liz straightened and gathered more magic. She pushed against Curtis's shield. She knew from experience that breaking it down would take a couple of minutes if she had time to focus, but he didn't give her a chance. He was barely giving her time to breathe. Liz managed to keep control over her magic, but she wasn't as focused as she would have liked. Curtis kept distracting her.

He came at her again, attacking and lunging and parrying, trying desperately to break past her defenses. Liz could feel Curtis's shield weakening, like glass slowly cracking apart.

Surveying Curtis's shield sidetracked her. She didn't quite notice when he brought his sword down, but she definitely noted when the blade cut into her left shoulder again.

"Come on, McKinnen!" Tolkien called out. "I don't want to lose to Dostoyevsky *again*!"

Liz enveloped Curtis's shield in her magic and flung the entire shield away, Curtis inside of it. He tumbled back in the air. Liz dropped her own sword and pried Curtis's blade from her shoulder, crying out as she did so.

She dropped his sword to the ground and picked her own back up, then ran toward him.

Curtis stood as she reached him and swerved to avoid her blow. He ducked around behind her and suddenly he had his sword in his hands again.

Damn it, Liz reprimanded herself. She had forgotten that Curtis and his sword were connected and that he could call it to himself. She cursed her stupidity and flung every ounce of magic she had at Curtis's shield.

She had never thrown so much concentrated magic at Curtis, so she was surprised when his shield shattered. Curtis seemed surprised, too, especially when the Spirit Magic exacted its price. It didn't incapacitate him, but Liz could see that it still affected him. Blood dripped from Curtis's nose and he swayed on his feet.

Liz didn't wait; she knew he wouldn't have if their situations were reversed. She stepped forward and started another bout with Curtis. He fought back, but he was weaker.

Curtis lunged, but Liz blocked him by cutting up at an angle. She felt his grip on his sword loosen, and Liz twisted her sabre and knocked his sword out of his hands.

Liz touched the point of her sword to the base of Curtis's throat.

"I win," she panted.

Liz heard Dostoyevsky swear loudly in Russian as the other authors cheered.

Curtis stared at his sword.

"Well done," Healer said. "That was impressive. I was nervous the whole time you—"

But Curtis apparently didn't think it was over. He raised both of his hands and caught Liz's sword between them, either hand on the flat sides of the blade. He twisted expertly, and Liz's own sword was wrenched out of her grasp and clattered to the ground.

Curtis leapt forward in an attempt to grab his sword, but Liz tackled him to the side, her left arm screaming in protest where Curtis had cut her before.

"Curtis," Healer called, "the fight is over, she beat you, stop—"

Curtis wrapped his leg around Liz's leg and twisted, throwing her onto the ground. He stood up and started to walk away, but Liz tripped him. He stumbled to the cobblestones, barely catching himself with his hands. He smiled and called his sword to him. It flew to his hand and he pointed the sword to Liz's chest. She froze.

"No," Curtis panted. "You don't win. Never assume a victory."

"Wait, who won?" Tolkien asked nervously. "I am not going to Poe's grave for the next decade!"

"Curtis!" Healer called. She ran up to them and shoved Curtis back. "What were you doing? Liz beat you. She did an exceptional job."

"Was I dead?" Curtis asked. "No. She hadn't incapacitated me. I was still in the fight."

"I had my sword at your throat!" Liz yelled. "If you'd been Kenric, you would have been dead."

Curtis started to reply, but Healer cut him off. "Liz is right. What did you want her to do, run you through?"

"Do you *want* me to slit your throat?" Liz asked. "Because at this point, I'm pretty tempted."

"Good luck getting that far," Curtis scoffed.

"I *did* get that far," Liz said.

"No, I think McKinnen still won," McCaffrey said. "Curtis just isn't used to losing."

Dostoyevsky swore again.

Curtis shook his head and lowered his sword. "Whatever."

Healer put her hand on his shoulder, her eyes full of concern. "Curtis, this isn't like you. What's going on?"

"Nothing," Curtis mumbled. He sheathed his sword. "Let's go. I'm done for the day."

He turned away. Liz couldn't let him leave without figuring out what was going on, and why he was so angry and impatient. Clutching her left shoulder, she stood up.

"Well *I'm* not done," she yelled.

Curtis turned back. "Yes you are," he snapped. "I've cut you apart enough today, I think."

"I don't mean that," Liz said. "You're going to talk to me and you're going to do it *now*."

"I'd like to see you try to make me," Curtis said as he folded his arms across his chest.

Rob chirped up from where he perched on his bench. "Healer, I think we should go."

Healer glanced back and forth between Liz and Curtis. "I'm not sure that's wise."

Rob shook his head. "They won't kill each other. Probably. But we need to let them work things out. Things have been tense ever since we went to Liz's place."

"What happened there?" Healer asked.

"Nothing," Curtis said.

"I'll tell you if you come with me and leave them to it," Rob said. "Come on. They'll be fine."

Healer didn't look convinced that she should go, but she finally nodded and walked over to Rob.

"All right," she said. "But I'm coming back in an hour. If you've killed each other by then I'll be very upset with both of you."

Rob and Healer walked away, Healer looking back every few seconds to ensure Liz and Curtis hadn't attacked each other again. Rob shooed the authors away. Austen seemed keen to stay and watch; she was absurdly interested in what was happening, but Rob managed to convince her to go. The other authors followed, Tolkien and McCaffrey cheering. Dostoyevsky was brooding.

"That's what you get for gambling," Hemingway said. "This is why I don't participate."

Soon, Curtis and Liz were alone in the courtyard. Curtis stood several feet away, staring at the ground. He flexed his fists and had a grim set to his mouth as he tightened his jaw.

"We're alone now," Liz finally said. She had meant to sound gentle but ended up sounding impatient. "Can you *please* tell me what's going on?"

"Nothing's wrong," Curtis said, not meeting her eyes. "I'm just trying to push you to your limits, to make you better."

"You forget: I know you. I *know* that something's wrong. Just tell me! Maybe I can help!"

Curtis laughed. "You can't help."

"How do you know?" Liz challenged.

Curtis rolled his eyes and started to turn away, but Liz ran up to him and grabbed his shoulder, forcing him to face her.

"What the *hell* is wrong with you?" she demanded.

Curtis gritted his teeth. "Let me go."

"No," Liz said. "Tell me what's wrong."

"I mean it. Release me."

Liz grabbed his other arm, grimacing at the pain in her shoulder.

"Damn it, Curtis," she yelled, "tell me what the problem is!"

He flung both of her hands off of him. "You!" he shouted. "You are the problem!"

"Me?" Liz yelled back. "What did I do?"

Curtis hung his head. "You wrote me as a hero and a lover. I could have had any girl I wanted. But I never stayed with anyone; not a single woman *really* caught my attention. And I didn't know why, not for the longest time. And then I came to your world, and I realized—the only person for me was you."

He walked toward her and Liz found herself backing away from him, toward the Castle.

"You're perfect, Liz; absolutely perfect. But then, then you had that confrontation with that *man*, the man you *loved*, and I couldn't stand it. And then you said there was nothing between us, and I didn't know what to do!"

Curtis grabbed the upper parts of her arms and pushed her against the Castle wall. "But I don't care. I don't care that you said there's nothing between us, and I don't care that you were with someone else. I love you, Liz."

He kissed her. The kiss wasn't gentle or hesitant. It was strong and passionate, full of the passion that he had been holding in since they had met. Liz knew she probably should be scared by that passion but she wasn't. His lips moved against hers roughly and she responded with the same urgency he felt.

His grip didn't loosen but his hands slid down her arms and held on to her waist, pulling her closer to him. He was hard and strong. All Liz could feel was the electricity of his touch. She just wanted him to touch her more.

She wrapped her arms around his neck and ran her hands through his hair. She barely noticed the throbbing pain in her left shoulder. All she felt was him.

Liz didn't know how long they kissed, but it must have been a long time. Still, by the time Curtis pulled back, she knew it hadn't been long enough.

Curtis didn't let her go, but kept her up against him and leaned the top of his head against her forehead. His breathing was heavy and intoxicating.

"I love you," he whispered.

"I love you too," she said. She pulled his head down to hers for another kiss.

CHAPTER TWENTY

Curtis and Liz sat side by side, leaning against the wall of the Castle, their hands intertwined between them. He had healed her shoulder and her thigh, and that, combined with Curtis's kisses, had left Liz feeling much better.

"I'm in love with a fictional character," Liz sighed.

"Life must be hard for you," Curtis laughed.

"So, so hard," Liz said solemnly. Curtis chuckled and squeezed her hand.

"Actually, I don't know much about your life," Curtis said. "It's not fair that you get to know everything about me but I know so little about you."

Liz winced. "I'm not sure you want to know."

"Are you worried about what I'll think?" Curtis asked. "I won't judge you, Liz. Honest."

"How can you say that when you don't know anything about my life?"

"I know *some* things," Curtis said. "I heard what you said yesterday in Shakespeare's office about Kenric being based off of you. And I remember the Imagination Room."

Liz hung her head and closed her eyes.

"Hey," Curtis said gently, "I don't think you're like Kenric. You're much more attractive than he is, and I wouldn't have spent the last forty minutes kissing him." Liz didn't laugh. Curtis sighed. "You may have developed Kenric's character from some of your life experiences, but I know both of you. You're not him. You've made different choices. Choices matter more than history and backstory. We're each accountable for our own actions."

"But I didn't always choose the right things," Liz said. "I struggled for a long time."

"Everyone does at some point or another," Curtis said. "And no matter what you did, the important thing is that you turned your life around."

"But you don't know what I did yet," Liz said.

Curtis shook his head. "It doesn't matter. I know who you are now. That's what matters to me... though I still want to know about your life."

Liz looked up at him. "Are you sure? You can't unlearn what I'm about to tell you."

"I want to know everything about you," Curtis said.

Liz leaned her head against his chest, trying to decide where to begin. There was so much—the days she and her sisters sat hungry and dirty in their house, the horrible nights where she screamed into her pillow, the times she'd shot up, the dizziness and the rush from the high. Did Curtis really want to know everything?

"My father died when I was very young," Liz began.

"Were you two close?"

"I don't know," Liz said. "We might have been, but I don't remember him. I'd like to think I was close to him. I'd like to think I had a good father figure in my life at some point. I want to believe that God wouldn't give me *two* horrible men as fathers."

"So your mother remarried," Curtis guessed.

"Yes," Liz said. "But not for a while. She was... incompetent. She neglected us. We'd go hungry for days, sometimes. Nothing was ever clean and we weren't very well taken care of. So at first it was a relief when she married Stan. I thought things would change. For a long time I had been the one taking care of my two sisters."

"How old were you when Stan came into the picture?"

"Eight," Liz said.

"So young," Curtis said softly. "And you were already taking care of your siblings?"

"I wanted them to be happy," Liz said. "I've always cared about people. Well, not everyone, but *certain* people. I'm very protective of those I love."

"You sound like Healer," Curtis said.

"I'd like to think that I put the best parts of myself in Healer," Liz said, "but in reality, I could never be as kind and selfless as she is. Healer's a much better person than I am."

"I think she's better than *everyone*," Curtis said. "Not that she thinks that, of course. She's far too humble."

"You two are very different," Liz said.

"What was Stan like?" Curtis prompted.

"He was great at first," Liz said. "I really liked him. He put on a good face. But I've learned that all abusers know how to put on a show. They know how to hide what they are."

Curtis tensed. "Your step-father... Stan... he's the man from the Imagination Room?"

"Yes," Liz said. Her mind flashed back to being in her room, crying softly so as not to disturb anyone else while her worst nightmare hovered above her. Thankfully, she managed to stay solidly in the present. Ever since she'd defeated Stan in the Imagination Room, she'd been able to avoid getting stuck in the past.

"Mostly he hurt my mom," Liz continued, "and I know it's wrong of me, but I wasn't particularly protective of my mother. In my eyes, even at that age, I didn't think she deserved my protection. She had all but abandoned us after my father died, and then she let Stan into our lives. I should have been a better daughter."

"You couldn't have done anything to help her," Curtis said. "You were a child. They were both adults. Your mother could have gotten out of that situation if she had been brave enough."

"I don't think it really had to do with bravery," Liz said. "As I got older I learned some things about people in abusive relationships. Stan really manipulated her. I don't think it was as simple as being brave enough to leave. Mom really thought she deserved what she was getting and somehow she still loved him. She couldn't make herself go. I don't think she thought she deserved anything better."

"But what about what he was doing to you and your sisters?" Curtis asked. "Did she think you deserved it?"

"I don't know," Liz said. "Maybe. But I think she just chose to ignore what was happening with us. It made it easier for her."

"Did your mother know what he did to you?"

"I told her once," Liz said. "I never made that mistake again."

"She didn't believe you?"

Liz thought back to the night she'd crept into her mother's room, crying, and told her everything that had happened. Her mother had looked away, shook her head, and told her to stop lying, and to stop being such a whore. It still twisted like a knife in her gut for Liz to think about those words coming from her mother's mouth.

"I think that, inside, she knew it was true," Liz said. "But like I said, she chose to ignore it. And she said that if he ever really did do something like that to me, that I probably instigated it."

"She said *what?*" Curtis said loudly.

"It's okay," Liz said quickly. "I—"

"It is *not* okay," Curtis said, his voice at a normal level again but still hard. "You didn't deserve what happened to you."

Liz chose not to answer that. "Things carried on for years. I didn't fight against... what he did to me... on the terms that he never touched my sisters."

"Did he really never touch them?"

"Sexually, he never did," Liz said, "at least, as far as I know. But I don't trust him. It could have been for nothing."

"I hate to tell you this," Curtis said gently, "but people like that don't usually have only one victim."

"I know," Liz said softly. "But I had to try."

"I know you did," Curtis said. "And I commend you for it, even though I wish that you hadn't. Or rather, I wish *he* hadn't."

There was a long pause as Liz worked to control her breathing. She stared at her hand in Curtis's and let the memories of the old dresser and the old man swirl back into the past.

"Do your sisters know what you did for them?" Curtis asked.

"No," Liz said. "And I'd like to keep it that way. I don't want them to feel guilty."

"Was Stan ever caught?"

"A school teacher noticed something was wrong and asked my sister, Jenn, about her home life. Jenn was the only one of us brave enough to speak up. The police came to our house and took Stan into custody."

"Did he pay for what he did?" Curtis asked.

"He was sentenced to life in prison," Liz said. "I testified against him and I think it was my testimony that sealed his fate. My mother never forgave me for that."

"She still didn't see him for what he was?" Curtis asked, incredulous.

Liz shook her head. "I think that if she had, she would've recognized that she was at fault. And she just couldn't face it."

"I'm sorry, Liz, but you shouldn't be justifying your mother," Curtis said. "If she had stood up to him in the first place, none of you would have gone through what you did."

"I blamed her for a long time," Liz said slowly, "but eventually, I decided I needed to forgive her. What she did wasn't okay, but I needed to let it go. So I tried to understand why she didn't save us. Eventually, with some meditation, I was able to get past it. I'm not trying to justify my mother, but I guess I need to believe what I just said so that I can let my anger go."

"Have you forgiven Stan?"

"No," Liz admitted. "I don't know if I'll ever be able to forgive him. I *can't* understand why he did what he did. I don't see any good in him at all. But I've at least gotten to a point where my hate for him doesn't consume me."

"So far you've only told me about the mistakes other people have made," Curtis pointed out. "I still don't see why you think you're so bad."

"That's because I haven't gotten to that part yet," Liz said. "But shortly after Stan's incarceration, I left my sisters alone with my mother and lived with my aunt, from my dad's side. I regret that decision. I should have taken Jenn and Anne with me. They were hurting just like I was. But I was too selfish, so I left. I was fourteen."

"It was about time you started taking care of yourself," Curtis said.

"But I wasn't taking care of myself," Liz countered. "I was just trying to escape. I got a part-time job at a bookstore, but pretty soon I was fired for drug use. I stole money from the bookstore so that I could get drugs for the next few months. My life continued to go downhill from there. I would have quit high school, but my aunt never let me. I enjoyed reading and English class, anyway, and it was an escape for me. But I eventually started prostituting myself. I felt dirty every time I did it, like I was being raped all over again. But I didn't know what else to do. I truly believed that was all I was good for."

"That's what Stan made you think," Curtis said. "You're worth a lot more than that, Liz."

"I didn't believe it at the time," Liz said. "The books in high school helped, like I said. I decided to try writing, and then, with the help of my teacher Jennifer, I was published. When I got that call from the publisher and they offered me a deal, it was like I could breathe for the first time in my life. It was a new beginning. With the advance they gave me, I cleaned up my life and I never looked back. Then with the award I was able to get my own place. Writing saved me."

"And you really did want to solve your problems through your characters," Curtis said. "You put everything bad into Kenric, and everything good into Healer."

"Yes," Liz said. "I also wrote Healer as a mother figure; the person I wished my own mother had been."

"So where did I come from?"

"I knew we'd start talking about you eventually." Liz smiled.

"Yes, well, it *was* inevitable," Curtis laughed.

"Don't let this go to your head or anything," Liz said, "but I basically wrote you as a dream. You were what I wanted a man to be like; what I hoped a man would treat me like some day. Someone beyond my grasp, but someone I thought would be *good*, and good enough for me. Someone I wouldn't have to be afraid of. Someone whom I could love, without being afraid of loving them."

Curtis was silent for a moment, and then slowly unwrapped his arms from around her. Liz frowned. She felt so safe when he held her. Why was he letting go?

But instead of leaving like Liz was afraid he would, Curtis turned to face her and gently cupped her face in his hands. "Elizabeth Christina McKinnen," he whispered. "I want you to understand a few things. I noticed that you didn't say anything when I said you didn't deserve what happened to you, and I want you to know that *I* know that what happened to you was Stan's fault, not yours. You were just a little girl trying to protect her sisters. Most children wouldn't have even thought about anyone but themselves. And even if you hadn't tried to protect them, you wouldn't have deserved what happened. I love you and I want you to know that I don't think less of you because of what that man did to you. Next, I promise that I will never, *ever* hurt you. Sparring wounds aside. But I will never harm you or abuse you or do anything to compromise your integrity. I want you to always feel safe with me. I swear I will protect you. I will never hurt you." Curtis looked desperate and helpless. "But tell me what to do. Let me make it better. Please."

"I just need you to be here for me," Liz said. "Stay by me. Hold me. And help me defeat Kenric."

Curtis leaned toward her and enveloped her in his arms.

"I'll never let anyone hurt you again," he promised.

"Are you happy that you made me tell you my life story?" Liz joked.

But Curtis's answer was serious. "Yes," he said. "Even though your past is hard, it helps me understand you. Sometimes you're so closed off, and I can't read you. Now I know why. And no matter what you've been through or what you've done, you're still mine."

"I'm yours," Liz agreed. She leaned up for another kiss, but then she heard multiple sets of footsteps echoing off of the cobblestones.

CHAPTER TWENTY-ONE

"You've definitely made up," Rob noted as he rounded the castle corner.

Liz sighed in relief that it was only Rob, then quickly jumped up and stepped away from Curtis. He stood as well, but kept her hand in his and didn't let her go far.

"So *that's* why you wanted us to leave them alone?" Healer asked.

"You've been around them more than I have," Rob said. "Haven't you noticed the sexual tension?"

Healer blushed. She didn't usually talk about these kinds of things in public.

"*So* much sexual tension." Curtis nodded vehemently.

Liz felt herself turn red. Rob winked at her.

"You got the girl again, I see," Rob said.

"The right one this time," Curtis said. He squeezed Liz's hand and she felt a giddy grin glide across her face.

"It took you long enough," Rob said. "Don't you think, Healer?"

Healer cleared her throat. "Well, I certainly noticed the... um... attraction there, but I haven't dwelt on it."

Curtis laughed. "Maybe we should change subjects to spare Healer. She seems extremely uncomfortable."

"*I'm* uncomfortable," Rob said. "Just look at you two."

Healer cleared her throat.

"Shakespeare wanted to meet with us now," she said awkwardly. "Even Rob is being forced to come."

"I'm not very happy about it," Rob said. "Meetings are boring. But can you two manage to control yourselves for a few minutes so we can go anyway?" Healer shot Rob a glare.

"For a *few* minutes," Curtis said. They walked together into the Castle. Healer kept her gaze firmly ahead of her. Liz could tell she was purposefully not looking at the two of them.

Curtis and Liz were still holding hands when they entered Shakespeare's office.

"Well it's about time," Shakespeare said, nodding at Liz's hand intertwined with Curtis's.

"Did *everyone* know?" Liz moaned.

"Pretty much." Shakespeare smiled. "But shall we get down to business?" He motioned for them all to sit. Curtis sat by Liz this time, keeping his hand firmly around hers. Healer sat in the chair to the side, Rob leaned against a bookshelf, and Shakespeare stood behind his desk, his fists planted against the wood as he leaned forward and studied the papers below him.

"I read through everything here," he said. "I can't really glean more from Kenric's character than you've already told us. I did find a few hidden things about him that may or may not be true, depending on what translated over from the page when he came to life."

"What are they?" Liz asked, worried. What had she forgotten? Had she created a monster even worse than she'd first thought?

"You've written a few potential powers on these pages." Shakespeare gestured down, and then stood up straight and started drawing in the air. Images appeared before him and Liz's mouth dropped.

"What?" she cried out, startled. "You have *magic*?"

"Yes," Shakespeare said calmly, continuing to write in the air.

"But... but... you're William Shakespeare."

Shakespeare paused and regarded her. "And you're Elizabeth McKinnen. I fail to see the point."

"How do you have *magic*?"

"It's not that big of a deal," Curtis said from beside her.

"But I… I just didn't think he… how did you get magic?" Liz managed.

Shakespeare raised an eyebrow. "I wrote that I had magic and it came true," he said. "It's really quite satisfying. I can become anything I want, as long as I put my mind to it."

"Including a sorcerer?"

"Including a sorcerer," Shakespeare affirmed. He pointed to the words in the air again. "If I may continue?"

"Sorry," Liz said quietly.

"Quite all right," Shakespeare said. "Now. We already know the following information about Kenric: one, he's a powerful Spirit user. Two, he has around fifty to one hundred dragons at his command. Three, he's an accomplished murderer and skilled fighter." Shakespeare pointed to each item in the air in turn as he said them and then, with a wave of his hand, he moved the words to his left-hand side. "Now, here are things that *might* be true about him. Liz already mentioned one yesterday: Kenric might be an Elementalist." He wrote "Elementalist" in the air. "I noticed some other notes scribbled here and there that may or may not be true. There was once a possibility of Kenric's mother coming back into the picture and teaching him a secret, darker power. How developed was that storyline, Liz?"

Liz shook her head. "I barely touched it. It didn't take me long to decide that that wasn't going to happen in the books. His mother abandoned him; she doesn't come back until later and he just ends up killing her. The idea of some secret, darker magic didn't seem realistic. It didn't fit. That's why I scratched it."

"Having dark magic doesn't fit magical law," Healer said. "Magic can be neither light nor dark. It just is; it is up to the person to decide how to use it."

"For example, Spirit can be used both ways," Curtis said pointedly. "Kenric uses it for evil but Liz uses it for good."

"It does seem unlikely that this will crop up in our reality," Shakespeare said, "but I'm going to write it up here just in case." He wrote "dark magic?" in the air and then wrote "new breeds" below it.

"Liz also noted at one point that Kenric might be experimenting with breeding new types of dragons," Shakespeare said. "If he was successful with this endeavor and has brought unknown monsters to our land, we will be highly unprepared."

"There are already seven known species of dragon," Curtis said. "How many did you make up?"

"The idea was never developed enough for me to come up with more," Liz said. "But maybe that's a blessing. We don't want Kenric to have even more of an advantage."

"But your lack of planning might not have stopped him from breeding dragons," Shakespeare said. "If the idea was planted in his mind, he might have done it."

"Can you imagine a Sampar and a Rokur breeding together? There would be no chance of survival. It would breathe radiation all over you before you had time to find a weak spot," Curtis mused. "There are so many possibilities. This could be disastrous."

"But what's the likelihood that he's *actually* done this?" Healer asked. "If Liz didn't finalize anything..."

"It doesn't matter," Shakespeare said. "The potential was there. And Liz wouldn't necessarily have had to come up with a concrete idea for a new dragon. Just the idea that a Sampar and a Rokur could mate and create something more powerful and dangerous would allow nature to create something new on its own."

"I hate my brain sometimes," Liz mumbled.

"Don't beat yourself up," Curtis said. "Your brain came up with me. You're clearly quite talented."

"We're not sure he's actually done this," Shakespeare said. "But we should keep it in mind as a possibility."

"And what if he has done it?" Rob asked. "We just march into his lair blind?"

"Not blind," Shakespeare said. "Just not quite at the advantage we'd like. We still stand a very good chance. Don't let questions discourage you. 'Our doubts are traitors, and make us lose the good we oft might win, by fearing to attempt.'"

"Are you quoting yourself?" Liz demanded.

"*Measure for Measure* was a good play," Shakespeare said.

Liz couldn't really argue with that, so she let him continue without further interruption.

"The last thing Liz wrote down that we didn't already know was that Kenric may have possibly found a way to block all forms of magic from hurting him while giving him ultimate power with Spirit Magic."

"That's not possible," Healer said. "Magicians *can't* have that much control of their magic. Magic isn't something to be possessed; it's wild, a life force of its own."

"But Kenric can subdue over one hundred dragons at once," Curtis said. "What's to stop him from completely ruling over magic?"

"Hopefully Liz's common sense," Rob said.

"How developed was this idea, Liz?" Shakespeare asked.

Liz's mouth was suddenly dry. She wasn't sure how she could admit this to them. At first she hadn't thought it would be a problem. She thought that since the final book hadn't been published yet, they'd be saved from this situation. But now that she knew that just a flimsy idea could change their lives, it was clear that this particular piece of the story had come to life with Curtis and Healer and the rest of them.

"Liz?" Shakespeare prodded.

Liz tried to swallow. "It's... in the last book."

Shakespeare breathed out heavily, Healer gasped, and Curtis tensed. Rob's reaction was more what she had expected.

"What were you *thinking*?" Rob exclaimed. "How does the series end? Kenric wins? We all die?"

"Back off," Curtis said. "I'm sure there's still a way to beat him. Liz must have written a way."

Liz stared ahead.

"Right?" Curtis asked, panicked.

She very carefully did not look at Healer. "You said that I could write myself some powers?" she asked Shakespeare. He nodded hesitantly, his eyes narrowed in thought. "Then I'll do that. I'll fix everything."

"But more magic won't work," Rob argued. "He's immune to it!"

"There's got to be a way," Liz argued. "I'm the writer; I'll figure it out. I'm in charge of my own story."

"Of course you are, dear," Healer said gently.

Liz's stomach plummeted.

"Hold on," Shakespeare said. "That *might* work, but it might not. It all depends on what else you wrote in that last book. How did Curtis get past this in the story?"

"Strange to be sitting here listening to my future in my other life," Curtis mumbled.

Liz just shook her head. "No. We're not doing it that way."

"Why?" Shakespeare asked. "Didn't it work?"

"Yes," Liz said. "Curtis beats Kenric. But I refuse to do what I wrote."

Shakespeare frowned. "You may not have a choice."

"But as the writer, I'm in control," Liz argued. "I *do* have a choice."

"But you already made a choice when you wrote the original story," Shakespeare said. "You can't change the consequences of your choices, even if you change your mind about them now. You've already set things into action."

"But I didn't know that you all would be alive when I wrote it!" Liz cried out. "I won't do it!"

"What's the problem?" Shakespeare asked.

She didn't answer but stared resolutely at the floor, trying to figure out how she could write her way out of this.

"Liz?" Curtis said gently. "We have to know. We can't let Kenric keep attacking everyone here. We can't let him win."

"What if I go to him, then?" Liz said. "That's what he wants anyway. I'll go be with him and I'll figure out a way to defeat him while I'm there."

"No," they all said together.

"I'm not letting you out of my sight if you're thinking that way," Curtis said. "You're not going to him. I won't let you."

"Stay put, Creator," Rob said. "You don't need to put yourself at risk like that."

"Sweetheart, nothing is worth compromising yourself," Healer said. Her voice was so gentle, so kind, so believing. "We'll find another way. You already have another way. Just tell us what it is and we'll make it work, no matter what."

Healer's soft voice broke Liz apart. She felt tears stream down her face.

Curtis wrapped his arm around her. "What's wrong, Liz? What happens in the book?" Liz kept crying. "If I have to die, I'll do it. I'll do that for you. I know what Kenric is like and I'll never put you in a position to be around a man like that again. Let me go. Let me die. I'm not afraid."

Liz tried to get control of herself and sagged against Curtis.

"What is it, Liz?" Shakespeare asked. "I can see that whatever it is will be difficult, but we *have* to know. We've got no time. Our spies have already discovered that he's planning another attack."

Liz couldn't let that happen; she knew that. She couldn't let more characters die. She had to do something. Closing her eyes, she fought to control her emotions and took comfort in Curtis's embrace. Maybe she could just tell them part of the truth and figure the rest out on her own.

"There's a way to get past Kenric's immunity," Liz finally said. Her voice shook. "I have to assume that it would have come through with him."

"Good," Shakespeare encouraged. "Tell us more."

"There's a secret pool behind a waterfall on the western coast of Shethara," Liz said. "It's difficult to get to; many people have died trying to reach it, and most don't make the attempt as they consider it legend. Kenric thought it was worth a try."

"What was the legend?"

"The pool can provide someone with whatever power they desire," Liz said. "When Kenric reached it, he asked for invincibility. This meant that he was granted immunity from magic, as he considered that his most dangerous weapon and his worst enemy."

"So a sword can still pierce him?" Rob asked.

"Sometimes," Liz said, "but with his magic as strong as it is now, I'm not sure a sword could get close enough to hurt him."

Rob rolled his eyes. "What were you thinking?"

"Let her speak, Rob," Healer said. "Patience."

"For your information, the writer doesn't always have complete control of her stories," Liz said defensively. "This just came to me, and it was strong. I couldn't fight against it; without this, the story didn't make sense. It was necessary. I couldn't change it and I'm sorry."

"This pool," Shakespeare said, "it could grant you and Curtis powers as well? The power to get through Kenric's invincibility?"

Liz hesitated, but nodded. "Yes. That's what happens in the book; Curtis is given the power to defeat Kenric. But it all depends on if the pool came through to this world."

"It makes sense that it would," Shakespeare mused. "If Kenric's power came through—and I'm certain it did—then the way to overcome it would have as well. There always have to be opposites. It's partly why Kenric and Curtis are both alive. Both had to come; it couldn't just be one of them."

"So where would the pool be?" Curtis asked. "We should find it and use it quickly."

"I don't want us to use it," Liz said. "At least, not yet. Let me try to change some things first."

Shakespeare folded his arms and studied Liz. She kept her eyes low, trying not to look guilty.

"The pool requires a sacrifice," Shakespeare said slowly. "All of the magic in your books comes with a price, so it makes sense that this pool would as well."

Liz didn't reply.

"What is the sacrifice?" Shakespeare asked.

Again, Liz remained silent. No one spoke; they were all eager to hear her answer. After the way she had reacted, they probably knew that the sacrifice was significant, and something that Liz was unwilling to give.

Of course, since Healer was an expert on magic, she was quick to figure out what the sacrifice was.

"To be given great power, you have to offer great power," Healer said slowly.

Liz froze. No. She didn't want anyone to know this. What if they actually *did* it? But, unaware of Liz's emotions, Healer continued.

"Kenric must have offered someone powerful to be given invincibility to magic. I don't know who he would have sacrificed." Healer paused, probably afraid to go on.

"What did he sacrifice?" Curtis asked Liz.

Liz cleared her throat. She knew she couldn't avoid this anymore. Healer had already figured it out.

"Paratheon was the strongest dragon he had, and with the power of their connection... the Sampar's life was enough to grant Kenric the power he wanted."

"And it would have been even more powerful because Paratheon was something he loved," Rob said slowly.

"And the person with the most power here," Healer said softly, "and who is expendable, is me."

Liz closed her eyes as a deep silence filled the room. She couldn't deny Healer's words, no matter how much she wanted to.

"Dear God," Rob breathed after a moment.

"Is there any other way?" Curtis asked, his voice rough.

"I'll figure it out," Liz said through her tears. "I'm a writer. I have magic. I can do anything."

"No," Shakespeare said quietly. "I'm sorry, but you've already established this. You can't write something that will negate what you've already founded. You've written that the only way you can defeat Kenric is to use this pool. You can't write your way around it because this path has already come to this reality."

"Yes I can," Liz argued. "I also wrote that Curtis defeats Kenric, but you tell me that *I* have to do it instead of him. Doesn't that mean I can change things?"

Shakespeare shook his head, a sad look on his face. "The laws of the Immortal Writers automatically put the writer into the equation. Of course, your hero still has to help you, but you become the hero of your own story. That's just how it works. And besides, you're not changing the means of victory, or the powers behind it. Your presence changes very little, actually; it just adds to the story. But trying to change the fact that… that Healer has to be a sacrifice so that you can beat Kenric… I'm sorry, but you can't do it. It would be futile. The path is set."

"Can we find another sacrifice?" Curtis asked. "Is there anyone else? Or any*thing* else?"

"It has to be within the realm of your story," Shakespeare said. "Healer *is* the strongest among you. Liz is powerful too, of course, but she cannot be sacrificed."

"Maybe I can," Liz said hopefully. "Please. Let me do it."

"There would be no point in even trying," Rob said bitterly. "Kenric would kill us all and this world would burn in dragon fire."

"Then give me time to find another way," Liz said. "Maybe I can find someone else or create someone else, someone who I don't care about killing off."

"You can't guarantee that someone will come to life," Shakespeare said, "and an entire character would take a long time to convincingly create. That won't work."

"But—"

"I will not let you sacrifice someone else in my place." Healer finally spoke up. "I will gladly die for all of you. I would rather it be me than one of you. Plus, you all know I've been sick. Not even Curtis can figure out what's wrong. I'm afraid I don't have much time left, anyway."

"No," Liz said. "*No.* I won't let you do this."

Healer gave her a small smile. "You will," she said. "You have no choice. As we have already established, it is the only way."

Liz's tears fell freely. "But I can't lose you, Healer. Don't you know I wrote you to be the mother I wish I had? I… I love you. I can't let you go."

Healer didn't cry. She was a strong person; she always had been. And she was kind. She wouldn't let Liz see any pain or fear she might feel. Liz knew this and it made her feel worse. Healer was too good to be sacrificed. It wasn't fair.

"You can do it," Healer said kindly. "I know you can. I'll always be alive, in a way: in your words, through your stories… through you. So *you* need to go on, and you need to survive. For me. I need that from you."

"I'll help you," Curtis said. His voice was heavy. "It won't be easy for me, either. Healer is my friend and has been for years. But I can see that this is necessary. We all have to make sacrifices for the greater good."

"I'm willing to do this," Healer said. "I have no regrets. I will play my part to defeat Kenric."

"But—"

"No, dear," Healer said. "Be strong. Remember, that is what *I* need from you. Let me do this."

Liz cried silently. She could be strong for Healer, but she wasn't going to give up, either. She would try to think of something. If it came down to it, she would throw herself into the pool first, just to try to spare Healer.

"As difficult as this is, we need to get moving," Shakespeare said gently. "The question is, where would this secret pool be located in our world?"

Everyone turned to Liz. She took a deep breath and wiped away her tears. Curtis put his arm around her shoulders and held her close to him. His touch helped her control her emotions.

"In Shethara, it's behind a waterfall," Liz said. "The waterfall was in the west. Should we look toward the west coast?"

"That might be worth pursuing," Shakespeare said, "but Shethara and the United States are completely different, if it's even *in* the Americas… though I would bet it is. The rest of your story came to life here. Still, it will be wherever makes the most sense physically… wherever nature would have had to make the least change to fit it in. Can you describe the waterfall?"

"It was the largest waterfall in Shethara," Liz said. "Thousands of pounds of water fell from it, so you can imagine the problem of passing under it to get to the pool. Like I said… most people didn't survive the attempt."

"So, thousands of pounds of water, a huge waterfall, and most likely in North America…" Curtis said.

"Niagara Falls?" Shakespeare suggested. "Specifically Horseshoe Falls?"

Liz nodded. "That closely fits the description."

Shakespeare walked behind his desk and sat down. "Perfect. I want you to leave tomorrow night."

Liz started. "What?" she exclaimed. That wouldn't give her enough time to think of a way to save Healer's life. She silently berated herself for telling them about the pool at all. This had all been a mistake. "Shouldn't... shouldn't we wait for a while? I'm not sure I'm ready..."

Shakespeare turned to Curtis. "How's her swordplay?"

"Perfect," Curtis said. "She beat me today."

"*Now* you admit it," Liz mumbled.

"Healer?" Shakespeare asked.

"She's ready," Healer said steadily. "Her magic is strong. Combining it with her combat skills and the pool's magic, she'll be able to defeat Kenric."

"Then you will all leave tomorrow," Shakespeare said. "As long as *you* are ready, Healer."

"I'm ready," Healer said. She stood up.

"Wait!" Liz begged. "Give me time. I'll figure something out. Just give me a couple of days. *Please.*"

"No," Healer said softly. "I will do this, Creator. I will do this for you. I'm not afraid." She turned to look at Shakespeare. "We will leave tomorrow." She left the room.

"Curtis, take Liz to her room and take care of her," Shakespeare said. "Work with her and get her to write herself some more magic. But don't let her waste time trying to change things that cannot change. Help make her stronger."

Curtis nodded and forced Liz to stand.

"If I can write myself more magic, why can't I write a way around the pool?" Liz demanded.

"You can write yourself more magic, but you can't erase the immunity the pool has given Kenric," Shakespeare explained. "Only the pool can grant you that power. You've made the pool the only option. You can't change that. I'm sorry, Liz. Curtis, go. Help her."

"What do you want me to do?" Rob asked.

"See to the pegasi," Shakespeare instructed. "Make sure they're ready for the journey. And then prepare yourself. You'll be going with them for extra protection."

Rob nodded as Curtis led Liz from the room. Liz tried to see where Healer had gone, but she couldn't find her. Liz wanted to tell her she was sorry, that she would make everything all right somehow... but with Curtis watching her, how would she ever get to her? She only had so much time left if she didn't figure something out soon.

"I want to see Healer," Liz said.

"I think Healer wants to be alone," Curtis replied gently. "And we have work to do."

"But..."

"Just come with me," Curtis said. "There'll be plenty of time for us to be with her and say goodbye tomorrow."

But Liz knew there wouldn't be. There would never be enough time to say goodbye. Too soon, Healer would be dead.

Amidst the grief and the pain, Liz felt an enormous amount of guilt. It was all her fault, *all her fault*. She had written thoughtlessly, without thinking about the consequences of her actions. But how could she have known she was actually going to kill someone?

Did her ignorance matter?

Or was she just like Kenric?

CHAPTER TWENTY-TWO

"I've never written about myself before," Liz said, tapping a pen against her desk. "I don't like to study myself. It scares me. I have a lot of respect for memoir writers."

"You're not writing a memoir," Curtis said. "You're writing a future. A very immediate future, hopefully. This should grant you some powers quickly."

"Like the ability to beat Kenric *without* sacrificing Healer?" Liz tried.

"You know that won't work," Curtis said, propping himself up on her bed. "And I'm determined to make you stop thinking about it."

"But what if I used the Imagination Room? Maybe it would help me come up with a way to save her."

"You can't," Curtis said. "Shakespeare already made that clear. Your attempts will be futile, and watching Healer die repeatedly will only make you worse off than you are. You don't need to see that."

"But I—"

"I know you're worried about Healer, but how about you just worry about making yourself as strong as possible?" Curtis suggested. "If you don't, Healer's sacrifice will be in vain, and it might affect me or Rob or Shakespeare. But, you know, no pressure."

Liz looked down at her desk. "Yeah… no pressure at all."

"I know you can do it. You're an exceptional writer."

"Not when it comes to *myself*."

"You've written two versions of yourself," Curtis pointed out. "Healer and Kenric. Now you just need to combine those two extremes and recognize who you really are."

"Interesting that I'll be killing off both parts of myself," Liz sighed. "Do you think I'm secretly suicidal?"

"I hope not," Curtis said seriously. "But I don't want you to think of it as killing yourself off. That's not what you're doing. If anything, you're making room for a new you to be created. Think of it that way. And we're going to write the new you *right now.*"

"How?" Liz asked.

Curtis lay back on the bed and thought about it for a minute. "I guess… try not to think of it as writing about yourself. Pretend you're writing for another character. Just make that character exactly like you."

"But I have to analyze myself first," Liz said.

"I can do it for you," Curtis said. "You already wrote a character profile for me. How about I describe you and you write it all down in your own words?"

Liz pursed her lips. "Okay," she said. "I'm not sure I want to hear this, but okay."

"It's good, I promise," Curtis said.

"Your opinion might be a little biased."

"Have I ever gone easy on you?"

"No," Liz admitted.

"That's not going to change," Curtis said. "I'll be honest. I'm not one of those guys who lies to his girl just to avoid conflict."

"I know," Liz said. She was pretty sure that would be a problem one day.

"Are you ready to focus?"

"It's hard to focus with you on my bed," Liz said.

Curtis grinned. "Think of it as incentive." He winked at her. "Just finish up first."

Liz cleared her throat. "Right." She picked up her pen and wrote, "Liz's character profile" on the top of a piece of paper. "I'm ready whenever you are," she said.

"Okay." Curtis cleared his throat. "Should we start with the physical stuff?"

"I know what I look like," Liz said.

"I think it's useful to find out how someone else sees you," Curtis said. "I mean, *I* know I'm gorgeous, but from what I understand most people judge themselves pretty harshly."

"Fine." Liz smirked. "Go ahead."

"Liz is five-eleven, with dirty-blonde hair and green eyes," Curtis began. "She used to be really skinny, but now she's strong. I like her strong."

"Why are you talking about me in third person?" Liz asked as she wrote.

"To help you think of yourself as a character so that this will be easier for you," Curtis said. "Now stop interrupting; I'm doing some hard work over here."

Liz kept writing.

"Liz has a long face with a strong chin. Her face looks best when she smiles. It always reaches her eyes because she very rarely smiles unless she means it. Her hair is long and pretty, but I think she could spice it up with some highlights or something." Liz rolled her eyes. "She has a few freckles. They're cute. Her nose is a little longer than most people's." Liz frowned but kept writing. "It's not terribly distracting, but… well, I guess everyone has to have a flaw. Liz's chest is a decent size. It's not overbearing. It's just right. I like it."

"Let's move on," Liz said quickly.

"You're interrupting again," Curtis said. "I can say what I want."

"If you make me write myself a bigger chest size I will kill you," Liz said.

Curtis laughed. "I meant what I said—I like them just the way they are."

Liz put her hands around her head. "Oh Lord. Can we please just move on to something else?"

"Okay, okay," Curtis said. "I like Liz's hands. They're not freakishly big but they're not petite either. They've seen work and I like that. Liz has a black tattoo on her back that looks like a phoenix."

"How do you know that?" Liz asked, looking back up at Curtis.

"I watched in the mirror when your shirt was off and you got rid of your bandages, remember?" Curtis asked, shifting himself to a more comfortable position on the bed. "*I remember.*"

Liz blushed. "I somehow forgot about that."

"I'll remind you later. But since we're talking about your tattoo... why a phoenix?"

"Because they rise," Liz said, picking at a scrape in the wooden desk. "They burn to ashes, but they come out of them new and vibrant and ready to live. After I signed my first book contract, I decided I wanted to rise again. I wanted a second chance."

"Hmmm," Curtis said. "I like that."

"Me too."

"But back to your character profile... you can write down your battle scars."

"Got it," Liz said after a moment.

"Moving on to personality," Curtis mused. He put his hands behind his head and studied Liz. "Guarded. Slow to trust and believe. Troubled. But kind, very kind. Protective. Funny, although not as funny as me. I'm pretty hilarious, and Liz isn't quite at my level."

Liz raised her eyebrow at that. She had given him his wit.

"Liz has a remarkable capacity to love people," Curtis said. "That's obvious just from what she did for her sisters. But it's carried over into her adult life, too. I've seen it and it makes me love her more. Liz isn't very confident in herself. I think she struggles to believe that she's worth anything, and I don't think she believes she can be a hero. But she should know that she already is one. She just needs to prove it to herself."

Curtis paused so that Liz could catch up with her writing. It was hard for her to do it. She just wanted to throw her arms around him. He was saying such nice things.

"Liz can be kind of self-absorbed, though," Curtis said.

Well, there goes the urge to hug him, Liz thought as she wrote.

"That's rich coming from Mister Arrogant," Liz mumbled.

"I didn't say I wasn't self-absorbed," Curtis retorted. "I'm just saying that you're that way, too. And *stop interrupting*. You can talk in a minute; I'm almost done."

Liz sighed as she finished writing "self-absorbed" on her character profile.

"She thinks a lot about her own problems and doesn't notice when someone's madly in love with her," Curtis continued. Liz shook her head. "She can be infuriating sometimes, but I'll take her anyway.

"Liz is strong. Not just physically—but mentally, too. She's good at sword fighting and is a strong wielder of Spirit Magic. She's even more powerful than Kenric."

Curtis paused and Liz finished writing "powerful Spirit User—stronger than Kenric" on her paper.

"Liz is also an Elementalist," Curtis added, and Liz wrote it down before she even realized what he had said.

"What?" Liz asked, looking up to face him. "No I'm not."

"I bet you are now," Curtis said. He sounded smug. "You wrote it down, didn't you?"

"Could it really be that easy?" Liz asked.

"I don't know," Curtis said. "But it was worth a shot. You've developed a pretty strong character profile for yourself… or rather, *I* have. Writing yourself down as an Elementalist might have worked." He nodded at her. "See if I'm right."

Liz gazed at him skeptically but reached out for her magic.

She was surprised by what she found.

There was still a vibrant, powerful pool of Spirit Magic in her chest, but there was a different element to it now. It seemed almost… wild. More earthy than it had been before. Something extra was there.

"No way," Liz whispered.

Curtis grinned. "Test it. Make it rain in here or something."

Liz wasn't sure what she was doing, but she figured it couldn't be much different than using Spirit Magic. She picked out the tendrils of magic that seemed unfamiliar. The Elemental Magic had a different texture than the

Spirit Magic. Spirit seemed almost silky and seductive; the Elemental Magic was rough and raw.

She sent the power up into the room, asking for rain.

Liz didn't know where she went wrong. Yes, it rained, but it felt more like a monsoon, and a very *hot* monsoon at that. She could swear there was a miniature earthquake as the rain started to fall.

"Okay, Liz," Curtis shouted over the wind. "Make it stop. The rain is scalding."

Liz pulled her magic back and called for the rain to stop. It did, and the price of the magic took its toll. She slumped back in her chair and gasped.

"You're definitely an Elementalist," Curtis said. "An incompetent one, but still powerful."

"That was my first attempt," Liz panted. "Give me some credit."

"Well, okay," Curtis said. "It was pretty impressive that you could separate the Elemental Magic from the Spirit Magic. But… can you sense the different elements *inside* of the Elemental Magic? Take time to study your power. Don't just fling it around."

Liz scowled at him, but closed her eyes and focused on the living pool inside her chest. The more she focused, the more she noticed differences in the strands of raw Elemental Magic. The textures of the power reflected the element it controlled. Fire was warm, wind was hardest to grasp, water was deceptively soothing, and earth was firm and cool. Feeling the separate strands, Liz could understand why most Elementalists used earth. It just *felt* better.

She opened her eyes after several minutes. "I think I can tell them apart now."

Curtis smiled in encouragement. "Good. Why don't you pick an element to use this time?"

"Earth," Liz said immediately.

Curtis nodded. "Okay," he said. "Uh…" He looked around and spotted the small lucky bamboo plant on her bedside table. It had been knocked over in the mini-monsoon, and the soil from the pot was strewn across the wood of the table. Curtis stretched and reached over to the bamboo, picked it up, and positioned it on the table. "Make that grow."

Liz nodded and focused on gathering the earth strands of magic. They came readily, cool and comforting. She sent them trickling toward the bamboo plant and watched in amazement as it shot up. She retracted her magic after a moment; she didn't want the bamboo to grow too much.

She barely felt the earth take her strength; she was in good shape, and she knew that using earth magic wouldn't hinder her in battle.

"You should probably water your ridiculously large plant now," Curtis said.

Liz reached out to water and directed it to the plant. It complied, but as it did Liz started to feel somewhat closed in. She reminded herself that she was safe and that this was just an effect of the magic. She calmed down, watered the bamboo, and then drew the magic back to her again. She felt a little thirsty, but fine.

"Very good," Curtis said. "I don't think we have time to train you on fire… from what I understand, that one's pretty rough, right?"

Liz nodded. "It's savage, and its price would leave me vulnerable in battle anyway."

"Then let's not worry about it for now," Curtis said. "But I bet air could be useful with all of those dragons." He picked up a pillow and threw it at her. She caught it with one hand, confused.

"Use air to pick that up and throw it at me," he said.

Liz frowned. "I could do that more effectively with Spirit Magic."

"Yes," Curtis said, "but I want you to practise using air. It might be beneficial."

Liz nodded and reached out for air. It was harder to hold, but she was prepared for that. She let air loose and it scattered itself around the room. She fought to gain control over it again. It was difficult, like trying to gather several balloons that were flying away at once. Luckily, Liz had a lot of practice controlling her magic due to her use of Spirit.

She guided the air into a tight band and forced it around the pillow. It shot up. Liz directed it toward Curtis and air gusted forward, smashing the pillow in Curtis's face.

Liz withdrew the magic and gasped. Air had exacted its toll from her: strength, breath, and sanity. She felt desperately anxious for a moment, but it passed as her lungs relaxed and breathing grew easier.

"Not bad," Curtis said. "But you could use more practice." He threw the pillow back at her. "Try again."

They practised earth, water, and air on and off for a while, but eventually Liz was too tired to continue.

"That's good enough," Curtis finally said. "I'm sure Kenric will suspect that you have some type of magic, but he won't be expecting you to be powerful in *two* areas. You may not be an expert Elementalist yet, but you'll be strong enough to catch him and his dragons off guard."

Liz nodded and fell back in her chair. "What else do I need to write for myself?"

Curtis frowned. "I don't know. I think you were pretty impressive to begin with. There wasn't much to improve upon. But now you have an edge, and that's something."

Liz took a deep breath and decided to try again. "You know, that was easier than I expected... writing myself a power, anyway. Maybe I can write around this thing with Healer's sacrifice and—"

"No," Curtis cut her off. "We've gone over this. It won't do any good. You'll just upset yourself."

"But isn't it worth a try?" Liz pleaded.

Curtis sighed and stared up at the ceiling, thinking for a moment. "You know I will miss Healer," he finally said. "She's been a support to me for a long time. I consider her one of my best friends. I don't want to lose her. I hate that we'll be escorting her to her death tomorrow night. I hate it much more than I'm letting on. But her sacrifice unfortunately makes sense. It's horrible, but it feels... well, not right, exactly, but necessary. And I know Healer. Admittedly, she's probably scared right now. But I also believe that she'll find peace with it. She knows that this is needed, and while I bet she's not happy about dying, she *is* happy to sacrifice herself for someone else, especially someone she cares for. It's in her nature. And she will always live on—in your words, in us. I'll miss her terribly, but with the circumstances as they are, it's not worth sacrificing your sanity on some fruitless attempt to save her."

Liz hung her head. Everything Curtis said made sense. She didn't want to accept it, but she knew it was true. And Shakespeare had made it clear—there was no point in trying to write her way out of this.

She closed her eyes against the dead weight in her chest and let the tears fall. When she had found out Healer was alive, it was like she had had a chance at having a mother, a *real* mother, one who was good and kind and nurturing. And now, because of Liz, that mother would die. She would never come back for Liz and believe in her again.

Curtis was beside her in a heartbeat, wrapping his arms around her. He bent down and gently picked her up, and then carried her to the bed.

"Now is not the time," Liz tried to joke.

Curtis shook his head. "I promised you I would never compromise your integrity, remember?" He set her down and covered her, then slid into the bed beside her. "And you asked me to hold you. I can do that now. I can keep you from falling apart." He wrapped his arms around her and held her close. "This will be hard for us both. But we can do it. Together."

"Together," Liz agreed.

His arms comforted her, but Liz couldn't find rest. Her writing was powerful—she knew that now. But why had she even started writing? First, she had created Kenric, a villain far worse than even Stan.

And now, she was single-handedly killing Healer.

CHAPTER TWENTY-THREE

Liz couldn't stop staring at Healer as they prepared to take off for Niagara Falls. She seemed so healthy, so alive, so vibrant, especially here in the beautiful moonlit courtyard. Several magicians from other stories had regrown and repaired the Castle grounds at an amazing rate since the attack. Liz was grateful for this act. It meant that Healer could be somewhere beautiful before she went off to die.

Liz didn't understand how Healer could head to her death so calmly. Her own nerves were on fire. She had eventually found peace in Curtis's arms the night before, but now that she was about to embark on this journey—this journey from whence Healer would not return—she found nothing but absolute panic.

"Just so you know, I have very different plans for the next time we're in bed together," Curtis said from beside her.

She knew what he was trying to do, but she still found herself pretty thoroughly distracted. "Oh really?" she asked, arching an eyebrow. "And what are those plans?"

"Well, you know," Curtis said. "I want to go past cuddling. I expect full spooning from now on."

Liz frowned. That wasn't what *she* had in mind.

"Don't I get a say in any of this?" Liz asked.

"No," Curtis said. "Cuddling is far too innocent. Spooning or nothing."

Liz laughed. "Spooning it is then."

She very much wanted to point out what *she* had planned for the next time they were in bed together, but she was distracted by Healer again. She had laughed at something Rob said. What a beautiful laugh.

Too bad it would soon be silenced.

"Do I need to take my shirt off again?" Curtis asked.

"What?" Liz asked, confused. "Why would you need to do that?"

"It was pretty distracting for you last time."

Liz sighed. "Is it that obvious?"

"That you enjoy it when my shirt's off, or that you're spiraling down into a deep pit of despair, guilt, grief, loss, and depression?" Liz stared at him and Curtis looked up at the sky in thought. "Yeah, it's pretty apparent."

"I do like your shirt off, but I think for the sake of everyone else it should stay on tonight."

"I bet everyone else would like it, too."

Liz shook her head. "Doesn't anything get you down?"

Curtis gave Liz a sad look. "Of course I'm upset," he admitted, "but I'm going to try to enjoy my last moments with Healer. I'm not going to gawk at her and make her worry any more about what she has to do. And you've been watching her... can't you tell that she's found peace? I don't know how she managed it, but I think she's ready to face this. She needs you to be strong right now. I need you to be strong, too. We can grieve together later. But for now we should try to enjoy the last little while we have with all of us together."

"One last ride into the night," Liz said. "I don't know if I'll ever be whole again, after this."

"But you're whole right now," Curtis said. "Focus on that."

"I don't think I'm whole," Liz countered. "As soon as I realized what had to happen I felt a piece of myself die."

"Then don't focus on that piece," Curtis said. "I know it's hard, but you've got to keep it together, at least for Healer. I'm not trying to belittle your pain. Believe me, *I understand* what you're going through. I'm hurting right now, too. But she needs us to be as close to normal as we can be."

Liz took a deep breath, held it, and then let it out slowly. "You're right," she admitted. "If she can be strong, I can, too. I can't be going through everything she's going through, and *she's* not a mess."

Curtis considered her words for a moment and then said, "I've never died, so I guess I can't be sure if what I'm saying is true, but… I think the people who are left behind hurt a lot more than the people who go."

Liz looked away from Curtis and took a deep breath. She had to agree with him, but she didn't have time to ponder his words. Shakespeare was approaching them, three pegasi trotting along behind him. The old author looked calm and dapper in his crisp, black and white suit. The pegasi were beautiful against the night, all silver and gold and white. They eased the pain in Liz's chest.

"Are you all ready?" Shakespeare asked. He looked at Healer as he spoke. She nodded.

"Good," he said. "I know this won't be easy, but for now I don't want you to focus on the pool at all. I want you to focus on getting there safely."

Liz hadn't considered that reaching Niagara Falls might be difficult. But of course, she knew that Kenric was watching the Castle. He would notice their departure and would almost certainly attack them once they were beyond its protection.

"How long do you think we have until we're attacked?" Curtis asked.

"It all depends on where the dragons will be coming from," Liz said. "But I wouldn't let our guard down. Kenric will have something waiting for us."

"We'll use evasive maneuvers in an attempt to throw the dragons off," Curtis said. "Take an unlikely route."

Rob nodded. "That's a good idea. Speed is nice, but if we can lose them altogether it'll be better. We don't want a dragon catching up with us while we're in the water."

"Remember that you have a couple of advantages here," Shakespeare said. "Kenric knew where the pool was in Shethara, but he might not know its whereabouts here. He'll undoubtedly know when you leave the Castle, but he shouldn't know where you're going. You might even be able to avoid an attack. Your company is small; you'll be hard to find after you leave, especially with the speed of your mounts and the cover of darkness."

"I wouldn't count on us being safe," Rob said.

"Agreed," Shakespeare said. "But have faith in the pegasi. They're fast. You have an advantage over the dragons when it comes to speed."

"But if the dragons find us, it would be unwise to just keep running," Curtis said. "We need to take them out as soon as possible. We don't want to risk them following us and trapping us later."

"That's probably wise." Shakespeare looked at the four of them and Liz followed his eyes. Rob, with his short sword and sais, his courage and flippant attitude; Healer with her bow and quiver of arrows, and endless expanse of magic and kindness; Curtis with his sword, his experience, his skill, his intimidating power. Finally Shakespeare's eyes rested on Liz. She wondered what Shakespeare saw when he looked at her. She hoped it was more than a scared girl way out of her league.

But he met her eyes with a smile. He looked confident in her. She hoped that confidence was deserved.

"It's time for you to go," Shakespeare said. "With how fast these pegasi travel, you should reach Niagara Falls in about three hours. It will be very dark when you reach your destination. Hopefully that will help you avoid any dragons."

"Won't people—mortals, I mean—won't they see us?" Liz asked

"Some might, if anyone's out by the time you reach the falls," Shakespeare said. "But most of them will think they're imagining things. Even if they believe what they see, no one else will believe them. The mortals are the least of your problems right now. In fact, I wouldn't consider them a problem at all."

Shakespeare released the reigns of the pegasi and they eagerly pranced up to the company. "Healer and Rob will be sharing Healer's pegasus. Is that all right?"

"Frederick won't mind," Healer said, patting her mount. "And then he can get to know Rob." She turned to look at him. "You'll take care of him for me, won't you?"

Rob swallowed. "Yes. Of course. You have my word."

Healer smiled. "Excellent." She swung onto Frederick's back and Rob clamoured up behind her.

Sinsus nudged Liz with his nose. Liz gave the pegasus a forced smile and rubbed his neck. "Are you ready to go?" she whispered. Sinsus snorted and raised his head in affirmation. "You're braver than I am," Liz sighed.

She mounted Sinsus. She felt some comfort sitting astride the strong pegasus. Sinsus was a good, smart animal. He would take care of her and would loan her some security during this hard journey.

"Good luck," Shakespeare said. He lifted a hand in farewell. "Have faith and be brave."

Healer and Rob took off first and Curtis followed behind them. Liz looked at Shakespeare.

"I'm not sure I can do this," she admitted.

The wise old writer looked sad, but understanding. "But you can," he said. "And you must."

Liz nodded, closed her eyes, and kicked her heels into Sinsus's sides. A small smile lit her face as they took flight. She could feel Sinsus's happiness at being in the air. What a wonderful thing it would be to have wings. Maybe she would write herself some one day.

She quickly caught up to the others. Curtis was now in the lead, undoubtedly on guard, searching the clouds for dragons that might attack. Healer led Frederick over to meet Liz.

"How are you tonight?" Healer asked her. Rob said nothing. He clung tightly to Healer, his eyes closed. He looked a little sick.

Liz considered. She was not feeling well, of course, but she wasn't sure honesty would be best for Healer right now. Curtis was right; Liz needed to be strong for her.

"I'm all right." Liz smiled. "How are you?"

"I'm fine," Healer said. "I am also honest. How are you *really*?"

Liz bit her lip and looked down. "I'm… feeling very guilty. And sad. I wish I could figure out another way that this could all work."

"Do not feel guilty. There is no need. This is not your fault."

Liz gave one short, sarcastic laugh. "Not my fault? How is this not my fault?"

"You once asked Curtis if you had taken away his agency by writing all of his history and his choices," Healer reminded her. "He said that you didn't take away our choices; rather, you provided a way for us to make those choices. You described what we would do instead of forcing us to do something. That is true. Sacrificing things is in my nature. This is a large sacrifice, of course... but I have come to terms with it."

"How?" Liz asked. "How could you possibly be all right with this?"

"It helps that my death is not pointless," Healer said. "It serves a purpose and it will help others. It will save many lives. This is how I would choose to pass on. Is it happening sooner than I expected? Yes. But none of us are ever really prepared for death. You have given me a gift, in a way: a chance to prepare, to know my end. And I am pleased with the purpose of my passing. It is better than dying to this mysterious ailment, at any rate."

"But don't you harbour any resentment toward me? I'm murdering you."

"You are not murdering me," Healer said. "You forget that I could have said no. I could have left the Castle last night and disappeared. You never would have found me. You wouldn't have had your sacrifice. I am choosing this."

"Why didn't you leave?" Liz asked. "That would have been... easier for you, I'm sure."

Healer shook her head. "It would not have been easier for me. I would have been leaving you all to a horrible fate. I couldn't live with myself if I betrayed my friends that way. And while it did cross my mind that I could make that choice, to me it wasn't really a choice at all."

"So you don't hate me?"

"No, Creator," Healer said with a smile. "You gave me life. I am grateful to you for that. I do not blame you at all for my death."

Liz swallowed and forced herself to keep her emotions in check. She refused to completely break down in front of Healer again. Somehow, miraculously, Healer had accepted that she was about to die. She didn't even hate Liz for it. Liz didn't think to doubt Healer's sincerity. Healer was a genuine person. She always had been.

"Don't be sad," Healer said. She stretched her arms out to her sides. "Enjoy the wind on your face. Don't you love flying?"

"You're insane," Rob moaned from behind Healer. His eyes were still squeezed shut.

Healer laughed. "Perhaps. But if being crazy means that I find joy in little things like riding Frederick, I'll take it."

Rob groaned. "Are we there yet?"

Liz couldn't help the smile that spread across her face. "For such a daring man, you're sure being a wimp."

"I prefer wheels," Rob said. "Wheels stay on the ground. You can *control* wheels. Who knows what this pegasus will do?"

"Have some faith in Frederick," Healer admonished. "He's a good boy. Aren't you, Frederick?"

The pegasus neighed and bucked in glee. Liz thought Rob was going to faint.

"Make it *stop*," he groaned.

Liz and Healer laughed.

"How do we even know where we're going?" Rob complained after a minute. "Curtis isn't familiar enough with this world to be leading us to this... Viagra Falls place."

"*Niagara* Falls," Liz corrected with a smirk.

"Pegasi are smart," Healer said. "Shakespeare told them where they need to go."

"And you trust that they'll get us there?" Rob asked.

"They will," Healer affirmed. "Won't they, Liz?"

"If we have any trouble reaching the falls it will be because of dragons, not the pegasi."

They rode in silence for a while. It was a little chilly riding through the night, but it was beautiful. They seemed so close to the waning moon that Liz thought she might be able to touch it. She followed Healer through some clouds a few times, laughing at Rob's complaints. They always came out of the clouds a little wet and very cold, but Liz took comfort in Healer's laughter and her company. She didn't sense any anxiety or fear from Healer, and that helped Liz relax.

Curtis was rigid in his seat, constantly on the lookout for some sign of attack. Liz wished he would lighten up and come be with her, but she recognized the importance of his diligence. They would almost certainly be attacked, and it would be best if they had some warning before the dragons ambushed them.

They were about halfway through their journey when Curtis suddenly veered to the left and dove. Liz tensed as Sinsus and Frederick followed Penelope's descent. She wondered how Rob was handling the dive.

Curtis swerved farther left and urged Penelope upward. She shot up and out, gathering speed. The other pegasi kept up with her easily. Liz was grateful that the dragons would have more trouble matching their speed.

"What's going on?" Liz asked once Sinsus and Frederick were abreast with Penelope.

"Dragons, to the right," Curtis said. "I'm trying to throw them off. They definitely saw us dive and I'm hoping they followed. Now I'm trying to get the higher ground. I don't think they saw us go *up*... we were too far away by then and the clouds gave us great cover. The pegasi are fast enough that the dragons wouldn't have noticed our ascent."

"How many dragons?" Rob asked. His eyes were finally open. He still looked ill, but his face was determined. He might have been scared of flying, but Liz knew he would fight bravely regardless.

"I saw two," Curtis said. "There might be more. I can't be sure."

"We can handle two," Healer said.

"Liz and I will attack," Curtis said. "Healer, Rob, I want you to hang back and wait. If either of us needs help you can come and join the fray, but for the most part I want you out of the action."

"I can at least provide Liz with a shield," Healer said.

"You need to shield yourself," Liz replied.

"I can do both." Healer shrugged.

"Keep your bow ready," Curtis commanded.

"Always," Healer affirmed.

"I'll have my sais ready, too," Rob said.

"They won't do much good," Curtis pointed out.

"I had one of the other characters enchant them," Rob said proudly. "I can use them like boomerangs now. They'll go do my bidding and then come back. I had—"

Whatever he had been about to say was cut off by a frustrated roar from beneath them.

"I think they've realized that we're not where they thought we were," Curtis said. "Healer?"

Healer nodded and notched an arrow to the string of her bow, taking careful aim.

"Let's go," Curtis said. He dove down.

Sinsus and Frederick followed, and as soon as the dragons were in range Healer let her arrow fly. It wasn't enough to hurt the dragons below them, but it caught one's attention. The dragon looked up and snarled. The three pegasi ascended again, Frederick taking the lead.

"Looks like we've got a Rokur and a Crystime," Curtis yelled. "Which one do you want?"

Liz looked back at the dragons. Fighting either one would prove difficult. The Crystime was a vicious attacker. It was the fastest of all the dragon species. It shot out lightning instead of fire. Getting hit by its breath weapon was far more likely to kill her than if the Rokur breathed fire on her. Liz already had experience killing Rokurs. If all else failed she could use the same tactics she had the last time.

"Are you all right taking the Crystime?" Liz shouted.

Curtis nodded. "I'd prefer it, actually. I don't like fighting Rokurs; they take too much patience. And I already know you can take one down by yourself."

"Just be careful," Liz called.

Curtis rolled his eyes. "Have faith in my awesomeness, Liz."

He jerked Penelope around and shot down toward the dark purple Crystime, his sword raised. Liz drew her own sword and swerved back to face the Rokur. The beast roared and belched fire. Sinsus flew to the side and narrowly avoided the flames. The Rokur had drawn much closer to them while they had dodged the fire, and Sinsus had to retreat quickly to avoid its clamping jaws.

"This one's faster than the other one, Sinsus," Liz said. "You're going to have to be quick."

Sinsus snorted and shot upward. The Rokur quickly followed suit, but it was a little slower than the pegasus. Liz flung her sword out and wrapped it in magic, planning to pierce the Rokur's eye and brain just as she had with the last one. She guided the sword with her magic, but the Rokur swerved and the sword missed its mark. Apparently this particular Rokur was smarter than its brother had been, too.

Liz cursed and used her magic to call her sword back to her. As it came, the Rokur blew fire and Sinsus once again had to back away. Liz reached out and grasped her sword as it emerged from the flames. She grunted in pain as the metal scorched her hand. Reflexively, she let go of the weapon. It started to fall.

Liz called out for her magic and had it surround the sword again and bring it back to her. She used her Elemental Magic to have water cool the hilt of the sword before she grabbed hold of the warm metal. She released her magic and urged Sinsus upward. The dragon tilted vertically and its right wing crashed into them. Liz lost her hold on Sinsus and fell.

"Sinsus!" she yelled in panic. "Sinsus!"

She struck the top of the dragon's head, smashing into the scales beneath her. She clamoured for a grip as she slid down the dragon's neck. The scales were too smooth to find a hold, but she managed to wrap her legs and arms around the Rokur's thick throat. She squeezed her limbs together so she could hold on as the beast roared and dove down. It had her and it knew it.

Liz couldn't think of what to do. She was panicking. She had failed. She was too afraid to let go of the Rokur and free-fall. Her fear conquered her.

The dragon roared and soared upward again. Liz looked up and noticed that Healer and Rob were advancing on the Rokur in an attempt to save her. They hadn't noticed that there was a third dragon behind them.

"Healer!" Liz shouted. "Look out—"

But Liz lost her balance on the Rokur's neck as the beast continued to climb. She tumbled along the monster's back and frantically twisted her sword around, trying to pierce something, *anything*, with it.

But of course, the Rokur was invincible to swords. What were the chances that she would find that one vulnerable spot while she tumbled to her death?

The tip of the sword scraped the surface of the Rokur's gem-scales. There wasn't anywhere the sharp edge could break through.

Liz was about to fall off of the dragon's back when her sword found a hold. Finally. The dragon's fatal point.

It was on the far left side, just above the back leg. A tiny, nearly invisible little niche about five inches wide. Liz's sword sank in, and the dragon roared in pain as Liz dangled off the side of the Rokur.

The dragon was dead.

Which meant it was falling.

Liz had to let go. She *had* to be brave enough to fall from the dragon. Sinsus would catch her, right? He had to.

She closed her eyes and, with a scream, she let go of her sword.

She discovered that she did not like falling nearly as much as she liked flying. For several seconds, she was sure she was going to die. This was it. This was the end.

But then she crashed clumsily onto Sinsus's back, and her hands clutched desperately at his mane just as she was about to tumble off of him.

Liz gasped. She resituated herself on the pegasus's back and leaned her head against his neck.

"That was the most terrifying thing I've ever done. Never again. Never. Again."

A scream from above made Liz look up. She grimaced. The third dragon had caught Healer and Rob by surprise.

"Come on, Sinsus," Liz said. "We need to go help them."

Sinsus flew up and Liz remembered that she didn't have a weapon. She looked below her at the Rokur that still tumbled to the ground. It was far away now, but she hoped her magic could still reach it and the sword that was buried in its flesh.

She cast her magic downward and told it to bring her sword to her. A wave of dizziness briefly confused her vision, but she returned her attention to the battles taking place above her. Curtis was absorbed in his fight with the Crystime. There was no way he could help Healer and Rob. If he turned his back on the dragon he was facing, he would die instantly. It was all up to Liz.

She and Sinsus had nearly reached Healer and Rob when Liz's sword finally whizzed up beside her. It was dripping with dragon blood, but Liz swallowed the bile in her throat and grabbed it.

Rob lost his balance on Frederick and started to fall. The dragon that was chasing them—a Grinliss, by the looks of it—hurtled toward him, determined to get Rob back in range of its breath.

Liz intercepted the dragon and sliced at its snout, then led Sinsus backwards. The dragon changed direction and snarled, licking the blood off of its muzzle.

"Healer, get Rob!" Liz yelled. Frederick and Healer dove after Rob while Liz turned her attention back to the Grinliss.

It was one of the largest dragons in existence with green, spiky scales and malevolent red eyes. It didn't breathe out a weapon; instead, when it inhaled, objects were pulled toward its gaping jaws.

It opened its mouth, and Liz pulled Sinsus to the side to escape the full force of its power. They were still slowly pulled forward. Sinsus beat his wings frantically, trying to stay back, but for the most part his efforts were next to useless.

The Grinliss stopped inhaling and snorted out in frustration. Liz took advantage of the reprieve and urged Sinsus up. He responded readily, eager to retreat from the dragon's powerful breath.

But the Grinliss was fast, and snapped its neck upward and breathed in again. Sinsus couldn't avoid being drawn in. Even the pegasus's powerful wings weren't enough to escape the draw of the dragon's breath. Liz and Sinsus were sucked into the dragon's moist, sticky mouth.

Fighting the breath that drew her toward the back of the dragon's throat, Liz thrust her sword upward, praying that her plan would work.

Her sword wedged itself inside the top of the dragon's mouth. The Grinliss choked and cried out in pain. Liz wrenched her sword out of the roof of its mouth and cringed when saliva and blood poured down on top of her.

"Fly, Sinsus!" Liz yelled above the dragon's cries. She spat out the blood that had oozed its way into her mouth. Sinsus wasted no time flying out of the Grinliss's jaws.

"Go up!" Liz shouted. Sinsus complied, and soon they were eye-level with the dragon.

The Grinliss snarled and snapped its teeth together, swinging its head upward to capture them again. Sinsus changed course and ducked under the dragon's head. Liz waited until they reached the thinnest point of the dragon's neck, and then, despite her promise to herself to never fall again, she jumped from Sinsus's back, her sword held high.

Her sabre connected with the underside of the dragon's neck. Liz's body weight forced the blade through the dragon's hide and muscle and veins.

The Grinliss wasn't decapitated—Liz's sword wasn't long enough for that—but it was grievously injured. The sword had gone about a quarter of the way through its neck, and blood spurted out from the dragon's veins and onto Liz as she fell.

Sinsus saved her again, neighing his complaints at what Liz assumed he considered stupid behaviour. Who jumped off of a pegasus in midflight?

"I'm sorry," Liz yelled. "But it worked, didn't it?"

It had indeed. The Grinliss was falling. It was losing too much blood to stay in the air. Liz and Sinsus panted in exhaustion as they watched the Grinliss plummet to the ground.

Once it was out of sight, Liz looked around. The battle had taken them away from the others somehow.

"Curtis?" Liz called. "Healer? Rob?" She turned Sinsus around. "Where are you? Are you all right?"

The night was silent.

Liz breathed heavily, straining her ears for some sign that the others had survived the attack.

And finally she heard him.

"Liz!" Curtis's voice was far away, but it sounded strong and alive.

"Curtis!" Liz yelled.

"Stay where you are!" he called. "Penelope will find you!"

Liz leaned forward against Sinsus and patted his neck. "We made it, boy. Well done. Well done."

She breathed deeply against him, exhausted from her battle. Only leftover adrenaline kept her upright.

"What happened to you?" Curtis yelled. His voice sounded frantic. Liz looked up. She could see him now. He and Penelope looked unscathed. Healer and Rob were behind him, safely astride Frederick.

All of them looked terrified.

"What's wrong?" Liz asked. She turned around, suddenly wary.

But nothing was behind her.

"What's going on?" Liz asked, looking back at them.

"You're covered in blood!" Curtis said as he and Penelope reached her. He looked worried. "Where are you hurt? We can heal you."

Liz had forgotten she was covered in dragon blood. "It's not mine," she explained. "It's the Grinliss's."

Curtis's face relaxed. "You're sure you're not hurt?"

"I'm tired, but I'm fine," Liz reassured him.

Curtis nodded. "Good." He looked back at Healer and Rob. Both appeared shaken. "Can you continue?"

"I think it's best if we go forward," Rob said.

"I agree," Healer said. "We can't just wait for more dragons to find us. We should get to the pool. Quickly."

"Then let's go," Curtis said.

They flew off in the night, anxiously watching and waiting.

CHAPTER TWENTY-FOUR

Niagara Falls was beautiful, even at night. The falls were turquoise and lavender, lit up by multi-coloured lights beaming up from the ground. They cast an ethereal glow on the roaring water beneath them. Only a couple of mortals stood on the docks beside the falls. They didn't look up to where Liz and the rest hovered in the air astride their pegasi.

Liz looked down at the mist and water in wonder. She could believe that something magical like the pool could be hidden here.

"Are you all ready?" Curtis asked. Liz looked over at Healer. The sorceress nodded calmly. Rob acquiesced a little more hesitantly. Curtis looked at Liz. She frowned but gave a shaky yes.

"We'll have to jump down into the water," Curtis said.

"I've had enough falling for tonight, thank you," Rob said.

"Seconded," Liz agreed.

"We can't take the pegasi into the water," Curtis pointed out. "And those mortals are more likely to see them if we bring them lower anyway. It's best if we jump."

"Where will the pegasi go?" Liz asked.

"They know to stay out of sight until they see you come out of the water," Healer said. "They're smart enough to take care of themselves."

"And how are we going to survive?" Rob asked. "I don't know about you, but I can't breathe underwater. And I *know* we'll be down there long enough that that's going to matter."

"Healer and I will maintain a shield around us that will keep the air in and let us breathe," Curtis said. "Liz can use her Elemental Magic to keep a fresh supply of air inside of the shield with us."

"The shield will also protect us from the force of the falling water," Healer explained.

"Tell me why we aren't just flying through the falls," Rob said. "Why do we have to go under the water at all?"

"There's a cliff behind the water, for one thing," Liz answered. "And the pool can only be accessed by going beneath the falls… that is, as long as it really is set up the way it is in my books. It's probably best to proceed assuming everything came through to this world the way I wrote it. Besides, Niagara Falls has some tunnels behind it for tourists. It doesn't make sense that nature would interrupt what's already there just to put in the pool. If that had happened, any mortal could get to it and that would cause trouble. I bet it'll be well hidden. We have to go under the water."

Rob sighed. "I don't want to jump first."

"I'll go first," Curtis said. "Then you, then Healer, and then Liz. Once we're all in the water, follow Liz's lead. She's probably our best bet at finding the pool's entrance." Curtis looked at each of them, staring at Healer for a long time. "Are you sure about this, Healer?" he finally asked. "You don't have to go through with this. It's your choice."

Healer just smiled. "I will go."

Curtis's chin quivered, but he nodded. "Then let us proceed."

He jumped off of Penelope, and the pegasus took off into the night. Rob jumped next, looking thoroughly unhappy. Healer hugged Frederick's neck.

"I shall miss you, my friend," she said. "Treat Rob well. Please remember me. I love you." And then she also jumped.

Liz blinked back tears as Frederick followed Penelope away. She patted Sinsus. "See you soon," she said, and then she let herself fall toward the dark water below.

The night was cool against her skin as she fell, and she worried that the water would be cold. The mist she was falling through certainly was.

She splashed into the water and immediately held her breath as claustrophobia attacked her.

"You don't have to hold your breath," Curtis said. Liz started, surprised to hear his voice. Then she realized that while she was wet and surrounded by rushing blue water, she was not currently in contact with it.

"The shield is up," Healer said. "You can breathe."

Liz took a tentative breath and was relieved to find that she wasn't drowning.

"Let's hurry," Curtis prodded. "You need to lead the way."

Liz frowned. "Since I'm not actually touching water, do I need to swim?"

Curtis rolled his eyes. "Yes. You still need to move through the water. Can't you feel the buoyancy of the water holding us up?"

Liz paid more attention to the way she felt. It was like she was wearing a life jacket. She still swayed with the water, even though it didn't touch her or pull her farther down.

"Just remember to keep the air fresh in here," Curtis reminded her. "We can still suffocate."

Liz nodded and felt for her magic. She sent wisps of oxygen out into the shield as she tilted forward and started to swim. It was an odd sensation, since she was technically swimming through air. The others followed along behind her. Liz was sure she was going the right way… she just followed the roar of the falls directly ahead of her. The water was dark and murky. There was a little bit of light coming from above since the falls were lit, but Liz and her friends were deep enough that they still couldn't see more than a few feet in front of them.

No one said anything as they swam forward. Liz figured everyone was anxious; she knew she was. They were only moments away from gaining a lot of power… and losing a very dear friend.

Now that they were so close, Liz once again felt pinpricks of guilt. Her mind raced as she tried to think of something to do. She had no way to write anything to change Healer's fate. She had lost that chance. She mentally kicked herself for not at least trying. She could have snuck out of bed and written *something*.

Maybe it wasn't too late. No matter what Shakespeare said, Curtis was more than competent enough to defeat Kenric by himself. Liz could be sacrificed instead of Healer. She felt a little better once she had resolved to enter the pool herself.

"Liz, stop," Curtis whispered from behind her.

Startled, Liz thought for a moment that he had somehow guessed what she was thinking. She looked behind her and realized that Curtis, Healer, and Rob had stopped swimming and were each peering through the water.

"What's going on?" Liz whispered back.

"Something else is in the water," Rob said.

"I'm sure there are... I don't know, fish or something."

"No," Rob said. "It's something bigger than that."

Then Liz saw it. Something large and dark swam past her on the right side. She turned around quickly but couldn't see what it was.

"Did you see that?" Liz whispered, staring.

"Yes," Healer whispered. "We're not alone."

"Did you have anything guarding the pool?" Curtis asked.

"There are some obstacles once we're out of the water, but here? No. I guess that wasn't very creative of me, but... no, there wasn't anything guarding it. Thousands of pounds of water were the biggest deterrent."

"Then what could possibly be down here?" Rob whispered.

There was more movement to the left. Liz whipped around. "Whatever it is, it's fast," she said.

Something else moved to her right.

"Is there more than one?" Healer asked.

They all strained to see through the dark water, and then Curtis gasped.

"No," he whispered. He sounded scared. He was *never* scared. "There's only one. And it's not fast... it's huge."

Liz looked around and with a jolt of horror realized that Curtis was right. They weren't surrounded by multiple creatures; one enormous body twisted like a cyclone and closed them in. Dark grey coils at least three feet thick trapped them. Liz could even see the black and white diamond shapes on the dragon's skin.

It was a Washer.

Liz had only created one species of water dragon. Washers were larger than Grinlisses. They didn't have any special breath weapons, so that, along with their unusual fear of fire, made some people underestimate them. But they were still very dangerous. They were strong, they were highly intelligent, and they had the upper hand in their element. In water, they could heal quickly. This strength made them almost impossible to kill. And they were always, *always* hungry.

They were also extremely rare. Kenric had control of the only one alive. Clearly it had followed him into this world and it guarded the pool. How had he known where to put it? How had he known they were coming?

The answers to those questions didn't matter. What mattered was that they were trapped.

"Is it just me or is it getting darker down here?" Healer asked.

"It's not just you," Curtis said.

"The Washer is closing in," Rob said.

"How long will the shield hold up against its coils?" Liz asked.

"With Curtis and I both holding it up, we probably have about three minutes before it collapses," Healer said.

"Is that all?" Rob choked.

"With all the power that thing has… once it starts squeezing its body against the shield, we really don't stand much of a chance. Three minutes is optimistic."

"Then what do we do?" Liz directed her question to Curtis. He was the fighter here.

"I… I don't know," Curtis admitted.

"What?" Liz demanded. "But you're the best dragon warrior in the world!"

"I've never fought a Washer before!" Curtis said. "And I can't breathe down here once the shield is gone. As soon as it goes out I'll be useless."

"We'll all be useless," Rob pointed out. "We'll all be *dead*."

"Calm down," Healer said, "we'll think of something."

"It's getting darker by the second," Rob retorted. "We don't have time to think. We might as well give up now."

A silky laugh wafted through the water. "Don't give up," a low voice hissed. "I sssssssso enjoy a fight."

Everyone froze. Liz was the first to realize what was happening.

"Oh my God," she whispered. "Kenric taught it how to speak."

"Yessssssss," the water dragon said. "What a delightful thing, to undersssssstand my prey'sssss fear and to be able to ressssssspond to it."

Liz swallowed. They couldn't even talk to each other to make a plan. The Washer was too advanced. Kenric had messed with its mind so much that it had become more human than beast.

"Don't sssssssssstop talking," the Washer said. "I want to hear your voiccccesssss before I sssssilencccccce them."

"Where are you?" Curtis called out.

The Washer chuckled. "I'm all around you, dragon warrior. Have your eyessss grown sssssso weak that you cannot sssssssee my body ccccccccircling you and your friendsssss?"

"But I want to see your face," Curtis demanded. "Let me see who I'm dealing with."

The little bit of light that was coming from above them suddenly dimmed. Liz looked up. An enormous reptilian face looked down on them from above. It was black and hard to see in the dark water, but its pearly white eyes glistened with their own evil light.

"You're ssssssso sssssssmall," the dragon sighed. "It'ssssss a pity I never get bigger vissssitorssss."

Liz reached out to her Spirit Magic and jabbed it into Curtis's mind. *I'm reading your mind whether you like it or not,* she sent to him. He jumped slightly, but thankfully didn't give any other indication that he had a secret way to communicate with Liz. *Do you have any ideas at all?*

Not really, Liz read from Curtis's mind. *My sword only does so much good here. The Washer can heal itself as soon as I cut it.*

Is there any way you can decapitate it or something? Liz asked. *Kill him in one clean cut? He can't recover from that.*

"What, no more wordssssssssssss for me?" the Washer asked. "It'ssssssss too bad. They were what wasssssssssss keeping you alive for sssssssssso long."

The dragon squeezed at the shield.

Both Curtis and Healer bent over in pain.

"What's wrong?" Rob asked.

"It takes a lot of strength to hold up the shield," Healer gasped. "It's hurting us to do it."

Liz flung her magic at Rob and Healer's minds to include them in the mental conversation.

Healer, how long could you hold the shield on your own?

Maybe a minute, Healer thought. *No longer. He's stronger than I thought.*

I won't let you do it alone, Curtis thought.

I hate Spirit Magic, Rob mused. *It's so strange to have someone inside my head.*

Shhh, Liz admonished. *Healer, hold up the shield. Rob, you're going to help me be a distraction.*

How? Rob asked.

Attack the Washer's body, Liz instructed. *Give him small cuts that he'll have to heal. That'll take some of his focus.*

Rob nodded.

Curtis, help hold up the shield until both Rob and I have sufficiently distracted the Washer. Then leave the shield to Healer and get to the dragon's head. Sever it. Kill him.

I'll do my best.

The dragon roared from above them, scaring Liz so badly that she lost hold of her magic.

"Of courssssssssssse," the dragon said venomously. "You are hiding your wordsssss with Sssssspirit Magic. Kenric ssssssaid I should be wary of it. He knew you would be a Sssssssssspirit ussssser, Creator."

Liz swallowed. "You're very wise," she said. "I am a Spirit user."

"Do not try to flatter me," the Washer spat. "I am above human trickery."

I sure hope not, Liz thought.

"Why do you want to kill us?" Liz asked. "I am your Creator. Maybe I could help you. Get you away from Kenric."

"I think not," the dragon laughed. "Kenric isssss much ssssssstronger than you. You will never defeat him. And I, I choosssssssse to be on the winning ssssssside."

It squeezed against the shield harder, and Rob gave Liz a significant look. Liz nodded.

Rob bounded outward and slashed a sword at one of the coils surrounding them. The dragon snarled, but it bled only for a moment before it healed over.

"Do you really think fighting is wisssssssse?" the Washer laughed. "I am sssssssstronger than any other beasssssst. I will kill you and eat you up. You cannot defeat me."

But Rob attacked again, this time cutting deeper. The water dragon growled and unconsciously loosened its hold ever so slightly.

"Thissssss will do you no good," it said as its wound sealed itself shut. "You are wasssssting energy. You are more foolish than I wasssss led to believe."

"Question," Liz interrupted. "Did Kenric say that I *only* have Spirit Magic?"

"What elsssssssse could you have?" the dragon asked, hissing as Rob cut him again. "You are ssssssso like Kenric. And you can only have one type of magic. Sssssso of coursssssse you are a Sssssspirit ussssssser."

Rob stabbed him deeply and the Washer cried out and twisted to get a better look at Rob.

"Ssssssssstop pessssstering me, little human. You will beg for merccccccy in the end."

"I hate to interrupt what I'm sure was going to be an excellent threat," Liz said. "But Kenric isn't as smart as you think he is." Liz held up a hand and produced a ball of fire. She was hesitant to use it because she hadn't practised fire with Curtis; they had thought she wouldn't need it. But it seemed the best way to distract the creature surrounding them.

"An Elementalisssssssst?" The dragon sounded stunned. "But how? You cannot…"

Liz flung the ball of fire at the Washer's head.

It backed away quickly in fear, temporarily loosening its coils.

Liz nodded at Curtis, and he dove out of the shield and into the water, using the small space between the coils to escape. Healer collapsed, undoubtedly suffering greatly from bearing the weight of the shield on her own.

One minute, if they were lucky. They could only survive for one minute.

Liz gasped as fire took heat, air, and strength from her, but she didn't focus on the pain. She called upon water and manipulated the liquid around her, punching the Washer with the element that it considered its greatest ally.

She called up the rocks and sand that were far beneath her and sent them sailing up to block the gills of the water dragon. With some luck it would suffocate the Washer for a moment. It was a shame that that wasn't enough to kill it.

"You think a mere Elementalissssssst can kill me?" the monster snarled. "Your shield is weak enough already. You are a fool."

The Washer plunged its head downward and the shield broke.

Liz gulped a breath as water poured in around her. The Washer snapped at her, but Liz swam to the side, narrowly avoiding its jaws.

"Come to me, little sssssssorcccceressssss," it hissed. "You cannot esssssscape me for long. Jussssssst give up."

It snapped again and managed to graze Liz's leg. She let out a cry, foolishly wasting some of her air. Rob still attacked the dragon, but it didn't care about him. It was too focused on Liz.

Where was Curtis? Liz couldn't see him. She just prayed that that meant the Washer wouldn't spot him, either.

The dragon flicked out its tongue and tasted Liz's blood in the water.

"Your blood appealsssssss to me, Creator," it said. "I think I will enjoy devouring you."

Liz kicked away from the Washer, but it reached out one of its arms and managed to catch her in its grasp.

"It wasssssssss ssssssssso niccccccce to sssssee who created me," the Washer whispered. "But I wonder, do you regret making me now?"

Liz could barely think. She needed air. She desperately, desperately needed to breathe.

The water dragon squeezed its hand and Liz tried to gasp as her ribs cracked.

But of course, there was no air.

She inhaled water and choked. Her lungs felt heavy and they burned. Everything was getting darker and darker...

Then the Washer suddenly let Liz go. She felt herself fall backward in the water. She tried to fight her way up, but the water dragon was sinking and its weight was bringing her down with it. Why was it sinking? Liz could barely see.

Then she saw a glint above her, and she quickly moved out of the way as the Washer's head sank down, detached from its body.

She dimly saw Curtis swimming down to her. He caught her around the waist and Liz was instantly surrounded by air again.

She cried out and sagged against Curtis. He pounded her back as she coughed water out of her lungs.

"Stop," Liz gasped, clutching her side. "Stop."

"Liz?" Curtis asked, frantically.

"My ribs..."

Curtis released her waist and stopped pounding her back, then gently placed his hands on her ribs.

"You have two cracked ribs," he said, feeling out with his magic. "I can heal them."

"Wait," Liz said. Her voice was raspy and hoarse. "Where are Healer and Rob?"

"They're coming." Curtis pointed and Liz squinted through the water. Healer had her own shield around her and Rob, and had almost reached Curtis and Liz.

"Now let me heal you," Curtis insisted. Liz felt warmth seep through her, and she gritted her teeth as her ribs snapped back into place and the cuts on her leg healed.

Curtis and Healer joined their shields and they all floated together in shocked silence, panting and shivering.

"Good plan," Rob told Liz after a moment.

"Quick thinking," Healer commended.

Liz shook her head. "How did Kenric even get the Washer out here?"

"I don't know," Curtis said. "But that explains why he only sent three dragons after us when we left the Castle."

"He knew the pool was protected," Liz said.

Curtis nodded. "I don't think he realized you were so smart."

"I couldn't have done it without all of you," Liz said.

"We should keep moving," Curtis finally stated. "It's tiring to keep the shield up even without the Washer's coils squeezing it."

Liz nodded and led the way again. They reached the falls without incident, but as soon as they did they were forced down by the weight of the water.

"How do we get past the falls?" Healer asked. "I don't mean to complain, but I'm tired enough that I can barely hold the shield up in normal water. Under thousands of tons beating down... I'm not sure we can make it. The Washer weakened me."

They were all silent for a moment, considering her words. Liz had no ideas. They would have been fine if not for the water dragon, but now...

"Can you lift the water's weight?" Curtis asked. "Or make it pause just long enough that we can slip through?"

It took Liz a moment to realize he was talking to her. "You mean with my Elemental Magic?"

"That's exactly what I mean," Curtis said. "I think it's our best shot."

"That's a lot of Elemental Magic," Healer pointed out. "Using that much water will undoubtedly cost you blood, not just body water. And you'll be extremely dehydrated afterwards."

Liz didn't like the idea of bleeding out a payment. The sight of her own blood didn't bother her as much as it had before she confronted Stan in the Imagination Room, but her blood still made her nauseous. However, she could think of no other solution. Except...

"Why not use Spirit Magic?" Liz asked. "Can't I use it to move the water without taking the effects of water?"

"Water will ultimately be less harmful," Healer said. "No one else can help you take the effects of Spirit when you use it on the water, and taking that much on by yourself will be more taxing than using your Elemental Magic."

"But I'll be bleeding out a payment," Liz said. "Are you sure Spirit is worse?"

"From everything I've studied, yes," Healer said. "And I can heal you from the effects of water. I can't heal you from Spirit."

Liz sighed. "All right. Hurry across. I'll follow you afterward."

"Just in case something goes wrong," Rob said, "what does the entrance to the pool look like?"

"What's going to go wrong?" Curtis asked. "Have some faith in her, Rob."

"I do have faith in her," Rob said, "but if she really will have to pay such a high price for using Elemental Magic then she might pass out."

"I expect you will lose consciousness, dear," Healer said. "If not from the exhaustion, from the loss of blood. Don't forget that water takes its price in liquid form, and I doubt you have enough water in your system to satisfy the magic. So why don't you tell us what we're looking for and then *you* go under the water first. That way you won't be trapped on this side when it gets to be too much."

Liz nodded, hoping she didn't look as scared as she felt. She didn't like the idea of magic rendering her unconscious.

"If everything is the way it was in my books, then there will be decoy entrances. There will be several tunnels of light. You want the one that is gold."

"Gold light." Healer nodded. "Anything else?"

"Just be careful," Liz said. "And don't go into the wrong tunnel. If you do, we will all die."

Liz looked up at the thousands of pounds of water tumbling down in front of them. "Try to hurry," she said. "I think this is going to hurt."

She grabbed hold of her water magic and told it what she needed. It heeded her but immediately started to take its price. The water above them halted, and Liz slowly swam forward. She was so thirsty. *So* thirsty. She felt incredibly heavy. How was she supposed to swim? Could she even move? She felt so claustrophobic. She could feel the weight of the water. The magic didn't want to hold it up. The longer she held it, the heavier it became. More and more water piled up, held back only by Liz's will.

She hadn't realized she had stopped swimming until Curtis pushed her forward. She could barely see him. Everything was hazy. What was all of that red stuff floating in the water around her?

Heavy. So heavy.

She felt like she was shrivelling up.

She just felt... *wrong*.

She didn't want to feel wrong anymore.

Something inside of her broke and the water crashed down again. She didn't have time to check if her friends had made it through the falls. She didn't care. All she knew was that she was thirsty and bleeding and very, very tired.

And then she knew nothing more.

CHAPTER TWENTY-FIVE

"I've done what I can," Healer said from far away, "but I can't replace all the blood she lost. We should have found another way through the falls. She used too much magic."

"What do we do now?" Curtis's voice was closer and clearer.

"Wait for her to regain consciousness," Healer said. "With any luck, it won't be long now."

Liz was vaguely aware that they were talking about her, but she couldn't remember to what they were referring or why she was just gaining consciousness.

"She's twitching," Rob said. "I think she's starting to wake up."

"Liz," Curtis said softly. "Liz, come on. We need to finish what we started."

Liz slowly opened her eyes. She expected to see her room in the Castle or Healer's tent in the courtyard. Instead, she was looking up at glowing golden rocks above her.

"How do you feel?" Healer asked.

Liz shifted her head to the right and saw Healer's worried face.

Healer.

Of course. That was why they were here at the entrance to the secret pool. They had been leading Healer to her death.

Liz sucked in a deep breath and shuddered. "I've been better," she said. Her voice was hoarse. "I'm thirsty."

"Unfortunately, we didn't think to bring the water from Sinsus's saddlebag with us," Curtis said. "It'll have to wait."

Liz nodded and sat up. She closed her eyes as the cavern they were in spun.

"Are you all right?" Curtis asked, steadying her under her elbow.

"Working on it," Liz said.

"Not that I want to get to the pool, exactly," Rob said, "but if we want to get back to the pegasi before sunrise, then we need to get moving."

"I know," Liz said. "I'm sorry. I'm trying."

"Take your time, dear," Healer said. "The most important thing is that you take care of yourself."

"But Rob has a point," Liz said. "We need to go."

She clumsily got to her feet, leaning heavily on Curtis for support. As she rose, she took a more thorough look around. They were in a large cavern. It was musky, damp, and abnormally warm. The cave had three tunnels leading away from it. There was a hole in the ground that led back to the water beneath them.

"Which way do we go?" Curtis asked.

Liz pointed. "The middle tunnel."

She shuffled forward, gaining strength with each step. Curtis was close by her side, and Healer and Rob followed along behind them.

The tunnel they walked through was long and narrow. Liz had to remind herself to keep breathing. She felt almost as claustrophobic here as she had in the water. Thankfully, the tunnel glowed with the same golden hue that the cavern had, so they didn't travel in darkness.

They reached another, smaller cavern. Liz paused. She might be walking on her own now, but her brain was still foggy. She looked at the two tunnels: one to the left, the other directly in front of her. There was so much to remember. Which way did she need to go?

"Why are we stopping?" Rob asked.

"I want to be sure we go the right way," Liz said.

"What happens if we go the wrong way?"

"We'll probably die."

"Great," Rob mumbled.

Liz frowned and peered down the left tunnel. She was almost certain that was the way to go. She remembered writing a lot of twists and turns. She doubted they would keep going forward. But she had to be certain.

"Stay here," Liz said. "I'll be right back."

She made it one step before Curtis grabbed her arm.

"Wait a minute," he said. "You're not going anywhere without me."

"I'm just making sure that's the right tunnel," Liz said. She twisted her arm out of Curtis's grasp. "I'll be fine."

"Just let me come with you."

"Stop being overprotective," Liz said. "Besides, I won't be going far enough that you won't be able to see me. I'm just investigating the tunnel for a minute."

Curtis frowned. "Be careful."

Liz approached the tunnel on her left. She stopped at its entrance and looked inside. It didn't seem sinister, but she was sure the other tunnel wouldn't appear malevolent, either. One of them had to be dangerous.

Hesitantly, she put one foot into the tunnel.

She felt the static before the lightning actually hit her, but she didn't have time to get her foot out of the way. Lightning shot from the back of the tunnel and rammed itself into the sole of her foot. Liz flew backwards and landed on her back with a sickening thud. She couldn't move and could barely breathe. Something was burning.

Curtis ran toward her and crouched down beside her. "I thought I told you to be careful."

Liz would have answered with a biting remark if she had been able to unclamp her jaw. She could still feel the electricity coursing through her.

"That was magical lightning. It's still in there. We have to get the electricity out of her body," Healer said. "Quickly."

"How?" Curtis asked. He sounded frantic.

"Maybe we can give it something else to go into?" Rob asked. "Another body?"

Healer shook her head. "One of us taking it doesn't make any sense. Then we'd just have to get it out of *us*."

Curtis reached out to stroke Liz's hair, but Healer caught his wrist. "Don't touch her," she warned.

Curtis withdrew his hand just as Liz started convulsing. The electricity was growing stronger.

"Do something!" Curtis yelled.

Rob took out a sai and moved toward Liz. Curtis jumped up and rounded on him.

"Don't you dare touch her!" he snarled.

"Calm down, dragon warrior," Rob said softly. "Metal is a conductor. I read it in one of Shakespeare's books. Maybe we can get the electricity to go into the sai."

Rob pushed Curtis aside and knelt down beside Liz. She shook uncontrollably now.

Rob held the sai horizontally above her chest for a moment and then dropped it. He hurriedly backed away from her. The sai clattered onto Liz's stomach and turned a strange blue as electricity surged into it.

"Did it work?" Healer asked.

"Let's find out," Curtis said. He grabbed Liz's left arm and jerked her to the side, allowing the sai to fall to the cavern floor. "Well, I wasn't electrocuted."

"Good thinking." Healer patted Rob on the shoulder and he smiled.

"Liz?" Curtis asked. He repositioned her to be safely enclosed in his arms.

"Ouch," Liz groaned.

"Healer, can you do anything?" Curtis asked.

Healer frowned. "I... I wish I could. But my magic has been depleted from holding up the shield and from healing her earlier. There's nothing I can do."

"Will she die?" Curtis asked. "What do we do?"

"Just because I can't do anything doesn't mean you can't," Healer pointed out.

"But I'm not as skilled at healing as you are," Curtis said.

"You're good enough to get her out of life-threatening danger, though she will still hurt terribly for a while," Healer said. "Go ahead and do what you can. But don't deplete your magic. You'll need a shield on your way back."

Curtis wrapped his hands around Liz's head and Liz felt that familiar healing warmth seep through her. Some of the pain started to go away and it seemed that she could breathe easier. But then, too soon, Curtis took his hands away.

"That's all I can do," Curtis said. His breathing was ragged. "Is it enough, Liz?"

"I feel better," Liz said hoarsely. "I think I might even be able to stand."

She disentangled herself from Curtis's arms and started to rise. She didn't make it very far before Curtis had to catch her. She felt like she had been in this situation a lot lately.

"I don't think you're going anywhere on your own, at least for a while," Curtis said.

Liz pointed to the tunnel that hadn't tried to kill her. "This way."

Curtis chuckled. "I certainly hope so."

They made their way down the tunnel, Liz leaning heavily on Curtis. They reached another cavern and, thankfully, Liz knew which way to go.

"That tunnel," she said, pointing to the one on her right.

"Are you sure?" Rob asked.

"Yes," Liz responded. "We went straight in the last one. This one is right. The next one is left. I just couldn't remember which one came first, but now I know where to go."

They ran into no further problems as they maneuvered through the tunnels and caverns leading to the pool. Still, everyone was tense. For Liz, it was because she was about to die. True, Curtis had taken her out of life-threatening danger from the lightening, but she was going to sacrifice herself in Healer's place. She found herself clinging to Curtis a little tighter than necessary.

"Do you see the golden glow up there?" Liz asked, nodding toward the end of the tunnel.

"It's hard to miss," Rob said.

"That's our destination," Liz said. "The secret pool is right in front of us. Once we reach it we'll be greeted by a spirit… assuming everything is the same as it was in the book, that is. Don't be afraid of her. She's not an enemy."

"So she's friendly?" Healer asked.

"I wouldn't say that, either," Liz said. "I created her to be the embodiment of magic and so, like magic, she is neither good nor evil. She just *is.*"

They emerged through the end of the tunnel and entered an enormous cavern. Dripping stalactites hung down from the ceiling. They looked sharp and dangerous. The cavern below the hanging rocks was covered in some sort of gold liquid, but there were narrow strips of land that spider-webbed through the pool to make it accessible. The golden water pulsated like it was a breathing, living thing.

Liz, Curtis, Healer, and Rob walked forward along a narrow strip of rock. They had to move in single-file. Liz stumbled frequently, despite Curtis's steadying hand. She fought against her fear. She couldn't go into the pool yet. It wouldn't do any good until the spirit asked for their sacrifice.

They reached a large oval of rough land in the middle of the cavern. Liz held up a hand for them to wait and they did, looking around warily.

Something rose from the water directly ahead of them. Like the water, it was gold and it shimmered and danced, making it hard to see clearly. But from what Liz could catch, she could tell that it was exactly as she had imagined: a spirit of a young, golden girl with long, flowing hair.

"This is the secret pool of Shethara," the spirit said. Her voice was more whisper than anything else, yet it could be heard around the cavern with ease. "It is magic embodied. It can grant you power, but you must offer a sacrifice of equal value to your desire." The spirit looked at each of them, her ghostly eyes seeing through them and into their souls. "Before you are permitted to proceed, you must present your sacrifice to the water."

Healer stepped forward. "Do I just jump in?"

Liz slowly let go of Curtis, making sure she didn't make any sudden moves so that he wouldn't notice what she was doing. She edged toward the water.

"The magic requires a live sacrifice," the spirit replied. "The sacrifice will walk into the water and they must do it willingly."

"I am willing," Healer said. She took a deep breath, and everyone was so focused on her that they didn't notice that Liz was almost to the water.

"So is the Creator," the spirit said, ruining everything as she pointed to Liz.

Curtis turned around and ran toward Liz. "No!" he cried. Liz kept walking forward. She would have run but she was still too weak. "Liz, stop! Stop!"

She was almost to the water. She was so, so close…

Rob slammed into her from the side and knocked her to the ground. Rob and Curtis dragged her away from the water. Liz struggled against Curtis, but she was still so weak that it didn't do any good. He had her arms pinned.

Healer walked up to them and put her hands on Liz's shoulders.

"This is not your sacrifice to make, Creator," Healer said softly.

"Just let me do it," Liz cried. She struggled against Curtis.

"No, Liz," Healer said. She leaned forward and kissed her on the forehead. That simple act of kindness took all of Liz's strength. She sagged down and wept, held up only by Curtis's arms.

"I'm so sorry," she cried. Healer stroked Liz's hair.

"All stories end," Healer said. "You wrote the end of my story beautifully."

"But you should have the chance to write your own ending."

"Do any of us really have that chance?" Healer asked. "We depart this life when our time is past, and that time is not up to us to decide. Still, I have chosen this. For Rob, for Curtis… and for you. I am ready."

"But it isn't fair."

Healer paused and Liz looked up into her face. Healer seemed to be struggling not to cry.

"No, it is not fair," Healer admitted. "But it is necessary."

Healer took a step back and walked toward the water.

"No, Healer!" Liz shouted. "Don't! Let me do it!"

"Keep holding her, Curtis," Healer said softly as she continued forward.

"I've got her," Curtis said. His voice was thick. "Goodbye, Healer."

"Goodbye, Curtis," Healer said. She turned her kind eyes to Rob. "Rob." Rob was crying, but he ran forward and embraced Healer. He whispered something to her that Liz couldn't hear and then stepped away.

Healer finally turned back to Liz as she reached the water's edge. "Goodbye, Creator. Thank you for everything. And remember, I have faith in you."

With a tear rolling down her cheek, she stepped into the water.

"No! No! HEALER!" Liz shouted. But Healer kept walking into the magical water until she was submerged.

Desperate to keep in contact with Healer or at least to let her know that she wasn't alone, Liz gathered her Spirit Magic and flung it out, trying to reach Healer's mind.

But where there should have been life, there was nothing. Absolutely nothing. The magic had taken her quickly, greedily.

Liz and Curtis sank to the ground, the grief too much for them both. Liz drowned in the darkness that enveloped her as the truth sank in.

She hadn't been able to save her.

Healer was gone.

CHAPTER TWENTY-SIX

"The sacrifice has been accepted," the spirit said emotionlessly after only a moment of letting them grieve. "Each of you may now request power from the pool."

This statement startled Liz enough to elicit a response. "Each of us?"

The spirit nodded. "The sacrifice had great power and can allow for three wishes."

"But I thought each person had to sacrifice something," Liz said.

"You each did," the spirit replied. She pointed at Liz. "A mother." The finger moved to Curtis. "A friend." Her gaze finally rested on Rob. "And a lover."

Shocked, Liz and Curtis turned to Rob.

"You and Healer...?" Curtis hedged.

Rob nodded, tears flowing freely down his face.

"Did you know?" Curtis asked Liz.

Liz shook her head. "I had suspicions, but... I didn't write that."

"You must hurry," the spirit said. "The power of the sacrifice will only last a few moments."

"What do we need to do?" Curtis asked.

"Tell me your desires," the spirit said, "and then dip your swords into the pool. Your wish will be granted as long as it is within the realm of possibility."

Curtis leaned toward Liz's ear. "Can I let you go?" he asked. "Do you promise you won't go into the pool?"

"It's too late now," Liz answered. "There would be no point."

"Promise me."

"I won't sacrifice myself."

Curtis nodded and let Liz go, then helped her to her feet. Liz still hurt both physically and emotionally, but she knew she had to go through with this. She didn't want Healer's sacrifice to be in vain.

She drew her sword and stepped toward the spirit. "I desire the power to defeat my enemies, regardless of who they are or what powers they might possess."

"Your request is acceptable," the spirit said. "But be warned: while the pool will grant you power, you must be wise enough to wield it. It will not do everything for you."

"I understand," Liz said.

"Then proceed."

Liz stepped up to the water's edge and dipped her sword into the golden liquid. She felt power buzz up through her sword and into her arm, and then seep into the rest of her body. She felt herself knit back together, at least physically. It was like she had never used water magic and hadn't been electrocuted. The power that seeped into her healed everything. She lifted her sword and stepped back, gasping. Her sword had turned from silver to gold, and she noticed that her body glowed with power.

"Dragon warrior, what do you desire?" the spirit asked.

Curtis drew his sword and stepped forward. "I desire the power to successfully protect others at all times… especially Liz. I want to be able to know when and how to help, and I want the abilities required to save others."

The spirit stared. "You have made more than one request. It is unacceptable. You may only wish for one power."

Curtis frowned in thought. "Then I… wish to be able to help and protect Liz. Always."

"That request is acceptable. But be warned: this will form a bond between the two of you that will be unbreakable. You must be sure that the Creator will allow it."

Curtis looked at Liz. "Please, Liz. Let me do this for you."

"Are you sure you want to waste your wish on me?" Liz asked.

"I don't think I'm wasting it."

Liz hesitated, but nodded after a moment.

Curtis turned back to the spirit. "She has agreed."

"Then you may proceed," the spirit said.

Curtis came to stand by Liz and dipped his sword into the water. His sword turned gold and his body began to glow… and then Liz felt something happen between them, like something snapped together. She was suddenly fully aware of everything Curtis felt: his grief, his power, his strength, and his longing for her. She stared at him in wonder and met his astonished gaze. He withdrew his sword from the water and stepped back.

"And what do you desire?" the spirit asked Rob. Rob stepped forward, his short sword shaking in his grasp.

"I wish for the power to bring back the dead."

The spirit blinked. "There is no magic that can resurrect the dead," the spirit said. "Your request is unacceptable. You must choose something else."

"That's all I want!" Rob yelled. "I want Healer back!"

"Your request is unacceptable," the spirit repeated, voice flat. "You must choose something else."

Rob swore and stared down at his boots. His knuckles were white around the hilt of his sword, and Liz could tell he was trying not to attack the spirit in his frustration and grief.

"You must hurry," the spirit said. "The power of the sacrifice is fading. If you want your wish to be granted, you must request it of me quickly."

Rob bit down on his lip and looked at Liz. "What do you need me to wish for?"

Liz shook her head. "It isn't my wish. What do you want?"

"I can't have what I want."

"Don't you have anything else you desire?" Curtis asked.

Rob shifted his gaze back to his boots and then seemed to come up with something. He looked back up at the spirit.

"Is it possible for me to have the ability to commune with the dead?"

The spirit nodded. "It is possible. But be warned: this power can become overwhelming. It could drive you into insanity."

"But will I get to speak with Healer again?"

"Yes."

"Then that is my desire."

"Your request, while unwise, is acceptable. You may proceed."

Rob jogged over to the pool and dipped his sword into the water. It turned gold, and Liz noted that Rob started to glow like she and Curtis had… but the glow seemed wrong somehow. It was tainted with… something. The golden hue was dark, and little black tendrils snaked around inside of it.

Rob removed his sword from the water and gasped. "Healer," he said softly.

Liz looked around, but could see nothing. "Rob?" she asked. "Are you…"

But Rob smiled and started talking quietly. Liz couldn't hear him.

"What's happening?" Liz asked.

"He's talking to Healer's spirit," Curtis said in wonder. "Or he's hallucinating."

"It is the sacrifice," the spirit said. "But one can commune with the dead only for so long before they begin to lose themselves and long to join them."

Liz and Curtis exchanged a worried glance.

"You are finished here," the spirit said. "Unless you have another sacrifice to offer, you must leave the pool."

"We're leaving," Liz said.

She started forward, Curtis at her heels.

"You seem better," Curtis noted.

"When I dipped my sword into the pool, I was healed," Liz said. "I'm not sure why."

"I felt better after dipping my sword in the pool as well," Curtis said. "Maybe it was Healer's last gift to us."

Liz gave a sad smile at that and turned back to answer Curtis, but noticed that Rob was not following them.

"Rob," she called out. Rob turned to look at them, a questioning look on his face. "We have to leave. Are you coming?"

Rob looked back to where Healer's spirit presumably was. "You're coming with me, aren't you?" he asked.

Liz strained her ears to hear Healer's voice one last time, but she heard nothing. She assumed that Healer assented because Rob trotted forward, a grin on his face.

They walked through tunnel after tunnel. Liz easily remembered the way and they soon reached the first cavern without any trouble—unless she counted the one-sided conversation from Rob. It made Liz's pain more acute. Rob got to talk to Healer, but Liz would never get that chance again. For Liz and Curtis, Healer was lost. It seemed almost unfair that Rob still had the opportunity to talk to her. He didn't have to grieve like the rest of them.

Curtis put an arm over her shoulder. It strengthened the bond between them and she became even more aware of what he was feeling.

"I agree with you," he said. "It isn't fair."

"I guess I should be happy for him, but it seems… wrong," Liz said. "Maybe I'm just jealous."

Curtis shook his head. "As much as I loved Healer, I concur. Rob is talking to his dead girlfriend. That will wear on him soon, I'm afraid. The spirit from the pool was right: his choice was unwise."

They stopped at the hole in the floor of the first cavern. "I'm afraid to get back in the water," Liz admitted.

"So am I," Curtis said. "Let's just hope the Washer couldn't heal itself from being decapitated."

"It shouldn't have been able to."

Curtis took a deep breath. "I'll go first, I think. Send Rob after me, then follow him."

Liz nodded. Curtis jumped down into the water.

"Rob," Liz said, "come on. Your turn."

He turned to her. Was she imagining things, or did he look pale?

"My turn for what?"

"To jump into the water."

"Oh," he said. "Of course."

He walked forward and sat on the edge of the hole in the ground. "Healer's all right, you know. She seems kind of sad, but she said dying didn't hurt."

Liz swallowed against a lump that had suddenly formed in her throat. "I'm... glad she's okay."

"She says she still doesn't blame you."

"Tell her I miss her," Liz said thickly.

Rob did, then cocked his head and stared ahead of him. "She says not to worry," he said after a moment. "And she loves you."

Liz closed her eyes as a tear fell down her cheek.

"You should hurry into the water," Liz said softly.

She heard a splash and opened her eyes. Rob was gone. Liz took a deep breath to steady herself and then dove into the tunnel of water. It took about a minute for her to find Curtis and Rob. Curtis held a shield together for them and Liz gratefully took a breath.

"How long can you hold the shield without... without Healer?" Liz asked.

Curtis shrugged. "I'm not sure. But we should hurry. We don't want to be caught down here without this shield. I'm not keen on drowning."

They swam forward. There were decoy tunnels above them. Purple, blue, green, orange, yellow, red, and white entrances gleamed at them from above. Liz thought they were beautiful, but she also knew they were deadly. Only the gold tunnel, which eventually led to the pool, was safe to enter. The rest would kill them.

They reached the falls and paused. "I have to do it again, don't I?" Liz asked.

Curtis nodded. "I'm afraid so," he said. "I don't have the power to maintain a shield through this. But with our bond I think I can help. I'm supposed to have the power to help and protect you, right? So I'll work on channelling that. With any luck it'll work and you won't lose as much blood."

"I just hope I don't pass out," Liz said. She turned her attention to the roaring water ahead of her and reached out for her magic. It responded to her eagerly and she sent it surging forward.

The price was immediate, and she started to feel dizzy and heavy and thirsty... but then she felt something else. Curtis. It was like he was holding her and loaning her some of his strength. She looked over at him. He was staring at her with a furrowed brow and serious eyes, concentrating.

Liz swam forward, checking back every once in a while to be sure Curtis and Rob were following her. Rob seemed distracted and distant, but at least he was paying enough attention to the world of the living to respond to what was going on around him.

She was relieved when they passed the falls. She was thoroughly drained and exhausted. The water magic had taken some blood from her again, though not as much. She was thirsty, *very* thirsty. She couldn't wait to get back to Sinsus and the water that was in his saddlebag.

Liz let the magic go and she felt Curtis relax.

"Are you all right?" Liz asked him.

"I'm tired," Curtis said, "but I'm fine. I can't manage the shield for much longer, though. We need to get to the surface."

They swam up, constantly on the lookout for danger. The encounter with the Washer earlier had shaken Liz, and she could feel that Curtis was also wary.

"Stop!" Rob yelled.

"What is it?" Liz jerked to a halt.

"Can't you see it?" Rob asked. He shrank back against the shield.

Curtis and Liz looked around. "See what?" Curtis asked. "What's going on?"

"The Washer," Rob said, and he pointed straight ahead of him.

Liz drew her sword and looked around. "Where is it?" she asked, confused.

"How can you be missing it?" Rob cried. He jabbed his finger forward.

Liz and Curtis swam forward a little, searching for some sign of the dragon. Liz even called up fire and threw some out into the water, surrounded by a small pocket of air, just to light up the murky depths so that she could see better. Nothing.

"He's already starting to go insane," Curtis murmured. "The Washer is dead."

Liz gasped. "He's not going insane. He's seeing the Washer's spirit."

"This could become a problem," Curtis whispered after a moment.

Liz turned back to Rob, sheathing her sword.

"Don't put your weapon away!" he chastised.

"Rob," Liz soothed. "Rob, the Washer is dead. You're seeing its spirit. It can't hurt us anymore."

Rob looked frantically from Liz to Curtis, unsure. He finally seemed to believe them and he straightened.

"Will I see everything that's dead?" he asked. "Is that why the spirit tried to warn me...?"

"I don't know," Liz said. "I bet you'll get to a point where you can control it. But for now, we have to keep moving."

Rob's eyes flickered back to where he saw the Washer. "But..."

"Trust us," Curtis said. "You might not be able to trust your own senses right now, but trust *us*. We need to get out of the water. I'm getting weaker."

Liz took ahold of Rob's hand and guided him as they swam up through the water. It was a relief when they broke the surface.

"I don't think I could have kept it up for much longer," Curtis admitted as he released the shield. "We made it out just in time."

Rob looked up. "Can the pegasi even see us? We're completely covered by mist."

"I can call Sinsus with my Spirit Magic," Liz said. She gathered her magic and sent *We're in the mist! Please come!* to Sinsus's mind. "They should be here soon."

Curtis swam over to Liz and embraced her. "You've done so well," he said into her ear. "I'm so proud of you."

Liz returned his embrace. "I still feel guilty."

"I know," he said. "But you'll heal from that. You did what you could to save her. And as disturbing as Rob's new power is... at least we know that she's all right."

They broke apart as Sinsus snorted above her. Liz looked up. The pegasi were flying right above them, three dark silhouettes in the pre-dawn light.

"How do we get on?" Liz asked.

"You can move things with your mind," Curtis reminded her. "Send us up."

"More magic?" Liz asked, already exhausted.

"Rob and I will take on some of the payment," Curtis reminded her. "Go ahead."

Liz wrapped Spirit Magic around Curtis and directed him upward. Penelope moved over and Curtis climbed on top of her. Liz directed the magic around Rob and lifted him up to Frederick. Frederick snorted in greeting.

Soon Liz was astride Sinsus and she let her magic go with relief. She could do without magic for a while, she thought. It was helpful, but it caused a lot of trouble.

"Let's go," Curtis said. He and Liz started upward, but then Liz noticed that, despite Rob's attempts, Frederick wasn't budging.

"What's wrong?" Liz called.

Rob looked up and shrugged. He looked terrified to be back on the pegasus.

"I don't know," he said. "He won't leave."

Curtis flew down until Penelope and Frederick were eye-level with each other. He reached out and touched Frederick's head.

"I'm sorry, boy," Curtis said slowly, "but she's not coming back. She... she had to do something that took her away from us."

Suddenly, Liz understood. Frederick was waiting for Healer to come back to him.

But she never would.

Frederick snorted and waved his head up and down in defiance.

"Shhh, Frederick," Curtis said soothingly. "I know. It's hard for all of us. But she… she's dead, boy. She's not coming back."

Frederick whinnied and bucked. The pegasus was smart enough to understand what was happening, and Penelope and Sinsus picked up on his grief. They all neighed in protest.

Curtis put his hands against Frederick's neck. "I'm so sorry. You don't know how sorry I am. But we have to go on without her, somehow. She told Rob to take care of you and she expects you to take care of him. Can you do that for her?"

Frederick slowly calmed down and finally snorted in agreement.

"Then we need to go," Curtis said. "Come on."

He took off again and this time Frederick followed. Liz noticed that he kept looking back to the water, looking for some sign of Healer.

But that sign would never come.

CHAPTER TWENTY-SEVEN

Liz was so numb from exhaustion and loss that she almost didn't notice when Curtis started to descend from the clouds. She spurred Sinsus toward him, squinting her eyes against the new day's light.

"What are you doing?" Liz asked. "We're not back to the Castle yet."

"We need to rest," Curtis said. "I'm exhausted. I have to get my strength back up or I'll be useless if we're attacked when we're closer to the Castle. I know you're feeling the same way. I can tell."

Liz said nothing and continued to follow him until they landed in a small grove of trees in what Liz guessed was the Winona State Forest. She looked behind her; despite his constant mutterings to what was presumably Healer's spirit, Rob had managed to follow them as well.

Curtis slid off of Penelope and removed her saddle. The pegasus was sweating but didn't seem too tired or over-worked. Liz hopped off of Sinsus and warily watched the dazed, distracted look on Rob's face as she removed the pegasus's saddle. Rob's behaviour was unhealthy. Everything about him seemed suddenly off. The fact that he couldn't seem to choose what dead being he saw worried her. Everything died. Wouldn't seeing and hearing the dead become overwhelming? How long would Rob be able to handle it?

"Worried about Rob?" Curtis asked from behind her. Liz jumped and turned around.

"You startled me," Liz said in surprise. "I didn't hear you come up."

"Sorry." Curtis grinned. He nodded toward Rob. "What do you think?"

Liz shook her head. "I'm concerned. It seems so unnatural. It's like he's not really part of reality anymore. He's ignoring everything around him."

"I agree," Curtis said. "And this is after only a short time with this new power. It's only been, what, an hour and a half? He can't keep this up indefinitely."

"What do we do?" Liz asked, turning back around to watch Rob. He wasn't by Frederick anymore—apparently his new power hadn't distracted him enough to like the pegasus. But he was still talking animatedly with what looked like air.

"I'm not sure we can do anything. The spirit warned Rob that his choice was unwise and that there would be consequences. But he didn't care. All he cared about was seeing Healer again."

"How did I not know that they were together?" Liz wondered. "I should know everything about all of you, and I barely suspected."

Curtis shrugged. "I didn't know either, and Rob and Healer are my best friends. Rob's a very private person, and Healer is—was—so concerned about everyone else that she hardly ever talked about herself."

"Part of me feels guilty about not wishing to bring Healer back," Liz admitted as she watched Rob throw his head back and laugh at something Healer must have said. "I should have thought to at least ask if I could bring her back. How could I be so selfish?"

"Selfish?" Curtis sounded shocked. "Liz. You tried to throw yourself into the pool before Healer could. I had to hold you down to stop you from sacrificing yourself. I'm still mad at you for that."

Curtis grabbed Liz's shoulders and turned her around to face him.

"What were you *thinking*?"

Liz blinked back tears. "I just, I couldn't help but feel guilty..."

"But don't you see, Liz?" Curtis put an arm around her and drew her close. "It wasn't about you, not really. It was about doing something for the greater good. Healer knew she had to do it. You know she didn't resent you or me or Rob or even Kenric for it. It's healthy and normal to be grieving for her right now, but it isn't okay for you to blame yourself. You did what you could to save her... much more than I wanted you to do. Even if you hadn't tried to kill yourself in her place, it wouldn't be your fault. It just happened. Grief is hard enough to bear on its own. You need to let the guilt part of it go."

Liz wept against his chest as she realized that Curtis was right. Ever since she discovered that they had to go to the pool, she had been feeling guilty. It had consumed her and eaten at her. It was getting in the way of her properly mourning Healer because she was so focused on how *she* was responsible. Curtis was right. She was making this about her, and it wasn't about her at all.

Could she really just let the guilt go? It wasn't that easy. It couldn't be that easy... could it?

Here in Curtis's arms it felt like it might be that simple, but Liz knew from experience that it would take time to truly heal from her grief. Maybe she'd need that extra love and support from him until she felt like she could let it go on her own.

"I love you, Liz," Curtis said. "Please stop blaming yourself. I can't stand for you to be in pain like this."

"It's not about you," Liz teased.

Curtis smiled. "Everything's about me. Don't you know that by now?"

Liz chuckled and reached up to touch his face. "I'm sorry I tried to leave you."

Curtis's face grew serious. "Don't ever do it again. I mean it. I need you. Promise me."

"I promise," Liz said.

Curtis leaned down and kissed her gently. It was very unlike their first kiss. The passion was still there, but it was controlled instead of wild. He meant for the kiss to be comforting, and it was. But it also ignited something inside of Liz, and due to their bond she knew Curtis could feel that fire as well.

She wrapped her arms around his chest and pulled him closer to her, needing him like she had never needed anything or anyone before. She needed to feel something other than the pain and torment that had been following her since that meeting in Shakespeare's office. She needed to feel *him*.

She could feel that need reciprocated through the bond they shared. His excitement, his desire, his passion, his heat... she could feel it all and her own need fed off of his.

Suddenly Curtis broke away from her and held her against his chest, panting heavily.

"We need to stop," he murmured.

"I beg to differ," Liz said. "I think we should—"

"I am very, *very* aware of what you think," Curtis said in a husky voice. "And, God, I want that. But not now."

"Why?" Liz complained.

"Rob is still here," Curtis pointed out.

"He's distracted."

"I don't think he's *that* distracted."

Liz sighed. "You're probably right."

"I'm always right," Curtis said. "And I don't want to do this just because you want to escape your grief. This will only happen when we both are in a good place."

"I was in a pretty good place a second ago," Liz said.

Curtis gave a throaty chuckle. "You know what I mean. Not yet. Not while you just want an escape. And not in the middle of a forest with a friend watching."

"You might want to step back, then," Liz said. "I'm not sure I can control myself."

"You almost died a few times last night. I'm not letting you go for a while," Curtis said. "And lucky for you, I *can* control myself."

"Curse you for your integrity."

"Whatever," Curtis laughed. "You love that I'm honourable."

"Not right now I don't."

"Yes you do," Curtis said. "Admit it."

Liz rolled her eyes. "You're right. I love you."

"I love you too."

They held each other for a while. Liz's heart was still racing, but her breathing was slowing down. The soft chirping of birds and the breeze that ruffled the leaves in the trees helped her collect herself.

"Let's get some rest," Curtis finally muttered. He pulled her down to the grass.

To Liz's deep disappointment, nothing exciting happened, but she did manage to sleep for several hours. The rest was sorely needed. Liz wasn't sure how long it was before Rob's voice woke her up.

"Guys, I hate to interrupt," Rob called.

"What is it, Rob?" Liz asked groggily, pulling away from Curtis.

"We have company." He pointed and Liz looked up to the sky. A small dragon was hovering above them and starting to descend.

"I don't recognize that species," Liz said.

"Neither do I," Curtis said. "But I know how to handle any type of dragon."

He and Liz drew their swords, waiting for the beast to come to them.

So much for getting some rest today, Liz lamented.

They charged.

CHAPTER TWENTY-EIGHT

They stopped short when the dragon landed. The brilliant blue beast made no move to attack. It seemed almost friendly. Liz found this odd at first; there had been no friendly dragons since Kenric's takeover. But then she realized that this must be a dragon from someone else's books, because a familiar form sat astride the beast.

"I have been looking for you since dawn," Shakespeare said as he slid off the dragon and onto the ground. He landed heavily and winced, looking down at his thighs. "I tell you... dragon riding is far more painful than horseback riding."

Liz, Curtis, and Rob sheathed their weapons. Curtis kept glancing at the dragon in front of them. He had been raised to respect dragons, and life experience had taught him to fear them.

A large eagle landed on the right side of the dragon. Tolkien and McCaffrey slid off the beast and landed on the ground, looking around warily.

"How did everything go at the pool?" Shakespeare asked.

"About as we expected," Curtis said. "Except all three of us were able to receive a power, not just Liz."

"Interesting," Shakespeare said. "And... Healer?"

Liz swallowed. "She's gone."

Shakespeare nodded somberly. "I'm so sorry to hear that. I know how hard it must—"

"But she's fine," Rob interrupted. "She really is. She says hello, Shakespeare."

Tolkien and McCaffrey gave each other a confused glance.

Shakespeare furrowed his brow and shot a worried look to Liz and Curtis. "Rob, are you all right?"

"I've never been better in my life," Rob said. "I never have to lose Healer."

"He chose the power to commune with the dead," Liz muttered. "But he can't control what spirits he sees. We know because he saw the spirit of the Washer we killed in the water."

"You had to battle a Washer?" Shakespeare asked.

"Unfortunately," Curtis said.

"Tell me what happened," Shakespeare commanded.

Curtis and Liz told him everything, from the dragon attack in the air to their landing there in the grove of trees. Rob never pitched in. He kept staring off into space, murmuring something every few minutes. Liz assumed he was looking at and talking with Healer, but she couldn't be sure. His complete inability to stay in the present made her worry.

"I can see why the spirit at the pool warned Rob not to choose this power," Shakespeare said, looking over at Rob with concern. "He's not really here, is he?"

"No, he's not," Curtis agreed. "The fact that he could see the Washer as well could be problematic. Who knows what else he'll end up facing?"

"He couldn't tell that the Washer was a spirit and not a tangible being," Shakespeare mused. "That could prove dangerous in the end."

"I'm afraid you're right," Curtis said.

"What if it distracts him while he's fighting?" Tolkien said. "Dragons are not something to be faced lightly."

"Indeed," McCaffrey said. "I know all of our dragons are different, but they're smart creatures. They'll take advantage of Rob's weakness."

"Maybe he'll get used to it by the time we fight Kenric," Liz said. "But… Shakespeare, what are you doing here? You look awful. All of you do. No offense."

It was true. Shakespeare's hair stuck up wildly in every possible direction. He had dark bags under his eyes, and he looked like he might fall over at any moment. His usually impeccable-looking suit was wrinkled and torn at the right elbow, and his tie was gone. Tolkien's white hair was also dishevelled, and it looked like, for once, he had forgotten his pipe. McCaffrey looked utterly exhausted, as well.

"Kenric attacked the Writers' Castle again," Shakespeare said. "And without either of you there..."

"Oh no," Liz breathed. "How bad was it?"

"We were able to drive them out, mostly with Tolkien and McCaffrey's help," Shakespeare said, "but the damage was catastrophic. Twenty-three people died and the Castle is in ruin. It won't take terribly long to repair, considering all the magic and technology at our disposal... but the lives lost cannot be replaced."

"Why did you come to us now?" Curtis asked. "What happened was horrible, but why not wait for us to return? What is it you need?"

"It is... strange that Kenric was able to inflict harm on us while you were not there," Shakespeare said.

"What do you mean?" Liz asked. "He's sent dragons to attack the Castle before."

"Yes," Shakespeare said, "but you were there. He shouldn't have been able to hurt us with you and Curtis gone."

"Why?" Curtis asked.

"The longer characters are in this world, the more a part of it they become," Shakespeare said. "So characters that were brought to life, say, one hundred years ago are fully integrated into the world, or as integrated as they'd like to be. But when a character first comes to life, they don't fit in right away. Nature is still trying to figure out a way to sew them into the fabric of this reality. Part of being not fully a part of this world is that they can only partially interact with others around them. That's why mortals haven't noticed your dragons flying around. They aren't fully part of this world yet... or at least, they weren't."

"They are now?" Liz asked.

"It appears that way," Shakespeare said. "They were able to attack before because it still fit into the scheme of their story, seeing as you and

Curtis and Rob and Healer were all present at the time. But with you gone, their ability to attack suggests that Kenric has somehow managed to force his presence into this world more quickly than any other character I have ever heard of."

"What does that mean, exactly?" Curtis asked.

"That we have to move quickly," Shakespeare said. "You know Kenric. He needs to get you out of the way, of course, but that's not his ultimate goal. He wants control. If we fail to stop him, the mortals will undoubtedly become aware of his existence, probably much sooner than we would like. And then Kenric will enslave them all, assuming he doesn't kill them first."

"So…"

"So you have to attack *now*," Tolkien said impatiently. "You need to get on your pegasi and fly to meet him. It helps that we killed some of his dragons last night. I'm hoping he's a little more vulnerable, and that he won't be expecting a counterattack so soon."

"But I don't know where his lair is," Liz said. "I suppose I could figure it out eventually, but we have the entire world to search."

McCaffrey shook her head. "I know where they are."

"How?" Curtis asked.

"My smaller dragons followed them," McCaffrey said. "They're hiding out in the same mountain range we are."

"They're in the Adirondacks and we never even noticed?" Liz exclaimed. "How did we miss that?"

"It's well hidden, much like it is in your books," McCaffrey explained. "But with the information my dragons gave me, I can get us there."

"You're coming with us?" Liz asked the three authors skeptically.

"I may not look like much of a warrior, but I've learned a thing or two over all these years," Shakespeare said. "I'm nearly as adept as Curtis."

Curtis huffed. "Hardly, old man."

"Well, I'm better than Rob."

"What?" Rob said, startled back into the conversation by the sound of his name.

Shakespeare shot Liz a worried glance but then offered Rob a smile.

"And your dragons are nothing compared to Smaug or Ancalagon," Tolkien said. "Trust me. I can take on your dragons."

"I know enough about dragons from my time as an Immortal Writer to fight alongside you," McCaffrey said. "If you've read my books at all, you know how intimately familiar I am with dragon lore."

Liz nodded hesitantly.

"We're going after Kenric now," Shakespeare said to Rob. "Get back on Frederick."

Rob gave the pegasus an uneasy look but nodded. "I can do that. Healer will help me."

He took off toward Frederick.

"Wait, we're leaving right now?" Liz asked. "Right this second? We're not going to... I don't know, plan or anything?"

"You're as trained as you're going to get," Shakespeare said. "As for a plan, you can think about that on the way. It'll take us a while to reach Kenric's lair. When we land, you can tell us how to get inside and how to beat him."

Shakespeare turned to mount the dragon again, but Curtis grabbed Shakespeare's shoulder to stop him.

"I'm sure this dragon is reliable and trustworthy, but Kenric has a way of getting into dragons' minds," Curtis warned. "I would not recommend riding it to his lair. It could possibly give him one more weapon to use against us."

Shakespeare nodded. "I hadn't thought of that, but you're right. I don't want to take any chances."

He walked to the front of the dragon and looked it in the eyes. "Go back to the Castle and to your rider. Let her know that everything is fine."

The dragon nodded and shot into the air. The wind from its wings sent Liz tumbling back a few steps before she regained her balance.

"All right," Shakespeare said. "Who shall I be accompanying today?"

"Not that I have anything against you riding with me," Curtis said, "but I think Rob could use an extra pair of eyes on this trip."

Shakespeare nodded and walked over to Rob, who was perched unsteadily atop Frederick. Tolkien and McCaffrey mounted the eagle.

"Are you ready?" Curtis asked Liz. Liz looked into his kind blue eyes and was encouraged to find confidence behind the exhaustion.

"Not really," Liz admitted, "but I don't think I'll ever be ready to face Kenric."

"If it makes you feel any better, I know you can do it," Curtis said. "You're strong enough, both physically and magically. You just have to believe in yourself."

"That's the hard part."

"If nothing else, believe in the power the pool gave you," Curtis reminded her. "You asked for the power to defeat your enemies, regardless of their powers. So somewhere within you is the power to defeat Kenric."

"But I have to be smart enough to use it," Liz said, doubtful.

"You are," Curtis said. He wrapped her in his arms and kissed her forehead.

"We need to go!" Shakespeare called from Frederick's back.

Liz sighed and stepped back from Curtis.

"I guess it's time."

Curtis nodded. "It's time."

IT WAS dark when they finally found the lair and descended to the base of the mountain. Liz was grateful that the pegasi were small enough to be silent and nearly invisible in the darkness, and thankfully the eagle was stealthy. They could not afford to be seen. She knew that the only chance they had for victory would be to infiltrate Kenric's lair and take on the dragons in small groups. If they gave away their position now and all of the dragons descended on them at once, they wouldn't stand a chance.

They slid off their mounts and huddled together, well hidden by the trees.

"Wait here," Curtis whispered to their mounts. All three pegasi nodded in silent agreement.

Tolkien glanced at the eagle and whispered to it in Elvish. The eagle nodded and folded its wings.

McCaffrey led the way as Liz, Curtis, Rob, Shakespeare, and Tolkien crept through the woods. They walked for ten minutes through red spruces, balsam firs, and mountain-ash trees. There was hardly any sound. Not even crickets were chirping.

Liz constantly checked behind her to be sure Rob was paying attention. She was worried that he would start talking to Healer at any moment and ruin their cover. Luckily, he seemed to understand that silence was imperative. Liz was sure he could still see Healer, but he had enough of his wits about him to be able to focus on what was going on.

McCaffrey held up a fist. They stopped. Liz held her breath, but after a moment McCaffrey nodded and beckoned them forward. They crowded around her and she pointed ahead. Liz peered around and gave a small gasp.

If she squinted, she could just see an enormous tower carved into the mountain. No, not carved in… it looked like it had always been there. No human could have created it. The front half of the tower protruded out of the mountainside. The rest of it was hidden inside the mountain itself, and extended deeper within its depths.

"Incredible," Liz breathed.

"What?" Curtis whispered.

"It looks exactly like I imagined."

"Good," Shakespeare said. "That means you can help us get inside and get to Kenric."

"There are two ways in," Liz said. "The first is from the ground, on the other side of the tower over there." Liz pointed. "Getting in that way is risky. It's more heavily guarded. It's possible to get through, but I doubt all of us would make it."

"What's the second way in?" Tolkien asked.

"It's harder to get to, but if we could reach it we'd probably be better off," Liz whispered. "It's up there at the top of the tower facing away from the mountain. We'd still run into dragons going that way, but we'd avoid all of the traps that Kenric has set up through the other entrance."

"But don't you know your way through the traps?" Curtis asked.

"Yes," Liz said, "but I'm sure Kenric would know that, so he would have changed them to prepare for my attack."

"So how do we get up there?" Shakespeare asked, nodding toward the top of the tower.

"Do we fly the pegasi up to the window?" Rob asked. Liz jumped at the sound of his voice. It was just a little too loud, but hopefully not loud enough to attract attention.

"No," Liz said, pointedly keeping her voice quite low. "The pegasi are small, but they'd be seen if we flew them up there. We need to remain undetected for as long as possible."

"So what do we do?" McCaffrey asked.

"I could use my Spirit Magic to send everyone up," Liz suggested. "Just like I did to get us out of the water and onto the pegasi."

"That's a long way up," Curtis pointed out. "Can your Spirit Magic hold us that far?"

"I think so," Liz said.

"Your confidence is reassuring, but I'd rather you *know* that we won't plummet to our deaths."

"Do you have any other ideas?" Liz snapped.

Curtis pursed his lips in thought. "Use your Elemental Magic to grow vines up the tower."

"Why would my Elemental Magic go farther than my Spirit Magic?" Liz asked.

"You could grow the vines as far as you could, stop and climb, and then keep growing them," Curtis said. "It could work."

Liz thought about it, but then shook her head. "I'd rather not let Kenric know that I'm an Elementalist unless it's necessary. I don't want to give it away too soon. I'd rather use Spirit."

"I think Liz is right," Shakespeare said. "Plus, we can take some of the effects of Spirit, whereas she'd have to pay all of the price herself for using

Elemental Magic. It's probably best to spread the pain around as much as possible so that it doesn't completely incapacitate one person."

"Okay," Curtis said. "Then what happens when we get inside?"

"Assuming everything is the way it was in my books—and the chances of that look pretty good as far as I can tell—we'll be in a sort of dragon lounge area. At most, there will be five dragons inside."

"Inside the first room we enter?" Rob exclaimed. Curtis clamped a hand over Rob's mouth and put a finger to his own lips.

"Keep your voice down," Curtis warned in a whisper. "You have got to stay focused, Rob. Remember where you are."

Rob nodded and Curtis slowly removed his hand from his mouth. "I'm sorry," Rob whispered. "But how is facing five dragons at once better than facing whatever is through the lower door?"

"Trust me, it's better," Liz said. "We can take them. They'll be manageable, things like Raknars and Callers. No Rokurs or Grinlisses or Crystimes, and especially no Washers."

"We can take on Raknars and Callers." Curtis nodded. "We just need to be careful."

"Those puny beasts?" Tolkien scoffed. "If you could come up with better dragons, McKinnen, you could be part of The Inklings. But this fight will be nothing like the time I took out Smaug. I had to—"

Curtis glared at Tolkien and cut him off. "I don't care what you've done as an Immortal Writer. I don't care who you've defeated. I don't know who this Smaug is, but it sounds to me like there was only *one* dragon. We'll face dozens, maybe hundreds in there. Are you sure you can handle it, old man?"

Tolkien gritted his teeth. "Trust me, dragon warrior, I can do this. You may have been fighting dragons all your life, but you haven't seen what I've seen."

"Enough," McCaffrey interrupted. "We need to focus. Liz, what's next?"

"Once we get past them, we should probably expect more trouble," Liz continued to explain. "For one thing, I doubt that initial battle will be quiet. If the entire tower isn't already awake, they will be after that, and they'll be on guard. It's crowded enough inside that they won't all be able to get to us at once, which is good, but it also means we won't ever get much of a break."

"How many dragons are in there?" Rob asked.

"I don't know," Liz said. "In my book there were hundreds, but that hopefully won't be the case here. Only three pegasi came to life amidst all of the thousands that live in Shethara. Who knows how many dragons came over to this world? And we've already killed some of Kenric's pets. He might not have that many left."

"I hope there aren't hundreds in there," Shakespeare said. "It sounds bad enough fending off five."

"You don't have to come," Curtis pointed out. "You're not a part of this story."

"Maybe not in the books," Shakespeare said, "but I am most certainly a part of this story now. Don't forget, they've killed people that I cared about dearly. I'd like to avenge them."

"Are you sure you can handle that, Shakespeare?" Liz asked.

Shakespeare sighed with impatience. "You clearly don't understand that being alive for hundreds of years changes a person."

"So what do we do after we go through those first five or so dragons?" Curtis asked.

"You follow me," Liz said. "While I'm sure Kenric has changed some things for defensive reasons, he can't have changed the entire layout of the place. I know he'll be in the war room, which is at the heart of the castle. It's where he's most protected. Just to warn you… the war room is guarded by Sampars."

"Those are the ones that breathe out radiation, right?" McCaffrey asked.

"Yes."

"Why in the world did you give them that power?" Shakespeare asked. "What were you thinking?"

"When I wrote about them I never thought I'd have to face them," Liz defended herself.

"So how are we supposed to survive their radiation?" Shakespeare asked.

"The radiation is only effective if it hits you directly," Liz said. "It doesn't just hang in the air and infect everyone like it would during a fallout. They could single-handedly destroy the world if that were the case. The key is to avoid getting in their line of fire."

"How do you kill them?" McCaffrey asked.

"Chopping off its head would work," Curtis said. "Or you could stab one of its vital organs. They're not like the Rokurs. There is more than one way to kill them."

"And once we get past the Sampars and reach Kenric?" Shakespeare pressed.

"We kill him," Liz said softly.

CHAPTER TWENTY-NINE

Liz planted her feet firmly at the base of the tower and drew on her magic. It wasn't difficult to grasp and seemed eager to be used again. She pointed at Curtis and he nodded. Liz surrounded him in magic and lifted him up into the air. Higher and higher she raised him. It was hard to see him in the dark, but she reached out with her mind to follow his progress.

Are you there yet? she asked him.

About six feet higher and I'll be level with the window, Curtis thought to her. *I'll tell you when to send me forward.*

Liz slowed her magic and inched him upward until he mentally called out for her to stop.

Now send me forward. Good. Now put me down.

She did. *How many dragons are in there?* she asked.

Five. They haven't noticed me yet.

That won't last long.

A distant roar sounded above them, and Liz retracted her magic from Curtis and surrounded Shakespeare. She sent him up, using their minds as communicators so that she could get him safely into the tower to help Curtis fight off the dragons.

Liz looked at Rob. He seemed slightly confused, but still more focused than he had been since he gained his new power.

Rob met her gaze and nodded apprehensively. Liz picked him up and sent him shooting upward. She was hesitant to enter his mind, but she made herself do it.

Are you level with the window?

Almost, Rob said. *Healer says I just need to be about three feet higher.*

Liz looked through Rob's mind, deeper into his psyche, until she was able to see through his eyes, and she saw Healer's spirit helping Rob up. Liz choked on a sob, but managed to stay focused as she lifted Rob the rest of the way up and into the window.

Stay focused, Rob, Liz warned. *You have to fight dragons now.*

Healer will help me, Rob said.

Liz brought her magic back and wondered if Healer would really be helpful. She feared that Healer's presence would be more of a distraction than anything else. Liz hoped Rob would survive this battle.

Liz sent McCaffrey and Tolkien up at the same time. She wanted them to stick together. She had read their works and knew they could handle themselves around dragons, but they hadn't been training for this fight, and she'd hate to be the one responsible for their deaths.

Another roar sounded from above. Liz shook her head in an attempt to clear it and lifted herself into the air. Since she was able to see where she was going she moved herself faster than she had the others, and soon flew through the window. She surveyed the scene quickly. Each person battled a dragon, though McCaffrey and Tolkien fought a Raknar together. Curtis was taking on two dragons at once. Liz soared over to the Raknar that was charging him and instructed her Spirit Magic to place her on the dragon's neck. She released the magic as she landed and brought her sword down in a strong swing, severing the dragon's head. She slid off the neck stump and ran over to help Rob, who seemed to be the one struggling the most with his dragon.

It was no wonder. The Caller was confusing him. Using its intuitive magic, it had taken on the voice of the one thing that was sure to distract Rob even more than he already was. It nearly stopped Liz in her tracks.

"Rob," the Caller cried out in Healer's voice. Pain shot up inside Liz's chest. The Caller wouldn't be able to cry out more than the one word— it wasn't smart enough to develop actual speech—but that one word was enough. It was so clearly Healer's voice.

Rob looked from the Caller to the space beside him, where Liz assumed the spirit of Healer was hovering. Rob shook his head, confused.

The Caller took advantage of Rob's hesitation and charged forward, snapping its jaws open and readying itself to breathe fire.

Liz reached it just in time and nicked the side of its snout with her sword. It snorted and turned around, angry at the interruption. It flicked out its tongue and inhaled again.

Liz ducked and rolled underneath the dragon's flames and open mouth. The Caller expelled fire and then clamped its jaw shut, turning to and fro, trying to find where Liz had gone.

She hefted her sword up and stabbed the Caller's belly. It groaned in pain and slumped forward as it died. Liz barely crawled out from under it in time to avoid being crushed by its weight. She ran over to Rob.

"Are you all right?" she asked him.

Rob nodded. He seemed shaky.

"Stay focused and you'll be fine. Now come on, let's help the others."

Curtis had already killed his dragon and was helping Shakespeare finish up his Raknar. In a matter of seconds it was done. McCaffrey and Tolkien stood over their Raknar, looking completely comfortable. It was somewhat unnerving.

"Everyone all right?" Liz asked.

"Lead the way." Curtis gestured. Shakespeare, Rob, McCaffrey, and Tolkien nodded and Liz ran forward.

Their footsteps reverberated around them in the large cavernous room. They had to be careful to avoid the streaks and pools of blood that now covered the marble floor. The gore made the room look grotesque, but Liz knew that it was beautiful when it was clean. Kenric might be evil, but he liked to be evil in style. The high, cathedral-like ceilings were proof of that.

They reached a large, light-beige double door. Liz grabbed one door handle and Curtis grasped the other. Together they heaved backward and the doors swung open.

"Duck!" Liz called.

Everyone dropped to the ground as two bolts of lightning shot from a purple Crystime's mouth. Curtis was the first to get on his hands and knees. He crawled forward, careful to stay out of the Crystime's path.

The dragon noticed his movement and aimed toward him.

"Look out!" Liz warned.

Curtis rolled to the side, the lightning curling around his shield. A black scorch mark scarred the floor where Curtis had been only a second ago.

"Stay back," Liz instructed Rob and the authors. She jumped up and sprinted forward. Curtis stood and ran on the opposite side of the Crystime, parallel to Liz.

The dragon snorted, clearly unsure whom it should attack first. It seemed to consider Curtis more of a threat. It turned its head and opened its mouth. Electricity surged forward and narrowly missed Curtis's swerving head.

Liz reached the Crystime and swung her sword. She would have hit it, but the Crystime's reflexes were fast. It swerved around and hit her sword with a large horn on its snout. It growled at her and pushed forward, backing Liz against the wall of the hallway in which they fought. Its horn pinned her sword, which was raised above her head, to the wall behind her.

The Crystime smiled and opened its mouth. Liz hated to let go of her sword, but if she didn't release her grip on it she'd be electrocuted. Gritting her teeth, she freed her hands and dropped to the floor. The lightning hit the wall above her with such force that the wall broke apart. A large piece of rock fell on her head and Liz saw black.

When she looked back up and could concentrate again, the Crystime was battling it out with Curtis. Somehow he had gotten its attention away from Liz, for which she was extremely grateful. She carefully stood up, a little wobbly at first, and looked around for her sword. It took her a moment to spot it. It was lying just behind the Crystime's front right claw.

Liz called on her Spirit Magic and beckoned her sword with it. It obeyed, and Liz felt a rush of dizziness again as she grabbed her weapon from the air. Perhaps it would be best if she lay off the magic for a few minutes, or at least until her head felt a little better from the blow.

She blinked rapidly and turned her attention back to the fight in front of her. To the untrained eye it would look like Curtis was losing the battle, but Liz knew better. He was feinting so that he could lure the Crystime into a trap. If Liz interfered, she'd only mess up his plan.

She stayed put, leaning against the wall and trying to make the hallway stay still. She was only vaguely aware of what Curtis was doing to fight the dragon. There was a lot of swerving and ducking. He ran around the back of the dragon and climbed onto its tail, balancing precariously as he dodged spikes and lightning bolts. He reached the neck and severed the head off neatly, then slid down to the floor, panting from exertion.

"Rob, Shakespeare, McCaffrey, Tolkien, come on!" Curtis yelled after a moment. He jogged toward Liz. "How's your head?"

"Ow," Liz said simply.

Curtis smirked and put a hand on her head. Warmth surged through her, and she felt her head clear and the throbbing sensation go away. Her balance miraculously returned to her as well.

"Thank you," Liz said as Curtis pulled his hand away. "Although you probably shouldn't be depleting your magic."

"I hardly depleted it from healing your concussion," Curtis said. "Besides, you can't fight dragons or Kenric if you can't even stand up on your own. So stop complaining and just be appreciative."

"I said thank you," Liz complained.

"Let's go," Shakespeare interrupted. "We don't have time for you two to banter."

Liz stood and took the lead again, jogging down the hallway and toward the spiral staircase that was at the end of it. They had just reached the top of the stairwell when Liz saw two large shadows coming up the stairs.

"Two dragons approaching," Liz whispered. "Get to either side of the stairway and hide. We'll take them by surprise."

Shakespeare and McCaffrey ran with Liz to the right while Rob and Tolkien joined Curtis on the left, their swords raised. The dragons scrambled up the stairs, claws clicking on the stone as they came. The clicking and scraping made Liz anxious, but she forced herself to remain calm as she waited.

Finally, the dragons breached the top of the stairs, and Curtis and Liz leapt forward and sliced off their heads. It took each of them only a single blow to kill each dragon.

"Good thing they were Raknars and not Rokurs," Curtis said, "or that wouldn't have worked."

The six of them ran forward again, Liz still in the lead. They had to hop over the dragons' bodies to reach the stairs, but aside from Rob stumbling a bit, it wasn't much of a deterrent. Liz was glad she wasn't squeamish any more or it would have been impossible.

She looked behind her and noticed that all of their boots were leaving dark red footprints on the ground, marking the path they had taken. There was so much blood. She wondered if she should feel guilty for all of the creatures she was killing. Why was it so easy for her to kill dragons? Not that it was physically easy; it wasn't. It took a lot of strength and skill. But she didn't feel any guilt or shame or hesitation when it came to slaying them. She worried about whether or not she would hesitate when it was time to kill Kenric. What if she did pause? Would he kill her if she did? Undoubtedly. He had no sense of guilt when it came to his actions.

She couldn't hesitate. She knew that. But still she wondered… what if she didn't hesitate at all? What would that say about her, if she were able to kill a human being so easily? She wasn't sure if she wanted to hesitate or not.

But she didn't have time to worry about that for long. When they reached the bottom of the stairs, they came to a large foyer with two hallways leading away from it. Liz turned to the right, which led to another large, cavernous room.

"You're sure this is the way to go?" Curtis asked.

"Yes," Liz called as she ran. "Just trust me and follow—"

She was cut off by a swooping sound from above her. Liz looked up and grimaced. A Grinliss hovered in the air above them. It was a testament to how huge the tower was that this dragon could fit inside with its enormous body and wingspan, which looked to be about twenty-five feet.

"Now *that's* more like it," Tolkien cried out in glee. Liz rolled her eyes.

The Grinliss opened its mouth and inhaled. The six of them were all lifted off of the ground, and spiralled toward the Grinliss's mouth.

"This isn't quite what I expected!" Tolkien admitted.

Frantic, Liz called upon her air magic and blasted it toward the dragon. The wind was too much for its wings and it careened backwards, letting them go in the process. They all tumbled to the ground. Liz felt her knees and shins bruise instantly but quickly rose to her feet, grasping her sword.

The Grinliss was on the floor now, clearly not trusting its wings to hold it up with unpredictable wind around. It ran forward and opened its jaws again. Everybody dove to the side, missing the full pull of its breath weapon.

Liz scrambled up and moved farther to the left, followed closely by Curtis, Shakespeare, McCaffrey, and Tolkien. It took Liz a moment to notice that Rob hadn't joined them.

She looked around and saw him stand up, flinging his sword wildly in front of him. The Grinliss was behind him and he had no idea.

"Rob!" Liz called.

"I've got this one," Rob shouted. "You take care of the Grinliss. These Raknars are mine this time!"

"Raknars?" Shakespeare repeated. "What—"

"He's seeing spirits," McCaffrey said. She sounded afraid.

"Rob, it's not real! Rob..." Curtis said.

"They have some sort of magic; they're invincible to my sword," Rob cried out. He was panting. He looked crazy, fighting the air like that. But he somehow looked brave at the same time.

"I know what I'm doing, Healer!" Rob yelled suddenly. "I've almost got them. Calm down. Healer, please, I'm trying to focus..."

Of course. Healer was trying to warn him, to protect him. But he wouldn't listen. The Grinliss was now right behind him.

Curtis ran forward and Liz trailed along behind him.

"Rob!" Curtis yelled. "Rob, turn around!"

"I've almost got this one," Rob panted. "It doesn't stand a—"

But then the Grinliss stooped low and inhaled, and Rob was sucked in. The dragon closed its mouth with a satisfied crunch.

Liz skidded to a stop, shocked.

No. Not Rob. Not him, too.

"Rob! No!" Curtis yelled. He leapt up and landed on the Grinliss's snout. The Grinliss immediately shot its neck up, trying to dislodge Curtis, but Curtis was steady. He jumped up, giving his body the force it would need to make the killing stroke. When he came down his sword point was ready and it sank deep into the dragon's skull, cracking it loudly.

The Grinliss started to fall and Liz backed up. She grabbed Shakespeare just in time and knocked him out of the way, rolling over him in an attempt to escape the dragon's crushing weight.

It crashed to the ground beside them, blood oozing from its head. Curtis jumped off of it and ran to the front of its snout, trying to pry the mouth open. He wasn't strong enough.

"Curtis," Liz panted. "Curtis, stop. It's too late."

"No it isn't," Curtis said, straining to open the jaws. "He's in there. I just need to let him out. Or you could. Use your Spirit Magic."

"Curtis—"

"Open it!" Curtis yelled.

Liz commanded her Spirit Magic to open the muzzle of the dragon. She looked away before she could see inside, choosing instead to stare at Shakespeare and help him up. McCaffrey glanced away as well, but Tolkien looked on, a grimace on his face.

She could still hear Curtis's reaction. He sucked in a gasp and choked on a sob.

"Close it," he said frantically. "I don't want to see him like that. Close it. Now."

Liz complied without looking at the dragon's mouth. She could imagine what was in there and she doubted it was pretty.

Liz hesitantly looked up. Curtis's face was pale, his lips set tightly together. Liz had to blink back tears. The adrenaline she felt helped her hold off her grief until later, but she was still shocked by what had happened.

"Curtis, are you—" she began.

"I'm fine," he said gruffly. He strode to the side of the dragon and grasped the hilt of his sword. He tugged and eventually it came out, completely covered with blood and gore. He wiped either side of the blade against the dragon's face and stepped back. He gazed at Liz with a look of utter despair.

"Can you keep going?" Liz asked.

Curtis nodded, straightened his shoulders, and hid his grief. Liz thought he was brave to be able to focus on his duty rather than the loss of his friend. Liz wondered why she wasn't a wreck right now. She supposed it wasn't real to her yet. A dragon had not just eaten Rob. That was absurd.

"How far away are the Sampars?" Tolkien asked. "How much longer is this going to take?"

"The Sampars are through those doors," Liz said, pointing behind Curtis. "Kenric is just beyond them, in the next room."

Curtis nodded. "Let's go." He looked past Liz. "You coming, Shakespeare?"

Liz turned around. Shakespeare looked shaken, and he couldn't stop staring at the dead Grinliss. Liz walked back to him and grabbed his upper arm, bringing him along with her as they walked with Curtis toward the doors in front of them.

"Keep moving," Liz encouraged them. "We're almost done. Just a couple more rooms, really. Then we can go home."

They paused outside of the doors and Liz looked at Curtis. "Ready?"

"Ready," Curtis said.

They pulled the doors open and then stepped behind them, using them for shields. It was a good thing they did. Three white Sampars were waiting, and breathed out as soon as the doors opened.

"Can you put a shield around all of us?" Liz asked Curtis over the roar of the Sampars. Curtis nodded.

"It's done. Let's go."

The five of them rushed around the doors and met the Sampars head-on. Surprised, the Sampars skittered back, but soon they recovered their footing and breathed out again. The radiation hit Curtis's shield hard, and Liz watched him stumble in pain as the shield wavered.

"How long can you keep it up?" Liz called to Curtis.

"Not long," Curtis said. "With three doses of that much radiation coming at me… maybe thirty seconds if they keep breathing."

"Let's get behind them, then," Liz said. Grabbing hold of Shakespeare, Liz feinted to the right, and the Sampar that wasn't focused on Curtis followed her with its head. McCaffrey and Tolkien headed for the third one. Liz rushed to the left and was just quick enough that the Sampar had trouble following her with its gaze. She managed to get behind the Sampar, and she watched the shimmering shield around her disappear.

"The shield's gone," Liz said to Shakespeare. "Keep out of direct range of the dragons' breath."

"That's the goal," Shakespeare said. He and Liz trotted back in a circle, staying just ahead of the Sampar's head and mouth. "What's the plan? How do we kill it?"

Liz pondered for only a moment. "I think it'll consider me more of a threat, so I'm going to distract it. You cut off its head."

"Me?" Shakespeare exclaimed. "Are you sure?"

"Be careful," Liz said. She darted out in front of the Sampar's mouth. It was caught off guard by this move and so, as Liz had hoped, it didn't immediately breathe radiation. It inhaled to prepare itself to attack, but Liz was already on the other side of its snout when it breathed out. The Sampar seemed to notice that its two victims were separated, and it paused for a moment, considering which prey to pursue.

Liz leapt forward and swung her sword toward the Sampar's neck. The white dragon hissed and turned toward Liz, shuffling itself away from her so that its neck remained unharmed.

Liz kept it distracted, feinting and lunging and constantly avoiding the dragon's breath. She had no idea where Shakespeare had gone. She didn't have time to look for him. All of her focus was on staying out of the Sampar's way.

She was so focused on her Sampar, in fact, that she had forgotten about Curtis's.

"Liz, jump to your left! *Far* to your left!" Curtis called. Liz leapt to her side, but she wasn't quick enough. She felt a blast of radiation hit her right side, and it immediately started to spread through her body. She screamed, and her Sampar caught her in its claws and pinned her down to the floor. Liz could see its needle-sharp scales quivering above her as it breathed in.

"Shakespeare!" Liz shouted. "Shakespeare! Hurry!"

Just as the Sampar started to breathe out, it sputtered and gurgled. Blood dripped from its mouth and splattered onto Liz's head. Liz looked around and saw Shakespeare standing under the Sampar's throat, his blade tucked neatly away into its flesh. Shakespeare had slit its throat and cut off its airways, rendering its breath weapon useless and killing it all at once. Liz smiled at him and tried to wriggle out of the Sampar's grip, but she couldn't manage it.

Shakespeare wrenched his sword free of the dragon's throat and the beast fell forward, pinning Liz solidly to the ground.

"Liz, are you all right?" Shakespeare shoved the dragon's head away and Liz gulped in a breath.

"The other Sampar... I wasn't paying attention," Liz gasped. "It got me."

Shakespeare frowned and turned toward Curtis. Liz followed his gaze. Curtis was just cleaning his blade off on his Sampar's dead cheek. McCaffrey and Tolkien had decapitated their dragon and were heading toward Liz, worried looks on their faces.

"Curtis," Shakespeare called. "It got her."

Curtis jerked his head up and ran toward them. He shoved the Sampar's claw off of Liz and she breathed a little easier. Still, she could feel her body growing weaker.

"I knew I felt something through our bond," Curtis said. "I thought you were just tired from running around. I should have paid more attention."

"I missed the worst of it," Liz panted. "You helped a lot."

Curtis pursed his lips and lifted up his hands. "Do you know where it hit you?"

Liz pointed to the right side of her waist. "Right there," she said, "but it's already spreading."

Curtis placed his hands on her side and started to heal her. Liz instantly felt better, and soon she was able to steady her breathing. Curtis pulled his hands away. He was sweating.

"No pressure or anything, but no more injuries, all right?" Curtis said. "If Healer were here she'd be able to heal you if something else came up, but getting rid of the radiation took everything out of me as far as healing goes. I might be able to manage a few shields for myself, but that's about it. So *be careful.*"

Liz nodded and sat up.

"Thank you again," she said.

McCaffrey and Tolkien let out a sigh of relief.

"Be more careful, won't you, McKinnen?" Tolkien demanded. "We're all dead if you're dead. I haven't lived nearly long enough for that."

Curtis and Shakespeare helped Liz stand. Curtis clapped Shakespeare on the back. "You took out a Sampar!"

Shakespeare grinned proudly and was about to reply when the doors behind them burst open.

"If you are quite finished massacring my pets," a deep voice said, "I believe we have something to take care of. Please come in."

Liz turned toward the sound of Kenric's voice. Holding on to Curtis for strength, she forced her way forward. Shakespeare, Tolkien, and McCaffrey followed behind the two of them, wary. They entered the war room and the doors closed behind them with a clang.

"How kind of you to visit me, Creator," Kenric said. He sat on a dark red throne in the middle of the grey room, surrounded by about twenty dragons, all of which eagerly awaited his command. His black hair was slicked back against his head and his dark eyes glimmered in the faint light of the room. Liz hated those eyes. They were the same as her stepfather's.

Kenric wore black leather pants and a dark jerkin. Blood red robes flowed around him. "But of course, I cannot welcome you with open arms. You've killed some of my favourite dragons. That is unforgivable."

Liz was too scared to say anything, but thankfully Curtis spoke up.

"All of the deaths *you* have caused are unforgivable," he said.

"Ah, yes," Kenric said, rising from his throne. "My old friend, the dragon warrior. Have you come to pay homage and swear fealty to your dragon lord at last?"

"I've come to kill you," Curtis said.

Kenric laughed. "Do not lie. It does not become you. You are not here to kill me." He turned his attention to Liz. "*She* is."

Liz lifted her chin and met Kenric's gaze, defiant and angry and incredibly scared.

Kenric smiled.

CHAPTER THIRTY

"Hello, Elizabeth," Kenric said as he strode forward. "I've been wondering when we would meet. Tell me, Creator, how does it feel to look at me and see the darkest parts of yourself?"

Liz swallowed. How could Kenric have possibly found out that he was based off of *her*? What else could he know?

"No answer?" Kenric shook his head and stopped about six feet in front of her. "You are less impressive than I imagined. Somehow I thought you would be... well, *better.*"

Liz pursed her lips and stared at him. "You know nothing about me."

Kenric cocked his head and raised his eyebrows. "Do I not? Are you sure?"

"You can't know me," Liz said. "I've never met you before now."

"Oh, but I do know you." Kenric smiled. "I know you so well. You see, something happened when I came over into this world. She didn't realize it at the time, of course, because she was unconscious, but I came here with Healer. I didn't hurt her; she was much more valuable alive. I just slipped a bit of my Spirit Magic into her mind and left it there. It never attacked and she never noticed... although you did. But you didn't recognize my eyes."

Liz gasped as she understood. She had seen Kenric's eyes through Healer, but had thought they were Stan's. If only she had understood sooner.

"You were in her mind," Liz said. "That's why she was sick and no one knew why."

"Yes," Kenric said. "And I was able to keep watch over everything. I knew when you arrived at the Castle. I found out about your connection to me. I read her mind when she read yours. I know you've somehow managed to make yourself an Elementalist as well as a Spirit user. I know *everything*.

"It saddened me when Healer died. I lost my connection to you. So I admit, you caught me off guard with your little attack tonight. I applaud you for it. I also commend you for sacrificing Healer. Maybe you're even more like me than you think."

"I am nothing like you," Liz said.

"Aren't you?" Kenric asked politely. "I've seen your past. I know what you've done. I've felt the darker part of you stirring inside, eager to lash out and break free. I know you. I know you because *we are the same*. Can you really kill me, Elizabeth? Do you really think you have enough power?"

"If you know so much about me, then you already know the answer to that question."

"You think you have enough power, but you are wrong," Kenric said. "I will always be stronger than you. You don't stand a chance."

He flung his arms outward and Liz was blasted with Spirit Magic. It knocked her off her feet and sent her flying backwards into Shakespeare. He and Liz quickly scrambled back to their feet, Tolkien helping them. Kenric laughed and Curtis leapt forward. Kenric drew his sword and met Curtis head-on.

"Oh, dragon warrior," Kenric sighed as their swords clashed. "This is no longer your fight. Elizabeth has to be the one to defeat me."

"As long as you end up dead, I don't care who delivers the final blow," Curtis growled. He shoved against the locked swords and sent Kenric stumbling back a few feet. Kenric smiled and took a few extra steps back.

"Then I'm sure you won't mind if I just engage Elizabeth on my own?"

"Why?" Curtis asked. "Are you afraid of me?"

Kenric laughed. "Hardly. But you have other things to worry about."

He raised both of his arms and the dragons around them sprang to life. Two Rokurs flew toward Liz, a Sampar and a Grinliss flew for Curtis, a Raknar and a Crytime went for Shakespeare, and four Callers went for McCaffrey and Tolkien. Liz hoped that the writers would be able to handle their dragons; it would be just her luck to inadvertently kill some of the greatest writers to ever live.

She didn't have time to think about that as the Rokurs came within firing range. Flames erupted from both of their mouths, and Liz backed up while she took control of her magic. She called on water and doused the flames before they could reach her. The Rokurs roared in anger. One enormous blue dragon landed in front of her, the other behind. Both inhaled and breathed out at the same time.

Liz ducked and rolled to her right, narrowly avoiding the flames that collided above her. She threw her sword toward the first Rokur and guided it with Spirit, hoping to plunge the sword through its eye. Kenric must have warned it about this strategy, however; it deftly dodged the blow. Liz continued guiding the sword with her magic, telling it to go for the eye of the dragon in front of her. The Rokur behind her roared and blew fire. Liz jumped away just in time to avoid the majority of the blow, but she had to pat fire off of her legs. Heat seared up her body, but she gritted her teeth and doused the fire with water magic before too much damage was done.

The Rokur spread its wings and jumped closer. Liz called on wind and directed it toward the dragon's wings. The sudden gust caught the dragon off guard and it rolled back, trying desperately to close its wings before it could go any farther.

Liz kept the gust up while she turned back to the first dragon. The sword was still trying to pierce the dragon's eye. Holding up the Spirit Magic and the Elemental Magic was exhausting, but Liz was determined to keep going. She ran toward the dragon, trying to distract it. It propelled fire at her, but she swerved and avoided it. The dragon snorted in frustration. Liz had her magic take the sword and jab it at the dragon's head. It didn't hurt the Rokur, but it annoyed it. The beast roared and turned its attention back to the sword. Liz checked over her shoulder on the other Rokur. It had managed to collapse its wings and was running toward her. Liz would have to hurry. She released her wind magic and turned back toward the first dragon. It still paid attention to the sword, and Liz took the opportunity to jump on the dragon's leg. She climbed its scales, but the Rokur didn't notice. Its gem-like exterior was too hard for it to feel her pulling herself up.

When Liz reached the dragon's neck, she called her sword back to her. The Rokur snorted and looked around, trying to find where Liz had gone. It swerved its head to the left, but Liz kept herself out of sight as she hid on the dragon.

The other Rokur, completely focused on its prey, gusted out fire. Liz took hold of her Spirit Magic and used it to divert the flames away from her. The dragon she was on roared in fury. It didn't understand why its brother had attacked it.

The Rokur flung itself forward and attacked the other dragon. Liz slid down its neck, careful to stay on top of the beast, and walked along its back to find its weak spot. It jolted to the side, avoiding its opponent's attack, and Liz fell to her knees. She crawled around, looking frantically for the weak point on the Rokur. The beast jumped forward and Liz slid back, ramming her head against the dragon's shoulder. She grimaced and fell forward, barely grabbing hold of the dragon's scales before she fell off. She was just swinging herself up when she noticed the place where one scale was missing.

Liz smiled and twirled her sword around, ready to plunge it into the dragon's flesh.

But the dragon fell to the side, caught off balance by a hit from its brother. Liz fell off the dragon and slammed into the ground. The dragon turned its head and recognition crossed its intelligent eyes. It turned away from its challenger and swung toward her.

Liz enveloped her sword in Spirit Magic and flung it at the Rokur's weak spot. It was partially hidden from view, but she prayed that the sword would find its target. If it didn't, she was dead.

The Rokur had almost reached her when it stopped and howled. The sword had pierced the dragon's flesh.

With its side dripping blood, the Rokur collapsed. Liz called her sword back to her and scrambled out of the way just before the dragon hit the ground.

Liz grabbed her sword out of the air and turned to the second dragon. It was almost upon her, and Liz had to dash forward to avoid being hit by its flames. The dragon couldn't see her now because she was under the fire's cover. She used this to her advantage. She lifted herself up with Spirit Magic and waited under the dragon's jaw until it stopped breathing flame. Liz didn't hesitate and hurled herself upward.

The Rokur didn't have time to react to Liz's sudden appearance, and Liz gritted her teeth as she swung her sword back to gain momentum. Just one deep thrust to the eye and she could help the writers or Curtis, and then get to Kenric.

Just as she was about to lunge, she felt something grab her from behind and pull her backward. She cried out in frustration and struggled to look behind her to see what had her in its grasp.

She couldn't see anything. What was happening? How could she be flying through the air unaided? Her Spirit Magic wasn't doing it.

Spirit Magic.

Of course.

She realized, too late, that Kenric's magic had control of her. She struggled all the more to get out of its grasp, but it was useless. She flung her sword around in a futile attempt to get free, but it clattered to the floor with sickening finality.

The magic slammed her into the ground, head first. High-pitched ringing filled her ears, and for a moment all she saw was black. The ringing cleared and she heard laughter echoing behind her.

She struggled to stand, weak from dragon fighting and fear.

Kenric walked in front of her, a wicked smile on his face.

"Oh, well done," he laughed. "Well done. I knew from Healer's mind that you were talented, but it was certainly exciting to see you in action in front of my eyes. Still, I didn't want you to kill my favourite Rokur."

Liz ran forward, calling her sword. Kenric just smiled and lifted his hand in the air, palm outstretched. Liz froze in midstride, incapable of movement. Her sword crashed again to the ground. Kenric had her firmly in his magic's grasp.

"Come now, Creator," Kenric said softly. He walked up to her and stopped only inches away. He was intimately close. "You should know better than to attack me like that," he breathed. "You should know better than to attack me at all. I'm too powerful."

He pressed his body against hers and Liz cringed. She desperately wanted to step back. Flashbacks threatened to overwhelm her, but she ground her teeth together and forced herself to focus.

"Don't you find power attractive?" Kenric whispered against her lips. "You used to, once. But now I hear that you're more into the hero-type. You're with Curtis, aren't you? My dear Elizabeth, he will never understand you like I do. He will never accept your darkness. But I, I can embrace it and mold it into something beautiful and more powerful than your wildest dreams. I can make you great. I can make you truly immortal. Join me, Creator." He pressed himself closer to her. "Join me."

He kissed her. It was nothing like the kisses Curtis had given her. These were power-hungry, lustful kisses. She knew what this type of kiss felt like.

Liz was powerless. She couldn't move. His magic and her terror froze her in place. His hands started to move in toward her and Liz gave in to her panic.

Not again, she thought. *Please, God, not again.*

There was suddenly a furious yell, and Kenric was stripped off of her and thrown to the ground.

"Don't you touch her," Curtis yelled. He stood in front of Liz, his arms thrown out in front of her protectively.

Kenric stood up, wiping blood from his lower lip and laughing. "I'll do whatever I want with her once you're dead."

"We both know you can't kill me," Curtis said. "You've tried and you've failed."

"The timing just wasn't right," Kenric said. "Trust me. I can kill you. And I will."

Kenric lunged at Curtis, his sword outstretched. Curtis returned his blow with one of his own, and then Liz couldn't keep up with what was happening. They moved too quickly, just a blur of swords and flesh.

It wasn't until Curtis knocked her out of the way to save her from being hit that Liz realized she could move. Kenric had released her from his magic. She didn't know if he had meant to or if he had even realized that she was free, but it didn't matter. She had to act before he hurt Curtis, or before he could compromise her again.

Liz shuddered and fought to hold back her panic. Kenric's touch had brought so many memories rushing to the surface, memories she had tried to bury and forget. She couldn't focus on them now. She couldn't afford to let her past haunt her. Not today.

She focused on her breathing and tried to make out what was happening between Curtis and Kenric.

Curtis lunged forward and stabbed straight through Kenric's thigh. Kenric screamed in fury. Curtis pulled his sword out of his flesh and jumped back, preparing to attack again.

But Kenric wouldn't put up with it.

"Enough!" he cried. He whipped his hands forward and pushed out his Spirit Magic. Liz watched as Curtis's shield shot up, but he was still so weak magically from healing Liz earlier that it was next to useless. Kenric pushed past it in seconds and Curtis flew backwards. He hit the ground with a horrible *crack* several yards away.

"Finish him!" Kenric commanded. Two dragons swooped down toward the fallen dragon warrior.

"No!" Liz called. She ran toward Curtis. She didn't know if he was unconscious or not. If he were, the dragons would kill him.

But Kenric wouldn't let Liz get that far.

He pulled her back with his Spirit Magic. She fell against his body and into his arms.

She was afraid that he would freeze her again, but instead he let the magic go, and just held on to her with his rough embrace.

"Now that he won't be around to save you," Kenric said gruffly, "we'll see how you do, shall we? I have to admit, I like them when they struggle."

Liz kicked back against the wound in his thigh. He cried out and loosened his hold on her. She grabbed his arm and pulled, swinging him over her head and onto the ground.

Kenric laughed. "You were right," he said. "I underestimated you. Be sure you don't make the mistake of underestimating me."

He wrapped his Spirit Magic around her and lifted her into the air. She struggled against the invisible bonds, which seemed to be centred on her throat. Liz reached out for her Spirit Magic and flung it at Kenric, but it didn't affect him at all. The pool had made him immune to magic, and now Liz was useless. Had Healer's sacrifice been for nothing?

Kenric stood and looked up at her, a twisted smile on his face.

"*You* made me this way," he sneered. "You filled my life with pain and fear and anger. You made me a villain. And now you will pay for it."

The Spirit Magic tightened and Liz choked. Liz tried to push magic out against him again, but it deflected off of him like water springing off of a trampoline.

"You... you came to my mind that way," she sputtered. "Evil is in your nature."

"But you didn't change it," Kenric snapped. "You didn't protect me from the evil thoughts in your head. You didn't save me. And so you see, *you* did this. Healer and Rob are dead because of you. Your lover's death is your own doing, and the inevitable fall of your world is all your fault."

Kenric's Spirit Magic gripped her throat tighter, and Liz's vision began to fade.

"Please..." Liz managed to whisper.

"No." Kenric threw his sword and it pierced Liz's side. Liz tried to scream, but only the tiniest bit of air escaped her throat. She felt blood trickle down her side. Tears flowed freely down her cheeks as she started to go numb and her vision faded away.

She was losing consciousness. This was the end. He was killing her. She hadn't won. And it was all because she had made him that way.

You didn't change it... you didn't save me.

Liz frowned. Something about how he had said it... something...

His face. His face had been contorted with rage and hate and... and fear. He still feared his past, just like Liz did.

Liz knew what she had to do. He had tried the same tactic on her only moments before, and she knew that the same thing would work on him.

With the last bit of energy she had, Liz closed her eyes and grabbed for her magic. She didn't bother with Spirit, and she didn't look for Elemental. She searched for the power the pool had given her, and she prayed it would be enough.

It took a moment to find, but she grasped the pool magic and flung it at Kenric as she opened her eyes. He staggered back from the force of it, and the hold on her throat loosened. Liz gulped in air and urged her magic onward, deeper and deeper into Kenric's psyche.

She could feel Kenric fighting back. He was trying to master her magic; control it with his will. But Liz had a powerful hold over her magic. She knew what she had to do.

"Memories," Liz said. Her voice didn't sound like her own; it was rough and strained, raw from choking. "The most powerful, harmful form of magic. The mind plays such tricks on us. It is our most dangerous weapon. My mind is more powerful than yours."

She finally found what she was looking for and brought it to the surface of Kenric's mind, slamming it against his consciousness and completely enveloping him in memory.

Images appeared between Liz and Kenric, and the dragon lord shrank back. He lost control of his Spirit Magic in his surprise and fear. Liz crumpled to the ground. She coughed and gasped, but kept firm control over her magic and made the images in front of her more concrete and active.

Kenric and Liz watched as Kenric's father advanced toward him. "It's *your* fault your mother left!" Henry yelled, and struck out. Liz made sure her magic forced Kenric to feel the blow. Kenric shrank back, astonished and frightened. "You drove her away! And you will pay for what you have cost me!" He beat Kenric violently. For a moment the dragon lord forgot that he was powerful, and that he had so much magic that he could easily kill his father. Instead, he reverted back to a scared little boy who just wanted to be loved.

"Please, Father," Kenric said. "I'm sorry. I didn't mean to do anything wrong—"

"Shut up!" Henry yelled as he kicked his son. "I don't want to hear your voice anymore. Stay silent. Take your punishment with some dignity. It will improve you. Or, it will kill you. I honestly don't know which one I'd prefer."

Henry bent down and lifted Kenric up by the collar of his robes. Kenric looked down fearfully at his father, and then his eyes spotted Liz on the ground, panting from the wound in her side and her excessive use of magic.

"This is… he's not really here!" Kenric shouted. "You're doing this!"

"Who are you talking to?" Henry asked. He shook Kenric. "Don't try to get out of this. It won't do you any good." He slapped his son.

"Stop!" Kenric cried out. "How are you doing this? Get rid of him!"

"I am a creator," Liz said. "I make worlds and men and dragons and monsters and heroes and gods. Who are you, with your anger and fear and hate, to think you can defeat me?"

Kenric winced as Henry hit him again. "I am the high dragon lord of Shethara."

"I created Shethara. I created you. I know what fuels you, what drives you, and most importantly, what hurts you."

The memory of Henry slammed Kenric to the ground and stepped on the dragon lord's throat. Kenric choked and struggled to get away from his father, but his fear incapacitated him.

Liz, focusing with all of her might on her magic, slowly rose to her feet. She wrenched Kenric's sword from her side with a scream but managed to stay upright. She walked forward and stopped beside Henry. He paid no attention to her. But of course, he wouldn't. He was just in Kenric's head.

"We're all just stories," Liz said, looking down at him. "Wonderful or horrible, we're just words and actions and plots and characters. Just stories. This is how your story ends."

Henry pressed down harder against Kenric's throat, and the dragon lord cried out in pain. Liz let her magic go and Henry disappeared. Kenric gasped and started to get up, but Liz didn't give him a chance.

She thrust his sword down through his chest, pinning him to the floor. Kenric's eyes widened as he stared up at Liz.

"Creator..." he gasped, "why? Why didn't you save me from him?"

Liz felt a tug of guilt, but she pressed down harder against the sword and twisted.

Kenric stared at her for a moment, his eyes wide with shock and pain. Liz forced herself to look as the light left his eyes. She wanted to remember this. She needed to remember that she had killed a man. She didn't want to forget that she was capable of such horrible things.

Kenric let out one final breath and Liz watched the last bit of light leave his eyes. He stared vacantly off into the air behind her, and Liz slumped against the hilt of the sword.

The dragons that were still alive in the room roared around her. She reached out with her mind and felt their fear and confusion. With Kenric dead, his magic had no control over them. They didn't know what to do on their own.

Liz tried to reach out with her magic so that she could comfort the dragons, but she couldn't find the strength. Why? What was wrong with her?

She realized that she was sinking to the ground. Why was she so weak?

She fell to the ground on her side, and the pain there reminded her that Kenric had stabbed her.

He had killed her after all.

She panted and looked up at the ceiling. Dragons flew wildly and without direction, breathing out fire and lightning and radiation in their panic and terror.

They're so beautiful, she thought.

She slipped into the waiting darkness.

EPILOGUE

Liz felt warm and comfortable. She was fairly certain she was dead. It didn't seem so bad. Sure, Curtis would be upset, but he'd manage. He had lost a lot of people in one short period of time. She wished she could comfort him or hold him one last time.

Liz sighed and rolled over, then grimaced at the pain in her side.

Pain?

If she were dead, why did she hurt? She frowned. Something was wrong.

Slowly, Liz managed to open her eyes. The lighting was dim, but she still recognized her surroundings. The soft pastel colours of the tent weren't hard to recognize.

Gasping, Liz tried to sit up. If she were dead, Healer would be here. She knew it. Healer would have come to take her to... wherever she had to go now that her life was over.

As Liz looked around Healer's tent, she knew Healer wasn't there. Her absence was almost as strong as her presence would have been. The pain Liz felt from missing Healer hurt as much as her side.

She slipped the covers off of her stomach and looked down. She wasn't wearing a shirt, but was instead covered with a large, thick white bandage. Well, it was supposed to be white. Instead, it was a gruesome red. It needed to be changed.

She looked up and glanced around. She wasn't dead, then. She should probably be happy about that, but all she managed to feel was numb and exhausted.

"Thank God," Curtis said. Liz looked over and watched him jog into the tent. Worry and exhaustion seemed permanently etched on his face. "You're awake. For a while I wasn't sure you would come back to me."

Liz smiled. "Of course I came back. The hero always makes it."

"Not always. I was worried this would turn into a tragedy."

"No way," Liz said. "I hate tragedies. This is *my* story. I'm in charge."

"So you planned to get a mortal wound in your belly?" Curtis asked.

"Well… no," Liz said. "Occupational hazard, I guess."

"I bet you thought you'd be safe at work when you became a writer."

"Nah," Liz said. "My mind has always been a dangerous place."

Curtis smiled and sat down beside her on the bed. He gently took one of her hands in his.

"How are you?"

"I'm in a lot of pain," Liz admitted. "And I'm exhausted. But… I think I'll survive."

"You were incredible," Curtis said. "I'm so proud of you."

Liz looked down. "He blamed me for not saving him. I did that to him. I made him a villain."

Curtis shook his head. "No, Liz. He was manipulating you. He was good at that."

"But I could have saved him," Liz said. "When I was being abused by Stan, I wondered why God didn't save me. Why didn't He step in and change my life? I blamed Him. Then I let the same thing happen to Kenric. How could I do that?"

Curtis leaned back against the headboard and swung his legs up onto the bed. He gently put his arm around Liz's shoulders and pulled her head against his chest.

"It goes back to what I said before," Curtis said. "You didn't make our choices for us; you just gave us a way to make those choices when you wrote out our lives. Henry made a choice to beat and hurt Kenric. That's not your fault, and you couldn't control his actions. Not without betraying your story and your role as a writer. You know, Kenric could have risen above what he chose to become, but he didn't. This wasn't your fault."

Liz nodded and lifted her hand to brush her tears away, but was surprised to find that she wasn't crying. She must have been too numb.

Curtis held her for a minute and Liz found herself growing tired again.

"How long have I been out?" Liz asked.

"About a week," Curtis said. "I couldn't heal you very well… I'm not as skilled as Healer was, and my magic still isn't fully recovered. I've only been able to do so much. I'm sorry. Please forgive me for not being able to fix you."

"Fix me?" Liz repeated. "You've saved me, Curtis. You protected me from Kenric, you taught me to be strong, you gave me confidence in myself, you made me believe that I'm worth something… you even made me forgive myself for things I thought I'd never overcome. Curtis, I love you."

"I love you too," Curtis said. He bent down and kissed her gently, then pulled back.

"How… how did we get out of there?" Liz asked. "The last thing I remember is the dragons going… rabid, almost, after they were freed from Kenric's magic."

"They were eager to get away from the mountain and the tower," Curtis said. "Once Kenric released them, they no longer cared about killing us. They were just desperate to get out. So the writers and I came over to you to guard you, and we waited until the coast was clear."

"And the authors survived?" Liz asked.

"Oh, yes," Curtis said. He grinned. "There's a lot more to them than I expected, especially Shakespeare. He's tough for such an old man. I can't wait to see what else he can do. I'm excited to work with him more. And he's excited to see what you come up with next."

Liz frowned. "Hasn't my writing caused enough trouble?"

"Definitely," Curtis said, "but that's part of the fun, isn't it? Besides, you're a writer. It's what you were born to do. You have to create. I think you'd go mad if you stopped."

"You're right," Liz sighed. "I write because I have to. I actually think I'm already a little crazy."

"Good," Curtis said as he squeezed her shoulder. "The best writers are usually the ones with a deep well of unresolvable issues."

"That's not always true," Liz pointed out.

"It is for you," Curtis said.

Liz laughed and wrapped her arms around Curtis's waist.

"So, Creator," Curtis said after a moment. "What will you write about next?"

Liz smiled. "Oh, don't worry. I have plenty of ideas. You won't like fighting any of them."

Curtis grinned. "As long as I get to be with you, I'll be just fine."

"You can stay with me forever, if you'd like," Liz said.

Curtis looked down at her. "I think I might do that."

He kissed her and Liz let all of her worries melt away. Everything would be all right. She was an Immortal Writer, after all.

It wasn't like any other writers could come and put the entire galaxy in jeopardy, right?

What could possibly go wrong?

BONUS CHAPTER - *IMMORTAL CREATORS* SNEAK PEEK

S cott clamped his hands over his ears as he sank down to the floor in a corner of his blue office. He rocked back and forth violently, his eyes squeezed shut, desperate to steady the flow of voices pouring into his head.

Save us!

The bomb only had one minute left before—

The man cocked his gun at the girl and smiled—

Red light, brighter than the sun at noon but far more sinister—

Save us!

"Scott!"

The wet rain whispered down the dark windows of the creaky hearse—

There was only so much time left before the god of this world discovered—

"Scott!"

His brother's voice broke through the cacophony of images and words in Scott's head. Scott gasped and slowly opened his eyes.

Dylan's dark face and worried light blue eyes stared at him.

"Thank you," Scott murmured. He cleared his throat and leaned his head back against the wall, exhausted.

"Another attack?" Dylan asked. He sat cross-legged on the floor in front of Scott and leaned forward, his arms tense across his knees.

Scott nodded and rubbed his temples. He was unsurprised to find sweat beading down his face.

"What's making them worse?" Dylan asked. "They've never been so close together before."

"I don't know." Scott shrugged his thin shoulders. "It's not like I'm doing it on purpose."

Dylan frowned. "I didn't say you were. I'm just concerned, that's all."

Scott nodded and focused on breathing deeply.

"How long was I gone?" he asked.

"I don't know," Dylan said. "I found you only a minute or two ago. I have no idea how long you've been here. What were you doing when the attack started?"

"I was just playing a video game on my computer," Scott said.

"When's the last time you wrote?" Dylan asked.

Scott craned his neck and glanced around the office. There were no windows; instead, the walls were painted like the sky to give some false sense of being outside. It was about as far as Scott went. He hated being outside. Ever since the Fever had started he hadn't felt like it was safe.

"Over a month," Scott admitted.

"C'mon, Scott," Dylan sighed. "No wonder the attacks have been so close together. You know writing is the only thing that helps."

Scott gritted his teeth. He had tried to explain to Dylan why he didn't like to write, but Dylan had never believed him about *them*.

"Dylan," Scott said. "Writing isn't safe."

He didn't look at his brother, but he could tell Dylan was rolling his eyes.

"Why won't you just accept that it helps you?" Dylan suggested. "You don't have to make up excuses if you just accept that it helps."

"I've written an entire book!" Scott growled. "What more do you want?"

"I want you to be healthy," Dylan said, "and—"

The ringing doorbell cut Dylan off.

"It's eleven o'clock at night," Dylan said. "Who would be dropping by at this hour?"

"Maybe it's one of your girlfriends," Scott suggested.

Dylan glared at him. "Yeah, because I have so many of those."

"Three, to be exact."

"Shut up, Scott."

The doorbell rang again.

"You should probably go answer the door," Scott murmured.

"They can come back," Dylan said. "I want to make sure you're okay."

"I'll still be here after you answer the door," Scott pointed out.

The doorbell rang a third time.

Dylan clumsily rose to his feet. "They're not very patient, are they?"

"Probably Sarah, then," Scott said.

Dylan smirked as he left the office, shutting the door behind him.

Scott leaned his head back against the wall, slid his hand through his sweaty dark hair, and chuckled, but the chuckle died in his throat as he heard Dylan's voice and the voice of another man—British, from the sound of him—coming from the other room.

The man's voice was familiar.

Scott swallowed. His throat suddenly felt so dry. What was *he* doing here?

"I said no," Dylan said. "He's not feeling well. You'll have to come back another time."

"There's no time like the present," the man said. "And I've come all this way."

"Hey, you can't just walk in there!" Dylan started shouting. "This is my house!"

"Thank you for the hospitality," the man said drily. His voice came from outside the office door.

Scott held his breath as he waited for the man to collect him. That's why he was here, wasn't it?

"Scott," the man said from outside the office. "You know why I'm here."

Scott grimaced.

"*Leave!*" he yelled. "You know I don't want you here."

"What's going on?" Dylan shouted through the door.

"I wouldn't be here if I had any other choice," the man said. "Now, are you going to come face me, or may I come in?"

Scott took several deep breaths and then forced himself up off of the floor. His hands curled into fists as he stomped to the door. Then, with a deep breath, he yanked it open.

An older man with a receding hairline and longish black hair stood before him. His black suit was neatly pressed, his thin black tie rested precisely in the middle of his white shirt, and he did not look nearly as chagrined as he should have.

They stared at each other for a moment.

"You don't look any older than when I last saw you," the man mused.

"What are you doing here?" Scott demanded.

"You know why I've come," the man said. "I would not have bothered you if there had been any other choice."

Dylan forced himself between Scott and the older man. He looked between the two of them, his brow furrowed.

"Scott, what's going on?" he asked.

The man raised an eyebrow at Scott. "You never told your brother?"

"I tried," Scott said. "But he never believed me."

"Tell me what's going on," Dylan demanded.

"Remember what I told you about Dad?" Scott said quietly. His eyes never left the man's face.

Dylan huffed. "Not this again. The *truth*, Scott."

"I knew your father," the man said. "He was a dear friend."

"Really?" Dylan asked.

Scott's fists tightened. "If you were his friend then you *never* would have let him die."

The man didn't look down, didn't break eye contact with Scott, didn't look ashamed at all. Scott gritted his teeth.

"It was not my fault, Scott."

Scott desperately wished that Dylan was out of the way so that he could punch the man in the jaw.

"What are you two talking about?" Dylan asked again.

The man turned from Scott and answered. "I need to take your brother away."

Dylan stood up straighter. "Why? Who are you?"

The man smiled. "You wouldn't believe me if I told you."

"You didn't believe me when *I* told you," Scott said.

"I need your brother to do something for me," the man said. "The whole world is in danger."

"You expect me to hand over my sixteen-year-old brother to a strange man who showed up at my doorstep?" Dylan laughed. "I don't know who you are, but you're not taking Scott anywhere."

The man sighed and turned his attention back to Scott. "Will you please persuade your brother to let me escort you to the Castle?"

"Castle?" Dylan repeated.

"I'm not going with you," Scott stated. "I refuse."

"Scott, we don't have a lot of time," the man said. "They're coming soon. They should start arriving the day after tomorrow. You have to come in now."

"He's not going anywhere with you," Dylan said sharply. "I don't care that you have a castle. He's not leaving. And if you take him, I will hunt you down. I can trace *anything*."

The man frowned. He put his hands in his pockets. "You will not come willingly?"

Dylan placed himself directly in front of Scott, facing the stranger. "He's not going at all."

The man sighed.

"I really didn't want it to be like this," the man said. "But the world is in danger, and I need you, Scott. If that means I take your brother, too, then so be it."

Scott peered around Dylan just in time to see the man pull a small round disc out of his right pocket.

"What is that?" Dylan asked.

"I'm terribly sorry for this," the man said.

Faster than Scott would have thought possible for someone his size and age, the man reached out and grabbed Dylan's shoulder, twisting him so that he had a good angle at Scott.

Dylan struggled, but he wasn't fast enough.

The man latched onto Scott's arm.

He tried to run, but he didn't even make it a step before he disintegrated.

AUTHOR'S NOTE

D ear Reader,

Welcome to the world of the Immortal Writers! I'd like to personally thank you for joining me in this adventure. I hope you enjoyed your stay in the Writers' Castle, and that while you watched the Immortal Writers learn to fight their villains, you learned to fend off your own.

The *Immortal Writers* world is a place where anything can happen. Every story you've ever loved has the potential to live here eternally. It is my hope that as you read and get to know authors—some from my own personal Imagination Field, and others who have actually lived and created beautiful stories—that you will feel encouraged to read, to write, and to live. I hope that when you read this book, and settle down to read the rest of the series, that you will get a taste for the magic of stories, and for how the Land of Story can save us all in unexpected but truly phenomenal ways. Remember that our imaginations are powerful… even powerful enough to defeat our own personal demons.

I also hope that you have fun! Think about what kind of Immortal Writer you would want to be, or what characters you'd like to meet, or what worlds you'd like to explore in the Imagination Room. Would you ride a pegasus? Would you fight dragons? What fictional character would you fall in love with?

I encourage you to reach out to me at any time via my website www. immortalauthor.com with questions about reading or writing, or comments about the "Immortal Writers" series. I would love to hear from you and to see what secrets you have discovered in the Writers' Castle. And Shakespeare would like to hear from you, too… he never tires of hearing from his fans (it comes from being the greatest writer in the world, I suppose).

Thank you again for joining the Immortal Writers. Welcome to our ranks!

ABOUT JILL BOWERS

Jill Bowers is a technical writer by day and a fantasy author by night. She is one of two composers-in-residence for the Westminster Bell Choirs and has a great love for all music. She used to be the writer and host for the award-winning radio show Olde Tyme Radio on the Aggie Radio Station at USU and has dabbled in stage play writing as well.

Jill enjoys attending Utah's Comic Con and Fantasy Con and has an unhealthy attachment to Netflix. She lives in Utah and has a lovely dachshund that needs to lose weight because she probably doesn't get enough walks and is too cute to not feed. Jill attended Utah State University for their creative writing program, where she actually specialized in creative nonfiction rather than fiction. However, Jill loves delving into different worlds in fantasy and sci-fi novels and is excited to have people enter the worlds she has created.

Visit Jill online:

Blog: http://www.immortalauthor.com/
Facebook: www.facebook.com/immortalauthorjill
Pinterest: https://www.pinterest.com/jilliard08/
Twitter: https://twitter.com/Jilliard08
Goodreads: https://www.goodreads.com/user/show/2509616-jill-bowers
Instagram: https://instagram.com/jilliard08/
Youtube: https://www.youtube.com/channel/UC4FH9bS51qVga7rPot7awTw

BOOK CLUB GUIDE

1. If you could choose any of your favourite stories to come to life in the *Immortal Writers* world, what stories would you choose?

2. If you could meet any author, alive or dead, as part of the Immortal Writers, who would you want to meet and why? What kinds of things would you talk about?

3. What types of things would you use the Imagination Room for?

4. There are three types of magic in Liz's world: Body Magic, Spirit Magic, and Elemental Magic. Which type of magic would you like to have? What would you do with it?

5. Each of Liz's dragons has a different kind of power. Which one would you be the most scared to face? Least scared to face?

6. Curtis's training methods may seem a bit harsh to some, since he's not afraid to hurt Liz while they're sparring. What do you think of his methods? Is building up a tolerance to pain a good enough reason to hurt her?

7. Why do you think Healer was so willing to be sacrificed? What about her character made her accept her death?

8. Rob refused to let Healer go after she died, and in the end his wish to stay in contact with her cost him his life. Why do you think Rob's choice so greatly affected his mind? What can we learn from Rob's refusal to let Healer go?

9. Liz couldn't save Healer because of the choices Liz had already made in her writing. The consequences of those choices were that Healer had to die; the path was set. What do you think of this idea? Do you think our

paths are set based on the choices we make, or is there hope to change our fate even after we've made certain choices?

10. Liz used Kenric's past against him in order to defeat him. Kenric tried the same tactic against her, but while it scared Liz, it didn't have quite the same effect. What do you think is the difference between these two characters, even though they have somewhat similar histories? Why did the past so greatly affect Kenric, but not Liz?

WRITE FOR US

We love discovering new voices and welcome submissions. Please read the following carefully before preparing your work for submission to us. Our publishing house does accept unsolicited manuscripts but we want to receive a proposal first, and if interested we will solicit the manuscript.

We are looking for solid writing—present an idea with originality and we will be very interested in reading your work.

As you can appreciate, we give each proposal careful consideration so it can take up to six weeks for us to respond, depending on the amount of proposals we have received. If it takes longer to hear back, your proposal could still be under consideration and may simply have been given to a second editor for their opinion. We can't publish all books sent to us but each book is given consideration based on its individual merits along with a set of criteria we use when considering proposals for publication.

THANK YOU FOR READING
IMMORTAL WRITERS

CPSIA information can be obtained
at www.ICGtesting.com
Printed in the USA
FSOW03n1853311016
26821FS